NORSKE FIELDS

A Novel
of Southern California's
Norwegian Colony

by

Anne Schroeder

Norske Fields
Published ©2020 Anne Schroeder
www.anneschroederauthor.com

ISBN 978-1-7348684-0-1

This book is a work of historical fiction based closely on real people and real events. Details that cannot be historically verified are purely products of the author's imagination.

All rights reserved. No part of this publication may be reproduced, stored in a retrieval system, or transmitted, in any form or in any means – by electronic, mechanical, photocopying, recording or otherwise - without prior written permission.

Cover design - Jennifer Hancey
Formatting - Rachel Rossano
Editorial suggestions - Robert Natiuk
All photographs used with permission.

Endorsement

Anne Schroeder is a loving member of the Olsen family of the Norwegian Colony of the Conejo Valley, being the granddaughter of Tracy and Oscar Olsen, and the author of *Branches on the Conejo, Revisited.* In this new book she writes, again, with the deep understanding of the hearts, feelings and struggles of all the Norwegian families, and the eventual arrival of future opportunities afforded through the growth of the Conejo Valley. She is such a caring and talented writer and I wish her well and thank her for including my beloved Pederson family in her new book.

Janet Pederson Reeling

Why this Book?

"Write what should not be forgotten."
—Isabel Allende

    As a young woman I saw a photograph of my grandfather, Oscar Olsen, watching county workers exhume the coffins of his six young sisters and brother from an old family cemetery at the corner of Moorpark and Olsen Roads. Grandpa's eyes held unfathomable pain of a brother remembering his long-ago childhood. I wanted to know those little girls and boy. I wanted to connect with my heritage.

    This story grew from thousands of facts known about the residents of the Norwegian Colony and the land that was later developed as California Lutheran University, in Thousand Oaks, California. The land was originally part of Jose de la Guerra's Spanish land grant. It held brief interest for oil speculators, lying as an untilled section of property nestled against rolling hills. Then in 1890, Norwegians put a plowshare to the hard-packed clay soil. Their efforts resulted in mutual support and a community of friends as they adapted to dryland farming that was strange and challenging to newcomers. The Norwegians endured tribulation, but their joy and satisfaction with their new homes was well recorded in diaries and letters home. They laughed, sang, played and celebrated life within their little colony.

    I began with a sheet of paper with a thick black border entitled: *"Those buried in the Olsen Cemetery and moved to Ivy Lawn Cemetery in 1957."* From this list of names, birthdates, deaths I constructed the struggles of new immigrants in a foreign land. Some of the dialogue came from diaries and stories passed down to grandchildren now in their eighties, who recalled attitudes, personalities and actual quotations. For the rest, well, that is for the reader to decide.

The Story Unfolds

Chapter One
    Heed the Call...1

Chapter Two
    Sweet New Land..11

Chapter Three
    Pretty Girls for Lonely Bachelors...23

Chapter Four
    Land of Sage and Rocks...29

Chapter Five
    Draw from the Hat..39

Chapter Six
    Bride of my Heart..51

Chapter Seven
    I Rock my Baby...61

Chapter Eight
    Drought is a Hard Master...75

Chapter Nine
    Celebrate the Happy Times..87

Chapter Ten
    The Land is Ours...95

Chapter Eleven
    Building Jorgen's Grade-Road..101

Chapter Twelve
    When Peddler Calls..107

Chapter Thirteen
    Cyclone..113

Chapter Fourteen
    Summer of our Sorrows...123

Chapter Fifteen
    Norska Strength..129

Chapter Sixteen
    To Bear the Farewell...135

Chapter Seventeen
    Make a New Beginning...145
Chapter Eighteen
    Bitter to Test the Marrow..159
Chapter Nineteen
    Sons of my Heart..167
Chapter Twenty
    Grade-Road Tragedy..175
Chapter Twenty-One
    A White Plague Tears our Hearts...181
Chapter Twenty-Two
    We Bend but Fear to Break...189
Chapter Twenty-Three
    Moorpark Promise..193
Chapter Twenty-Four
    The Sons Make Courtship...203
Chapter Twenty-Five
    Vexed..211
Chapter Twenty-Six
    Two Become One...219
Chapter Twenty-Seven
    A Father's Place..229
Chapter Twenty-Eight
    Between Rock and Hard Place...239
Chapter Twenty-Nine
    Depression Years..245
Chapter Thirty
    The Final Years...255
Chapter Thirty-One
    Quitclaim Transfer...263
Chapter Thirty-Two
    Shoes and Sheepfolds..271
Chapter Thirty-Three
    Promise Years..277
Chapter Thirty-Four
    A Hard Farewell..287

People of the Norwegian Colony

Ole Overaa Anderson — Drew Lot #1. Never farmed. Sold land to Lars Pederson by 1900 and returned to Norway.

Lars Berge Pederson — Farmed Lot #2. Died in 1901 at 38. Buried in Olsen Cemetery.

Karn (Karen) Pederson — Lars's wife. Farmed the Colony with her sons. Died in 1960 at 92.

Ole Ansok Nelson — Farmed Lot #3. Moved to Suisan in 1903. Died in 1945 at 81.

Elizabeth Berge Nelson — Ole's wife. Lars Pederson's sister.

Jorgen Overaa Hansen — Farmed lot # 4. Died in 1901 at 39. Buried in Olsen Cemetery.

Lina Hansen — Jorgen's wife. Returned to Norway with daughter Ella in 1902-03.

Nils Uren Olsen — Farmed Lot #5. Lived on Colony and Moorpark until his death in 1941 at 82.

Ellen Fjorstad Olsen — Nils's wife. Died in 1923 at 60.

- *Oscar Olsen* — Oldest son. Remained on the Colony until his retirement in 1956. Died in 1972 at 77.
- *Theresa Kelley* — Oscar's wife. Died in 1987 at 86.
- *Ludvik "Lud"* — Middle son. Married Hazel Mundel; Irene McAfee. Died in 1947 at 47.
- *Nicolay "Nick"* — Youngest son. Married to Sarah Davis; Jenni Pitello. Remained on the Colony until his death in 1989 at 82.

Paula, Nora, Emma, Nora, Laura, Ned, Thora	Olsen children who died in childhood. Buried in the Olsen Cemetery.
Lars Pederson's Children	Remained on the Conejo until 1958.
Peder "Pete"	Oldest son. Married to Frances Larsen; Rheta Lawler. Died in 1976 at 84.
Rich	Second son. Married to Ruth Pearson. Died in 1976 at 81.
Anna Pederson Albertson	Daughter. Married to Benjam. Died at 58.
Lawrence	Youngest son. Married to Vida Landru. Died in 1977 at 75.
Henry, Petra, Ella	Jorgen and Lina Hansen's children. Older two buried in Olsen Cemetery.
Harry, Mable and Alma	Ole and Elizabeth Nelson's children. All survived.
Martin Overaa, Oscar Overaa	Brothers. Carpenters and hired men.
Mary Ansok	Santa Barbara relative of Ole Nelson.
Suzanne (Susie) Jacobson	Karn Pederson's sister. Married to Ross.
Ross Jacobson	Died in 1901. Buried Olsen Cemetery.
Martin Peterson	Hired man. Buried in Olsen Cemetery.
George Ness	Lina Hansen's brother. Suspected suicide. Buried in Olsen Cemetery.

Chapter One

Heed the Call

March 30, 1884. Stranda, Norway. My friends heed the call to America. I will keep a diary to record the things I see. Nils Uren.

From across the Størfjørd, the pealing bell of Stranda Church tugged at yet another memory holding a young man to this ancient land. The last tone faded. Nils Uren gazed over the bow of the small wooden *færing*, capturing every detail. He saw wispy clouds staining the horizon where morning thrust a cautious shadow across winter-clad mountains. On the alpine slopes, scattered trees shook off their snowy coverings light as a dusting of flour. *Seems everything recalls the hungry belly.* He closed his eyes and inhaled the tang of frost. "We will feel the sting of our late arrival," his mother fretted from under the thick oilcloth wrap she shared with her nearly-grown daughter.

"*Ja.*" He bent his thick shoulders to the oars and continued rowing.

He dragged the boat into the boathouse on the opposite bank. Taking care not to soak his boots, he saw to his bundle of dry Sunday clothes before wrapping his mother's worn shawl around her frail shoulders and helping her into their changing shed. Her eyes were fringed with worry, but theirs wouldn't be the last tardy boots to tromp into the church on this frigid March morning. More than one family struggled on steep paths still slippery with spring frost, or crossed the icy water in a stiff wind. Still, he had caused the delay with his dark mood. His mother usually asked little of him. Her Sunday visit with friends was a bright spot in her week that he was glad to provide.

1

He shook off his frustration. When it was his turn, he traded soaked clothing for dry and hung his soaked oilskin on a hook.

A blast of air announced their arrival. He glanced around to see which of his friends was there on an overcast winter day with the sun not long up and cold blistering the cheeks. Each month it seemed someone else left for America. Even his sister, Olave Marie, scanned the room to see which marriageable man might be left.

"Today, none but my friends to pull your braids and tease you, sister." He grinned at the elbow she dug into his side.

He nodded to his friend Lars, sitting in the pew alongside his girlfriend and her family. Contentment wrapped his face. Good for Lars. At least one of them would enjoy the sermon. On the other side his friend Jorgen glanced back, grinning before his mother frowned and shushed him out of habit. Nils offered a wink and an exaggerated scowl that earned a snort from his friend, a grown man, the same as the rest of them, nearly twenty-five years.

The entire community seemed to be here today. A space opened up at the rear for his mother and sister. From the back wall he had a clear view of Ingeborg sitting up front. No chance to slip in beside her, with the pew filled up and the preacher already started. An opportunity to hold his sweetheart's hand lost to a long morning with early rising and a scant breakfast after the goats were milked and fed.

A long sermon and the lazy heat from the woodstove proved irresistible. He jerked awake again to find a girl watching him from the seat next to Ingeborg. He felt his face warming after she turned around and faced the minister again. From the back, the two girls looked like sisters with their sable braids fastened to their crowns, a strand of hair on the girl's nape hinting of escape. Her dark eyes and smooth cheeks glowed with health, but it was her matter-of-fact look that intrigued him. *Pretty for sure. But no more glances her way. It is Ingeborg I will convince to marry me and move to America.*

When the service ended, he cornered Lars and Jorgen in the fellowship room while the girls clustered together, laughing and talking. He feigned a playful jab at Jorgen and hitched a thumb toward the girl. "Who is she?" He kept his tone light. His friends would be heartless if they detected a weakness.

Jorgen smirked. "The girl with Ingeborg? *You* know her. It's Ellen Fjørstad. From the farm up the valley."

"Iversdatter? *Nei.*" He took a closer look. "*Nei.* Not the same girl we know. This one is grown up. Not a simple farm girl any longer."

Jorgen chuckled. "So much has changed since you left for the army? All that marching and training leaves you confused. You come back and everything is different."

"Not much—!" He bit back his protest when he realized his friend was right. Much had changed. Not his choice, the mandatory military service, but a lifesaver in the way it had opened his world. He tucked his hands under his arms and. glanced up to see his friends grinning. "I am having a hard time fitting myself into my father's small house again. Not much interests me since coming home. I think all the time about America."

Lars nodded. "You too? I think how I can save enough money for the voyage. I talk with Ole Ansok. His brother is in California now. Santa Barbara. He and a dozen others from this region. I think to join them."

"And Ole?"

Lars nodded again. "He says it will take us two years to save up enough money. But when our pockets are full-up, we could sail together from Bergen."

Excitement lit Jorgen's face. "In two years then! We sail to Liverpool and take the White Star Line to New York City. The plan is set?"

"I have saved my *kroner* from the army pay. I add every bit I can." Nils lowered his voice when he realized others were listening. "In another year I be twenty-five. No time to lose."

Lars nodded. "So, we have a plan, the three of us? Four if my cousin Ole wants in?"

Jorgen laughed. "Of course Ole comes. People think the two of us are brothers, Ole Ansok and me. We even make the agreement not to get in the way of the other, no hard feelings if we both court a girl and she chooses one over the other."

"More likely she chooses neither of you," Lars teased.

Nils hesitated. "I hear Ole Overaa thinks to go. He is a strange fellow, but a hard worker. What do you say?"

"If his money is good, then who cares?" Jorgen grinned. "But I don't envy you, Nils, having to tell your sweetheart you are leaving."

Nils watched Ingeborg laughing with her friends. "Mind your own concerns, brother. I will convince her to come. You will see. What good is it to build a home in America without a sweetheart?" He gestured to the women laying out a buffet for all to eat. "A sweetheart who cooks the good foods from home."

He turned to the sideboard, distracted by aromas of pickled vegetables, boiled eggs, *flatbrød*, creamed potatoes, salted fish and dried cherry cake that made his belly grumble with anticipation. When it was his turn, he filled his plate and joined Jorgen to find seats next to the girls.

Later, he managed to capture Ingeborg's hand when one of the men picked up a Hardanger fiddle and another fellow a Jew's harp. The impromptu band kept the toes tapping and boots stomping. Ingeborg's toes kept time to the rollicking tunes while she returned the pressure of his fingers.

"If this was not church I would ask you to dance," he stammered. When she shook her head firmly, he felt relief. "Come, get your shawl. We find a place to talk."

Outside, a stiff breeze tempered their attempt at conversation. He felt her shivering and he thought of the boathouse where his dry wool coat hung on a peg next to his sodden oilcloth. Inside, he was encouraged by the warmth of her hand in his.

"The others and I are planning to go to America when we have enough saved. Maybe you and I—we can go together. That is my hope." He waited for her to reply, but it seemed she listened with more politeness than interest. "We can be married in Stranda, and find a farm in America." He hesitated. "If you want, maybe your brother will join us. Or your sister?" He explained about the farmland in California and the weeks it would take to reach it.

Finally his sweetheart had heard enough. "America! Everyone is mad for America. What is wrong with this place? I care for you. But I care for my home here as well. My goats and my friends. The traditions. The hiking. The snow. You wait and see. America will not be *Norveg*. We would trade what we have here for something else, who knows what? We cannot have both." She stood with her hands grasping her shawl as the wind tugged at the corners.

He saw tears of frustration in her eyes. "We have time to decide. Two years. Maybe by then you will change your mind."

She studied him with a look of uncertainty. "Maybe." She laughed. "Or who knows? Maybe the mountain will slide on top of our house tonight and pffft, all gone."

He grinned. "No more avalanches this season. The big rock over your father's farm is almost bare of snow. Soon enough we will have wildflowers and picnics."

"Promise me. When the midnight sun arrives."

Later, when Ingeborg left with her family, he signaled to his sister that it was time to go.

On the windblown journey back across the fjord he steered the boat toward the hillside where their stout farmhouse set wedged on a narrow shelf between the tall cliff and the water's edge. The place they leased, the old Uranes Farm—another memory to carry with him to America. Stones formed the foundation of the house and barn, sheltering the thick logs from melting snow. Generations earlier, part of the cliff had slid off in an avalanche that brought death and destruction to the family living there. The falling rock caused a tidal wave that ripped across the water and pushed the church off its foundation. Parishioners searching in the debris found the baptismal font in the mud. They gratefully reset it in the church they rebuilt mostly from the timbers of the old one. The house his family leased had been reset as far away as possible from the sliding hillside.

Nils scanned the water for ice and debris from the latest storm. Spring was a dangerous time to cross, but what choice did a tenant farmer have, trapped on a shelf while the outside world existed across the fjord? He sometimes felt as though he might suffocate in his father's stale routine. The talk with his friends at the church had convinced him. America was no longer a distant dream but a chance. His older brother would inherit the goats and his father's tools. A younger son had no hopes except to hire out as a laborer—or maybe if he were lucky, a tenant farmer working for shares. For his father, every season was a struggle to find enough food to feed the family: grain purchased by the pound and hauled to the gristmill for milling; flour saved for Christmas cakes and delicacies. *Flatbrød* did not fill the belly like the thick loaves of wheat bread he had tasted in the army.

"What is this talk of you leaving?" his mother asked.

He kept his head down, glad that he had the excuse of the boat. But she had saved the question until they were nearly home.

"I know what you will say, Mother. My brother."

She nodded. "I recall this son of my heart, my grown son. He leaves for Australia on a sailing sloop like you intend. Your father and I wait three years without word—but so far nothing. It is as though Hans has dropped off the edge of the earth."

Nils shook off his fear of a similar fate. "I will write you often. You and Father."

"And the sweetheart? She is willing?"

He shrugged and put his body into rowing. On shore again, he secured his boat and followed his mother and sister up the path to the house.

"The cherry trees will soon be swelling," his mother commented.

He glanced over, glad to see her tears were gone. She understood that his staying would mean poverty and want for all of them. He vowed that his letters home from America would tell of hope and good fortune. "*Ja,*" he teased, giving her a wink. "My mouth already waters for the pies you make."

His father's *melkegelts* bleated from their pen in the gathering darkness. He lit a lantern and joined his sister in the barn. "In America, they say the sun shines even in winter until it is bedtime. That would be a wonder," he commented over the goat he was milking.

"She won't go with you," Olave Marie said.

"What do you know about Ingeborg? About marriage? You're a *kidd*." He began milking another goat but his mind was on Ingeborg's soft hand.

Olave Marie peered over the goat without pausing her milking. "She's like me. A homebody. We'd rather be without a husband than without our homeland. Ellen Fjorstad thinks we're foolish, but that's the way we think."

⁓

February 6, 1888. The ship in the Bergen harbor seemed alive to Nils, with sails flapping in the wind, listless and eager. His friends followed him up the gangplank—Lars, Jorgen, Ole Elias Ansok and Ole Overaa—some carrying more money in their pockets than others, but each with the same dream. He gripped a carpetbag filled with a spare shirt, undergarments and a spare pair of britches for the two weeks' journey to New York. His wooden trunk was already stowed below deck, filled with everything he owned: his carpentry tools, his knives, a wooden carving from his childhood, salves, and enough spare clothing and heavy woolen socks to last until he could afford to replace them. The lack of clothing in his rucksack did not concern him. He would buy a farm and earn enough to get the things he needed. No problem. In America, they said the fields were planted with gold.

Below, Lars reached to help his sister Elizabeth with her bag until she waved him away. "Mind your own pack, little brother. We agreed that if I accompanied you, you would not make a fuss over me. I am capable and more. You will see."

Jorgen followed them up the boardwalk, laughing. At the railing he turned to watch the noisy dockside bustle. "Maybe it is your sister who protects *us*, Lars! When a pickpocket steals our passage, we beg her for the loan of a few *kroner*."

"No chance!" Elizabeth snorted a laugh as she fought her hat in the wind. "I plan to trade my *speciedalers* for American dollars when we reach New York. It will be a hard exchange, the old coins for the new, but necessary."

"Our old money as worthless as our old ways, I suppose," Nils said. Ole Ansok nodded, preoccupied with the crowd gathered on the waterfront. His fiancée had said her goodbyes back in Stranda, but he scanned the waterfront in hopes of seeing her familiar face.

Lars reached to give his friend a cuff on the chin. "She doesn't come, Ole. Face it. Your Anne inherits her father's land. She can have the pick of the bachelors who stay behind, all wanting such a fine farm. She will forget your sorry face as soon as you are out of sight." He batted at his friend's hat and laughed as Ole bent to retrieve it before it blew off the deck and into the sea.

Ole chuckled. With his hat safely on his head, he watched the gangplank being raised. "Nah," he teased. "Those fellows will be gathered at the Gjerde farm, watching your Karn hang out the washing in her fresh blouse. You soon find yourself a lonely bachelor—alone and feeling the fool. She will be married and fat with her third when you return to fetch her to America."

Lars scowled. He had known Karn Gjerde from the time they were schoolmates. She'd had plenty of time to make up her mind about the other fellows. Still, she'd driven a hard bargain. *I don't intend to be a land widow like some of the others, waiting here while we both grow long in the tooth. You write me often and let me know how things go,* she had demanded. *We make decisions for the future together. No surprises, you hear?* He had agreed and he intended to keep his word.

Nils turned from listening to his friends to watch the dockside workers unhook the ship and toss the ropes to waiting crewman. Jorgen leaned over the wooden railing beside him as the sails unfurled and the ship eased from shore. Jorgen had spent time after church each week with Lina Ness. She had protested that she had no interest in a fellow who was leaving in a few months. Finally, she relented. *Jorgen, if you choose to write me about life in America, I promise to read your letter before I wrap the fish in it,* she told him. Good and enough for Jorgen.

The brisk wind whipped Jorgen's thick dark hair as the ship got underway. "I hope we are making the right choice. Not every new suit turns out to fit the wearer. I will be hard-put to convince Lina if I am uncertain myself."

Nils laughed. "We are men without money for even an old suit, my friend. So how can we lose? You will see. We show the girls back home that America is the place for them."

They remained unmoving as the ship plowed the dark water, until darkness obscured the coast and a crew member ordered them below.

Four days later the ship reached Hull, England, where the railroad would take them to Liverpool. They had scarcely time to secure their luggage and find a berth before the train started rolling. The nine-hour railroad journey kept Nils riveted to the window. He counted thirty-six bridges and three tunnels, but it was the beauty of the countryside filled with flatland and abundance that left him mesmerized. He wrote his thoughts in a letter.

> Ireland, February 11, 1886
> My beloved Ingeborg,
> At 11 in the morning I was in Liverpool and I went to board the White Star Line, a very big steamship with four masts, one of the biggest between England and America. It was very comfortable on board. They had very good food and whatever we needed. We left England and went to Iceland and from Iceland we will go to New York and America. I was so lucky that I could leave so quickly, otherwise I had to stay another six days in England. Our Lord gave us very good weather on the whole journey.

In New York City, they secured a modest room for the night and stowed their luggage so they could explore the streets. They agreed. No money to spend on frivolous pursuits such as a fancy eating house. Nils followed his friends to gawk at the strange accents and brash joy of immigrants like themselves who arrived from all corners of the earth. He found himself trying to memorize the sights and sounds of a town that offered a surprise on every corner.

February 22, 1886
My beloved Ingeborg,

    I stayed in New York one and a half days. During my time there I traveled a lot in this town and I saw many excellent things, some are of very great importance and I visited the town and I saw the lovely things around me and I paid very careful attention to the things I saw because I was only a very young man and haven't traveled earlier so therefore I looked very carefully, perhaps more carefully than other people who have traveled a lot would do.

    We maybe have worn out our shoes with sightseeing, but now we will sleep well on the railway going up the country.

Despite his words he sat up late, watching the countryside from the window.

    One thing I did soon realize, the land here isn't flat, but has many hills and valleys. In the morning the train came to Elvant, a very big city and this city had eight stations which I could see and I do not think there were any others and in the evening I came to another very big city some name being Binghamton and the nearest town is Orvegon. And a week later I came to another town called Sikago where the train halted for three hours.

In Chicago, the clock in the tower rang the three o'clock afternoon hour. Earsplitting piping and alarms commenced from the factories and carpenters as though a fire alarm was sounding all over the city. "If I had to work in such a town, the time would pass very quickly for me," he shouted to Lars over the din.

He fought sleep as the train rumbled across the dusty prairie, land as endless as the seas had been on the crossing to America. He kept his diary close and captured his impressions on its pages, noting the passing days. By the time the train arrived in Sacramento, twelve days later, he felt equal to any task his new country might demand of him. "We are here. California," he announced to his friends as he stepped from the train."

They engaged a stagecoach to take them on the next leg of their journey, a swaying, cramped ride over bogs and ruts that caused

Elizabeth to shriek as she gripped her hat to keep it from being crushed by her brother's flying elbow. The stage took them through wide valleys filled with waterfowl and native grasses, huge ranches with grazing cattle, and bogs and canyons rife with wild game. Nils watched as the noises of their horses flushed deer from hiding.

The journey was broken by hasty meals of strange lima beans and sourdough bread at way stations. Occasionally, a ferry waited to transport them across a swollen river. Slowly, the chill of Northern California and Oakland gave way to clear skies and sunshine that caused Nils to squint in the brightness. Elizabeth removed her coat in favor of shirtsleeves and a hastily-made paper fan.

The rolling hills and sand dunes in California seemed to have been dropped from the sky, or thrust up from the bowels of the earth. Trees stood huge and spaced thirty feet apart from each other as though their roots needed space in the arid land.

"Everything is upside down from what we know," Nils said.

Lars laughed. "We are Norskes. We will learn."

Ellen Fjorstad's sister, Pernille, remained behind.

Chapter Two

Sweet New Land

March 5, 1886. Santa Barbara. A welcome home-coming in this sea town. Old friends greet us. Fine land and climate here, and good wages—$1.25 per day.

THE COAST STAGE swayed from side to side, hurling dust over the winding track to the top of the San Marcos Pass. Following a quick changeover to fresh horses at the Cold Springs stop, the stage raced down through the rugged, brushy hills and onto the Coast Road. Yellow mustard crowded both sides of the road and wildflowers covered the hillsides. Cattle grazed in grass to their underbellies. Oak trees spread branches wide enough to cover a cottage back home.

"Isn't it wonderful!" Elizabeth's laughter filled the coach.

Some of the Norwegians clung to the top of the stage for a first glimpse of the Pacific Ocean in the sparkling sunlight. "There it is!" Ole shouted. "As blue as Jorgen's eyes!"

A few hours later the stage slowed on the outskirts of town. A Spanish adobe with patchy whitewash walls stood where the sweet, heady smell of citrus and the hum of bees filled a sandy courtyard. "Oranges!" Elizabeth clasped her hands together and laughed.

When the stage rocked to a stop, Nils fumbled with the latch without waiting for the pull-down steps.

"Break your neck, Nils, there be no purpose in coming," Lars called.

Nils grinned as he launched through the opening. He landed feet-first on the cobblestones with his woolen cap tilted to one side. The cap threatened to slide off his thick sandy hair, tousled and filthy from a poor man's journey.

He tossed his cap in the air and let out a whoop. "Steps be for ordinary men, my friend. Today Nils Uren is not one of *them*!"

"*Nei*! No ordinary *Nordsmenn*! Not us!"

His friends sailed their caps down from the stage. They jumped to the ground to join him in plucking them from the dirt and giving them swipes across their dusty trousers before rearranging them on close-cropped heads. Nils joined them, his cheeks already burning from the windy ride south from Sacramento, and now the late afternoon sun. With their fair skin and light eyes, surely each would need to buy a felt hat, or a woven straw like the Spanish men wore, before their faces burned to the shade of the adobe tiles that covered the roofs in this town.

"A strange homecoming, this Santa Barbara" one of them muttered to himself.

Nils agreed. He knew the town from the relatives' letters, passed around from farm to farm and digested over coffee and *lefse* since the time the first man left Stranda twenty years past. *Norveg* might be home, but America was the land for opportunity. Everyone wrote letters saying the same thing: *Come to America and prosper.* So here he was with his threadbare worsted suit and worn boots that would have to do for work as well as church.

Lars slid from the coach. "We be in agreement there, my friend! A day to celebrate."

Elizabeth stepped down cautiously, her skirt bunched in one hand, ladylike, her movements sure and agile from her early years as a goatherd and servant girl on the Berge farm. She turned to admire the view with a broad smile wreathing her fine face.

Nils considered what he knew—what everyone knew—of her misfortune. Elizabeth Berge. A girl good enough to work for the farmer—and even to take the farm's name as her own in a land where a person's surname was connected to the farm and not the family—but not good enough in the eyes of the farmer to marry his son, despite the two young peoples' love for each other. A girl to work beside a man. A clever girl whose green eyes carried only hope and optimism. She had made no agreement with a man after the Berge farmer spoiled her hopes for a match with his son, all over a few dollars or a cow. *No secrets in a small town. Not for a girl spurned.*

The young woman standing next to her brother showed no signs of sorrow or regret. Her face radiated with life and expectation. No matter what happened later, this day would mark itself in their memories forever.

Nils turned with his friends to watch the sailboats gliding beyond the pier. "There it is, brothers."

"Look, Lars, isn't it something!" Elizabeth spoke to her brother, putting into words the emotions that stuck in Nils's head without a way of expressing themselves.

Nils turned to the wide plaza where the stagecoach was moving down the street. Baskets of red geraniums draped the low adobe walls of Spanish houses. Brightly-garbed children ran about and proud roosters flapped their wings in the afternoon sun. The street heading east held a row of wood-framed houses with ornate gingerbread trim, plentiful windows and gabled roofs. Wide porches supported blooming bushes planted close to the foundations. No two houses looked alike, as though every homebuilder had a different notion. He craned to see a farmhouse like those dotting the valleys in *Norveg*, but the Americans here seemed to prefer thin wood planks and whitewashed adobe brick to the stout logs of his homeland.

In the plaza, a vaquero reclined on a low wall. The man hiked his foot up to support himself, purposely showing the stiletto knife tucked in his boot, its white cow-horn handle glinting in the sun. He spat as he rolled a cigarette, not once looking down at his fingers, but keeping his eyes on Elizabeth as he grinned and showed his stained teeth, the few that remained. A breeze riffled his long black hair under his black leather hat, stained at the band from years of sweat and dust.

"*Hei!*" Elizabeth greeted him. Nils moved to stand beside her.

She got a wide smile back from the vaquero. "*Buenos dias, señorita bonita!*"

Nils took her by her elbow and led her to the others. From the plaza, grim-faced Americans bustled across the dusty road as though they had somewhere important to be. Elegant Spanish ladies strolled at a slower pace, in dark, full skirts that swept freely above the dusty street. Elizabeth turned to watch until they turned a corner and disappeared.

A tall man with a trimmed beard gave them an inquisitive look and made a quiet comment to another man wearing spectacles. "Norskies!" he muttered.

Nils reached to restrain Ole Overaa before his friend could confront the two Americans. "It makes no matter that we be green arrivals," he whispered. "Take no shame in being a Norske. Even a poorly dressed one."

A low-hanging branch laden with ripe oranges partially blocked their path. Nils reached to twist one off, took a deep whiff and began peeling a section. With his first bite, the juices engaged his senses and he sighed.

Ole Ansok glanced at Elizabeth and returned her amused shrug. It was a secret bet between the others that Elizabeth might yet set her cap for Ole. They would make a fine couple if anything came of it. But Ole had thoughts only for his Anne back in Stranda. Everyone said the same: *That Ole is one lucky fellow.*

Elizabeth moved to pick an orange for herself. Her low laugh reminded Nils of the girls back home. He had seen her talking to Ellen Fjørstad on their last Sunday before departing. The two were similar in their dress and manners, but Ellen was more practical and he liked that about her. Elizabeth was like a hummingbird, too quick of mood for him. She would be a handful for any man she set her sights on.

He had made no progress with Ingeborg. She had promised to write, but beyond that, nothing. Her farewell at the boat seemed guarded as though she didn't trust his promise to write and to send money for her passage. Her eyes were guarded and her lip trembled when she bid him farewell without a kiss, but he saw the tears that she tried to hide. In the boat he had turned to wave and saw her standing with her arms crossed, her shoulders hunched in dejection before she turned away into the crowd as though she had already dismissed him. Perhaps he should have tried harder, but it had taken every bit of money he earned to make his dream happen. Little time or energy left for courting. She was happy with her life in Stranda, she claimed. But maybe absence would change her heart.

He wondered for a moment whether Ellen Fjørstad would ever set her path for America. More likely she would find a fellow back home who suited her, but maybe not; so many marriageable men had already left for America—thousands each year. Maybe she would join them. She had talked of coming, he remembered *that.*

He shook off thoughts of Stranda and shifted his attention to the bustle of the new California town. *Time enough to mend the path with my sweetheart, after I find my own way.*

Elizabeth still bubbled with excitement. Women, it seemed, had a way with words that failed the farm boys. She smoothed her crumpled travel suit while her eyes drank in the sights and sounds of the town before calling to her brother in her open, guileless manner. "Look, Lars, the sand as white as a Norska's braids."

Her brother laughed. "You *would* think of your hair, Elizabeth. But the Norska's braids? I think you have wool for a brain. You don't have the white braids since you were a child. But you are right to think of the water. When we find our lodgings we see if the wading is warmer here than back home."

Nils avenged himself with an elbow to his friend's belly and was satisfied when he heard Lars's sharp expulsion of air. "*Ja*, sure," he joked, "you write home that you swim in the ocean in early March, your people will think you catch the brain fever. They never believe the air is so mild this early in the year."

Elizabeth plucked a geranium from a bush and sniffed it. "Or the flowers blooming like they see no tomorrow."

"Everything serves the thief, I see." Jorgen Hansen's eyes crinkled with laughter as he made an unsuccessful grab for the flower.

"*Nei*! It is mine now! Pick your own," Elizabeth teased.

Nils watched the teasing between the two. The girls back home agreed that Jorgen was the best looking of their friends, with his dark hair growing flat to his head, his hearty dark mustache and his bright, inquisitive manner. But he held no regard for his looks. He had spent the journey from Sacramento seeing only the farms dotting the valleys, the glory in the land. Jorgen was an easy fellow to like—and a good friend to be sure.

"Such a growing season for a farmer," Jorgen said. "Time for two hayings each summer. That would be really something!"

"And the length of the days! Who would think? Seven o'clock at night and the sun still casting light over the water? How does a Norska manage without the long evenings for darning her socks? And the farmer without darkness to sharpen his hoe?" Elizabeth asked.

"Time enough for farming when we find our land. For now, we better worry about paying for it. First a bed, then a job. That is the way I see it," Nils said.

"You worry like a Norske uncle," Elizabeth joked. "*Onkel Nils*, please do not send us so soon to bed. We will be good girls and boys!"

Nils's grin crinkled the edges of his smooth face, giving him, as he had been reminded by his older brothers, the look of a fresh lad rather than the twenty-six years his entry visa claimed—and as it further certified; neither blind, insane, a pauper, nor a criminal. He waited for the stage driver to throw down the worn valises and boxes tied with twine before he plucked his satchel from the pile. Case in hand, he straightened and grinned at a group of men and women hurrying toward them. "Look, Ole—the Ansoks! Your brother comes to meet us."

A moment later he and his four weary friends were engulfed in hugs and handshakes, accompanied by whoops and squeals of welcome. One of them grabbed Ole and shouted, "Brother, you made it. I make a cot ready for your sorry rump. Tell us, are there any pretty girls left in *Norveg*? You should have brought your Anne with you. You will need a good wife like mine. If I had my way, the whole of Stranda would jump on the boat and come to America."

Ole laughed. "Then who would farm our mother's farm? It is in our family four hundred years, now. Good our oldest brother don't think the same as you. He sends his regards." Ole dusted the travel grit from his baggy wool coat before meeting his brother's grin. "By the way, I go by the name *Nilson* now. Too many Ansoks already in this country." He looped an arm around his older brother's shoulders and took a firmer grip on his heavy canvas rucksack.

Ole's sister-in-law, Mary, pressed through from behind with her good-natured manner and plain, kind face, her bosom heaving from the effort of her brisk pace as she hurried to give her brother-in-law a crushing hug. "Anyway, we call it 'Norway' now, little brother! Like the Americans. No more '*Norge*' for us. Only in letters home do we use that spelling." She urged them forward with a wave of her hand. "Come, follow. I bake a cake to celebrate."

"A *kransekage?*" Ole teased.

Mary Ansok laughed. "Not a tower cake. I save that for your wedding day. I make a cake filled with American jam and the cream of good American cows. You will see soon enough, little brother, how we adapt to new ways."

"I will be happy to eat my share," Jorgen laughed.

As they started back, Mary made space for Elizabeth at her side while she fussed about the girl traveling so far in the company of five rough bachelors.

"The best friends are the fewest. Besides, they make good protection," Elizabeth protested. "Especially my brother. Lars knows much of the world. More than is good for him at his young age. And the others are like brothers now. We sit in the same church pews since we are *kidds*."

Mary clucked and nodded for Ole to carry Elizabeth's suitcase. Soon they were walking along a side street toward the rooming house. "The furnishings are not fancy, but more than we are used to," she said.

"Part of the reason we left the old country—no room for us to spread our blankets in the wintertime," her husband joked.

"Nowhere to plant the plow, more like it," Lars muttered.

Elizabeth gave her brother a look. "Don't start, Lars. It was never for you to inherit a farm, even if our father had not drowned in the storm. Others suffer more than we. And you have much to look forward to." She gave him a playful jab. "A certain girl, for sure, if she can be convinced the American West is not filled with bandits and wild Indians." Her brother's ripening face encouraged her to explain for the others' benefits. "Karn tells Lars to be careful he don't get scalped by the wild Indians she reads about in the stories."

Mary turned to study Lars. "Is that the Gjerde girl you speak of?"

Lars remained silent, his head downcast.

"*Ja,* Karn Gjerde. They are *sweethearts!*" his sister teased.

Laughter at Lars expense fanned his irritation. "We are engaged," he blustered. "The matter is set. She waits for me to settle here." He jammed his fists into his pockets and scowled at his sister. "You're just addled about your own marriage prospects."

"You're to be married?" the older woman asked. "I thought—"

Elizabeth's chin thrust up and her face took color. "Nothing has changed. His parents require the dowry. There is none."

"No wonder. Your poor mother thrown off the crofter's land. Having to remarry scarce before your father was cold. And no room for you olders in the new husband's house." She cast her arm around Elizabeth and gave a squeeze. "It makes a hard way to grow up, with no family for comfort, only the work. How old were you, thirteen?"

"I was twelve. Me and Lars were lucky my stepfather finds us a place at the Berge farm. Their son and I—we have deep feelings for each other, but the parents don't budge. I leave the farm when there is no reason to stay." Elizabeth struggled to keep her face brave.

Nils watched through tight lips. *The girl spends enough hours on tears. Time now for a new beginning.*

Mary turned her knowing gaze from Elizabeth and nodded briskly. "The old ways are not always the best. Here in America there will be no need of a dowry. A woman's part is equal. You will find a husband and he will be glad to have you." She laughed. "He will work hard to woo you. You are a strong, handsome woman."

Nils noticed the look Ole Nilson gave Elizabeth, easily hefting her suitcase as well as his own to impress her with his strength. The two exchanged glances and Ole skirted his eyes. The look of embarrassment surprised Nils. His friend had spent the voyage studying a small photograph of his Anne, reading and rereading her letter until it seemed he would be washed overboard by a wave while he daydreamed. *Better to know rightly than to hope wrongly.*

Her husband opened the door to the rooming house where the smell of meatballs simmered in a pot on the woodstove. A good-sized fish lay ready for poaching alongside fresh peppers and onions.

Nils joined the other men in hooting their appreciation. *"Tørrfisk!* My mouth drools."

Mary laughed. "Ah, the table catches the hungry man! It is not proper stock fish, but only cod. You find we eat American food now. We use spices and peppers like our Spanish neighbors. They are good. Just different. You will see."

"The beggar does not choose!" Ole twisted away from the misplaced swat she aimed at his rump. He laughed on his way out of the room. "You are used to my brother and his slow ways. I be back with a kiss when your old man is not looking."

The room erupted in a roar of laughter. Even his brother laughed at the jest at his expense.

After stowing his gear and bedroll in the corner and finding his way to the outhouse, Nils accepted Mary's offer of coffee to tide him over. "So many new mouths to feed. We will be a burden for you good people," he said.

"Not to worry. A working man can afford to fill his belly here. Not like at home where we had to curb our hunger. Look at me—a dumpling who has forgotten the size of her dinner plate!" Mary patted her ample waist and laughed.

"*Ja*, for sure." Nils felt his face heating, but her words, even spoken in jest, were true. Back home there was seldom enough to go around. The old people laughed and said compact people could better fit in the old, low houses.

Mary patted a ball of dough into a flat mound and began rolling *flatbrød*. "The *middag* meal will be ready shortly. We serve potluck soon." She snapped off a piece of flatbread from the griddle and held it out. "Here, take a bit and get yourself out! Elizabeth and I will manage here. She will catch me up on the news."

Savoring the nutty flavor of rye flour, Nils headed for a trio of men engaged in conversation. He found himself listening to a former neighbor who had news of work making new adobe walls for the Catholic Mission. He scooted closer and nodded when the man explained, "Not here the rocks and stones like Norway. Here, they make their own bricks from the red clay earth."

Nils laughed. "I learn this brick-making with one hand tied behind me. I take the job."

⁂

With a first week's wages pinned inside his pocket, Nils paused to mop his brow with appreciation for the job that had fallen into his hands. They were lucky that the foreman valued their experience. A few weary Mexican men formed the adobe bricks in molds and laid them in long rows to dry in the sun. Byyack-breaking work for less pay.

"We spend time building rock walls back home. A wall is a wall," he admitted. "Honest labor to justify the strain of shoulders at the end of the day."

Jorgen nodded in agreement. "The work hones our muscles." He grinned. "We get soft on the journey to America."

They walked home to find Ole Nilson waiting on the worn stoop while the fading sun laid a track across the water.

"My brother talks me to staying in Santa Barbara," Ole confessed. "My job at the stables pays one dollar and twenty-five a day. If I cinch the purse, I can marry in only three years. You go ahead—find a farm and a wife. Everything I need waits for me back home."

Nils watched the setting sun slide behind a cloud and emerge to cast a long reflection across the quiet sea. "The land is everything. Something to pass down to our children. Something to be proud of."

Ole nodded. His cheeks grew red and he glanced around. "I guess this isn't what I have on my mind tonight."

Nils grinned. "Lovesick? I wish you luck with *that*." He felt his own face heating and he turned away, embarrassed at the talk of girls. He had written a letter to Ingeborg. Her response burned a hole in his pocket.

Ole laughed. "The billy-goat knows he has horns! You will see when your turn comes, Nils, my friend." He grinned as he stared at the sunset. "A wife is what you need."

Nils thought on his friend's words the next day. *A farm and a wife in that order.* He paused as he waited for a fresh load of bricks. "Hey, Jorgen, this Sunday makes a day to visit farmland for sale. Are you thinking we get lucky?"

Jorgen grunted. "God's promise, maybe. But Santa Barbara has what people call a land bonanza. We will be lucky to put together fifteen acres. A man don't survive on that!"

"Give it time. We cool our heads and let our beggars' pockets fill." Nils turned back to his work. It would not do for the foreman to think he was a slacker.

"None too soon for my taste."

Nils grinned and slapped a half-inch layer of mud mortar on his row of sun-warmed bricks. "Poor Ole, shoveling *hesteskit* from the stalls of stubborn horses. Do you see the bruise he brings home last night?"

Jorgen nodded. *"Ja.* Elizabeth sees it as well. She gets handy at mending his sorry skin. One would say she likes it."

Nils laughed. "He has blinders for that girlfriend of his back home."

Jorgen paused to gaze out at the seagulls fighting over fish scraps being dumped by a lone fisherman on the wharf. A raft of otters joined the fray and the bay erupted in a chorus of barking. Below, Lars was already finished with work, on his way to the wharf with a fishing pole slung over his shoulder. "Lars is one lucky man. He trains horses for the rich men now—come up in the world for sure." He laughed and placed a brick. "The boss says we Norskes have the touch."

Nils bladed a thin layer of mud across another row of bricks. "Praise don't fill our pockets. At the rate the job pays, we will be yet another year saving to buy our land."

"Maybe so. But Lars makes up his mind to bring his fiancée over. She writes to say she is ready to make the journey this winter. He leaves at the end of the month."

Nils tried to quell his rapid heart. "Any others speak of coming?"

"If they do, all are welcome."

Nils continued working without comment. He had received a letter. His sweetheart had told him that she had no wish to travel to America. She claimed she was sorry to disappoint, but her mind was fixed.

He spent the evening after supper walking along the beach, thinking about how his life had changed with the arrival of a single letter. If he were home he could convince his sweetheart to change her mind. But he was no letter writer. His letters had not talked of his heart or his hopes for her. A sensible girl would know without having to read a man's feelings. Better that she should hear descriptions of the land and of his progress to earn a farm. But neither had impressed her.

When the sun slipped into the horizon he turned and made his way back home. Tomorrow was another day.

At the rooming house, Ole Nilson clutched a crumpled letter in his shaking hands. His words rushed out in a torrent of anguish. "Anne's sister writes that she does not survive the fever. They buried her at Stranda Church, and the sister takes over the farm." He twisted the letter and stared at the hateful words. "What am I to do? I have no future. No wife, no nothing."

Nils sat quietly, unsure what he should say. Anne Marie Ringstad had been the oldest, set to inherit her father's Nygaren farm, but her father was unyielding in his insistence that any husband must pay her sisters for their share of the property. Ole had made no secret about it. He was here to get rich so he could return and marry the fiancée he spent so much time thinking about. Now that dream was over. "Will you be going back then?"

Ole rocked back and forth, considering. "Nothing for me there. It seems I am destined for America after all." He folded his letter and set it in the pocket over his heart, his hand resting against it as he turned to face the sea with set lips and dry eyes.

Nils rocked on his heels in silence. Both of them without a future, it seemed. He felt the last rays of daylight shutter into darkness and the breeze die down. The sound of seagulls quieted. Only the steady lap of waves and the occasional bark of a dog filled the void of silence surrounding them. From somewhere a man coughed and a woman made a quick, agreeable laugh, the sound encouraging and hopeful.

When the lanterns inside the house were extinguished, he urged his friend to his feet. "Come, brother. We put this day behind us. Enough trouble for today."

Chapter Three

Pretty Girls for Lonely Bachelors

October 7, 1889. Lars will arrive soon with three pretty girls for us lonely bachelors. Looks to be a wedding soon.

NILS SHARED LARS'S letter, written after his friend's arrival in *Norveg*. "He writes that nothing much has changed. The quiet farms as neat and proper as they been for five hundred years. He says the deep snow seems like a prison. He tries the ski slopes, but it seems he left his youth behind when he departed for America. His mother is in good health, but she is busy with her husband's farm and barely the time to chat. He and Karn will set off as soon as weather permits." He abruptly scanned the part added for his eyes alone. *Ingeborg has married an old farmer. She will not be coming with us. Don't buy any land until I arrive.*

Nils handed the letter to Ole, even the private part. Ole looked up, but no words were needed. His friend had watched a dozen ships leave Santa Barbara without boarding any of them to return home. Ole would make a fine neighbor—if they could find the land. But the search seemed no closer than when Lars left. Each time the men found property, the asking price was higher than it had been a month earlier. The labor contractor had found them another job, the town's main street would have cobblestones before long. Their money grew in their tins and mattresses.

"So what is next for us?" Nils asked.

Jorgen suggested they find a bank to deposit it in. "I ask around. Mr. Ansok says there is a man who may be trusted."

"Good. We go see him while we wait for Lars to return."

Mr. George Edwards invited them into his office while his assistant scrambled to find chairs. While they waited to be seated in the richly appointed room, with its dark mahogany desk big enough to sleep a man on top, he inquired as to whether they would need an interpreter.

Jorgen proudly shook his head. "I . . . know the English pretty good," he stuttered.

The investor glanced at the paperwork from their new savings accounts. "Have you gentlemen considered investing in a fishing boat?" he asked. "A formal company where each own shares of stock in the vessel?"

Nils exchanged a look with the others while Jorgen studied his shoes. Ole clearly remembered his own father's death in a storm. "Fishing boats sink. We have seen this back home," Nils said.

"*Ja.* Farming is in the blood. We rather work our own selves to death than let the fish do the job," Jorgen said. The banker earned a living by loaning his money out, secure in the faith that his profits would increase. For Norskes, the land was the only way.

"I have a suggestion," Mr. Edwards said. "My family possesses acreage at the northeast end of Ventura County. The land would suit for dry farming. Perhaps we might ride over to see the prospects."

"How much you think to ask?" Ole Overaa voiced the thought on Nils's tongue.

"The payment could be amortized over say, seven years. I would ask four dollars per acre for the flats and two for the bluffs." The banker's smile mocked their unsuccessful attempts to hide their interest.

Ole Overaa scowled. "I don't want land suited only for goats and sheep. That be the case, I stay back home."

"Some of each," Edwards said. "The majority is good, flat farmland. Good water."

At the mention of water, Nils leaned in to better hear the banker's words. "When could we see it?"

"We could leave as soon as your friend returns. That would allow sufficient time before the rains." Edwards lifted his ink pen and examined it while the men considered. "I will keep it off the market. Give you fellows a chance to see it."

Outside the bank, Jorgen swung onto a lamp stanchion and gave a yelp of joy. With one hand holding onto the base, he pulled a flask of aquavit from his vest and took a swig. *"Bonden er ikkje gås fordi han er grå!"*

"The farmer is no goose because he is grey? A proverb for old men, not five green fellows with a lot to learn," Nils said, laughing. He took a swig, grimaced and took another. Clearly the drink was turning him upside down. "You think searching for farmland on Sunday is a sin?"

Ole frowned and reached for the flask. "Sure. But God isn't the one trying to make a living." He raised his hand in a toast. *"Skål!"*

"Skål, brothers. We are bound to be rich men. There is no help for it. Rich and good-looking—both!" Jorgen jumped to the ground and pocketed his empty flask.

A shout went out for the big four-mast ship sailing across the horizon. Nils joined the throng waiting at the pier to help Lars and three laughing women disembark. Lars was nearly a foot taller than his fiancée, Karn Gjerde, a tiny, energetic girl with sensitive, intelligent eyes and a neat coil of braids on top of her head.

Nils craned to see the faces of the other girls climbing from the small transfer vessel. He recognized Lina Ness from her small form. His heart raced as the third girl hesitated, her hat covering her face as she fought to keep it attached in the stiff breeze. When she looked up, he released his breath when he saw the stray hairs escaping her tight coronet of braids. *A farm-girl no more.* When the sound of people jabbering and laughing broke his concentration, he shook his head to clear his confusion.

Ellen Fjørstad met his eyes and smiled before she turned to whisper something to Lina Ness. The two girls moved easily along the pier. Ellen's sensible skirt whisked from side to side with each stride of her tiny, stout boots. She met his glance again and he managed to smile. Next to him, Jorgen gawked at Lina like a schoolboy. *Three pretty girls for the lonely bachelors.* Jorgen was already pressing a kiss on Lina Ness's small hand. The girl's face flamed with color, but she showed no sign of objecting.

Nils glanced at Ellen and hesitated. He was no *flørter*, eager to show off for a girl. He would ask her to walk with him on Sunday—to know if he had a chance with her.

At the small neighborhood street dance that night, Ole Nilson sat with Lars's sister, Elizabeth, discouraging strangers from asking her to dance. Jorgen tried to talk Lina into joining a folk dance, but she shook her head in protest.

"I think it's not the Lord's way, this dancing. It makes me sick to see them out there like that," she said.

When the music halted, the men moved aside to speak among themselves of weather and the chances of finding a good team of wagon horses. They agreed that they would put their money into quality farm wagons until each could afford a good spring buggy.

Finally, Ole broached the subject that had been turning his stomach in knots. "Lars, my friend! What do you say to having me for a brother-in-law? I have settled in my head that I wish to marry your sister."

Lars smiled and clapped his friend on the back. "Elizabeth has been on her own for many years. I have no right to decide for her. This is her decision."

"But you have no objection?"

"None. If she don't see you for the fool you are, then who am I to tell her," Lars teased.

"She frets the three years she has on me."

"She is not so old. Time enough left for children." Lars fumbled with the frayed edge of his jacket before meeting his friend's eye. "But no woman should live in the shadow of a dead girl. Or a grieving man."

Ole blushed. "*Nei!* Your sister has put my grief to rest. Time now for the living."

Nils returned to where the young women stood chatting and laughing. When the fiddlers began playing a traditional *halling*, Nils joked to Ellen that he had wooden legs more suited to watching. Apparently she agreed because when the dance began, she remained at his side. As they walked back to the rooming house, he was careful that their hands didn't touch lest he seem too forward. "We leave in a few days to visit the Conejo Valley. A farm has been offered us for purchase," he began, searching for something to fill the silence.

"So—farmers all? Soon you will be land barons!" Ellen laughed. "This is how you say that valley? Cone-nay-ho? How long do you be gone?"

He detected admiration in her teasing, a good sign. "About a week. We see what happens."

"Then I wish you safe travel." She turned toward him, her green eyes showing wariness. "Maybe you get so smitten with your Norske fields you forget your heart yearns for our friend Ingeborg."

Chapter Four

Land of Sage and Rocks

October 15, 1889. A land of sage and rocks. Not hard to prosper if you have good health and strong will. Thanks be, the good Lord grants us both.

NILS SAT HUNCHED in his wagon seat beside Ole Overaa as the team fought the harness in the early morning fog. "I would sooner walk the sixty miles to the Conejo Valley than trust these dumb brutes I buy at a bargain. But they need the practice."

Ole smirked. "And you as well!"

Nils held the two horses with muscled forearms honed by months of hard work. His wagon held bedrolls, food and cooking pots—nothing that a green team could damage—time enough for risky loads after he and his horses learned each other's ways. Jorgen rode with Mr. Edwards, already deep into a story that brought a hoot of laughter from the other man. Ole's team was already broke to harness. Elizabeth sat with them in the buggy.

Edwards had arranged the trip for late fall before winter rains filled the rivers. Now they took their place on the sand road. When the tide receded in the morning light, exposing the hard-packed sand, the buggies and freight wagons started forward. Horse tracks in the sand filled as quickly as the horses vacated them. To distract himself from the chilling fog that cut through his work coat, Nils turned to watch wagons loaded with families on outings. A stage hurried to get a better position in the line. Drays carried goods and supplies to the next town. Jorgen leaped from the buggy, his trousers rolled up to the knees, to fill his pockets with unbroken sand dollars until the tide receded and the line started forward. By the time the fog burned off and the sun announced itself, the traffic was spread out along the beach.

The small village of Ventura lay like a bright shell on the shore—an isolated town, smaller than Santa Barbara but with the same Spanish adobes and wood houses cloistered around a mission church. Nils trailed Mr. Edward's buggy through a narrow street crowded with Chinese men in loose clothing wearing long black braids down their backs. Their quaint stalls were surrounded by hanging ducks and dried fish. Smells of pickled pork and incense permeated the air.

Jorgen turned to his friends, his thumb and forefinger pinching his nose. Nils smirked, but he felt better when Elizabeth's fingers brushed a basket filled with familiar bread and cheese.

That night he joined the other men throwing their bedrolls in the dried grass alongside the river, leaving Karn and Elizabeth the wagon bed. At sunrise the girls served strong coffee doused with held-over milk to go with the thin crisps of flatbread, butter and boiled eggs Mary Ansok had sent along.

Their conversation on the travel that morning was of the dark, rich soil and the eucalyptus trees that formed windbreaks along farm boundaries. "Blue gum." Edwards paused to relight his pipe. "You might consider planting a grove. The wood makes an even cooking fire. Even furniture if you've the talent."

Jorgen craned his neck at the tidy farms they passed. "Even a fool could make his fortune on this rich land."

"Too late for that," Edwards said. "Eastern speculators have claimed much of it for oil drilling. Organizing a company for the speculation and extraction of crude oil from underneath the surface as we speak."

"Oil?" Elizabeth asked. "Like the whale and fish oil we use?"

Edwards nodded. "They'll find uses. Wait and see."

Nils drove past a farm with a three-story house trimmed with ornate lintels and sconces. Even the barn looked grand. From the seat next to him, Ole Overaa muttered, "What chance do five Norwegians with paper in their soles have against men with money?"

In the late afternoon they climbed a steep grade into the Conejo Valley. Nils's weary horses plodded in steady cadence, their footfalls accompanied by the creaking of harness. He stood to ease his muscles at a section of road where grain had already been threshed and cattle grazed on the stubble. A line of gnarled pepper trees shaded a water trough in a land bleached from the summer sun.

"There's less rainfall here. You should know that," Edwards warned. "Bean and barley land for the most part."

The sun was low when the wagons halted near a rocky hillside overgrown with stunted cactus. A rabbit ran across the ground in front of them. He set the brake, tied off his team and looked to where Edwards was pointing out the boundaries of a square mile of land covered with desert vegetation. He swallowed. "There sure is a lot of rocks and sagebrush here." For once, not even Ole Overaa contradicted him.

Lars knelt to crumble hard-packed adobe earth in his hand and looked up, frowning.

"It will require effort. But the land has potential," Edwards said. Nils looked from one man to the next, seeing their hopefulness and greenhorn optimism. A meadowlark called from a bush. A rabbit ran from cover and skittered to a halt. Edwards directed the teams toward the west. They traveled through the brush to a willow thicket surrounding a small pool. "The water source," he explained. "I believe you'll find it adequate."

Nils stripped two willow saplings from a nearby bush and crossed the witching sticks in front of him as his father had taught him. He started off toward the east for a dozen paces before he changed course. When the sticks dipped of their own accord, he looked up, satisfied. "Close water here."

A gust of wind tore across the field, lifting soil in a dramatic zephyr that held them spellbound for several minutes. Edwards nodded. "Gentlemen, you witness the east winds. They will seem vexatious in the late summer."

"Better the wind to turn the windmill than a fool to tote the bucket." Jorgen laughed. "This wind reminds me of the fjord."

Edwards produced a map. The men started around the perimeter, marking the boundaries with stakes and rags. Someone added a line-drawing of the creek to the line map, and later an artesian spring they discovered that provided slightly alkaline water. "Fresh enough for cattle and garden. Horses might be a little more choosy," Ole said.

Nils found Indian paintings on a stone cave protected by a rocky overhang. He joined Lars beside a scattered collection of broken bowls and arrowheads. "These people were here when the Vikings rode the sea."

At the highest point, the men paused to study the sagebrush land sprawled before them. "How would we divide the land to be fair to all?" Jorgen asked.

"Maybe we put names in the hat and each name pulled in order chooses his lot," Ole Overaa suggested.

Edwards checked his pocket watch. "Those details can be determined later. You're fair men. You'll find the way. But are you gentlemen in agreement on this parcel?"

"Yes." Nils joined the others, his agreement spoken in English to commemorate the occasion. He looked around at those who had yet to commit. Ole Nilson glanced at Elizabeth, biting her bottom lip as she considered, arms folded over her breasts. Finally she nodded. Lars and Karn whispered furtively until they looked up, eyes shining. The agreement unanimous.

At dusk Nils heard the harsh, insistent call of small brown towhees settled in the bushes for the night and the clicking of spoon to plate over a cookfire. Common sounds. Familiar sounds. It seemed as though the land was choosing them instead of the other way around. He recalled Ellen's words, that he had a strong heart. *Maybe for farming, but for a wife as well.* He sat with one ear trained on the conversation and the other on the sounds of the land. The winds died down. The air carried the musky scent of sage and the shrill cries of coyotes. He stood to stretch his legs and added a branch of dried sage to the fire. The crackling release of the pungent herb served as a backdrop while the men delayed sleep, debating the land's prospects. From somewhere to the east a neighbor's cow bawled from a canyon.

Spirited debate peppered the ride back to Santa Barbara the next morning. Each man had an opinion about how the section might be divided.

"We will need supplies—everything from needle to nest, as my mother used to say," Elizabeth joked from the bouncing wagon.

Karn nodded, her eyes dark in thought. "We will wait to marry. Lars needs time with this wild new land."

Marriage early would work better, in Nil's opinion, but he held his tongue. The men would be consumed with small tasks and big thoughts —as would the wives. But surely they would enjoy facing the challenges together.

Jorgen apparently felt the same. "I will need to do some fast talking to talk Lina into this place."

Nils smiled. "I think you are up to the task, brother. When you describe the land she will think you take her to Eden itself."

In Santa Barbara, Nils walked with Ellen. The question of marriage waited on the tip of his tongue, but he was afraid of what her answer might be. He spent the walk telling her about the sage and rocks, the adobe and the need for corrals and a well.

"Is the land so poor?" she asked when he paused to catch his breath.

"Poor?" He shook his head. "Only much work at the start. Once the land is ready, it provides five families with all they need. Space for children to run and play. We will have good times there. A life filled with joy and bounty such as we have never seen in our lives. We make a fine community. This is what I see awaits us." He waited for her to make a jest of his eagerness, but her eyes seemed thoughtful.

"Karn waits to marry," she said. "I think this is a good plan."

He nodded. The question he had intended to ask would wait.

By the end of a week, Mr. Edward's map was nearly worn through from fingers tracing imaginary lines where each man's farm would begin and end. They consulted other farmers about American ways of farming. Earlier arrivals explained the process for changing their names and becoming citizens. The five listened to warnings of green immigrants being swindled in the past. Before long, both their business acumen and their English began improving.

Nils led the way to see Mr. Edwards with their down payment.

"You gentlemen understand, I'm selling you the entire section, six hundred fifty acres as a unit. If you quarrel among yourselves, the others will still be responsible for the payment. If you default, all of you lose the land. Is this agreed?"

Nils nodded with a glance at the others. The room crackled with unspoken fear until, one by one, they shifted and studied their feet. *If any one of us has doubts, this is the time.* It would be like a marriage, a union of farmers. When the last man looked up and nodded agreement, Edwards produced an official-looking document.

"Gentlemen, think carefully how you sign. The name as it appears on this document will reflect your American status."

Each signed his name. Lars Berge became Lars Berge Pederson. Ole Overaa signed Ole Anderson. Nils signed Nils Uren Olsen. Ole Ansok Nilson signed Ole Nelson and Jorgen signed George Hansen.

"Letters from *Norveg* will have a hard time finding us if they are addressed to the old names," Jorgen joked.

"We keep the old ways among ourselves. Too many changes otherwise," Ole Overaa Anderson grumbled. He glanced at Edwards. "We have decided how the land is to be divided. We wish to have the lines drawn on the map."

"As you wish," Edwards responded. "But until the land is paid for nothing will be legally binding. At that time you'll each sign quit-claims giving up your right for a parcel, and transferring it one to another. You'll sell it to each other for a fixed fee—say, a penny."

The map was drawn up, with lot No. 1 on the north end at 199 acres because it contained the largest amount of hillside, some of little value. Lot No. 2 for 111.16 acres. Lot No. 3 for 97.03 acres. Lot No. 4 for 105 acres. Lot No. 5 for 139 acres because it contained a vast field of cactus on a rocky hill.

"We do the draw after we arrive on the land," Ole Anderson explained. "From the hat." He spanned the map with his thumb and little finger. "I hope to hell I don't be getting the end pieces. I'm a farmer, not a goatherd. Still, I take my chances."

Over supper, Ole explained to Elizabeth how the land would be divided. "Not enough you take a chance on me as a husband, but also on the farm I bring. You are a brave Norska," he teased.

She smiled. "Don't forget, I also settle myself to a new American name. I will be Mrs. Nelson to my neighbors. I won't know myself!"

"You'll be a fine wife, this I know. Never a doubt for me."

After dinner Nils asked Ellen to accompany him to the beach. "A fine winter day," he began. She nodded, but her silence gave him no encouragement to broach the topic of his heart. Just ahead, Ole held Elizabeth's hand. When he turned with a kiss, his hand brushed her breast. Nils felt a stab for the day he would be able to do the same.

Elizabeth's face blazed when she saw that they were watched. "Look, Ole! Look at the seagulls. So like those at home that I am homesick. Do you think we ever see *Norveg* again?"

Ole lowered his lips to her ear. "Who can say? Would you have a liar for a husband?"

Elizabeth's eyes welled, even as her laughter spilled over. "Such good things here. I feel selfish for having a thought of home. Do you think we will one day forget?"

"We will have two homelands." He stared off into the sea, his hands tucked into his armpits. "Home is where you will be, wife. This is all I know."

Nils glanced to see Ellen's reaction. She turned and happiness shone in her face. "America is our future," she whispered. Nils felt his heart swell with hope. He was glad when the wind whipped her shawl and he could settle it close around her shoulders where a small vein throbbed near her ear.

When Ole and Elizabeth's wedding day arrived, Mary Ansok made a *kransekage* cake with donut-shaped layers of whipped egg whites baked to golden crispness, and a pile of whipped cream between each layer. On the sides she placed Norwegian flags, and at the top, an American flag to mark the solemnity of their future.

Mary produced a carefully wrapped *bunad* from her trunk. It was old and worn, a one-piece jumper in formal black with vibrant embroidery on the yoke and around the hem. She had sewed a snowy white blouse with puffy sleeves. Someone before her had woven the double-shuttle wool skirt and the decorative yoke for a beloved daughter. Now she pressed her lips against the colorful embroidery she had spent many hours mending to look new again. She produced a colorful embroidered purse with a crisp white handkerchief inside. "For the tears of a happy bride," she said as she handed everything to Elizabeth. "The *bunard* is not complete without the little purse."

Elizabeth's eyes glistened with joy as she pressed the fabric to her cheek. "How I have dreamed of this. I never dared to hope."

Mary laughed. "It seems we immigrants are more sentimental than the folks who stay behind. Try it on. See how it fits."

Lars returned to fetch his fiddle from the parlor. "You look beautiful, sister. Ole is a lucky man." With Elizabeth's hair freshly braided and her garments pressed and scented with rose water, she looked as worthy as any girl on her wedding day.

The wedding procession began at the rooming house, with two fiddlers leading the way and the bridal couple following to the Lutheran Church. Lars escorted his sister. Jorgen and Lina followed, their shoulders brushing each other—and sometimes their hands, but no one dared to tease; Jorgen had developed a jealous streak in the weeks since Lina arrived.

Afterward, Elizabeth raised her glass of aquavit. "Even at home I would not have such a wonderful wedding," she confessed. "My family will know of this day by my letters and the photograph. By my heart."

Later, Lars picked up his fiddle and joined other musicians. The street filled with laughter as a few guests danced the ring dance, the walking dance, waltzes and stomps. The food on the *koldtbord*, the cold table, disappeared. Aquavit, vodka and wine came out of hiding. Some of the bolder men sang bawdy drinking songs they devised on the spot for the bride and groom.

The moon was halfway across the sky before the *nattmat*, night food, was brought out. At some point the bride and groom excused themselves, but the music continued until the last of the dancers pleaded the need of rest.

Nils woke the following morning to a bare spot where Ole's bedroll had laid, and remembered that their numbers had been reduced by one. "Ole is one lucky man. A wife to cure his headache!" he groaned from his bedroll.

"I would not mind being Ole today, myself," Jorgen teased.

"Shhh. Everyone cannot become pope in Rome. Go back to sleep." Lars snarled.

Nils smiled at the old Norwegian proverb. But he was of the same mind. Ellen need not think he still pined for his old sweetheart, Ingeborg. That time was forgotten. His future held feelings for a joking, practical girl who already claimed his heart.

Elizabeth Berge Nelson

Ole Nelson

Chapter Five

Draw from the Hat

March 20, 1890. The Conejo Valley. Today we draw from the hat to determine our farms. Friends first and always, no matter the outcome.

ON MOVING DAY, Nils joined his team to the line of wagons and buggies waiting for low tide on an ocean that lie glassy in the crystal-clear air. No sign of fog for their sending-off. No sign of carelessness, either. His buckboard was piled high with plow blades, spare leather for harnesses, water barrels, tools and provisions.

When Ellen appeared at the edge of the small crowd, he leaped down and doffed his hat, conscious of everyone watching. His words felt halting and awkward in the presence of their friends. "So, I am off. I write you often with news so you will see our Conejo through the eyes of one weary farmer."

Her eyes glowed with intensity and intelligence. Her green eyes flashed beneath a fringe of bangs she had woken early to curl on a curling iron. Her hands fluttered as though searching for something to grasp. She turned and saw others hurrying past to their wagons, and her fingers stilled. "You will take care? Eat proper and give a thought to the dangers? A weary farmer can make a misstep."

He laughed. "I will take care. I plan to build a farm that a wife would like to share."

Ellen's face reddened. "Then you best take your seat like the others. I will wait to read how you get on with your new farm."

He hesitated, grasped her hand and pumped it in a firm handshake that left his own tingling when he leaped onto his buckboard a moment later.

Ole and Elizabeth followed, already in a lover's quarrel from the sound of it. "Ole, hold up a minute. Stop talking about the farm. We are barely wed and already you have forgotten me."

"Barely wed? Nearly two months. You are not satisfied I spend my nights in your bed—you would have me spend my days there as well? In short time you would be a widow with no land!" He laughed. "Once we arrive and empty our wagon, I make a trip to Hueneme to pick up two loads of wide redwood boards—and shingles for the roof of our home."

"Two wagons? You would build me a *herregård*?" she teased.

"A mansion? No, sorry. A shack, more likely. Two rooms to begin with. Smaller than I would like, but with a wooden floor to satisfy my fussy wife."

"*Absolutt nødvendig!*" she teased.

"Everything is necessary with you, wife," he retorted. "I will build you an outside fireplace with a good inside hearth to hang your cooking pots."

She nodded. "The boys agree to build me a cooking shack if I feed them until they have their own wives. Do not concern yourself. A sad little crofter's cottage with its plain boards will do until we have a real house."

The crowd was already dispersing. Nils's heart sank when he saw Ellen edging toward her house. He turned away and vented his disappointment on his companions. "Come, Nelson. At this rate the horses will need another feeding before we start. Tell the wife to take her seat and let's be off!"

Lars followed in his own wagon and team. Karn had met the Solanos and she was happy working for them as a maid and cook. When his shack was ready and the first crops harvested, Lars would return for her. In the meantime she would earn money for their household furnishings. It had seemed like a good idea when she suggested it, but now the two stood at the loading, pretending that their whispered conversation was essential.

"What will you do with the money you make when I am gone?" he asked.

She laughed. "I buy chickens. And sugar for my thin butter cookies that you love so. No Norska can run a proper household without poultry or cookies!"

He folded her into his arms, his body looming over her tiny frame. "The months will be long. But I turn my thoughts to the horses and the plow and maybe I forget you."

Her tinkling laughter made him smile. "There never was so bad a crow that it did not want a mate."

He heard the old adage spoken in her crisp Norwegian tongue and his tongue thickened. "I return as soon as everything is ready, my little Norska. Promise." He gave her a kiss and moved reluctantly onto his wagon.

Jorgen stood atop his wagon seat, wearing a new knitted scarf that matched the one draped over Lina's head. He stood and waved from the seat, keeping his balance as his team lurched. He had spent the morning with his head close to hers, sharing conversation. They had dawdled at the table in the rooming house until his breakfast was cold and his coffee colder.

Nils turned to wave at Ellen as she stood at the edge of the crowd. She had agreed to write him. He was satisfied. She would make no contract with any other man until the two became better acquainted. It was something, he decided, as he turned to his team. Still, he spent the hours upbraiding himself for his stupidity. A kiss would have been something to remember her by.

In New Jerusalem, they watered the horses before going inside to purchase flour, sugar, canned sardines, soda crackers, and other supplies from Samuel Cohen's mercantile. A small purchase of farmer's cheese would last them until they could cure their own. Nils bought bags of oats for the horses and seed corn for planting.

Elizabeth passed among the shelves, trying not to yearn for the simple basics she would do without until the first crops came in. Tins of macaroons, red apples, skeins of taupe woolen yarn, bolts of soft flannel and mother-of-pearl buttons caught her eye as she wandered the aisles in search of baking soda and kerosene. She was glad to help select bare-root fruit trees, including a fig, loquat, quince and two peaches, and three nut trees to start an orchard. But it was hard seeing the beautiful ginghams and baskets without experiencing a bit of regret.

Her husband noticed. "When the harvest makes we will have coin for your needs. Until then only basics such as God provides."

"There is nothing here I need." She caught his smile and his warm eyes told her he was grateful. "We have wedding gifts to occupy me. I am content."

Nils bought a few cents worth of paper and ink for his letters and a notebook for his journal. Lars made the same purchase. Jorgen had bought a stack of writing paper in Santa Barbara and the stamps to send them. Ole Anderson bought his supplies without speaking. If there was a man for silence, it was Anderson. He lived on the edge of their company as though he feared he would get burned if he stood too close. But he had always been so. At his core he was an honest man, a good worker, and not one given to idle gossip.

As the Conejo came into sight, Nils craned to see the land as a resident, not a visitor. Elizabeth waved her handkerchief at a farmer's wife who stood beside a small wood-frame house to watch them pass.

"I reckon you make her acquaintance before long," Ole commented.

"If she has the good fortune to speak Norwegian, we become fast friends," Elizabeth teased. "But until then I have my little troupe of men."

"I will learn to juggle and we can earn a penny with a traveling show if our crops fail," Jorgen laughed.

That evening, Elizabeth ground coffee beans and brewed a pot of coffee over the open fire. She heated tins of beans to be served with flatbread and butter while the men unharnessed their horses.

Nils carried a pail to the creek while the others led their horses to drink. On their way back he pointed to a place where the creek overflowed in wet years. "Here, we plant the blue gum."

"On whose land? No right until you know," Ole Anderson growled.

"Makes no matter," Lars said. "Blue gum will give us all good firewood. Without the splitting of oak." He laughed. "No sense in wearing out the axes, right?"

"Lars thinks to save his energy for other things once his bride arrives," Jorgen teased. The men smiled at this. They looked around at the flat, treeless land and nodded their agreements to planting the grove.

The sun had scarcely topped the hill when Nils rolled out of his bedroll, too nervous about the morning's business to think of the breakfast Elizabeth set out. He filled his plate and joined the others eating in silence.

Finally, Lars drained his coffee and cleared his throat. "We remain friends, whatever the draw. Agreed?"

"*Ja.*" The four men's voices dropped in apprehension.

"No time like the present," Jorgen added.

Elizabeth collected the breakfast dishes while her husband produced his hat. Nils brought out a sheet of paper. Each man wrote his name on a scrap, folded it and dropped it into the hat.

"First name takes first parcel—are we agreed on this?" Ole Nelson studied the others for signs of agreement. When everyone nodded, Lars pulled the first name from the hat.

The sound of five men and one woman breathing was the only sound until the slip was unfolded. Lars read aloud in a steady voice, "Ole Anderson."

Ole jumped to his feet and strode off into the sage, facing the dreaded hillside with its imposing bluffs so reminiscent of home—and an Indian cave that reminded them they were in America. "I am no damned goatherd. I am a farmer," he shouted.

His words were harsh and angry. Of all the men, Ole Anderson had been the most certain of what he wanted. And now this. Nils considered for a moment the possibility of trading lots when his name was called; but a man couldn't spend his days herding goats. Maybe someday the farm would provide for sheep or goats, but not yet.

To curb the rising tension, someone reached into the hat and pulled the next slip of paper. "Lars Pederson."

The largest portion of flatland, over one hundred and eleven acres. Luck was with Lars this day, Nils thought. He watched as Lars inspected his land with his thumb absently rubbing the sleeve of his coat, an old habit. He was anxious for the others and sorry for Anderson.

Another hand reached into the hat and retrieved a name from the dwindling pile. "Ole Nelson."

Ole and Elizabeth Nelson smiled at each other. Less than a hundred acres, the smallest parcel of the five, but good flats fit for barley. Back home they would be considered wealthy with such a landholding. Nils exchanged a glance with Jorgen and relaxed. No matter the draw, they would remain friends, unlike Ole Anderson who had stalked away, ranting to his horse.

The next name was drawn. "Jorgen Hansen." Jorgen glanced at Nils and gave a wry smile. He was happy with his draw. The flats would provide a living. He would be Nils's nearest neighbor, a happy coincidence.

Nils turned to study his land nearly a mile distant. On the edge, cactus grew to the height of a man's head. Nearby, clumps of sage dotted land interspersed with dove weed and stunted thistles. Two years of drought had left the soil parched and barren of any desirable grass. His horses would be reduced to eating dried weeds until the rains came. From the south, a small wind funnel raced across the land. Overhead, a lone buzzard glided in the wind currents, looking for food. He cleared his throat and said, "Well, we better get to clearing."

The men shook hands all around except for Ole Anderson who had mounted his horse and was riding toward his land. The others spread out to walk their fields, making note of the stones and brush that marked their boundaries. Nils began cutting a fire line across the field. By the time Elizabeth rang the bell signaling the *midden* meal, he had a pile ready for burning.

As the others ate, Ole Anderson sat with his head downcast, ignoring the chatter. Nils caught Lars's eye. They knew their friend's stubborn streak. He was not happy with his lot.

"We will be drawing from your creek, Anderson. It is good, sweet water you have," Lars said.

"Help yourself to it. I go back to Santa Barbara. I can't make a living on that place. Better I get my old job back at the stable." Anderson spewed while the others sat in silence. After all the months of talking and planning, dissatisfaction was claiming a heavy toll.

"There is for sure, forty acres of flats on your piece. Maybe more. A man could make something of it," Jorgen said. "Wait and see what the day brings. Maybe we find gold on your land when we dig the well."

"Anyone wants to farm my flats is welcome. Take the profits for my share until the land pays off. After that, we see." Anderson stood and tossed out the last dregs of coffee from his cup. "I start out daybreak. I let the folks know."

The next morning, Ole Nelson brought the news when he returned from harnessing his team. "He's gone. He won't be back. I see this in his eyes when his name is read first. He shakes the dust from his sandals on this place."

Nils attended to his meal in silence. Back home, Anderson would have supplemented his farm with goats, cherry trees, fishing, lumber, even some blacksmith work. But this land was too new. *They* were too new. Back home everyone knew each other. Here, relationships were yet to be made, markets established.

"Everything needs its time. Maybe he sees how the rest of us fare, Anderson will return," Ole said. "In the meantime, we clear and plant his flats with our own. Income from his land will support the loan until it is paid off. Any extra goes to the feeding of the horses and the men."

Nils nodded. "The terms of the agreement are fixed. I will chain my wagon behind yours for the first trip to pick up lumber as soon as the burning is finished. We will need a cook shack to prepare and store the food. And no more gossip about our friend."

Lars and Jorgen remained behind to begin preparing their land for clearing. Ole and Nils started on the two-day journey to Hueneme to buy redwood lumber off the pier. On the way home they would stop at the post office to pick up citizenship papers.

By late afternoon of the following day, Nils and Ole were back with a load of lumber and the iron required for forming nails on their common anvil. They had stopped for their mid-day meal alongside a huge valley oak that grew along the road and picked up broken branches for cooking wood. After supper they spent the evening giving reports of the washouts, the steep grade and the watering tanks offered by ranchers along the route.

The next morning it took three men to hitch the plow behind the steadiest of the teams while the other horses balked and pitched their heads. Nils started off at a near run, cutting a firebreak through waist-high sage around a section of the field. By nightfall his shoulders felt wracked by the stress of handling the draft horses. His hips ached from pitching back and forth on the uneven land. As one patch was burned, the men moved to another, gathering the brush into a pile with hoes and pitchforks. The smoke-filled valley brought a few curious neighbors who stayed to lend a hand. When the ground was burned, the men put their backs into stump pulling, careful to remove every chunk. A fist-sized root would break a plow tooth.

Each night they scrubbed soot off faces and necks before hunkering over plates and mugs. Elizabeth carried water and food to the table. At the end of the day she led tired horses to the creek. She dug holes and planted her young fruit trees, watering them with dish water after each meal. When the land was prepared, she carried precious seed corn in her apron and dropped it into the ground, in hopes of a late spring rain. If no rain came, they would haul water with their milk buckets. The land payment did not allow for drought.

There was no flour to be spared for cake and only a few black pots to cook it in. Elizabeth made do with an open fire while Ole worked in the evenings pounding the cook shack together. Like Nils, the Nelsons had little energy for laughter, but judging from the spring in his step, Ole seemed to save a bit of vigor for quiet time before the sun rose.

One morning Nils heard Elizabeth laugh at something Ole said.

"No talk of a dowry with this one," she teased.

"*Nei*. Only thanks from a grateful man," he replied.

Later that morning a rare spring shower teased the newly-sown ground, enough to set the seed and to give hope. Ole tossed his cap in the air as the first drops hit his face. "Thank the Lord," he called out without looking to see who heard.

Elizabeth ran into the field, spinning in circles with her dingy white apron drawn up over her head. She laughed and ran to her husband's side. Jorgen joined them in the middle of the field where small green shoots would soon be breaking through the soil. Together, the three of them began a Norske folk dance, Elizabeth taking turns on the arms of the other two. "We did it! We beat the rocks and the brush. We beat the naysayers," she shouted.

Nils paused to watch, hoping for all their sakes that the sprinkles might build to honest rain. He wouldn't mind if his tent was soaked and his spare clothing wet. Summer would bring plenty of heat to dry things out.

When Jorgen returned to his field, Nils turned back to work whistling a marching tune he recalled from his army days. He spent precious time hiking to the top of his bluff, fragrant with the scent of sage and damp earth. The land spread out before him like humpback whales in a golden sea. His musings returned to Stranda and Sunnmøre, places that had comforted him in the past. The sea was such a place. He had spent childhood days standing on such bluffs as this one, watching fishing boats and the occasional navy vessel cut through the fjord. He had dreamed of serving, but the Navy needed no untried farm boys.

Now he lived far from the water. But on this overcast morning he could see the faint line where the Pacific Ocean touched California, twenty-five miles distant. In his mind he smelled the salt tang. The sea had been his dream, but this land offered riches. He imagined his land in a few short months, a field of grain bowing and bending under the unseen force of the wind. In a few months his threshed grain would ride a ship back across the ocean.

In the north field, the Butterfield stage cut across the land between his land and Jorgen's with a thick cloud of dust and the crack of a whip. Jorgen stood watching until the horses passed and the dust settled before he urged his team forward to finish his planting. He was under pressure because others waited the plow. They needed to forge another plow in their shared blacksmith shop. Another in an endless list of jobs before they could seed the fields to barley in the fall.

A week later Lars hurried to finish his field while Nils inspected the new heifers he had bought with his lumber money. The price of redwood hewn from Northern California forests was cheap. It was the glass windows and doorknobs shipped from Boston that cost dearly. Lars's shack would have two rooms, including a bedroom; walls hammered in single thickness planks, one inch thick and twelve inches wide, nailed vertically for strength with joints sealed with narrow redwood battens. The cook shack would soon be finished, but the rest of the houses would wait until they had time and money. Nils had made a decision to buy cattle with his money and bunk with Jorgen until the first crop was in.

"Some of our American neighbors build bigger shacks," Lars observed that evening as he threw down his bedroll in the back of his wagon bed. "But at the cost of plank floors . . . " He stood to survey the night stars in the darkness of the valley. "I would like a bigger house, but I cannot bring a wife to such a place. Her relatives in *Norveg* would tell her, 'better to lie uncomfortably than to cover yourself with a rag.'" He laughed.

"And they would be right. Give her good floors to scrub," Nils joked from his own camp nearby.

"Tomorrow we make a trip to pick up my lumber. And afterwards, a stop at the mercantile for good brooder hens and material to build a strong henhouse." Lars's voice trailed off into a soft snore.

At New Jerusalem, the following morning, they heard news that three wagons loaded with wool had gone over the grade when the brakes failed on the narrow road near Round Mountain.

"Better the bend than the bump," Nils warned. "You intend to take the horses back the same way?"

Lars nodded. "Too late for second-guesses. I have good horses. Mine will do their jobs." He added a sack of feed oats to his order before leaping onto the seat and gathering the reins.

Nils rode the brake hard on the return trip, while the weary horses plodded with their heads down, to the base of the grade and into the last leg of the journey. With the grade behind them, Lars halted to water the horses.

"*Stor klapp på skuldra,* Lars." Nils gave a light clap to Lars's shoulder.

"*Ja. God hester da.*" The horses *had* done well. Lars might have said more, but like Nils, he sounded too weary to jest.

After a day to unload the wagon and rest his horses, Lars collected a wagonload of fist-sized rocks he had unearthed in his field during the first pass of his plow. Now they would do service as the foundation of his shack. Locals had told them of a sandy wash at a bend in Santa Rosa Creek where they would find fine sand for the foundation and the stone fireplace. Later the wives could stretch cheesecloth across the inside walls to trap the dust. When they married, Karn might be annoyed with the constant grit in her food, but she would find ways to make the shack comfortable.

Ole Overaa Anderson and friend.

Lars and Karn Gjerde Pederson, 1891.

Chapter Six

Bride of my Heart

March 2, 1891. Jorgen takes the bride of his heart in marriage. We are each eager to follow. Wives and families will make our colony complete.

ONE EVENING ELIZABETH spilled grease on her apron and broke into tears before slamming the door of her shack. Ole's gaze followed her before he turned back to join the others in a game of whist. Elizabeth had been moody of late. None of the men had escaped her ill humor. She often climbed the bluff to stand with her face turned toward the Pacific Ocean. Afterwards she would return and Ole would tease her out of her moodiness. Clearly, he enjoyed his position as the only married man. More than once Nils had caught Ole's frown when he spent time talking to Elizabeth. For the first time Ole seemed anxious about his wife spending time with the bachelors.

One day he strode around the corner of his shack with Nils following, intending to show off his new harness. They surprised Elizabeth as she stood on her tiptoes, giving Jorgen a kiss on the cheek. Ole stopped abruptly, the summer sun burning his cheeks with anger. "What is the meaning of this?" he demanded.

The two of them looked up and Jorgen held out a letter to his friends.

"Lina has written. It is good news, this I tell you. And I share it first with your wife Elizabeth that soon she will have another friend to live on the Conejo with her. She is so happy she forgets herself." Jorgen laughed.

"Although I don't much care that she did. But I am glad my news makes her so happy. Your wife is a fine woman. She is due a good turn."

"*Ja.*" Ole replied, but without a smile.

Nils saw the hurt and disappointment in Elizabeth's eyes. Ole lowered his gaze, ashamed because she had done nothing to deserve his distrust. Nils stood without knowing what to say that would make things right.

Finally, Jorgen folded his letter back into his pocket and picked up his hoe. "Thank you for the drink, Elizabeth. It surely hit the spot." Whistling, he walked off into the field holding his hand over the pocket where his letter rested.

Elizabeth turned back to her chores without acknowledging her husband. She pushed her hair back with a weary gesture that surely sent a flash of pain through his heart.

"Elizabeth . . . I am a blockhead, it seems." Ole waited for her to turn and smile, but she seemed close to tears. Sighing, he turned back to the field without remembering what it was he had intended to show Nils.

At the end of the week, Nils suggested a trip to New Jerusalem for supplies. Elizabeth turned and began washing dishes with greater force than was needed. He saw the tightness in her shoulders, as though she were holding her tears back. Her husband could spare no time away from the barn he was building. He needed to finish so the next man could use the tools.

Jorgen cleared his throat as though an idea had just come to him. "Elizabeth has a list of things she needs. What say she rides along? She could use a day away from here. It would do her good."

Nils's tongue refused to work. He choked back his objection while he searched for something to fix his gaze on. His fingers gripped the hoe he was sharpening as though it were a good Nordic walking stick.

Jorgen looked from one to another before guessing the reason. "Nils plans to visit Santa Barbara for a few days. There must be a girl there he misses."

Elizabeth looked up and nodded as her eyes filled. Ole took a breath. "Maybe our friends will take you along, wife? It would be a fine visit on your birthday. And when you come back, your pickles will be ready for brining."

She gasped and hugged him in front of everyone, not caring that the kiss on his cheek caused embarrassment. She was that happy. The next morning she climbed aboard the wagon while her husband reminded for the third time, to be sure to pick up the windowpanes ordered and paid for at the mercantile in New Jerusalem. Without waiting for an answer, he picked up his hammer and began pounding nails.

When they reached Newbury Park, Elizabeth craned to watch children lining up to salute the flag outside Timberville School. "It is good that both girls and boys attend. A girl should know to read, not just to herd goats."

She waved to a young teacher shading her eyes from the bright sun. The girl smiled and called, "Hello!"

Elizabeth half rose on her toes before she remembered the moving wagon. "*God Dag*! Hello. *Snakker du norsk?*"

The American girl laughed and shook her head. "No. Only English. And you?"

"Some little bit," Elizabeth said. "I learn."

The teacher moved closer to the wagon to hand them a handbill that clearly one of her students had made. "We will hold dances at the schoolhouse each first Saturday when the harvest is finished. You're invited. We are only two hundred people in the entire Conejo Valley, and most are men—registered voters. We need every girl for dancing." She smiled and added, "Bring something for the potluck."

Elizabeth nodded uncertainly and bent her head to examine the paper. She knew enough English to understand *Saturday, dance*—and *potluck*, which was the same in their language. "I should bring a dish that would let people know our ways. The *flatbrød*?"

Jorgen laughed. "Maybe you make *frikadeller* from rabbit meat and pork? That shows our neighbors what we mostly eat on the Conejo."

Elizabeth poked him with her elbow. "Do you complain about my rabbit meatballs, Jorgen? You are welcome to do better. If you are cooking, I have poached cod on a bed of new potatoes, pickles from jars and cake made of egg whites to melt in the mouth. And a dozen other things we do without in our little colony."

Jorgen reddened. "I tease you, Elizabeth. Do not take offense. Your garden already produces radishes and cabbages. The potatoes are soon ready for digging. Without you, we be eating beans from tins and drinking bad coffee."

Nils turned to look back at the disappearing school. "We make time when the harvest is in. Even though we don't dance, it makes a chance to meet our neighbors. We been so busy we forget to be social."

Elizabeth settled back into her seat. "Ole will agree. When I return, he sees he needs to take me dancing."

"If it were not for Sunday rest, we would work ourselves to a frazzle. It is hard, a day spent under the shade, reading letters from the folks or the Bible—when there is another weed to hoe," Jorgen joked.

"Or a meal to cook," she said.

"Maybe one of us takes a turn," Jorgen suggested. "But not me. What do I know about griddles and batter?"

"Everyone wants to put the axe in the bear-skull, but nobody wants to hold the axe handle," she snapped. "I miss the church back home."

"The traveling preacher comes soon. We have a proper service." Nils was cautious to keep his eyes trained on the road. He had respect for Ole's wife and her strange moods of late, so he kept his silence and concentrated on the horses. He waited until they reached the bottom of the grade before he continued the conversation. "Ole frets about his window panes. He will pace the field waiting for the sight of our wagon, and the first words from his mouth will be for the windows."

Elizabeth smiled. "It is not window glass that sets him to pacing. That is not what fills his head while I am gone. One day you will see!" Nils felt his cheeks heat until Elizabeth took pity on him. "You will be happy to spend time with Ellen, I think," she said. Nils grunted and made no more comments about Ole's temper.

At the boarding house, Mary Ansok rushed to offer chipped blue mugs of strong coffee with thick cream to the shivering arrivals. Cup in hand, Nils looked to see who occupied the parlor. He was happy when Ellen set aside her knitting with a smile and reached for her shawl. On the boardwalk, he took a deep breath and spoke the words he had come to say. "So what's it to be, Ellen Fjørstad? Have you decided if you are a town girl or a farm girl?" He waited as she considered his words.

"Maybe."

Her answer was not convincing. What did *maybe* mean? That she was happy here, or she was not? He tried again. "You have a town man in mind to marry?"

She sounded hesitant. "There are plenty of men looking for wives. The town is growing by bounds. You see how the railroad is changing things."

"A farmer's life is not so noisy as a train man's," he muttered. She would have to decide for herself. She smiled and rearranged her shawl. Her cheeks were rounded and full of health. Her hair was slightly disarrayed. He realized how pretty it looked bound in a loose bun on her head.

Her eyes sparkled with impudence. "You remind me of home, Nils. Your eyes see everything so clear. But you have a stubborn streak like my father's. My stepmother would say the same."

Did she say he reminded her of her father—that old man? "I would marry you if you would have me, Ellen. This is what I come to tell you." He straightened so she would not see his nervousness. "I am not the train man you are hoping to meet, but I have a farm and soon, a house. I intend to become a citizen and vote in each election. I will work hard, and rarely drink, read my Bible and keep the Sabbath. And when children come, I will be a good father to them." He waited for his heart to slow before he continued. "But you will need to set aside the idea of being a train man's wife."

She smiled. "I do not know any train man. I know how to make soft cheese. This is what I love. I want a man who will keep goats for cheese."

He considered. "I keep cows now. Will that satisfy you?"

She nodded. "I stay here another year. I like this town and the people here. I will like the country, too, but this is a happy place for me. But still, nothing lasts forever. I write my family and prepare them. You must write the folks. This will take time. We will exchange letters, talk. Get to understand each other before hard work becomes the only thing we know."

Nils nodded, hoping the sound of his racing heart wasn't obvious to her. He had failed with his last sweetheart; he would not trust letters to make his case to this one. *Thirty years old and still acting the fool with a girl.* He dropped his hat and took her into his arms for a proper kiss. The next minute he was pretty sure he had made a good choice.

On the way back, he kept her hand tucked in his arm, conscious of each brush of her wind-tossed skirt against his trouser leg. Pride lifted his chin when he saw a passerby smile at them. Ellen felt the moment as well. Later, he lingered outside the boardinghouse, unwilling for the evening to end. She had agreed to marry him, but he needed to see if she felt the same. When her eyes softened and she leaned toward him, he wrapped his arms around her in an embrace that quickened his heart. When she finally pulled away he saw in her eyes impatience for the future.

"Our lives together will be more than hard work. We will have good times. Laughter. And children, if God provides," he promised.

He waited to tell Jorgen the good news, but Jorgen surprised him. "Lina and I get married. I stay behind to prepare. We rent a small house from her former employer for the ceremony. Friends will loan us cups and tablecloths . . . all we need for the celebration. The minister will marry us there with all our friends in attendance. She says she prays over the matter and the Lord shows her that she shuns her duty, letting me work all alone."

Nils pumped his friend's hand. "That is fine news, brother. Fine news."

"*Ja.* I slip the ring on her finger before she knows me for the fool I am. Afterwards it will be too late!" Jorgen gave him a hasty one-handed hug and grinned. "Don't you warn her I am no great catch!"

Nils set out the next afternoon with his buckboard filled with Lina's trunks and boxes. The newlyweds planned to come later, bringing Elizabeth and a cousin who would remain as a hired man.

❦

When Elizabeth didn't materialize from the wagon, her husband stood glaring accusations at Nils. It was late and the journey had been tedious. Nils was in no mood for a lecture and he was quick to tell Ole so. The next morning he was awakened by hammering. It seemed that Ole's windows were being set into their openings with a great deal of foul language on the disappointed husband's part. Nils helped his friend until his ears rang with abuse.

"Ole, I leave you to your bad mood—*and* your bad cooking. I, too, will be happy to see your wife back home." He turned and walked off, but the sound of hammering had ended for the time being.

The newlyweds arrived a few days later. The photographer had attended the wedding and produced a fine photograph of the newlyweds in borrowed clothes and finery. Jorgen's worn work boots were visible in the photograph beneath his suit and waistcloth. His fine dark hair lay close to his head, framing the happiness in his eyes for all to see. Lina looked lovely in her wedding outfit; both of them posed in an elegant manner.

The Ansoks had sent along a wooden box filled with salted fish. The women set out a supper of potato soup, hardboiled eggs, late season cucumbers, cheeses and hearty breads and butter, and later, a plate of sliced pear and apple wedges. When supper was finished, Ole and Elizabeth disappeared in the direction of the creek. Nils smiled at the contrition he saw in his friend's face. Clearly there was more to being a new husband than met the eye. He would have much to learn when the time came. Not too soon for him.

Lars unwrapped his fiddle from its flannel blanket and fitted it against his chin, testing the fit of wood worn smooth with use. He pulled the bow across the strings and began a light tune while his toe tapped the rhythm. The lateness of the hour and the aquavit created a melancholy longing in his strings. He played a soft Norwegian folk tune while Nils's thoughts returned to his brothers back home and a hem-hawing girl in Santa Barbara who would maybe marry him—but maybe not. A lot could happen in a year. His mood drove him to request another melancholy tune until Jorgen complained. "This is my wedding week, not my funeral. Time now for happy music."

Much later Ole made a spot on a log alongside his wife, whispering words that were meant for the two alone. Nils tried to temper his embarrassment with a question to Lars about the barley. Lars put down his fiddle to answer. "Mr. Borchard is happy to sell us seed grain when we plant in December. Also starter pigs. The market for our grain is good. America will soon feed the world, he says."

"You saw him at the school dance?" Nils asked.

Lars shook his head. "His son, Antone. Those Germans work like Vikings. Always a new invention to follow the last. They will harvest our crops if we can afford to pay. They have a thresher pulled by thirty-two draft horses."

Nils leaped to his feet in his eagerness. "This I will see for myself. We should ask the cost if we carry our sheaves to them for threshing. Every penny counts for me."

Lars smiled. "And me as well. Karn and I marry at the end of harvest. In Santa Barbara."

Nils pounded his gladness onto his friend's shoulder. "Soon another happy married man." On his way back to his bed he thought of how Ole Anderson must have felt, out of step with the rest of them. He, Nils Olsen, was a five-legged horse now that the other men were all taking wives. It was time for him to start cooking his own meals, spending time in his own company. He would be a burden to no man, even a friend.

※

At the end of harvest, with their barley sewed into heavy burlap sacks, the three men washed the grit from their best clothes, lined up at

Elizabeth's door for haircuts, and readied themselves for the long haul to the wharf in Hueneme. The crop would make the land payment, with maybe enough left to pay down their tabs at the mercantile. They would need Mr. Cohen to open a new tab for the coming year. Necessities only. They would ignore the fresh-ground vanilla and cardamom on the shelves. No money this year for spending on spice cakes and reminders of home.

Ole and Elizabeth waved the men off with ill-concealed longing, but the late-term child growing inside her wouldn't stand the journey. Nils clucked the horses to start the double wagons rolling. Everything depended on this trip. He felt his hands sweating inside his thick leather gloves as he adjusted his hat and checked to see that Jorgen and Lars were at their places.

While they watered their teams at the Borchard trough, another wagon and team passed them with a wave from the farmer headed in the same direction. Jorgen cocked a thumb at Lars and grinned. At the incline they bound chains to their hubs like the farmer in front of them did, so their wagons would drag rather than free-rolling.

At Hueneme, the wagons were unloaded and the sacks stacked on the wharf while the broker, Mr. Archille Levy, oversaw the weighing and the payment. He kept up a friendly patter as he recorded the weight and wrote out a check. A man for fair dealing, others had told them.

"We travel to Santa Barbara to make our payment," Lars explained.

"Long way for that. One of these days I'll give this county a bank," Levy assured them as an assistant carried in steaming cups of coffee.

Nils thought of what waited for him in Santa Barbara. No distance was too far if it meant spending an evening with Ellen. Her letters were welcome, but an hour of hand-holding and conversation would be a boon for a lonely bachelor like himself. And maybe, if she was willing, another kiss.

Mr. Edwards was in his office when the farmers arrived at the bank. He glanced at the draft Nils held. "You've made a good investment in sweat and labor—I'm gratified." He smiled. "The next step is to diversify. There is a new packing house being considered in Oxnard for drying prunes. This is something you should try."

Nils remained silent. He didn't need a banker to tell him what he should plant. Four farmers could do the thinking for themselves. But he reminded himself that the land still belonged to Edwards. Until it was paid off, they were only tenant farmers, crofters like Lars's father who had died leaving ten children with nothing to hold on to.

"And so a weight off the shoulders," Jorgen teased on the way back to the rooming house. He plucked three oranges from an overhanging limb and juggled them as he walked.

Nils smiled to himself. "Still practicing for the traveling circus if our crops don't make? You have no faith in the Good Lord's plan for us?"

Jorgen smirked and tossed an orange to Nils. "Always good to have another trade. Keeps me from becoming *kjedelig*—like you."

"Better boring than a rooster—" Nils's words were cut off by a friendly jab from his friend. The scuffle that followed ended when they reached the boarding house, winded and grinning.

Nils took a seat at the kitchen, accepted a cup of good black coffee, and waited for Ellen to ask how the meeting had gone.

The next evening he asked her to accompany him to Lars's wedding.

The ceremony was lively, with music and foods from the Spanish culture as well as their own. Karn's employers attended. She proudly raised her glass to them when the time came for toasting. "I thank you that you help me to learn proper English. Even though I still do not speak it so good, it is not the fault of the teacher who tries to get the English into this blockhead." She waited for the laughter to subside before she continued. "I will miss you. I so enjoy my time with the children as their cook and nurse-girl." She flicked away a happy tear and raised her glass. "I remember your kindness for all my life."

Ellen sat near Nils while they listened to the music. He knew by the smiling looks that people expected an engagement announcement from the two of them any day. He waited for a sign from Ellen that she was ready to formalize their agreement, but it was hard with only a few minutes here and there in a crowded sitting room, or the occasional walk on a beach with others lending ears to their sweet talk. The evening stretched into the early hours without an opportunity. He walked her home with Jorgen and Lina close behind, not even a chance for a lingering kiss.

He started home the next morning in a sour mood.

Chapter Seven

I Rock my Baby

April 11, 1892. We share such good times here. Good friends and growing families make work seem like nothing. If only my sweetheart were here.

THE WOMEN CREATED *smalahove* from a ewe's head fresh-butchered for their Christmas feast. They rendered whey in their black kettles to make *mysost*, the nutty, sweet tasting brown cheese. After it set, they peeled thin curls from the block and piled it on slabs of flatbread. The women wore their best clothes, kept in trunks against the moths, with the addition of their best white aprons.

On the evening of their Christmas celebration, Elizabeth held up her new son for Nils to admire.

"Strong, big hands. This is good if he is to one day replace his father on this land," Nils managed. All eyes seemed to be watching him. His face burned by the time he returned the baby to its mother and urged Lars to pick up his fiddle.

Two of the hired men danced with each other, acting like fools for the others watching. The women tapped their toes in their white stockings and shoes blackened with soot for the occasion. When it was time for Lars to take a break from his playing, Nils presented each of the wives with a set of wooden spoons.

"Your gift makes a teething toy as well!" Lars laughed. He glanced at his wife. "We too will be blessed with a baby in early summer."

"You waste no time, Lars," Jorgen teased.

"Well, we don't get no younger." Lars stood with his arm around his happy bride.

Nils glanced away. When he looked back again, Karn was watching. "Nils?" She leaned toward him, a smile in her eyes. "What do you say I write Ellen and invite her to stay with Lars and me this spring? To see for herself how we get on? I could use help with the coming baby."

Nils started. *Ellen here?* He saw everyone grinning and managed a surprised "*Ja. Ja!*" in a loud tone that startled the baby. He could think of nothing else to say—the idea was too new.

Karn laughed at his confusion. "After the spring crops are sowed, you take the buggy to Santa Barbara. Fetch her things. You can be married right here on the Conejo."

"The traveling preacher?"

"Reverend Leach will come from Hueneme. Your vows will be legal and spoken before the Lord." Karn's eyes glowed with excitement. "When Ellen sees our good lives here, she will want this—you."

⁓

January crept on slow legs, and February no swifter. No rain fell, a wonder for men and women used to snow. Their new land held no threat of avalanche as happened when snow piled deep on the Stranda hillsides. But neither a frozen pond nor snowy slope for skiing.

The cold months were so mild that they kept their thick woolen socks packed in trunks. The women made pillows of the spare goosedown they pulled from their lofty comforters, after the husbands complained of the heat. They set aside their heavy wool coats and the women knitted baby sweaters from light wool. The men planted winter barley and watched as sparse seedlings broke through the crusty soil in the dry winter months.

They spent the long evenings honing and sharpening hoes and axes in the common blacksmith shop they built together. Nils wrote letters home to his brothers describing how he milked his cows in sunlight, morning and night. He bragged how his barn lantern needed filling only once a week. Lars bought horses and trained them to work, and sold them for a fair profit.

Their pride in the land expressed itself in spontaneous song and laughter, jokes played on unsuspecting neighbors and picnics on the bluffs. They hiked the hills until they knew the land like the trails back home. They took walks in the dusky evenings, feeling like they had a second life handed to them with so many extra hours in a day.

Ole and Lars planted the blue gum grove on a false spring day in January when the hard clay earth fought the spade and the horses whinnied to be set to harness. Their wives placed the eucalyptus stock while Nils followed, breaking the soil with chisel and shovel. Afterward, the women visited the spindly starts with pails of water.

"Rain does not come soon, this may all be in vain," Karn murmured.

Nils smiled. "Faith, neighbor. That is the coinage of the farmer. The rains come again, sweet like a Norska bride."

Karn ventured a weak smile. "Your own wedding will be here soon."

Elizabeth straightened and ran a hand across her lower back. "*Ja*. Tonight, if the Lord wills, my baby will sleep through the night and I will have some much-needed rest." She glanced down the road to where Jorgen's shack was barely visible in the distance. "Lina's baby will be the next to join us. She is ready. She told me so just two hours ago."

Above them on the bluff, Jorgen pushed his cattle in search of grass.

"In a few years 'twill be our sons up there," Nils said.

Karn ran her hand across her own rounding belly. "Farmer thrives among farmers best. Our sons will learn from example."

Elizabeth laughed. "If we grow nothing else in this drought, we grow babies. Soon each house will have its nursery."

Nils turned away, hoping his ripening face wasn't seen by the women. They would make a jest of his embarrassment.

Karn stopped by later in the week with news that Lina's baby had arrived safely. "Both healthy as horses," she hollered to Nils across the field as she made her way home.

Nils raised his hat in salute and clicked his horses forward. Ellen would be glad to hear of the safe birth. It would set her mind at ease.

He spent restless evenings making four sturdy chairs to match the table he planned for Ellen. His hands sanded the fine wood while his mind made plans for his future. His barley was already breaking through the soil. When spring arrived, he would hurry to plant the new crops. Karn had already set up a daybed in their kitchen. When the day arrived to leave, the wives put together a box of butter and fresh eggs for him to take to the Santa Barbara folks. Ole and Elizabeth rode with him. Elizabeth was eager to show her seven-month-old baby to the relatives, and although no one said anything, she would act as a chaperone on the trip home.

When they arrived in Santa Barbara, Ellen showed him her dusky blue trunk. She owned two dark skirts and white blouses that would be suitable for every day, and a black taffeta dress for special occasions. She had stitched together a pair of aprons, white for easy bleaching—and owned a pair of sensible shoes for walking on the dusty roads.

Before they left, they visited W.J. Rea's Photography to have a wedding picture taken. Nils posed in a suit borrowed from the studio wardrobe so that he looked prosperous for the folks back in Norway. The photographer acted as though they were already married and Nils made no effort to correct him. He sat proudly while Ellen positioned her hand on his shoulder as the photographer indicated.

They started home on a beautiful spring morning. The journey took them through blooming orchards and fields already green with row crops just sprouting. Lupine and clover, mullein, mustard and Johnny jump-ups filled the wild areas along the roadways.

"So much abundance in this country. It is clear why they say America is the farmer's paradise." Nils pointed out a windmill in the distance. "So much innovation. I doubt my brothers will believe me when I try to describe all I see today."

Ellen spent her first days arranging her belongings in the home Nils built for her. The rough-cut boards were strange and crude, but she bit off her disappointment. In time they would build a house like the ones back home—after they owned the land. She spread her newly-finished quilt atop the double mattress. She ran her hand over the smooth table and chairs Nils had set in the small area near the window. The room was cozy. It would be easy to prepare food and read the Bible with the same candle. A fireplace for heat and windows favoring the sunshine. *He has built these four walls for living, not show.*

She pulled a length of chintz from the bottom of her trunk and set it aside. The fabric would become curtains during evenings at the Pedersons. When she finished hemming them, she would thread each on a willow stick that Nils had provided for curtain rods. He hung hooks for her cooking pots with a joke about suppers of steamed cabbage, rabbit stew and meatballs. Later, he set a water barrel at the back door with a caution for the labor required to refill it.

Norwegian Colony. Ellen heard the words the first time she rode with Nils to Newbury Park to pick up the mail. They stood outside the Grand Union Hotel and peered through the grainy glass windows at tables holding fine napkins and fancy tablecloths. She studied the menu for clues as to what she might order, had she the money to do so. She moved aside to avoid a couple entering and heard the woman whisper, "That's some of those *Norskies* formed a Colony over yon. Quite a few of them there now."

She wasn't sure if the *Norwegian Colony* was a good thing or a bad, but she was shamed that people felt the need to set them apart. They were Christian people, same as everyone else. She gripped Nils's arm and pretended to read the menu until they passed. She made out the words for fried chicken and mashed potatoes. When the door shut again, she whispered, "I make us fried chicken for far less than they charge here." During the ride home, she admitted that her English was lacking. "I practice with Karn while we work together to make her baby clothes."

On a weekday in the last week of April, Nils arrived at the Pederson shack in his carefully brushed suit and a wool cap pulled over his neatly trimmed locks.

Ellen carefully latched the door behind her and climbed into the wagon. "A rare thing, a buggy ride for just the two of us," she teased as she settled in. "People will think we are scandalous!"

"With no notion of anything but each other," Nils added.

After they paid for their marriage license at the courthouse in Ventura, Nils carried their picnic basket to a spot near the pier where fishermen and yachters were setting off on the water.

Ellen stared at the sea, her thoughts at odds with the happiness of the day. "Do you think we ever go home again?"

Nils cast a questioning look that brought heat to her cheeks. "For me, *this* is home. You. The farm. What more is there?" He sounded so certain.

"Does it bother you," she persisted. "the missed strands we leave behind? Do you ever wish for—?" She wasn't sure what she was asking for. She was happy here. "Your brothers and sisters? Your father? Mother?"

"For me, leaving home was not a choice. I was a burden if I stayed." Nils squeezed her hand and she felt his warmth. "Our lives—here together—will make up for the things you miss. Wait and see."

His certainty countered her lingering doubt. "We have letters and photographs. Perhaps someone else will come over. My sister inherits the farm—she will stay. But perhaps—"

Nils moved to fold her into his embrace. "We will make a big family. And we will write home so often that they get tired of hearing from us. You will see."

She nodded, convinced by the truth she saw in his face. The sun overhead had begun its afternoon descent over the endless horizon, she stood and shook the sand from her skirts. "Such a beautiful thing, this ocean. But we have a long journey home. And a wedding to attend."

Nils lifted the picnic basket and set it in the wagon before turning to the long boardwalk that fronted the shops. A few coins jingled in his pocket. "We buy a root beer. Something to remember the day." Root beer or not, he would not forget this day—or the happy, bright girl who reached to take his arm.

Preacher Leach arrived on horseback two days later. Ellen carried a bouquet of mustard and wildflowers that she and Nils had collected. Some of the Santa Barbara folks arrived to spend a few days, bringing pickles, cakes, meats and hard cheese. Mary assembled her *kransekage*, the traditional wedding cake, using Nils's fresh cream. Ellen was proud to provide miner's lettuce and wild strawberries she had found on her ride from Ventura—proof that other parts of the county were not as dry as the Conejo.

The ceremony was simple. Before she realized it, Nils was giving her a proper kiss in front of the others. Now she was a wife—28 years and no longer a spinster in the eyes of the world—with a good, kind man who smiled as he faced the jests and applause of his friends.

With the first bottle of aquavit, the men shed their suits and rolled up their sleeves. Someone brought out a fiddle and everyone clapped and hooted when Jorgen began dancing alone. People laughed and toasted the newlyweds, saying that theirs was a fine wedding. Nils offered a toast to thank his friends and good neighbors. "God has blessed us with abundance. We will fill our home with joy."

Ellen led the wives inside to exclaim over her wedding gifts, including the goose-down comforter and knitted woolen socks from her family. She set out other gifts on the table: a fine pewter sugar dish, a rosemaling-painted butter server and candlestick holders. Nils had made her a rocking chair with a high back and a deep seat. It set proudly beside a blue domed trunk she had brought with her from *Norveg* that now held her precious woolens. She ran her hand across the wood of the rocker. "My Nils is a fine woodworker. Like his father."

Karn nodded. "Nils said it well. This will be a fine, happy place. The same as our mothers' back home."

Ellen glanced outside where the fading sunset colored the hills in stripes of orange and red. "I have a good man. A good home. And friends to share it with. Surely God has blessed us."

The next day she and Nils joined the others for a hike across the hills. Their first stop was the Indian cave with its symbols painted with campfire soot and crushed flowers. She hid her smile when Nils helped her cross a rough patch; she, a farm girl who had hiked with her two sisters in far more dangerous places than this gentle, rolling land. Their picnic on the bluff was a joyous event with leftovers from the wedding feast and cold coffee—good and satisfying with laughter and ribbing, songs and stories shared about the old country.

One of the men had fashioned a sled for the children, made with smooth boards. "I make blades if we ever get snow here," Nils quipped as the mothers piled their toddlers in for a well-deserved break from riding on weary hips. One of the men pulled the rope along the new grass.

Karn lifted her arms in praise. "You keep your snow, *Norveg*. I choose my garden! I have seen enough snow for one lifetime. I love it here. Every seed I toss in my garden grows with no effort."

Lars rose to embrace his wife. "Agreed. This is our promised land."

Ellen spent her first weeks as a married woman learning tips from the other wives for managing a home in this new land. Elizabeth called on her with a bar of lye wash soap and the loan of her wash tub. She showed the proper way to light a fire in the yard with cow chips and sagebrush, and poured a bucket of spring water into the heating tub. "Always start your fire early. You will need to dry the clothes before the afternoon wind comes up. Here, I'll shave the soap while you sort the clothes into three piles, whites, coloreds and those horrible filthy britches."

Ellen blushed. "Is it only just *my* husband who comes in so grimy each night?"

"Heavens, no! Rainy season, the farmer fights the clay soil that clings to shirts and trousers. In summers, dust and grime everywhere—even in the rice we boil."

"The rice? We wear our teeth down! Is there nothing we can do?" Ellen glanced at the corn-straw broom she was well to wearing through with her efforts to keep her little shack clean.

"The summer heat shrinks the wood walls. Thank God for the laths nailed over the cracks or we would see daylight."

"What can be done? My mother would be ashamed of my—"

Elizabeth paused to hug her. "Do not think such thoughts. Your mother knows nothing of our circumstances. Back home everything is settled. Here, we must find our own way." She smiled at Ellen's teary face. "We make mud to caulk the cracks. At least there is something the soil is good for. And when it falls out, we do it again until we afford muslin to stretch across the walls. Or wallpaper. I see this done at a hotel once. It looks so lovely."

Ellen smiled. "Look, I scraped a knuckle on the washboard. The same as I do back home."

Elizabeth glanced over at the cactus growing in Nils's forage land. "When we finish hanging the clothes on the ropes Nils has strung for you, I show you how to burn the spines from the cactus apples. You will enjoy their flavor."

"So much to learn! Each morning I wake with new surprises waiting. Karn's baby arrives soon. Am I expected to act as midwife? I have had little experience with births."

"No, silly goose. You will cook up a pot of potato and meatball soup and leave me to help with the birth." Elizabeth smiled and patted Ellen's flat belly. "Your turn comes soon enough!"

"The Pedersons name him Peder," Ellen told Nils later. "He makes a playmate for our own when it arrives."

"Our own child?"

She smiled. "One day, God willing."

※

The winter barley was patchy and stunted—a worry, Ellen thought as she carried her skimmed milk to the just-weaned shoats squealing their hunger in the new pigpen. After each meal she lugged her rinse water to the orchard to douse a different tree each time. In another year the trees should be rooted and strong, but the drought was proving to be a clever adversary for man and tree alike. She was watching her latest bucket of rinse water soak into the earth when Nils arrived from the field. "I start the trees proper and in time they reward me with cherries and peaches—better than the home country," she said.

"Home country?" Nils frowned in the lighting of his pipe.

She blanched. "I meant to say, 'old country.' Of course this is my home. With you, where my heart is."

In the kitchen again, she diced fresh butter into flour for a pie crust. When Nils left again, she set the pie to baking in her Dutch oven with a strange heaviness in her chest. Her digestion was off. Her breakfast threatened to come back up again. Her mood was melancholy. Something wasn't right.

At the end of the week, by the time Nils finished the last slice of the dried peach pie, she was certain. "Nils, what would you want first, farmer or goat maid?"

Her husband's confusion was quickly replaced by a flash of understanding. He rose to wrap her in an embrace that lifted her from the floor. "It makes no difference to me. Children are pauper wealth. We are sure enough paupers. I will feel rich."

She laughed. "We tell the others tomorrow."

He was staring at her with wonder in his proud eyes. She had never seen him so happy except for the wedding day not so very long ago. She slipped her fingers through his hair and pressed an errant curl back, "You will be a fine father, Nils. You have a good heart." He closed his eyes as she plied her fingers through his weary scalp, the touch enough to bring drowsiness as he slumped in the rocking chair before the fire.

Summer brought changes to her body, but to the land as well. In high summer she sat in the shade of the house, knitting booties until the heat set her to doze. She was jolted awake by a loud boom and heard the men in the field shouting. "What now," she mused aloud. "Never a dull moment in this sunny place. And now the sky is falling."

"Sounded like it came from west. I ride over to see," Lars shouted from his buckboard when he arrived minutes later.

"I join you. Maybe we are needed." Nils mounted the seat beside him.

Ellen gathered with the other women to watch a column of smoke rising five miles away to the west. "The fields between us hold grain and beans awaiting the thresher," she fretted. Wildfire would take their entire summer crop. She was glad when, two hours later, the sound of horses broke the chatter of their waiting.

Nils arrived with news that a neighbor's boiler had blown up. "Dynamite stored too close to the heat. No one injured, praise God. But the boiler sits four hundred yards from where it laid this morning. And it did not sprout legs!"

"Good news—the smokehouse made it through." Jorgen's joke brought a smile from his wife. "Mr. Borchard's hams are safe."

"If anyone could afford one," Nils muttered with a glance at the cloudless sky.

"Maybe they have a fire sale on the hams? A good break for us."

Jorgen's joke was hushed by his laughing wife's hand over his mouth.

The summer stretched without rain. The young orchards and vineyards clung to life, one dishpan at a time. The cows grazed the hills in search of a blade of brittle, scorched grass. The cattle searched for food, but nothing would touch the pepper trees that grew along the ridges. Nils resorted to stripping the delicate cactus spines and feeding them to the cattle. His horses supplemented their grazing with scant feedbags of oats bartered for Ellen's butter and eggs in New Jerusalem. Twice monthly she rolled the butter made from her cow's rich cream in long rolls, wrapped in wet cloths and set in heavy wooden boxes for Nils to haul to the mercantile.

Sometime she rode along. Even in the drought there was much to appreciate. Riding beside Nils, watching him handle the horses and greet neighbors in his hesitant English brought pride to her heart. "Such a life as this. Who would have thought!" she found herself saying again and again.

The Fourth of July celebration was held in the shade of the eucalyptus grove. Men spread cloths to hold the watermelons and sliced meats, pickles and eggs that the women provided. The Santa Barbara folks brought pepper starts for the women and seashells for the children. The sounds of laughter and conversation filled the colony with energy.

Someone brought a much-used *kubb* set that one of them had made: pins and a crowned "king" from hardwood blocks and batons shaped like fat dowel rods. The men set the pins along parallel lines they drew in the roadway, five pins for each team, with the king squarely between the teams. When the field was prepared, they argued good naturedly who would be on each side.

"Not just the men," Elizabeth protested. "My aim puts you all to shame—you will see. I call foul if you do not choose me for a side."

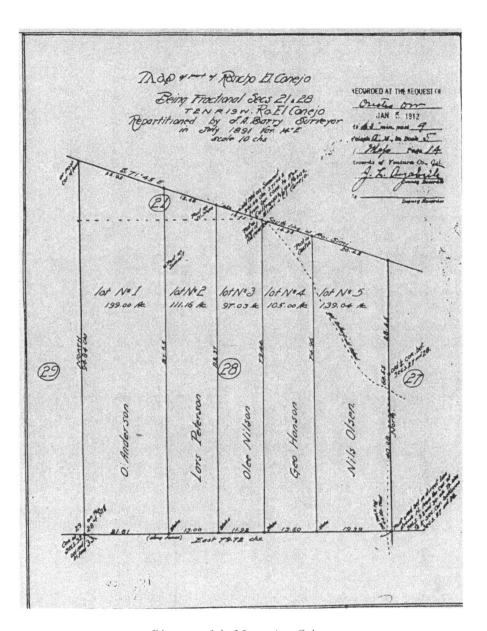

Plot map of the Norwegian Colony

Lars nodded for her to join his team. Nils glanced to see if Ellen wanted to join them. When she shook her head, he took his turn on the opposite line and threw the first set of pins.

He managed to knock two to the ground, and Elizabeth joined her teammates in tossing them back to the opposite side, a penalty against her team, but easier to hit when they stood crowded so tightly in the line. When it was her turn to throw the batons, she fixed her aim on the pin she intended to hit—at a distance of eight meters, no small challenge. The men had the advantage of strength, but her eye was unwavering. The hoots and encouragement from the other women added to the fun, especially when she sent the first baton sailing end-over-end and managed to drop two pins in one toss.

"Take the woman's weapon away. She will slay the field," Jorgen protested. Elizabeth laughed and lobed her next toss at the pin nearest him. He jumped back in mock terror. "You try to kill me. This is certain."

She squinted against the sun and threw again, but this time her throw missed, as did the next. Her last baton claimed another pin. The game continued for another hour, until Nils's team claimed victory.

"Not bad, Opponent." Nils shook Elizabeth's hand with exaggerated vigor that brought a flush of color to her cheeks. "I make a set of kubbs for us this winter. I had forgotten the fun of beating my foes in competition."

She laughed. "Spoken like a true Viking. We welcome the next battle."

That night some of the men fired off their revolvers, but fireworks were saved for the sandy beaches and safe waters of Santa Barbara where a stray spark would not torch the ripened grain. Ellen joined the other women singing familiar folk tunes from the old country while they celebrated her new America.

"Nils," Ellen asked as they prepared for bed. "You will soon be a citizen. Then the country's celebration will truly be our own."

"And I will vote my convictions. Something to look forward to in this big new country of ours. I like it here!"

Ellen nodded, thinking of the day she might learn English well enough to become a citizen herself.

The next day the Moorpark men and some of their Santa Barbara relatives helped harvest the barley while the women sat in the shade, crocheting or working on their laces while they read letters aloud from back home. They celebrated again that night with whipped cream and berries, and rowdy circle singing that brought tears of laughter when the men substituted bawdy lyrics to the songs they had sung since childhood.

"Ssshh. The children will hear you," Lina warned.

"Where do you think we learn these feisty words if not from our own fathers? It is the way of things," Lars teased. "Even you, Lina, must take joy in letting the hair down now and again."

The Santa Barbara people began a song that sent everyone into another round of laughter. It was the way of their little colony to celebrate, tonight and all the other days.

When the last wagon left for Santa Barbara at the end of the week, Ellen waved them off from her front door.

Ellen Fjorstad Olsen

Nils Olsen

Chapter Eight

Drought is a Hard Master

August 1, 1893. Drought is a hard master. Each day brings some little thing that keeps our eyes turned upward.

A WILDFIRE BEGAN in the canyons between Los Angeles and the ocean, filling Nils with apprehension as the winds shifted and smoke enveloped the valley. He stood long into the night, watching ridges glow as fire crept toward them. Over the next two days neighbors worked together to dig fire breaks to the west. One night a fleeing mountain lion set the dogs to baying. Nils brought his rifle to his cheek and took aim, until Ellen placed her hand on his.

"Let it be. It only wants safety. The same as us. Let it be."

He lowered his gun and watched the animal slip into the darkness. "We will be short a calf next week and wondering the cause," he muttered.

Ellen remained silent. Perhaps he was right, but the deed was done.

Finally, the winds changed, sending the fire back on itself until the red line of flames faded and the skies cleared again. Nils drove his cattle over the ridge in an attempt to find new grass. When he returned, Ellen applied calamine to his poison oak and buttermilk to his sunburned cheeks.

"A *Nordsmann* is not made for this heat," she murmured as she placed a dampened cloth on his skin. "It will make an old man of you."

"A farmer must cut the meadow grass while the sun shines," he murmured, smiling. "I will be glad when the baby arrives."

The baby inside her pressed against her at odd hours until, finally, her labor began. Karn assisted in the birth after shooing Nils out to spend the evening with her husband. When Ellen took the baby into her arms and set it to breast for the first time, it had trouble lifting its neck to suckle.

"I fear for this one. Something is not right," Karn whispered as she tucked the baby into a fresh piece of flannel.

Ellen took the bundle and began singing a song her mother had sung to her. "Last year, I herded the goats in the hills. This year, I rock my baby in the cradle. . ."

Karn said nothing, but sadness filled her eyes.

Ellen shared her fears with Nils later that night.

"What does one woman know?" he consoled. "The other women will have assurances for you. Best wait and see."

"You think a lie will relieve me—and not the truth? Karn is a midwife and she knows."

He smoothed a strand of her hair back and leaned close. "Wait and pray. All we can do."

Her neighbors offered advice for easing the baby. They tried massage, manipulating the small limbs, sugar tits and even spooning the milk, but the problem seemed to be more than just the lack of nourishment. The baby's spine was nearly rigid.

※

Eight weeks later, Ellen tearfully hemmed a baby blanket made of a flour sack, printed with the words: "New Roller Process" in bold letters across the front. She placed it in the bottom of a tiny coffin that Nils had nailed together from scraps of redwood, and pressed the blanket down with quick, helpless jabs. *Such a shabby comfort, this stiff sacking for the tiny bundle.* "Better the millers leave their names off," she sobbed. "At least we mothers would be spared the shame."

"Not our shame. We did nothing wrong!" Nils turned away, slamming the door behind him. When he returned, he carried a small wooden marker that read, *Paula Olsen, aged 2 mos. 1893.*

Night dragged on slow limbs as Ellen sat rocking, afraid to leave such a tiny bundle alone in the dark. The sun awakened her from a dull drowse when she felt the pinch of her corset against her ribcage. The darkened fireplace held embers. She added a log and watched flames illuminate the small coffin on the table.

Outside, Lars and Ole arrived with shovels slung over their shoulders. Ellen pulled on her shawl and slipped outside to watch them dig a small grave. *Such generosity to spare Nils the necessity.* After the brief funeral, she watched the men shovel dirt into the tiny grave. From her window the new cemetery seemed a smudge at the edge of the grain field. The men began setting a line for a small fence around the edge, while men and horses worked the field, ever closer with their plows.

Ellen ran outside, waving her arms. "Set that fence back. I won't have her disturbed by an errant pass of the plow. Give the baby space to be. Give her space!"

Nils opened his mouth, checked himself, and nodded to the men to set the fence line back another few feet while Ellen watched, fighting to breathe. He fretted for his wife, needing the comfort of her mother and sisters back home. The baby's death had set her back. A small soul only just taking hold in her heart—withered like the seedlings in his field. He turned from the oversized plot, big enough to bury a dozen more souls. *Please God the space will not be needed.* He started toward the house and halted. His wife would prefer to find her own peace.

The next morning a sour taste coated his tongue before he had finished filling the last milk bucket. Side-by-side on the sideboard, the buckets represented an hour of his life. Butter, to be sure, but more valuable, time.

He plunged his knife into a stack of waiting hotcakes without looking up. When his plate and cup were empty, he pushed back his chair, hitched his trousers and left the table. The day was barely started and already a rash of irritation wore at his good humor. His woolen socks itched with the heat. The goose-down comforter sent as a wedding gift by his wife's people caused him to wake in the night sweating, but his wife clung to the comforter as though it were necessary to her sleep. No argument there. His wife was right. *Alle ting har to sider, minst.* At least two sides to a thing—but sometimes more. There would be more babies, of this he was sure. Not all life was a sorrow.

Normally, he woke each morning filled with immigrant joy, as the others called it, the feeling others described in their letters to *Norveg.* He sent letters home describing his pride when his barnyard came alive at daybreak with the sounds of hunger and purpose. His roosters and hens, cattle and pigs. A seed tossed into the soil grew grain to the height of a man's waist. Aching muscles and new calluses were a light cost when stacked against the promise of first crops. Better to live with certainty than in the hope, his mother claimed. But hope filled his days with sweetness—his and soon again, Ellen's.

The barn was his comfort, smelling of new redwood and the sweet tang of oats. A place for milking and storing fresh-cut hay if the growing season proved worthy of the land agent's claims. He plucked his harnesses from their pegs, started toward the pasture and halted. Time to clean out the corrals. Good manure and straw tamed the hardpan, but maybe this time better intended for the kitchen garden—something to please a still-grieving wife. The land could wait for the garden to thrive.

Everything here was new, untried. Even the horses fought his harnessing and refused to lift their hooves for trimming. The earth fought his attempt to lighten the clay with straw and offal, accepting the burrowing of gophers easier than the cut of his furrow. Everything in this new land fought a Norwegian. The rattlesnakes coiled and hissed at his approach. The cactus tore, and the winds skimmed the topsoil from under his feet. This farm would test the mettle of a stubborn Norwegian, but it would not conquer him. *A man carries his own saddle*, his father used to say. A strange saying because he'd never seen his father ride a horse. Like himself, his father distrusted horses and only used them out of necessity.

In the distance, Jorgen was hitching his horses to the wagon while his wife Lina scurried about with baskets and shawls. He saw Nils and shouted across the field, "Tell your wife to pack a picnic. I get the others. We go on a sleigh ride. No work today."

Ellen reacted with a flash of annoyance when he conveyed the plan. "Sleigh ride? In the summer? We have no snow!"

"Hayride, then. Jorgen's right. Too much brooding these past days."

Nils turned away before she thought to object. Half an hour later, they were crowded into the wagon on blankets and crates. Jorgen handled his team while Nils helped Ellen up on the seat beside him.

"Where do we go?" someone asked.

"That is for you to find out. A farmer's holiday." Jorgen clicked his horses forward. In the wagon box behind him, women began singing and the men took up the refrain. They rode past the old stage stop, pausing to water the horses at a ranch pond. Their harmonies caught the ears of farmers at the houses they passed. Elizabeth and Lina called out laughing "hellos" to strangers who paused in their wagons to return a wave.

Jorgen pulled up in a shady spot where a spring fed a patch of grass. He unharnessed his horses to crop lush green grass while the women carried their babies and the men carried picnic baskets to a copse of oaks. The potluck caused much laughter with its sad choices of dry bread, fatty meat, warm cheese and limp carrots and cucumbers. Hunger and exhilaration brought gusto for the last of the summer pickles and the small slice of leftover cake that Lina divided into eight equal pieces.

"Husband, you have mine," Karn offered as she collected crumbs from a piece of flatbread broken into pieces by someone's leg against her lunch basket.

"*Nei*. All for one and one for all. That's the way of it, wife." Lars pushed a bite of cake into her mouth.

She laughingly accepted it. "Who has sugar left in their larder for making cake? If I knew this, I would already be knocking on the door with my cup in hand to make a loan."

Elizabeth smiled. "Too late. Now we are all in similar straits. Enjoy the treat. We shall see no more until husband has a pig to trade the grocer."

"Better take care. I hear gypsies are hereabouts. They will run off with the young hogs."

"I hear they steal the laundry from the line," Ellen said.

"They are welcome to it. I darn Ole's undergarments until they stand up for themselves in the wash water!" Elizabeth joined the laughter bought at her husband's expense, but he was a good sport and his situation no worse than the others.

Ellen watched each of them showing a happy side that carried them through the tribulations. Maybe it was a Norwegian thing. If so, she thanked God for her good friends. She felt her sorrow lifting. "How do you find this place, neighbor?"

Jorgen laughed and his face reddened. "I hear someone at the post office complaining about people who use his land for range. The postmaster reminds him that the people are only taking their rest on a long journey. I think to myself, if my hungry horses graze while they wait for us to finish our picnic, how can this be stealing?"

"So all this is for the horses? Jorgen, my friend, you are as wise as a judge."

The trip home was made lighter with the bottle that someone drew from their pocket. Not enough aquavit to do anyone harm, but enough to take away the sharp edges.

That night, Ellen reached for Nils for the first time since the baby died. "It is time to put the sorrow behind us, husband." She felt his throat constricting before she heard him swallow. A good new beginning for a man and wife.

⁂

Winter brought no relief from the drought. Christmas arrived and the friends shared *sweet soup* made of tapioca, apples, dried fruit, lemon juice and prunes from their own cellars. Ellen made *lopskus*, meatballs from lamb, served over steaming noodles with eggs stored in straw from late fall. The women gathered at Lina's to make the traditional *lefse* for the celebration.

"We Norskes always find the sweetness in the vinegar," Karn teased.

"The sweetest pickles made from the tart fruit," Ellen agreed. She held Karn's baby while her friend poured coffee for the others. The baby's sweet face brought a pang, but she was happy for the health and vigor in the little cheeks. Her time would come again.

In the early months of the New Year, with no fresh eggs and the calves weaned, Nils fed the surplus milk to the sows in a slop of ground corn, sad pumpkins and gourds not fit for the table. He joined the other men in butchering hogs for cash money. Ellen stoked a fire in the yard while she rendered the lard for soap. Each of them worked hard to keep the others from despair. Small kindnesses reminded them of their blessings. They were a people used to scrimping. The joy of friendship made each day a golden treasure, and the land a constant reminder of God's provision.

Nils pushed his cattle down the farm road to forage on blackberries and willows along the creek. He stood with Lars, watching the hungry animals tearing at shrubs. "There is much poverty in the world."

"Well, we got our good share, that's for sure."

"Back home, when I was four, we climb the cliff to cut grass for the goats," Nils recalled. "We put it in rope bags and lower it. It was no job for a child, but we do it. That or the strap, for sure."

Lars nodded. "In the summers, our goats go into the mountains, and we go with them. Sometimes one is stuck on a ledge. My father lowers me on a rope to find the goat bleating in the dark. He expects I should hold it while he pulls me up. I can see nothing, it gets so dark."

"My sisters take Father's *aja* and cut the grass—and often the leaves from the trees. It is our job to spread it all out to dry before stacking it in the barn for the winter." Nils watched the cows reaching into the lower branches. "No matter how hard we men work here, it is better for the children. This, I know."

"'The farmer himself the best, and his wife the next,' the old timers used to say." Lars's nostrils flared in recollection. "I pray we can give our children more."

"No worrying, my friend. We are land barons in a fair valley. Our children and theirs will have a good life. Just wait and see!" Nils laughed.

A year later, the third without rain, Ellen delivered a perfect little blonde baby she named Nora. Karn arrived with her two-year-old Peder and a kettle of chicken and pillowy dumplings for the evening meal. She stroked the baby's fine hair and curled the tiny fingers around her own. "A healthy baby is proof of God's goodness," she murmured.

"Praise God." Ellen felt hot and itchy, in need of a damp cloth and basin of tepid water. A slight breeze blew through the window, but the effect was slight and the house stifling, even with her nightdress on. "I have decided. I leave my corset in the trunk for the summer. What difference does it make out here?"

Karn shook her head. "*Nei*. We don't allow ourselves to become undisciplined. What will our husbands think? You will regret it later. And here I carry another child in this heat." She laughed. "Not that I complain. I am happy."

"A girl baby to play with mine!"

"I pray so. Lars is hopeful for another son. Either will suit as long as it is healthy." Karn hesitated as Ellen glanced down at her own baby. "She will be fine. Don't fret."

Ellen fanned her baby's downy hair and caught a bubbly smile. "This one has claimed my heart from the moment I feel her inside me. She will be my favorite; this I can already know. Is it wrong to feel love so strongly?"

"Never. A blessing for a mother. A source of hope."

"Less so the land. Nils says there is no point to plant anything. It is only May and already the land is so dry."

Karn searched the sky for the sign of a cloud, but there was none. "So many years without God's tears. How can this be? We pray for rain, but none comes."

"They say no marriages take place because there is no grass for the young folks."

"It will be a hard year for us, but at least we have food set aside. It is something, for sure. People trade at the mercantile with exchange values and markers because there is no money circulating."

"Nils says the adobe earth is as cracked and broken as he has ever seen it. He fears for his horses if they step wrongly." Ellen pinched her lips to hide her fear. "Every day a fresh worry. I must plan what I put in my letters home, so my family don't fret." She smiled. "A baby is always happy news." She reached to accept a piece of crumpled dried grass from Peder's hand. "What is this? A wildflower?"

Peder nodded. "From the hill."

"Where God watches to keep the children safe," his mother added.

Ellen bent over and stroked his silky blonde hair. "You know," she said, "when Mr. Olsen was small, his mother ties a small rope around him when he plays above the fjørd. So if he falls, they pull him back up. So you see, we must all be brave in some way."

※

Summer arrived, sealing their hopes for a late spring rain. June flowed into July while the women served noonday meals in the shade of the eucalyptus trees and tried to keep up the spirits of their worried husbands. They played hide and seek among the blue gum grove with their toddlers. One morning the women dragged a child's sled to the top of the bluff overlooking the colony. For half an hour Ellen felt like a girl again. She closed her eyes and saw the snowfields of Stranda and the whip of the sled while she shrieked with laughter. At the bottom of the run, her friends waited to snatch the sled for their own run. With squeals and laughter, they took turns sliding down the slope with their skirts tucked in their waistbands and their shoes hooked in front of them.

Below, some of the men paused to watch and listen. Lars loped up the draw to see for himself the reason for his wife's laughter. He took his turn, gliding to a halt with his son held high in his arms and the women laughing. "Soon you will have your own sled. And one for your brothers," Lars assured his son.

"Talking of the future again, husband?" Karn bent to give him a kiss. "We have good and enough in the here-and-now."

Summer brought sunshine and happy outings punctuated with the worried grumblings of the men who watched the sky with a hope of seeing a cloud. In the last months of summer, with stunted grain and drought heavy on their minds, the women curbed their words lest grievances flare into discord. They rejoiced over a ripe watermelon, a blooming chrysanthemum or a child's first tooth. They organized an evening of Bible verses and hymn singing. Anything to break the monotony. Some days they joined their husbands when a foal or calf was born. Small miracles or large.

"Even though it seems the rains have forgotten us," Karn reminded them one evening while they met for a communal supper, "our land will not fail us." She smiled at the children playing in the yard, the husbands reclining after a hard day's labor spent deepening the well. "Remember to thank the Lord for blessings both hoped-for and unrealized."

Sometimes memories of *Norveg* returned in their daydreams. Nils relived his dreams during his journey to America—

> *A fine place for clearing the head, topside of a four-mast ship bound for America. Waves lashed the ship, sending spray over everyone curious enough to brave the decks. The bow pitched upward, lifting the ship. He braced his legs against the ship's movement, feeling odd amid the crush of men dressed in Wellingtons and Mackintoshes. His old worsted wool suit was soaked from the mist and wanting a thread where the cuff had caught on his worn heel.*
>
> *He stood beneath a storm jib, its sail snapping full in the wind. Sea spray peppered his lashes until his eyes closed of their own volition and irritated tears washed the corners of his eyes. Exhilaration flooded his lungs. An hour on deck offered welcome release from the long days below deck. An unattended stairway provided an opportunity to see the upper deck while below, steerage teemed with sounds and smells of unwashed bodies and discordant languages. A glorious storm show for the cost of steerage. He heard the shrill piping of the ship's warning horn over the steady drum of ropes on the rain-slick deck. A well-dressed stranger pointed him out to a crewman. He heard the exchange: Topside! He glanced at the stairway leading below, but the beauty of the storm immobilized him.*
>
> *From the stairwell, Jorgen shouted, "Come, Nils. It is not permitted that we are found up here. We must go."*

A white uniform approached, whistle blowing. He found a place in the shadows where he blended with the darkness. The sound of running feet and the whistle again, closer. A rough hand jerked him from hiding. In the moment before the gate was secured, his Viking blood sang a song of the majestic White Star sailing ship, its bow plowing the storm trough in the storm raging overhead.

Downstairs, others cast him doubtful glances before returning to their cards and stories. His suit would carry the wrinkles of this day, even as his memory would carry this one, perfect hour.

"Nils Olsen, wake up! The cattle wait their melking. A farmer makes no dallying between his cow and the bucket!" Ellen's impatience was more than about the milk needed for cheese-making.

Pulled from sleep, Nils opened his eyes to a picture of a White Star sailing ship hanging on his bedroom wall. It was an advertisement plucked intact from the gangplank and fitted into a frame he'd tacked together in his workshop. He paused with his trousers half-buttoned to study the photograph of the four-mast ship under billowing sails.

"Nils?"

"*Ja.* Coming."

In the following months, farmers struggled to keep livestock producing and food on the table. Finally, winter again brought hope, as the skies darkened with rain clouds. Children gathered in their yards to watch promising clouds fill a sky that had seen nothing but blue for three years. The smell of ozone filled the air, quickening the hearts and offering hope that grasses might emerge for starving cattle. The children's laughter burst forth like the buds of the lilac bushes that held on through the hard years.

The storm gathered, only to pass over the Conejo on its way east.

Another sadness occurred. Jorgen's daughter, Petra, took ill with a childhood disease that sent her to bed. Five days later the father stopped by to ask, in a halting voice, if they could bury their little girl in the fenced plot. The next morning, neighbors made another journey to the cemetery.

Ellen carried her year-old Nora in her arms as she walked beside the grieving mother. *Poor Lina, with a mother's grief for her dear Petra, a daughter half grown and already a helper.* She absently rubbed her mounding belly as she tried to think of comforting words.

Lina looked up, eyes red. "Your turn next!"

Not my little Nora—scarcely walking! Ellen felt her blood freeze until she grasped Lina's meaning. "Mid-April, we think. Nils hopes for a son to name Oscar."

"We join our prayers for you a healthy little boy. And for more rain. Always we pray for rain."

Chapter Nine

Celebrate the Happy Times

December 25, 1896. We celebrate the happy times.

NILS AND ELLEN celebrated their son Oscar's first birthday with a wagon trip to the County Courthouse in Ventura. Ellen pulled her corset from the trunk and donned her good wool skirt and jacket, heavy with the scent of mothballs. She shined their shoes with soot and rubbed them until they shone. Nils wore his suit and fresh-shined shoes to stand beside his neighbors as they recited the Oath of Citizenship in clear, strong voices and signed their names to the form that made them officially American citizens. Afterward they celebrated with cakes and flags, people talking and laughing as though they had known each other all of their lives. German men, Polish and Irish, a Jewish family, two Dutch brothers and other Norwegians joined the conversation in as many accents to enjoy a slice of cake. Nils allowed his son to wave the flag for a moment before he took it away and rolled it carefully in his pocket.

"This is not a toy, son. This is the symbol of a great nation. To be honored, always. We keep it for holidays and celebrations."

Jorgen searched the room for other faces he might recognize. "Strange, Ole Anderson did not attend. He signed his intentions when we did."

Lina slipped her arm through his and smiled. "He must take his oath in Santa Barbara. Surely he does not give up on America!"

"No, only the Conejo."

They spent the day on the beach, basking in the cool ocean breezes. The children sat on a blanket and ate a picnic from a basket—cheeses and bread, and fruit from the trees the women had struggled to keep alive with wash-water and prayer. Afterward, the children chased seagulls through the foamy swash while their mothers pulled off their stockings to wade.

"I feel like a school girl on a holiday!" Karn called from further down the beach, her words nearly lost in the sound of crashing waves and childish laughter.

"I miss the summers in Stranda, this is for sure." Ellen tugged off her last stocking and allowed Nils to pull her to her feet. "So much we took for granted." When Nils arched a questioning brow, she smiled. "But even *Norveg* did not have this wonderful sand for the children to play on. Such a beautiful, happy day."

"The rains will come. Wait and see. Even in the driest year we are better served than in Stranda." Nils's voice held determination.

She smoothed her husband's hair. "We wait together, husband. The Lord will provide."

A sparse harvest was delivered to Hueneme in the fall. The bank draft carried to Santa Barbara was scarcely enough to satisfy their land payment. Some of the wives rode along, making a cause for holiday. They pointed to the bare ocean cliffs where a plume of fire burned from a slit in the land where natural gas seeped out of the earth. A grassfire years earlier had ignited the seepage and it continued to burn, unabated. Sweeping fields of mustard covered the mesas. When they arrived at the ocean, gentle waves lapped the wheels of the wagons while they waited for the tide to go out. The children played tag along the hard-packed sand and collected shells. Their fathers fished the surf for their supper and watched the otters barking from the rocks. The change of scenery, clean ocean air and the bright, clear sunshine served to break the monotony of dust and drought during the hard summer months. The brief stay in Santa Barbara was a celebration. The Colony families camped in the yards of their friends and shared news of the homeland. When they packed to return, Mary saw that they carried copies of the Norwegian newspaper to pass among themselves.

Nils spent what remained of his harvest income in New Jerusalem, paying off his bill at the mercantile. After Mr. Cohen agreed to extend credit for the following year, he loaded sacks of flour, sugar and oats into his buggy.

Lars hurried home to greet the new baby Karn had delivered in his absence. He traced the fine lines of his daughter's brow and remarked how different a little girl seemed alongside her two spirited brothers.

On a December afternoon, a sudden thunderstorm opened the heavens to a torrential storm. Ellen heard the first drops hit the shake roof. She opened her door to hear Lina's and Jorgen's shouting joined by other neighbors to the end of the colony. She tucked her daughter under her shawl and started toward her neighbors, already standing in the roadway beside her husband. The child squirmed, batting at the fat drops washing her cheeks. Ellen danced the toddler in a circle. She didn't care that her feet were bare, or that mud covered her toes. Behind her, Nils lifted his head and roared at the sky. Jorgen stood frozen as though capturing the moment in his mind.

She wrapped her shawl tighter against her sodden clothing while the memory of summer lingered on her parched skin.

Jorgen returned from his shack with a small bottle of spirits. "I save this for when the rains come. Right on time, at the start of the *jul* season." He handed the bottle to Nils, laughing like a boy again. "Now we see what this land of ours can do!"

"*Ja.* We planted deep this fall, knowing the land can't hold out forever. The drought knew it was no match for the four of us." Nils pushed his cap back and glanced at the darkened sky. "I sleep good tonight in my snug house with the rain. My little girl, she doesn't know what to make of this. She has never seen rain before."

Lina turned back toward her shack as though she were thistledown instead of heavy-burdened with child. Her face was wreathed in joy when she turned to wave. "Sweet Norske rain, Ellen. Sweet with the promise of more to come."

Ellen inhaled in the smell of freshly planted fields. Norske fields —the tang of earth poignant and cleansing. The air filled with the tang of electricity that frizzed her hair and made her blood pulse. She returned to the house to set Nora in front of the fire, but she left the windows open so that the smell filled her home. She unloosened her bound hair and toweled her sodden tresses with a piece of scrap linen, pressing her nose to the towel afterwards. When Nils returned and took a seat in the rocker, she toweled his hair while he rocked with eyes closed and a satisfied smile.

The Christmas celebration at Ellen's house was a noisy affair, accompanied by crying babies and talk of the dark clouds that filled the sky. Candles lit the corners and the fireplace crackled with welcome light for the houseful of guests and the full table of special foods.

"This will be a year for rain," Nils predicted. "Already we have had enough to set the seed. The drought is broken."

"Praise God." Lars said, raising his glass.

"A year for babies, this is for sure," Karn added. "Two in the last month." She glanced at Lina and Elizabeth soothing their newborns.

From her spot on a chair Lars had brought from their own shack for the many people celebrating Christmas tonight, Ellen watched her Nora dancing around the new little kitchen troll, a gift from Santa Barbara, its wry expression so perfect that her breath caught in homesickness. Her daughter's fine blonde hair curled around her shoulders, highlighted by the fire like a halo as she spun. The child climbed into her lap. Ellen pressed her nose into the fine baby hair and whispered, "Tonight we put out a milk saucer to remember those who have passed. And to bring us luck in the New Year. But we have no need of luck, do we, my precious? We have God and each other."

One of her favorite seasons, the sharing of stories, the songs, special foods and the squeals of the children as they listened to the traditions that filled the month long *jul* season of Christmas in the old country. She had made a special rice pudding to leave out for the *nisse* spirit. Nora had helped by placing a fat pat of butter on top. Good luck for the coming year, she could feel it.

By middle January, the Colony was bursting with childish laughter. Ellen resorted to playpens and harnesses while she did her laundry—using a sliver of soap sparingly, as with everything. Spare flour sacks were treated like fine-spun silk for her children's clothing and underwear. Time seemed to be in short supply as well, with hog butchering, sausage making, cheese rendering and the other tasks that accompanied the wives. One afternoon she invited the other wives to her kitchen to paint pickle jars with elaborate rosemaling patterns they had learned from their mothers.

"Our homes will have such color we won't know them," Elizabeth remarked as she lifted a glass jar to inspect her work. "Rosemaling gives me satisfaction. As if I have created something lasting."

Elizabeth nodded. "I paint my beams with rosemaling patterns. To brighten the dark walls." Her eyes glowed with excitement. "You must come to see my colorful little house. Little *Norveg,* Ole tells me."

"I look to the day I teach my Anna to paint," Karn said. "The boys don't sit long enough. They are eager to be outdoors."

Lina turned from watching the children playing on the floor. "Your Oscar likes his blocks. Maybe he will be a carpenter like his father and grandfather."

Ellen smiled. She had a fine family, for certain. But it was her girls she looked forward to teaching. Nils would teach the boys what they needed to learn.

The following day a thick layer of clouds emptied onto the thirsty land. When rain continued through the following days, the cattle mooed and lifted their heads to catch the rain on their long tongues.

"It is thanks to God that we had faith to plant the barley seed. It is safe in the ground, waiting warm weather to sprout. Woe to the naysayers who keep their seed in bags this winter. Too late for them," Nils told his wife over coffee.

"Nils, for shame!"

"I only say what every farmer is thinking. Faith is needed for this occupation." He untied the sack of his carefully hoarded corn seed. "I plant the spring crops as soon as the soil dries to where I can crumble it in my hand."

In March, Ellen gathered with the other wives to watch their husbands begin the spring tilling. "Just smell the earth," she said. "Praise God!"

When the first grasses covered the ground and wildflowers pressed through crannies in the rocks, Nils hauled the children's sled to the bluff. He rode down alone, laying a path in the soft grass for others to follow. He was scarcely on his feet before Elizabeth careened down the slope on another sled, giggling under a bunched-up skirt and a clutch of petticoats. When she stood, flushed and shaky, Lina and Karn took their turns. For an hour everyone lent their laughter and shrieks, even fathers who took their infants down in their arms and returned for another turn. It was nearly noon before the men turned back to their fields.

"Take picnic with us first," Karn said. "You will be hungry and there be no wife at home to prepare your meal. Bread and boiled eggs will do for now. And later, hot coffee and good meat and potatoes."

The women spread their picnic while their husbands surveyed their land with barely contained pride. "I wish my father could see this," Nils murmured.

"*Ja.* They would not believe our good fortune. Worth the sacrifice—whatever it be." Lars spoke without looking to see who heard.

Ellen stretched out in the early spring sunshine, idly pulling petals from a fragile snow flower that her daughter dropped into her lap. Above, an eagle soared in the air currents without moving a single feather. Sluggish bees buzzed in the emerging clover. *Too early for snakes. This is a blessing.* She watched her children trying to follow the older ones. "Nora, hold on to your brother." Her son was scarcely two, and small for his age. It was difficult not to compare the children—Karn's boisterous boys seemed healthier than her own. Her Nora tumbled in the dirt as she tried to keep up with Lina's son, two years younger and already running after the older ones.

Karn's eyes flickered to Ellen. "Give the child time. Feed her rich cream and new strawberries." She smiled. "The best cure meets the disease before it enters the home."

A month later Karn discovered the secret Ellen had held off sharing when she dropped by one afternoon. "You didn't tell me. Any of us!"

Ellen tucked her worn shirtwaist into her dark serge skirt. She refastened her hair coil with a weary gesture that spoke more of weariness than a want of fashion. "Another child, so soon after the last."

"Ellen—"

"But enough of this! One more payment and the land is ours. Nothing must happen to spoil the dream we carry for so long."

Karn nodded. "Lars is filled with plans. Already he speaks of the day. There are legal matters that must be attended to."

"Nils talks of nothing else. Everything must be done proper and legal."

Karn laughed. "I hear Nils's voice in what you say. "Each man must sign away a portion to each other for a token fee of a penny." Her voice boomed in a passable imitation of Nils.

Ellen joined her friend's laughter. "Nils already carries in his shoe the four pennies he uses to buy his land from the others." She turned sober as she confessed, "For Nils, this land is everything. Sometimes I think more important than his children."

Karn shook her head. "Never that. But for these Norse-Americans, without the farm there would be no family. One cannot be separated from the other." She didn't continue, but Ellen understood. The children would not have to work as maids and nurse-girls for strangers. One day they might even hire a nurse-girl of their own.

In early July, Jorgen returned from Newbury Park with news of a fiesta at Mission Buenaventura set for the middle of the month. "They will have a bull and bear fight. I would like to go."

Nils glanced at Ellen to see if she would agree. "Oscar is young to watch the contest," she protested. "I would not have the children frightened."

"He is already curious. A farm boy sees nature as it is."

The women filled a farm wagon with blankets and baskets of food for the two-day trip. They arrived to find the fiesta underway, with brightly-garbed Mexican riders in colored sashes racing their horses in death defying stunts. The plaza was rife with the smells of grilling meat, the chants of the crowd and the growling of the enraged bear. The women found places in the grandstand built for the occasion a safe distance from a sad, hungry bear tied by its hind leg to a thick post.

Across the plaza a bull was dragged out by horsemen on fast-charging horses trained to keep the men's ropes taut and the bull from charging. The bull caught the bear's scent. It lowered its head, stomping and pitching, mad to escape the ropes. Nils glanced over to see how his son was reacting. The caballeros released the ropes and the bull charged. Out of harm's way, Nils lifted Oscar to his shoulders to better watch the bull shake its head and plunge toward the bear. Before any harm was done, the bear sunk its teeth into the bull's neck, sending it backing up with an enraged roar. The crowd cheered encouragement while Oscar twisted for a better view. The bull charged again, and this time the bear drew blood.

The battle raged with no clear winner as the bull charged and backed off, bellowing. It tried to muster energy for another charge, but in minutes the bull sagged. The bear reared on its hind legs and gave a final, fatal bite to the bull's neck. The crowd booed the victor. The vaqueros lassoed the bull carcass and dragged it out on a piece of cowhide. Men in the plaza began exchanging money for the bets won and lost.

Nils collected his family before several men with knives began to butcher the bull for the poor. A shot rang out nearby and he saw a mounted man dispatch the wounded bear with his gun. The crowd moved into the plaza where a mariachi band was entertaining. Nils took Ellen's hand and led her to an area where bougainvillea draped a trellis at the ice cream pavilion. Oscar's eyes were big and round over what he had seen.

Nils smiled. "Oscar thinks to be a cowboy."

Ellen shook her head. "Enough of cruelty and death. We watch the dancers and singers. They are more to my liking."

Two weeks before Christmas, Ellen gave birth to another girl with green eyes and a cradle of dark hair that would turn blonde soon enough. This one she named Emma. Karn helped with the birth. Afterward, they watched the baby suckle.

"A healthy baby girl," Karn whispered over the sleeping baby. "This one will be a helper."

Oscar and sister Emma Olsen, 1896 or 1897.

Chapter Ten

The Land is Ours

May 24, 1898. What we have worked for has come to be. The land is ours. We are each free to farm as we see fit from this day forward. Thank the Lord!

IN THE LAST week of February, Nils slipped outside in the early dawn to milk his cow. He caught the tang of cold in the air—and something more elusive that set his blood pumping with excitement. He climbed the hill behind his house and scanned the far mountains to the north. When he saw what he was searching for, he dropped his bucket and turned back to the house. "Snow! Snow! Snow! Over near Filmore. There's snow on the hills, Ellen. Snow!"

He laughed as she joined him in the yard, clad in her sleeping gown with her feet bare and the baby in her arms. As the children climbed the hill, he lifted first one and then another to his shoulders and pointed to where a range of white-capped peaks barely showed in the distance.

"What is snow?" Oscar asked.

Nils turned toward Ellen and saw the question in her eyes. He nodded. "Get dressed. We go tell the others."

He turned toward the barn without waiting to see if they followed. A few minutes later he dumped the milk to the hogs and reached for the harnesses. When the horses were hitched to the buggy, he lifted Oscar onto the seat and urged him to shout their news until Jorgen came to the door and looked in the direction the boy was pointing. Lars was already outside when his wife and sons piled from their shack, barefooted and shivering. Ole and Elizabeth slipped outside fully dressed, holding their coffee mugs. At the last house, Nils reined his horses to a halt and stood up. "Get dressed. Let's go have a look."

Within a half-hour the buggies were loaded with blankets and eager children. The horses pulled the spring buggies west to Newbury Park, where the snow-topped peaks were visible in the distance. On the way, the children listened as their parents told them stories of their childhood. They were hoarse from singing, from laughing and storytelling when they arrived home again with the sun high overhead. Not possible to travel to Ventura to visit the snow for themselves, but everyone agreed that even a glimpse was something!

That night Ellen waited beneath their comforter for Nils to secure the door and join her.

"That was some good day."

⁂

The last field was planted. Nils joined his neighbors for a trip to the courthouse to sign the quit-claim transfers. Ole Anderson had agreed to meet them there.

"Nearly eight years!" Jorgen shouted from the back of his buggy. "We prove to everyone that we are no slouches."

"No offense, neighbors, but I will feel better when I take my own counsel," Nils quipped.

"Yes, but now you have a fool for a boss," Jorgen joked. He pounded Nils on the back. "We are each man equal to the Borchards!"

"Word will get out to the mercantile in New Jerusalem."

Lars laughed. "*Ja!* Samuel Cohen will show us respect when we stop for supplies. He will bow and offer the children a lollipop when we pay the bill at harvest time."

Some of the Santa Barbara folks arrived to celebrate, along with the Moorpark relatives. Karn made a cake with American flags rimming the top. Ellen added a small silk Norwegian flag in the center. Ole Anderson stood apart, fidgeting in the presence of his old friends with their easy camaraderie and laughter before he left to take a long walk across his property. Nils noticed and started out after him.

"Best leave him to his mood," Lars murmured.

Nils stared after the retreating Anderson and nodded. Their friend had always been a loner. Maybe this was just his way.

Anderson waited until the evening meal had settled and the music began before he approached Jorgen. The two disappeared along the dusty track. Lars met Nils's gaze over the top of his fiddle. It was good to see their friend again. This day was a celebration for each in equal measure.

The party continued for several days, until the Santa Barbara folks left with a promise from the farmers to visit soon. "This year we celebrate Thanksgiving in Santa Barbara. You will need to let us repay your hospitality," Mary Ansok insisted. Nils nodded agreement. A trip to the coast would suit his wife.

He woke Ellen the next morning with a kiss.

"What's that for?"

"For the heaviness that no longer rides my shoulders. The summer crops will carry us this year. You will have wool for your children's sweaters. No more land payment."

"We can save for an iron cook stove?"

Nils's eyes crinkled. "A husband can provide this in exchange for lighter cakes!" He sobered in thought. "Our needs are few. The cows and horses are bred and we soon have an increase in our herd. The children are healthy and growing."

Ellen hesitated. "Some, but not all." She turned away, but her voice trembled. "Something is wrong with our Nora."

"Ellen, you brood too much. Let her be." Nils glanced to be sure the bedroom door was closed. He retrieved his shoes and jammed his feet inside before he ventured a look at his wife. He tried to think of something to ease her fears, but his nerve failed him. With a sigh, he softly closed the door and turned to his children.

He sat Nora on his lap and gathered the other children around him while he read from a tattered copy of *Norske Folkeeventyr*, purchased used from a bookstore in Santa Barbara. The children sat quietly as he read the stories of *Kari Trestakk, Hanen gauken og århanen,* and *Gutten og fanden* by the light of the newly stoked fireplace. Oscar stood beside his chair, studying the clues to the fairytales in the woodcut illustrations. When the children fretted for breakfast and the cows mooed for their milking, Nils set bread and cold milk on the table and escaped to his barnyard.

Ellen served the midday meal in an impassive manner that didn't encourage conversation. She was glad when Nils ate without speaking and returned to his field.

That night she waited until the children were asleep to tell her husband the troubling news that had consumed her thoughts that day. "Lina's son Henry has taken to bed, quarantined. She fears diphtheria."

Nils drew her close. "A large family is protection against the childhood diseases. Wait and see."

She turned away without responding. After wiping the last coffee cup, she made her way to bed while he finished his smoke and banked the coals for the night.

A week later, Ellen watched from the window as some of the men buried the Hansen boy. Her thoughts strayed to something her mother had often said: *The burden of someone else is always light.* Her Nora stood against her skirt. She reached to touch her daughter's curls without conscious thought. "The day is a warm one to hold a burial, isn't it, Nora? No Pastor Leach this time. Having the service read by a true man of God would have been a blessing for Mrs. Hansen."

Lina Hansen and her last child, Ella, were still in quarantine to protect the others. Only the father was present, helping to dig the hole. *The boy's death goes hard for Jorgen, his hope for the farm. Praise God the little girl is healthy. The child will keep her mother from despairing.*

⁂

Ellen's baby arrived on the first day of April. She sent her son to fetch the midwife, and afterward, to keep his sisters occupied collecting eggs and playing with the kittens in the barn. When Nora grew weary and fretful, Nils carried her to her bed.

Later he greeted a healthy son. "We name him Peder Ludvik," he announced. He glanced around with satisfaction. The baby flailed until the mother cocooned its tiny arms in a swaddling blanket. From the daybed near the fire, Nora fretted for a glass of water.

Before Karn left, she made a comment about how frail the child had grown in the past months.

"We pray for a miracle." Ellen busied herself in the motions of her suckling newborn.

"Did you try cow's cream for nourishment?" Karn reddened when Ellen's sharp look pointed out the hollowness of the question. Ellen had tried rich milk. She had tried canned milk, goat's milk, medicine from the apothecary. "The child is nearly six, a strange time for lingering illness. Usually fever takes a child quickly," Karn pressed.

Ellen offered a weary smile. "Go home to your children, Karn. There is nothing you can do here. I thank you for everything." Nora's bright little nature made it impossible to believe that God intended to take the child. She felt her heart grow numb with her neighbors' good intentions—their need to buoy her with false hopes. Her Nora was happy and interested in everything around her. But it became clear that her prayers for her daughter's sake were not being heard.

"Nora lives between one world and the next," she told Nils. "Like a sprite in the forests back home." As the summer commenced, she tried to find things to occupy her daughter's time. She taught Nora to knit, and fried *ableskivvers* served with jam to make her daughter smile. But it seemed the Norwegian Colony had other problems to worry about.

Norwegian Colony (Olsen Road) Looking west.

Work on the Grade
Hired man, Nils Olsen, Nick (age 4), Oscar, Hired Man

CHAPTER ELEVEN

Building Jorgen's Grade-Road

February 4, 1900. We are in agreement to begin work on Jorgen's grade-road.

"You're not driving your load, Jorgen?"

"*Nei*. My cousin figures to take a turn. I'll sit back and handle the brake this time. Take a breather."

Jorgen's new hired man had already climbed into the seat. He looked eager as he juggled the harness reins and looked around, grinning.

"A keen one, this cousin of Jorgen's. Just over from the home country and wanting to prove himself," Nils whispered to Ellen from the seat of his own double wagon as she handed up his lunch pail. "Taking a team down the grade isn't like the simple wagons the new fellow used in the old country," he muttered, not caring that the new man noticed his warning look.

"He does fine, Nils." Jorgen balanced in the buckboard, like a man finding his sea legs, before he took a seat at the brake.

Nils shrugged and turned to give his team their command. The Indian summer day held the remembered heat of summer. Dust roiled across the track until it was hard to tell where the road lay. He was hot and sweaty by the time they arrived at the Borchard watering tank. He dipped his kerchief and wiped the sweat from his brow while the new man remained on his seat waiting for his horses to water. "Better cool yourself while you have a chance. The grade will take the starch out of you," Nils called.

Jorgen climbed back to his spot in the second wagon while the man ignored Nils's warning. Instead, the man hurried his horses ahead of Nils's team to avoid the dust.

"He's an eager one, for sure," Lars joked. "He takes that hill once and he'll have more respect for the sharp bank at the bottom. Every one of us has learned a hard lesson on that one."

"He's some distant relative of Jorgen's. Our friend thinks kinship is good enough."

At the Potrero Grade approach, Nils cocked a thumb at the other driver and grinned at Lars. "The man should have cooled off when he had a chance. He don't look so good."

"Maybe Jorgen trades off, they come to the hill. I would if I wore the shoes."

At the top of the grade, Jorgen gripped the brake and stood, legs braced against a bulging corn sack while the horses started down. As the wagon's speed increased, he strained to keep the brake pulled back. The driver glanced back and gave a cocky wave.

"Keep your eyes forward," Jorgen shouted. Nils heard his friend's nervousness from the top of the hill.

The man hollered when he saw the approaching bank, but the weight of the load made slowing impossible. The front wagon caught the edge. The wagon listed as the driver bounced off his seat and came down hard. The second wagon hit the bank hard, shifting the load. Jorgen cursed and grabbed for the brake lever as he somersaulted out of the wagon and landed in the road seconds before the edge of the wagon caught him across the back. When the dust cleared, he lay on his back looking as though he were dead.

Lars leaped from the wagon and began running down the hill while Nils tied off his team and followed. Their friend's eyes were blurred with pain and fear. The hired man shouted that a rider approached from the north.

Before the rider could dismount, Nils was on his feet, shouting. "Man down. Get the doctor!"

They gave their friend a drink of water and tried to keep him comfortable, but every movement caused a wave of agony in his spine. Someone removed his boots and saw that he could wiggle his toes, a good sign.

They loaded Jorgen into the wagon and left their corn lying on the side of the road. The three men arrived back home after dark and presented themselves at Lina's door to explain what had happened. Nils was for letting the relative do the explaining, but the man's shame was punishment enough. When the doctor arrived in his spring buggy his patient lay in his bed, strapped into a pile of blankets.

"He'll live," the doctor told them. "I've cast him up in plaster. See he stays in bed. No walking, no sitting. His spine needs to mend." He held out a bottle of painkiller. "I don't have to tell you to feed him well. Lots of fresh cream and red meat. Honey and citrus. Avocados if you have them."

"If we had the money for those, we would have the money to pay you for your good work, doctor. Both must wait to see if I live." Jorgen muttered, a wave of pain thwarting his customary good humor.

The next day, after seeing Jorgen settled with a dose of laudanum for the pain, Lina threw her shawl on and started for the barn.

Nils met her as she emerged with a bucket of milk. "What you doing?" he asked.

"Milking. Someone will need to do it. I think that someone will be me."

He looked up, glad that Lars had arrived in time to hear this last. They exchanged glances and Nils shook his head. "Lina, I help with Jorgen's duties. We are family. I don't take no for an answer."

She considered with a grave expression. "You may help. But I do my share in the fields. It is what I must for my husband's honor. We—Jorgen and I—will carry our share."

"Agreed. But I do the milking starting tomorrow morning. You may thank me with a cup of coffee when I bring the bucket. *Ja?*"

Her chin jutted and she threw her hands up in defeat. "I suppose the east wind travels where it is supposed to. So *ja.*"

Nils returned within the month with more bad news for Jorgen. "One of the hired hands tries to take a load down the Butterfield road and he don't do so good. Turned a double wagon on its side. No man hurt—they jumped free. But some of the horses are hurt bad."

"Mine?"

"*Ja,* Jorgen. Yours and everyone else's. Lars tends to them."

"And the men?"

Nils shrugged. "Nothing more than a bad sprain and aching ribs." He pulled off his hat and mopped his forehead. "I tell you, Jorgen, these fellows we hire, everyone wants to do the thinking, but nobody got the brains."

"Things are different here than back home. There is much to learn. The Americans have a word for it—'trial and error'. More the trial, I think. But we learn in good time. Nothing so dire that we don't take it in stride. The Norske way."

Nils shook his head, too weary to temper his disgust. "Easy for you to see the good. We spent the day unloading and righting the load. Some of the horses will lose the summer until they can work again."

"There is nothing so bad that it cannot be worse. Let me think on this." Jorgen struggled to raise himself. "I'll call a meeting. It gives me a purpose other than merely to feel my body itching."

At the meeting a few days later, Nils listened as Jorgen offered a suggestion from his bed. "Before all this happens, I speak to the fellow who owns the hill beyond Nils's. He is willing that his land be used for making a road down the mountain. He thinks it can be done, and so do I. No matter that I am in no condition now. The doctor says I recover. We need to cut a road that holds less danger. A route to the train depot in Moorpark."

"It will be hard work, and slow, but we work together, we get it done. *Ja?* Maybe the County will supply men and tools," Lars said.

Ole Nelson paced in agitation. "We think about this from the day we arrive. Ten years and more. It is past time for talk. Time for building before one of us gets killed."

Nils glanced around the room. "We should take a vote."

"We should talk about other routes," Lars said.

"Widen the Butterfield Road," one of the hired men suggested.

Jorgen's voice was raspy with pain. "If it could be done, the Butterfield people would have done it. But it suffers from washouts now that the stage route is switched to Santa Susanna and the road abandoned. We drill and blast the rock road—the only way. Once built it will remain in place for a thousand years, the same as back home."

"Take the time to do it right!" Ole shouted.

Nils joined his voice to the chorus of cheers that followed.

"We work in the off-season, after the crops are in." Jorgen said. "I spend hours in this bed thinking on the solution. In my mind, this is the only way."

Nils looked over the group. "All in favor, say *ja*."

The room resounded with *"ja's,"* and enthusiastic *"ja ja's,"* but no *nei's*.

Jorgen slumped back with a satisfied smile. "Then it is settled. I write a letter to the County people and see if they make good for the dynamite. Ole will call on our neighbor and settle the details. We get a legal right-of-way so the neighbor don't claim it for a toll road and charge us for the use." He winced and shifted to a more comfortable position. "And when I am out of this damned bed, you can be sure I do my share. No more wagon accidents."

When the letter from Ventura arrived in early summer, Jorgen called another meeting.

"The County folks say they provide sixty dollars for dynamite. But they spare no men or machinery. With that we are on our own. The folks who own the mountain sell us the right-of-way for forty. That makes the cost ten per man."

"We don't get nothing out of Ole Anderson. He has dusted his shoes of this place."

Nils smiled, but his thoughts were weary. Even the folks back home were writing of troubles and death. It seemed as though life was a struggle no matter where a man lived.

Jorgen hesitated. "Lars, you joke about Ole Anderson, but before the accident, I make agreement with him. He sells me his farm. He makes plans to return to *Norveg*. For him, the dream of America is no good."

The friend of all is the fool of all! Nils glanced over to see Lars's face heating. Lars had spoken for the land, but now it had been offered to Jorgen. He turned to the bed where Jorgen lie soaked in sweat, his wife's white cotton coverlet wrinkled from hours of restless twisting. The others would be farming Anderson's parcel now—along with the rest of Jorgen's land. But it would not be Lars who benefited from his own hard work.

Nils was glad when Lars managed a weak smile. Friendship was the most important thing—harmony among neighbors.

"That's good news, Jorgen. Another few months you'll be right as rain." Lars offered his friend a hearty handshake and a wink. "Your wife does a fine job in your stead. Maybe you should think to stay in bed another year." He turned to the door and Nils laughed at the wooden coffee mug Jorgen threatened to chuck at his head.

CHAPTER TWELVE

When Peddler Calls

August 29, 1900. Ellen is glad that the peddler has found our little farms. We are known to outsiders as the Norwegian Colony. Who would think?

IN FEBRUARY, ELLEN pleaded with Nils to wait for a pause in the rain before carrying Nora's coffin to the cemetery. She followed with the children bundled in their sweaters and scarves, her eyes trained on the road to discourage the other women from speaking to her. Words had no place. Her heart lay heavy, forsaken in the long hours of darkness while she had sat beside her Nora and crooned Norwegian songs until the sky quickened in the east. At sunup she halted only when the children's door opened and Oscar stole out to climb into her lap and whisper, "Why are you sad?"

Nature required this stark, plain service; her grief had no space for argument. The preacher would ride his circuit as soon as the roads dried, but his presence here today would make the burial no easier. The hired men attended. Some recited from the Bible and sang hymns from the Lutheran hymnal. It was the best they could do, and God would understand. *Nora Olsen 1894-1900.*

During the days that followed, the crackling fire called to mind winter days with Nora practicing her stitches on a little knit scarf while the younger children played at her bedside. Now childish laughter rang silent in the room. *The burnt child fears the fire*, Ellen thought, and wondered why she should have such a notion. Was she suffering melancholy or madness? Would it matter to Nils if she took sick? Matter to anyone?

She thought back to the first years of their marriage, a moment when she emptied a sloshing bucket of cow's milk into her copper kettle before simmering the milk to near boiling and adding rennet. Her soft cheese would set as her mother's had, and her grandmother's before her, a comfort in this land. Everything seemed topsy-turvy here, from the weather to the outlook about common things. Americans rushed about, eager to earn money and acquire more. Even her own husband in a hurry to make up for the years of want.

"Rather free in a foreign place than a slave at home," he often told her in the evenings when she reread the letters from across the sea.

It would get better; Nils promised it would. Her husband struggled as well in this place. She could see it in the way he turned his shoulder to the draft horses each time he drove them to the field. He was used to hard labor, but the small farms back home held with the seasons. Haying in summer meant cutting wild grasses, not coaxing seed from the hard soil in a drought year. Cherry picking lasted a week. The trees required trimming only once each year. The cold season freed a man for carpentry, building a wall or a cabinet when a customer presented himself. And in the between-times a man busied himself with catching fish. Nothing so backbreaking as this harsh land demanded. Here, over a hundred acres to be broken, plowed, seeded, hoed—and later harvested, threshed and hauled to market across the hills. Too much for one man. She saw each day the worry in her husband's eyes that he would injure himself or one of his horses, and all this would be for naught.

She recalled a day in her first months as a new bride, turning to stir the milk. Proud of her contribution—eggs and butter to trade for supplies at the mercantile in New Jerusalem. Working in the satisfaction of knowing that they couldn't make it without her efforts.

The door opened and Nils entered, looking worn and damp beneath his battered hat, but so young and handsome to her mind. "Back so soon?" The words were out before she considered how they might sound —like a criticism.

"*Ja.* Lars hits a snag. He makes need of my team today."

"Just today?"

He smiled and glanced down at his dusty trousers. "He tries to pull the rocks, but the stones seem happy where they lay. We work together."

"You? Two Norskes make a plan together? One of you will likely find yourself sprawled in the dust."

Nils reached for the plate she set before him. "We make trial and error with each new challenge. Everything does not go as we think it might. After the *midden* meal, we harness the horses." He sighed. "So much trouble, the straps, doubletrees, collars, reins that weigh as much as a small child."

"It is best to stop when things go well. My mother's saying, tried and true." She leaned to brush a kiss across his cheek. "This will pass. I know it for a fact."

He nodded. "The seasons of joy get pushed aside when something bad happens. But we need to keep a thought for the good times. We have a happy life here, no matter what."

⁓

Lina stopped by on one of the last rainy days of the season with a warm cake and news of the Conejo. Ellen set aside her toddler, just finished taking the breast and now restless and eager to be on the floor taking his first steps. A nursing child would delay the possibility of another pregnancy. Every woman knew this. Ellen bent to wipe the child's hands before he stuck a bit of cake into his mouth. "My little Ludvik is all the time into something. I wish I had his energy."

Lina's eyes watched the little boy play with a stack of blocks his father had cut from scrap wood. Across the room, Oscar drew a bird he had seen on a walk. "It is nice, having a boy around," she said wistfully.

Ellen's eyes welled. Lina's daughter Ella—looking so like her own Nora— sat next to her older son, helping to color the bird's wings. "It seems we want what we do not have."

Lina's attention turned to Emma shuffling across the room. "Is . . . does she . . . is it the same with her?"

Ellen bit her lip before trusting herself to nod.

When the silence grew heavy, Lina stood. "So, let us set out the cake and have a coffee party. Oscar, do you like a little coffee with your milk?"

"Oscar is a clever boy. He already counts to ten," Ellen said. Her son nodded and set his drawing aside. She turned to encourage him in his shyness. "Show Mrs. Hansen how you count. Go. Take your eyes off your boot tops and show her."

He began haltingly. "*En, to, tre, fire, fem, seks, sju, åtte, ni, ti.*"

Lina clapped and exclaimed, "Wonderful!"

Her neighbor's gaze turned and Ellen saw that Lina had discovered the secret she was hiding. Her fear was realized when Lina asked softly, "Ellen, are you . . ."

Ellen felt her eyes filling. She dabbed them with the corner of her apron and nodded. "In late summer. I don't tell Nils yet. He will tell me not to worry. How is that possible?"

Lina nodded. "It is not the bearing of children that tears at our hearts. It is their loss." She leaned closer and whispered, "I am so fearful for Ella. I don't allow Jorgen to speak of sending her to school. I school her myself when the time comes. At home, where she will be safe."

Ellen glanced at Oscar, watching, and straightened. "Enough of being down. Now we speak of happier things. And take our coffee with this delicious cake you bring. Complaining never changes a thing, only makes us ungrateful for our blessings."

A soft summer breeze stirred the wheat across the fields when Ellen delivered her sixth child. She held the baby in her arms for many minutes before she trusted herself to face her husband. The weight of her request caused her heart to skip, but her voice was certain. "I cannot bear the house without the sound of my Nora. We all loved her so. Is it wrong that I name this one Nora, too? Please, Nils, I need to hear myself calling my Nora again. Please."

Her heart eased when Nils nodded. She wasn't sure what the neighbors would think, but it felt as though she could breathe again for the first time in many days. Later, she sent the children outside under Emma's care and lay down on the daybed to muster strength for supper preparations. "Please, Lord . . . ." She lacked the will to continue.

Early the next morning, the milk had scarcely been strained through cheesecloth and set to simmering when a horse and buggy pulled up outside the door. Ellen glanced out at her children staring at a strange man in a felt hat. The leather seats of his buggy were filled with goods like a traveling tinker. The name on the side of his door read something she couldn't understand. A peddler? She stepped off the porch and hesitated when she saw a sample tin in his hand. He introduced himself and showed her his surrey filled with goods—his English too quick and clever for her to understand.

She sent her oldest to fetch their father. Nils noticed the man from the barn and made his way forward, wiping his hands on a rag he tucked into his pocket. At the buggy Ellen ran her hand over a bolt of soft creamy flannel. Together they looked over the tinker's supply of threads, scissors, cook pans, liniments, pain salves, flavoring, and even something the salesman called *chewing gum*. "We won't need that," Nils muttered.

"But maybe we use the liniment," Ellen suggested. "You are all the time stove-up. You work so hard."

The salesman handed them a fresh tin from his supply. "Here, you take it on a trial basis. If you like it, I'll collect for it on my next trip over here to the Norwegian Colony."

There is was again, that name. Clearly someone in Newbury Park had told him this name for four simple families living and farming together.

Nils took the tin and added a bottle of vanilla for his wife. "Thank you, but we pay as we go." He fished the coins from his leather coin purse and waited for his change.

They stood together with the children while the man continued to the Nelson house, where Elizabeth watched with one hand on the sodden sheet she had just finished hanging. A visitor to their homes was such a rare event that even the dog had forgotten to bark.

The wives discussed their purchases later over coffee. Ellen shared the vanilla and joined them in dabbing a spot behind their ears. Lina had purchased a bottle of cough syrup to have on hand for Ella, and pain tonic for the days when Jorgen's back acted up. Elizabeth whispered to Ellen that Ole had decided to wait to see about the hog mix. She vowed that next time the salesman stopped by, she would have coins handy.

Having an outsider call on her made Ellen feel less isolated. She counted her blessings: The new baby was thriving. Emma seemed healthier, spending the spring days with her brother, chasing after their father's plow and collecting bird nests in the grass. Emma was in charge of feeding the chickens and gathering the eggs. Oscar would take over the milking in another year when he turned eight. He had recently brought home a baby rabbit and gave it to his sister for a pet. The Pederson boys brought their donkey cart and gave Emma rides so she could keep up with the other children. Ellen found herself pausing in her tasks to stand at the door, pressing images into her memory so she could remember. Lud was a bundle of energy, always pleading to follow the older ones into the field. Ellen allowed him. It gave her time to spend with her infant Nora.

The doctor arrived from Oxnard to remove Jorgen's body cast. Ellen learned the good news as she passed the Hansen's door and saw Jorgen outside taking his first stiff steps, his body erect and carefully balanced.

"The back has healed good enough to plow my land this spring," Jorgen announced. "I start juggling again if someone brings me some ripe oranges."

She told Nils the news that night while she inspected her small hands, protected from the sun by the gloves she wore for gardening. "How Lina's hands suffered from handling her horses. The other men do the heavy work, but Lina and Jorgen's pride has been a hard cross to bear."

Nils nodded. "But it is over now. Praise God. With another man to share the workload, we make progress on the grade road again."

"Jorgen says they throw a Christmas party to thank their friends. His humor is back. Only today he tickles his daughter with a handful of feathers from the henhouse. For him, laughter is all the medicine needed. Laughter and good neighbors."

"Let us pray that nothing else happens to our little colony."

Jorgen and Lina Hansen (and Ella)

Chapter Thirteen

Cyclone

December 19, 1900. Nature has some good surprise for us. Cyclone. Trouble in the night for sure. We are thankful to God who helped us so that all went well.

ELLEN RAPPED ON Lina's door and let herself in. "I drop by to see which special treat I should bring to your Christmas party. The last of the old century! This is a special occasion." She noticed a carved *hexe* woman on a broom near the fireplace. "Does the old woman tell us good weather or bad?"

"She says good today, but who knows? Maybe tomorrow the sky falls!" Lina offered a slice of *krum kakke* fresh from the black Dutch oven hanging over the fire. "Jorgen has taken my butter and eggs to trade. We will have provisions for the Christmas celebration and to sustain us if the rains come and the roads become impassable—not to mention the river we must ford each time we go to market."

"Truly, it will be a wonder when the new bridge over the river is built. They say it should happen this year. The trip to Ventura will be easier then."

Lina nodded. "Popcorn. You should bring popcorn. The children are eager to try such a treat."

"Good enough. I leave the baking to Karn. She has the touch."

"I make ableskivvers for the children. They will like the new jam." Lina laughed. "Last night, husband falls asleep while I babble of my plans."

Outside, wind whipped the eucalyptus trees, making it hard to hear and hard even to see. A quick glance at the sky convinced Ellen to hurry home. "The first rains are fierce when they come late like this. Don't try to make the *julebord* by yourself. We all share in the cooking." The pitched whine of the wind caught her words as she struggled to keep her ankles covered and her shawl on her shoulders. She was breathless by the time she collected her children and hurried them home.

She woke in the night to the sound of a loud crack, followed by a rending of wood. "Nils, are you asleep?"

"Hardly. May be one of the neighbors' barns collapses. Best I get dressed if I am needed."

A heavy pounding on the door woke the baby. Nils opened it to a windblown and worried Lars, panting from exertion. "Jorgen's house has collapsed."

Ellen clasped her robe tightly around her as Nils asked, "Are they—?"

"Safe and warming at our house. But rain is starting. Everything they own is in harm's way. Hurry."

Nils rushed from the house still fastening his coat against the storm. The next morning Ellen dressed her children and hurried to the ruined shack to see for herself. When the Hansens arrived for supper, Lina's eyes were still bright with shock. Her story tumbled out to a curious audience including the Olsen children stretching their bedtime.

"In night, I wake to wind shrieking and rattling the shack. You know how we insist to build on a ridge with a view of the Colony—who would know this happens? I grip my blankets and pray aloud as wind shakes the bed. 'Stay calm. It will pass,' my husband whispers. I take heart in his words, even if my head says otherwise. Then something in the yard breaks loose and hits the barn. Husband jumps from his bed and carries the lantern outside."

"Still in my nightshirt," Jorgen added with a wink at the youngest children. "With my knees knocking in fear." Everyone laughed and Lina continued.

"I force the door closed when he leaves. Outside, everything swirling in the darkness." She paused for a breath. "Soon he returns. 'Too dangerous!' he shouts and fights the door behind him. 'Nothing but to wait for sunup!' He crawls back into bed, but neither of us can sleep. Impossible—as you know for yourselves. Instead we huddle together—me, his scared-rabbit wife. Walls rattle and things fall from the shelves. We feel a shudder and hear a scraping sound like a tree falling on the house. My husband bolts upright. I do the same." Lina paused to sip her coffee.

"What happened then?"

"We find ourselves staring at the night sky where the ceiling was. We look up and see stars but also where clouds hide the moon. I think maybe I am crazy because for a minute it's wonderful."

Ellen smiled at the faces of her children, engrossed in the story as Lina continued.

"Suddenly the walls fall outward—like playing cards! The boards no longer hold each other up! I scream for my Ella and give a glad cry when she answers with a wail. I follow her sound and thank God I find her safe. My husband searches for his boots while I grope for my clothing, but my dresses are all hanging on hooks. And the hooks are lying in the darkness! God only knows where my dresses are. 'Where are you, wife?' Husband calls. I answer, I'm here. Ella's safe. I have her.

"We stand on bare floor while the wind tears at our night things. What to do, I think to myself. Then I remember the small rug I keep on the floor. I slip it over my nightgown and tuck the ends around Ella, hush her fears. My husband finds another rug and there we stand, wearing our floor coverings."

"Did you look like a bird, Mrs. Hansen?" Oscar asked.

Lina smiled. "Yes, just like a big bird with wings flying. I search in the dark for my stockings—nowhere to be found. But thank God my fingers find the shoes." She took a sip of coffee and continued. "My eyes have grit in them. It is terrible windy. 'We need to leave!' Husband shouts, grabs my hand. 'Careful! Here, take my hand and follow me!' He leads me around the fallen boards and I see moonlight shining on my unbroken window—lying on the ground—or I might have stepped right on it!"

"Praise God!" Emma's eyes shone with excitement.

"Exactly so, Emma." Lina smiled. "Suddenly, like a miracle from God, I see a light in the Pederson's window. Look, husband! I point and shout. He tells me what to do, but his words are not necessary. 'I have a lantern in the barn,' he says, 'but no dry matches. Let's go,' he says.

"The road is dark. We feel with our toes over the jagged cracks in the earth. I am thinking, what happens if one of us wrenches an ankle? Or trips? Ella's hand tugs at mine and I hold tight, praying out loud. The tiny light in the window grows brighter. A miracle! I say to myself."

Jorgen shifted and took over the story so his wife could drink her coffee. "I take up Ella when she can walk no farther. She shivers so. I tell her: You soon see your friend, Anna. Then everything will be okay. My pounding at the door sounds like another thunderclap. We worry they will not hear, until Lars—" he glanced over at the children. "Mr. Pederson bumps across the floor and we hear the children. The door opens and Lars stands there looking at us as if we are apparitions from Hades. He holds a shotgun, him as fearful as us. But I push my family forward—or maybe the wind does the pushing. Who can tell?"

The children laughed at this. Even Nils smiled.

"Mrs. Pederson cries out, 'It's the Hansens—something has happened.' Lars opens the door wider and his papers blow around the room. Everything is chaos. I am saying, we see your light. My wife is saying, 'Thank God. A miracle for sure!' Mrs. Pederson stares as though we are strangers. Until she sees Ella. 'Here,' she says, 'give me the child. Let's get her warmed. Tell us what happened.'

"The roof—it is gone. The house, gone! In a moment—gone. I stand with my rug still around me and the children all staring at me and my wife until we are silent. Mrs. Pederson settles Ella in her bed and sees us trembling as well. 'Quick, climb into our bed and warm up. You catch consumption and that will be worse than the loss of the shack,' she says, and it is true. Lars quick dons his coat and turns to go saddle his horse. I think to follow, but Mrs. Pederson calls in her firm tone, 'Jorgen, you do nobody any good, sick and ailing. You climb into this bed.' So I do!"

Laughter all around at the funny face Jorgen made for the children.

"Mrs. Pederson has hot coffee ready by the time your father arrives with our neighbors. Thank God they each bring lanterns. I have to borrow spare trousers before I can go see what the wind has left me."

"And what did you find?"

"The roof is where we saw it today—still intact. The walls are there, too. Fanned out like playing cards, the windows unbroken."

"A miracle," Ellen said.

Nils joined them and helped himself to coffee. "The wind makes a cyclone. We know this from the old farmers. The winds are fierce when the rains come late."

Jorgen nodded and took a sip of coffee. "The wind tears at our coats like on the ship. Ole—Mr. Nelson—poked a toe at a corner of the roof like it will sprout legs and run off." He grinned at the children and continued. "When the rain begins, we scatter like chickens, some collecting the feather tick and others the mattress still lying on our four-poster bed."

"My husband made the bed for me as a bride-gift. Thank God it survives," Lina whispered.

"We carry all into the barn and lay it on the straw. Then we run back and forth fetching clothing, books. A winter's food provisions. Piling all in the barn. Afterward, we search the ground with lanterns. This is when we find Jorgen's precious deed. We find most of the dishes broken after the shelf fell."

Jorgen gave his wife a quick, apologetic look. "Someone rights a crock with the last of the season's chicken and duck eggs packed in straw. Some are cracked or broken, but the rest survive. Bring them along, I tell them, or they do nobody any good but the foxes and skunks. We eat them for breakfast."

Lina smiled. "A good breakfast, it was. When first light arrives, I hike up my borrowed skirt and walk to see the damage. Mud and rain on everything, but I cannot think beyond what might have been. I see the overturned bed where my Ella was sleeping. Trees uprooted by the wind. I search the mud for small items. In the barn I find my corset, petticoat, and my best black dress and I wonder which of the men has found these things! My muddied curtains—whipped from their willow rods." She brushed off the events of the previous night with a quick flutter of her hand. "I collect what we will need and carry all back to Karn's." She glanced at the children and corrected herself. "Mrs. Pederson's."

Her story trailed off, to the dismay of the children.

Jorgen added, "Your father chases off the coyotes that think to eat our hens after the henhouse is destroyed. But they are too smart for the wild dogs. The hens flew into the trees. We will have a job getting them back once I rebuild their little coop."

Lina confessed that she clasped her daughter close and thanked God for His mercy. She found her journal and wrote about the events while they were fresh. *God was with us,* she wrote. *God gave us strength.* She and Ella made a game of wiping the mud from her baking table. "Too clean has no taste," she joked. "But I don't think the wise woman who said that meant our table!"

The event was written up in the *Moorpark Enterprise.* Lars purchased a copy for his neighbors to read. Lina wrote to the folks in Santa Barbara and in the old country about her adventures. In her journal she added: *We are thankful to God who helped us, so that all went well. We praise God that our horses and cows were spared. God has spared our lives and made everything good again. We are well satisfied.*

The Hansens made a ceremony out of choosing a secluded site in the shadow of the blue gum grove where they would have protection from the wind. Ellen joined the others in picking up a corner of the roof. The horses dragged it across the field while everyone carried the walls to the site of the new home. Nils helped hammer the walls.

"Make sure the nails are long enough. No cobbler's tacks do I use this time! I learn my lesson," Jorgen joked.

"You make a better farrier than a carpenter, this is for certain!"

With the walls sturdy once again, they used the draft horses to help lift the roof back on before bracing and nailing it. Lina washed curtains and bedding. Some of it never came clean, but even her ruined shirtwaist would have a story. The first evening in their new home she glanced up from her knitting to find the lantern illuminating two pairs of men's shoeprints on the ceiling. She climbed her stepstool with a scrub cloth, but no matter, the ceiling refused to relinquish the size-eight bootprints.

The Christmas celebration was held at their new home a few days later. Lars and Jorgen waited for the children to receive their treats before they shared their news. "We have been offered a situation this spring," Lars began. "My wife's sister Susie . . . she and her husband Ross have leased land in Filmore. They've offered us to farm the land beside them. On shares."

Nils glanced at his shoes before replying. "The two of you will farm across the hills?"

Lars nodded, unfazed. "*Ja.* The rains come stronger over that way. We will make income to tide us over. We are thinking for you and Ole to remain behind. Water the stock and haul tree branches and cactus to fill the bellies of the cattle and horses. Keep the orchards alive. Make butter for trade. Together we will help each other through this hard time."

"*Ja.* This is possible. The land as it is now sure won't support four families. Will you take yours along?" Nils asked.

Lars shook his head. "*Nei.* They stay here. If this is acceptable, my friend."

⁂

Jorgen spent the days before his departure tending to his wife and daughter. Lina came down with dysentery first. Ella was the sicker, curled up in her bed, fevered and pained. Jorgen spent his nights beside the child so her mother could recover. "Time for rest," he told his daughter one night, when he fought the need for sleep. "The sun is so long setting in this country that we forget how late it grows."

"It's not late. I see the gum trees."

"In the old country, we would be so sound asleep the kittens would be looking to see if we still breathed," he teased his daughter.

"*Nei!* kittens don't do that."

"Ask your mother. She tells you about the cats that steal your breath. This is why you clean your teeth before you go to bed. Don't forget!"

On the day he left, he gave Lina a last quick peck. They had said their proper goodbyes earlier, while the sun was just peeking over the hill. He would not soon forget the early morning exchange, but a quick peck in front of the neighbors was still a comfort. He turned to his neighbor and grinned. "Lars, you see to it Lina rests. She is not yet recovered. And we see you in a week or two, after your baby is born. Four for you! Maybe you be taking lessons from Nils!" He winked and gripped his valise. Leaving was hard, but it was a good plan. The storm that accompanied the cyclone had proved to be the only rain they received all winter.

Lars spent the first weeks of spring planting forage. His older sons were seven and nine—the same as Nils's boy, Oscar—good ages to tag along and ask questions. The two fathers carried their younger sons on shoulders across the sun-scorched fields while Lars explained his plans for improving the land. In the blue gum grove they chopped wood so the family would be well-provisioned. The eucalyptus was still green, but Lars claimed it would be ready for winter.

"Isn't that how squirrels do it? Collect their nuts early?" he asked his son Peder while Nils and Oscar helped load the wagon.

"So the squirrel will have nuts when it's time to eat," his son said. Lars nodded and tossed another piece into his wagon.

He spent the evening reading the Bible aloud and hearing the boys recite verses.

A few days later, Ellen helped when Karn delivered their son Lawrence. Lars held his baby and gazed at its clear blue eyes. He saw his father's strong forehead. "Three strong boys to farm the land and a daughter with her mother's flaxen braids and spunky demeanor."

The birth freed Lars to leave, but it seemed to Ellen as she busied herself with the Pederson children's supper, that his heart was not that of a farmer this night.

The next day Karn insisted her husband keep his promise to her sister. "We will be fine. I do not understand your reluctance to leave us. The change will suit you. Keep you from pacing a trail to the barn and back this dry summer." She laughed her bright, tinkling laugh—a sound he claimed had filled his heart from the time he first heard it as a boy. "And God knows, we can use the income. You don't regret it each night when the baby fusses. You will soon remember what to do with a real night's sleep."

He set his cup down and took the baby from her arms. "I am glad that I go back to Stranda to fetch you."

From her birthing bed, his wife sighed. "These past ten years have been the happiest of my life."

"Then we see that you have ten more."

"Only ten?" she teased. "With God's grace, I live to be an ancient crone. I will need at least seventy more years with you."

He brushed his lips across her forehead. "When I am old, wife, I will see you as you are now—beautiful."

Karn laughed. "The eye is the first thing that is blinded, husband."

Ellen arrived the next morning in time to see the four small faces and their mother lined up to kiss him farewell. He drove his team off in the direction of Moorpark, carrying a worn valise filled with his work clothes. At the top of the bluff he turned and took a long look at the barren fields. With a last wave to his family, he turned down the track past the cemetery where so many of his friends' children were buried.

Karn stood waving, but her face showed apprehension. Watching, Ellen sympathized. They needed the income that farming on shares would bring, but a wife's selfish desire was to have her husband home. Karn and Lars had not been separated for more than a couple of days since they married. A trip with the barley to Hueneme and back was a long separation from her husband. His joy was at his family's side. *The eye wants to be where it is dear; and the hand where it hurts.* An ancient proverb, Ellen thought as she watched. Women understood its meaning.

Karn turned to her brood. "Who will help me gather peppercorns from the trees along the road? We fill this old tin can and see who can pick the most." She tucked her skirt into her waistband and fastened the baby into its carrying cloth while the older boys raced down the road ahead of their sister.

"I have a bit of chocolate for anyone who recites their verses correctly," she called.

Pederson Family
Peder, Anna, Lawrence, Karn, Richard

Chapter Fourteen

Summer of our Sorrows

September 30, 1901. This has been the summer of our sorrows.

AFTER THE SCANT spring planting was finished, and between loads of water in a water tank pulled by their horses, Nils, Ole and the two hired men worked on the grade road. Ole took charge of the dynamite. He spent his days drilling holes, setting charges and blasting rock for the others to clear. Nils manned the Fresno grader. The hired men were glad to put their shoulders to any task that would push the road through.

In late June, Lina and her daughter made the short walk to the Olsen house for the children to play together. Ellen had just served coffee when they heard a rider pull up outside the door.

"Excuse me, ma'ams. I'm looking for Mrs. George Hansen."

Lina stepped forward. "I'm Mrs. Hansen."

The man doffed his hat and slid to the ground, his eyes heavy with regret. "Ma'am, I'm sorry to bring you bad news. It's your husband."

Lina's face paled. At first it seemed impossible, but they had both heard him correctly. The doctor had seen him and his report confirmed the fact. Jorgen had died the previous night.

"How?" Lina's question seemed little louder than a squeak.

"Too early for a cause, Ma'am," the man said. "But best guess is most likely typhoid."

"Typhoid fever? From bad meat? How does this happen? My husband is careful with these things. He is not one to take risks. You have made a mistake. Maybe he takes the dysentery."

The man shrugged. "The body will arrive on the afternoon train, ma'am." He tipped his hat and turned back in the direction he had come.

Ellen sent Oscar to the field to fetch the men. Nils arrived to help Lina into his wagon for the slow journey across the ridge to Moorpark. Lina sat motionless in her work-stained shirtwaist and skirt, her mended shawl draped across her bowed shoulders.

Ellen pressed a hand against Lina's. "You'll want to look your best. For Jorgen."

Nils held the horses until Lina reappeared with a fresh dress and her hair braided and tidied. At the station, Moorpark buzzed with speculation. Nils shrugged off the inquiries of the curious and hurried the coffin onto the wagon while Lina sat alone with her thoughts.

On the ride home, Lina stared straight ahead, voicing her thoughts aimlessly. "The cause makes little difference. Jorgen is dead in his prime, only thirty-nine. We were happy in our little shack. What purpose is served in taking such a fine man? What will I do? And the child—Ella?"

It seemed as though a storm had broken inside her. At her house Nils helped her inside, still weeping. He glanced up at a frame hanging prominently on their wall, a photograph of the three of them: Lina, Jorgen and Ella. Her other children, Petra and Henry, were missing, dead before the photograph could be taken. Now even Jorgen was gone.

Nils stood awkwardly clasping his hat. "Lina, you best come down to our place tonight. Ellen will have supper ready. We can have the laying-out at our place if you like. Or in Jorgen's shop."

Lina collapsed into her rocker without looking up. She shook her head. "No need for everyone to fuss," she said. "This is God's will for me. My husband's *begravelsen* will be held tomorrow. Put him in his shop and see to your supper. I will sit in the darkness and ask God why this happens. This terrible thing."

When the Presbyterian minister from Hueneme arrived, Ellen fed him pie and coffee while he waited for mourners to gather. Friends from Moorpark came offering their condolences. Lars returned to help with the burying, and to give his version of how Jorgen had succumbed with a fever and a bellyache that grew worse with the passing hours. He led the *risting* with a long salute to Jorgen's memory that left Lina weeping. The next day Lars left again to finish the job that he and Jorgen had begun.

Lina slumped at her kitchen table and began crying. Tears streamed down her face until her hankie was soaked and another pressed into use. She sat at the table, refusing to be led into bed until one of the others carried her child away to sleep with their own. Her nervous fever continued for the next twenty-four hours in spurts of unrelieved distress. She refused to eat or drink until she became too exhausted to sleep. The other women worried for her sanity.

She seemed scarcely aware when she was lifted onto a spring buggy for a journey to Santa Barbara. Mary Ansok opened her home and her heart. Long walks on the beach and memories of happier days helped to ease Lina's nerves. When she returned, two weeks later, her color was better and her tears had been replaced by timid determination.

Nils insisted to help with Lina's chores. At first Lina protested, but she soon found that as soon as she finished her own tasks it was time to do her husband's work again. When Karn sent her oldest son to help with the feeding, Lina protested that the chores were too much for a young boy. She sent letters to her brothers, asking for help with the farm.

Her brother Alfred was still in Alaska. Her brother, George Ness, sent word from San Francisco that he would come as soon as he recovered from an illness he had contracted in the Yukon, earning money by carrying goods over the Chilkoot Trail.

When George arrived, edgy and exhausted, Nils tried to get him to talk of his troubles in the wild country of Alaska, but he wouldn't speak of it beyond a few facts about the Ice Road and the weight of the packs he had carried, the poorness and scarcity of the food, and the taste of horsemeat after it had died under a crushing load and had to be butchered before the flesh froze to a hard brick.

Nils learned about the frozen horsemeat when George broke down sobbing as he attempted to break loose a piece of hard adobe from a hole he was digging. He had jabbed and jabbed at it until his moans brought Nils running.

George shared later how a stubborn rock could take a man so easily back to the frozen land of unhappiness. He managed to help out with the scant harvest and his brother-in-law's small herd, letting them out to graze on the rolling bluff overlooking the flats. In the afternoons he took his gun and shot rabbits in the grain field.

Lina needed the meat, that was for certain, but she complained that her brother seemed uninterested in eating it. She talked to Ellen about him.

"Let him be, Lina. The chores will keep him occupied. He has purpose, helping you. Give him time."

Nils attempted to include George in conversations about the farm. It seemed that their kindness had an effect. George took long walks.

Several times he brought home rattlesnakes he had killed for his niece to show her friends.

By early August, it seemed as though the year of calamity was over. Karn shared the good news that Lars would soon return from Filmore after the barley was threshed and sold. His cattle grazed the sparse stubble of the Colony land. The gardens were filled with squashes and pumpkins, soon ready for picking. Cucumbers were brining into pickles.

Lina attended Ellen when her seventh baby was born, a girl she named Laura. "This baby girl seems healthy, Ellen. No worries here."

Ellen took her gaze from the bundle in her arms. "No. It is Emma who worries me. I see the same symptoms that took our first Nora." The mother watched her older daughter struggle to walk across the dirt toward her father's workshop. "I do not make the suggestion lightly, but it is best you keep your Ella away. Until the doctor tells us the cause of our problems." Ellen ignored her friend's surprised glance. "It is hard to welcome a new soul without thinking on the fragility of life," she mused. "It seems our little Colony is plagued by joy and sadness, hope and despair."

"I miss my Jorgen with every fiber of my being." Lina's cheeks deepened with fervor. "I miss his joking . . . his way of making everything seem good and right." She hesitated. "I miss his touch." She looked up and shook herself as she realized she had spoken aloud. "You are right. I must protect Ella. And my brother, George."

Ellen set the baby into its cradle and took her friend's hand. "Pray that with God's grace he will recover his health, both in mind and body."

"God willing." Lina gripped her shawl and turned to stare out the window.

⁂

Ellen walked alongside the sparse grain crop nearing harvest, on her way to return Lina's empty pan, brought filled with leek soup and sausages to feed the family during her confinement. From a crook in the hill, a wagon approached, one of the Norsemen from Moorpark who attended the Methodist Church until they should be enough in number to build a church for the Lutherans. She stood staring while he drove straight to the Pederson house. The sun was behind her as she stood in the road, leaning to hear the words the man was saying. Karn came to the door drying her hands on her apron.

Suddenly she heard Karn's shriek, "*Nei, nei, nei!*"

Ellen caught herself against Lina's fence while a shiver ran down her spine. At her side, Ella Hansen watched with a question in her bright green eyes. Ellen heard herself speaking in a tone that brooked no disobedience. "Ella, go find your uncle. Tell him he is needed."

She waited until the child disappeared before gathering her skirts and running the short distance to the Pederson place. When she arrived, Karn was standing over her sink, her eyes vacant while the messenger stood awkwardly twisting his cap in his hands.

Lina arrived to stand in the doorway next to Ellen. Outside, the sound of children's laughter contrasted with the tension in the room. Ellen heard people in the distance—the little Hansen girl arriving with her uncle George.

Karn slipped into a chair beside her table, absently wiping crumbs that were not there. "Lars is in the wagon. We must carry him to bed. One of yours needs to ride for the doctor. My husband will not die from lack of care." She rushed to flip back the comforter on her bed. "Put him here. I get wet cloths to take his fever down. They say typhoid, but they are not for certain. Maybe Jorgen's trouble persists." She pounded the table with her hands. "Why did he not return after the deaths? Why did we not realize that danger remained? Don't tell me this is God's will! I know my God, and this is not his plan for us."

Karn picked up a basin and began pumping water so quickly that it seemed the lever could break. The Pederson children arrived from the henhouse, their baskets filled with eggs and Ellen slipped from the doorway to intercept them. George Ness arrived and stood waiting to be told what to do. *Nils! Nils must be told.* Her husband was not in his field—probably inside with his coffee and his pipe. Ellen turned to shoo the children from the yard.

Hours later the doctor arrived with his black satchel and words of advice as he examined the patient. When he finished taking Lar's temperature, probing his stomach and listening to his lungs, he straightened and nodded in Karn's direction. "You have done what you can. I suggest I take him to the hospital in Ventura. Better medicine as we have for this. With good care and the grace of God, he will recover."

"No. We keep him with us here at home. It is up to God whether he recovers. But we will care for him in the home he loves."

Karn stood watching as the doctor drove off. The children went about their chores in silence, gathering eggs and pouring milk to the hogs without bothering to bring it to the house. At mealtime they returned to eat the cornbread and beans one of the women prepared. The next morning, Elizabeth brought a kettle of cooked oats and helped to clean up the dishes while the older boys took their milk buckets and disappeared. Days passed. Karn remained at her husband's side until she was exhausted.

Ellen arrived with a pot of chicken soup. She entered without knocking and saw Karn asleep in the chair. At first she thought to slip out quietly to give her friend a chance to rest, but a glance at a the bedroom door told her that her suspicion was correct. Karn stirred and her eyes opened. Neither of them spoke while they adjusted to the reality of his passing.

Finally, Ellen whispered, "You will need to meet the train for the coffin, Karn. Take your children so they remember what you did for their father."

George brought Lina's spring buggy and waited until Karn emerged with her children who clambered up behind her, subdued and teary-eyed. The oldest sat with his shoulders hunched as though protecting himself from a blow. George crouched in the seat, gripping the reins with trembling hands. At the last moment Ole took the reins from him.

Ellen was nearly home when the horses passed her and halted at her shack. Her husband came out, wiping his mouth before pocketing his handkerchief again. His sandy hair was plastered to his head from sweat.

He glanced at Karn's stricken face and those of her children, his fading smile revealing that he understood what had happened. Ellen rued not arriving in time to soften the blow. But misfortune liked its story told in details and re-tellings that made the event seem natural. Later the men would recount the day and their story would be different, the gaps filled with the details each thought important. A woman understood death in a way that no man could. Wives were the victims, no matter who died.

After the wagon started to Moorpark, Nils slipped his arm around his wife and watched it disappear. "God's will, this. No use thinking."

Chapter Fifteen

Norska Strength

October 1, 1901. Our broken colony. It is now the Norska strength that holds us together. May God sustain us in our trials.

Ellen nursed her newborn in the pine rocker Nils had created for her firstborn. Lina sat nearby, neither of them speaking until a cough broke the silence.

"Remember the day Jorgen and I planted our precious prune-plum trees? Husband digging a straight line of holes while I set the trees and tamped the dirt around them? Afterward we use the horses to pull the water tank, giving each tree a soaking?" Lina wiped a tear without looking up. "We prepare the soil with straw and last year's manure. Mix it with the adobe so the bare roots will have it easy to grow." She smiled. "Our children playing nearby, getting themselves muddy with the watering, but it does not matter. We all laugh when my husband slips in the mud and falls. The day is a happy one, all of us together. A day of promise."

Ellen nodded. *Too much sorrow for such a small, hopeful group. I pray God that something good comes of our trials. Something good.* She quickly covered herself when the door opened. "I told you children to stay outside and pl—" She broke off when she saw Elizabeth.

"Ole has returned with the coffin."

Ellen rested her head against the rocker. "Who is to be next? My husband? Yours?" She rose and laid the baby in its crib. "What are we to do? We have not yet resigned ourselves to losing Jorgen and now this."

Elizabeth glanced around. "In Moorpark, Karn hears her name and she looks up to see her sister. She braces herself for Susie's words of sympathy. Instead, the sister coming toward her seems as off-tilt as she. She remembers something the messenger said earlier—that another man had died. Karn sees her sister's dark circles and distraught bearing, and the idea slowly registers—they both wait at the station on the same errand."

"No!" Lina rose from her chair, struggling to grasp this latest horror.

Elizabeth ignored the interruption. "Some say because they drank from the same well. But others did likewise. There is no way of knowing. Rumors claim a dead squirrel was found in the well after Jorgen. Who can know?"

"Are the children safe?"

"The baby, Clara. They will be burying her with her father."

The funeral procession the following day began at Lars's workshop. The women walked behind a wagon carrying two coffins, one holding Lars Pederson and another holding Ross Jacobson and his infant daughter, with a marker waiting to be placed in the loose soil: *Ross Jacobson 1873-1901. Clara Jacobson 9 mos 1901.*

Lina stood apart, praying at Jorgen's grave where the loose soil still showed the shovel marks of three months earlier. "I will never marry again, husband. This I promise you. Never. You are my love forever."

Perhaps she didn't realize she spoke aloud, but Ellen heard and moved away to give her privacy.

The eulogy concluded and the burial began. These latest casualties would lie near Jorgen, but not so near as to prevent Lina from being buried next to her husband and her children when her time came. There was even space for their daughter. Ellen turned her head to stave off the dizziness that accompanied the thought. *Not Ella. God would not leave a mother with none.*

Lars Pederson 1863-1901.

When the service ended, she led the widows away before Nils and the hired men began the awful task of covering the coffins. The finality of death seemed caught in that first, ugly shovelful of dirt. Ironically, tradition dictated that the wife sprinkle the first handful, perhaps so she could blame no one else later.

The women started back down the road in silence alongside cattle nosing in the scant stubble, searching for grain. What a blessing, Ellen thought. The animals had only themselves to think of. At Ole's house, the women spread sparse lunch fixings on the table and fixed plates for the children. No celebration, this meal. Simply something to fill the stomach since no one had the heart to eat. The men brought out their elderberry wine and toasted their departed friends with sentiments that brought tears to men and women alike. When the bottle was emptied, the men eased out of the yard toward Lars's barn and the horses he had loved.

Ellen watched from the window while she washed dishes with Lina. "So many times we hear the *begravelsen risting*. Saying farewell to good men takes the heart from the ones left."

"They pour their sorrow into words of praise for their friends. Not like ordinary farmers. Like poets," Lina said. "We should paint the fence around the cemetery—white."

Lina nodded. "I will plant a rosebush when winter comes." She spoke of the early bloomer she kept alive with buckets of rinse water through the hard summer. The bush was from a cutting Mary Ansok had carried from Santa Barbara on one of her first visits. Mary had also brought bougainvillea that bloomed so abundantly at the corner of her rooming house, but an early frost had claimed it. Lina pruned and tended it though another season in hopes it would revive, but it never did.

Ellen paused, her hands chapped and red from the harsh soap. Karn sat motionless, her small form dwarfed by the black shawl around her shoulders and the baby in her arms. When she sagged from exhaustion, her son took the baby with the seriousness of an older brother who had already assumed the role of man of the house. He carried the blanketed bundle outside where one of the hired men was conjecturing about the cause of the latest deaths.

Karn heard it as well. She rose from her chair, anger flaming her cheeks at the constant talk that claimed the men's time. Their gossip was upsetting her children. She slapped her hand on the open door with enough firmness that the talk halted. "*Alle saman likning ar haltar!* No more talk of mistakes or foolishness! The children will know their fathers for heroes. It is the only thing we can give them now—respect for these kind and caring men."

Lina nodded, reacting to the weight of gossip that had settled on her during the past three months. "*Alder vil ha ære!*" Age wants honor! She glanced at the two hired men and was gratified to see their glances fall. They nodded in agreement.

Later, when the dishes were finished, Lina took Karn's hand in her own and whispered, "This needed saying. Now I can breathe again."

That night Ellen woke from a bad dream. She tossed fretfully, trying not to wake her baby in the cradle next to her, but her fears kept her from sleeping, even though her head ached with exhaustion. Beside her, Nils tossed in their bed. Finally he woke and turned to see why she lay with the lantern still burning.

"Nils, my heart feels heavy. Like we just wait for the next bad thing to happen. I can scarcely lift myself from bed each morning. My body aches. My soul aches."

Nils stilled. Was this some strange sickness his wife spoke of? What would he do without her? What if she fell ill and died? How would he care for an invalid daughter and a baby? Oscar was only seven, and although he was strong and capable, small for his age.

"Nils?"

"Ja."

"No more waiting. Tomorrow you see about school for Oscar. No more waiting."

Nils hesitated. "The Moorpark school is seven miles away."

Ellen shook her head. "No more excuses. You talk to the teachers. If they will take him, then we see he goes."

The next morning Nils left his fields to ride over the hills along the narrow track of land where a herd of longhorn cattle grazed. At the squat little schoolhouse on Peach Hill, the teacher explained that Nils would need to take the matter up with higher authorities.

When he found the superintendent at home, the man explained that the school term had already started. The man strained to understand the broken English Nils had picked up during his days in Santa Barbara, his dealings with the grain broker and the mercantile people. Nils blushed at how ignorant he must seem to such an educated man. He considered how remote his people lived, comfortable with their own language. They had not given thought to the children, who spoke only Norwegian. Now his Oscar would suffer the consequences of a father's ignorance.

Nils took a deep breath and began speaking in his best English. "My wife and me, we pay taxes to support the school. It is important that our children become good citizens."

After considering, the superintendent offered a compromise. "Send the boy to school for the rest of the term to learn English. If he does well, he can start first grade in September."

Nils nodded and backed out of the room, considering the problems that a simple "yes" created. The men had halted work on the grade road with Jorgen's death. Now with Lars gone as well, he could not see how the remaining men could do the work. He had planned to finish the road during the winter, but now there were not enough backs for the heavy labor.

He fretted over the demands already falling to him: the scraping of the road, the carrying of water, the cows that got out, and the sheep that needed shearing for women with no husbands. Lina Hansen had her brother helping, but when the brother's horses balked or he fell behind in the plowing, it seemed the person to ask was Nils Olson. It wasn't their fault, the widows, but both he and Ole were feeling the burden of keeping everyone in firewood and water, butchering the pigs, clearing the creek when the rains threatened, and all the other jobs that needed doing. He had been careful to control his exasperation, but the grade road was the last straw. And now his wife hinted that he should ride his son to school every morning?

His report to Ellen that evening was filled with questions he had no answers for. Who would take the boy? He didn't trust a child on a horse—too much could go wrong. But walking? And who would help with the chores Oscar was already doing? His younger son was only five. The older girl was scarcely able to walk without stumbling. She should be helping out, but she was failing.

Ellen listened without betraying her thoughts. Her husband was a stubborn man. He had grown up with a father who put him to work at an early age. He didn't understand that there was an easier life for small boys. She had grown up with sisters who didn't carry the weight of their father's expectations on their small shoulders. Her daughter might be failing, but her sons were strong and smart, and they deserved a chance.

"I walk with him part of the way," she said. "He catches a ride with others. And some days you take him as far as the turnoff. God provides a way. You will see."

Nils scowled and slipped his trousers off while the baby stirred in the crib. He needed sleep if he was to finish the repairs to the fence that Lina's cows had pushed through. The brother, George, was no help. He could scarcely walk, crippled as he was from frostbite and malnutrition. And his mind was troubled. He was no farmer—that was for sure. But at least he kept the cow milked and the hog crib filled.

"I haul him to school for a few days, starting Monday. We give it the rest of the year and see how it goes." His wife rewarded him with a kiss and, more welcome, a backrub with the liniment that the peddler left on his last trip through. He sighed and allowed her ministrations to work on his sore muscles. He was forty-two and he felt like an old man.

Chapter Sixteen

To Bear the Farewell

October 22, 1902. Ellen struggles to lift the children's spirits as another friend leaves us.

THE WIVES MET to harvest the black walnuts near the creek.

"You look tired, Karn," Ellen whispered as she showed her youngest children how to collect the nuts before the squirrels got them all.

"I guess I am. I wake each morning determined that my husband's hard work does not be squandered by a wife who lacks discipline!" Karn slipped to her knees in search of nuts. "Each night I promise God that every action I take from this day forward will be for Lars."

"He would be proud."

Karn continued as if she had something she needed to say. "My sister weighs on me. She gives up their farm. Their children are young, and she has no one except me and this farm. She comes to live with me next week. We must make life cheerful again for our children's sakes. We owe it to them."

"Are you sure of this? Eight children under the age of ten? Your shack is small."

"We are used to each other's ways. And Susie likes outside work. She will be good in the orchard."

Ellen said nothing further. Karn was stubborn; she would do as she pleased.

Karn straightened and ran her hand over her trim backside to ease the strain of bending. "Time enough for moping! I think what is needed is a trip to Santa Barbara. We spend time with the relatives. This spell of heartbreak will devour us if we are not careful. Yours as well, Ellen. Sadness is not who we are. Let us take the children and visit the folks. Maybe Nils will drive us? When we see the ocean, we remember what it is to have faith in the future, *ja*?"

Ellen slowly nodded, even though everything inside her formed excuses. "*Ja*. Your men will do the chores for a few days. What will it hurt if Nils misses a few milkings?"

Sitting in Mary Ansok's front room sipping coffee and eating jelly roll baked in her new cast iron oven, reminded them of better times. "Sharing with friends is the best medicine. We ease each other with our laughter— the way of women everywhere." Ellen spoke from experience. Her mother had died at her birth. Her father's second wife had raised her with a mother's heart, teaching lessons of love and friendship.

At the beach the women sifted sand through their fingers while the children raced along the shore. Seeing the children's' joy seemed to settle Karn. Her forehead softened and she smiled. "Lars and I had good memories of this place. I would like my children to know the peace I experienced living here."

They left for home three days later.

"The farmer's chores rule his existence," Mr. Ansok joked as he helped lift the last child into the wagon and reached to shake Nils's hand. "Easy judgment for a man who is off to work his wage-day," Nils joked. "While I enjoy a quiet drive with a load of sunburned babies and two fretful women."

"I show you 'fretful' if you don't get me home safely," Karn teased. She looked better for her trip. Something had changed with this brief vacation.

Ellen sat beside Nils as the horses made their way along the sand road to Ventura where the low tide exposed dozens of seashells and rocks. "One day we will be able to leave at our will, not at the tide's bidding," she murmured. The older children ran alongside the wagon, collecting shells for their little sisters. Otters barked and seagulls honked in the distance. The flat, calm sea soothed the troubles of the past. *Whatever awaits us doesn't bear thinking on.*

Susie drove her wagon past Ellen's shack a few days later with her meager belongings and a look of determination. Karn's oldest son announced that they would increase their holding of chickens and ducks. He was now milking their cows, the same as Oscar. His mother and his aunt now made cheeses and butter, jams and canned fruit from the stone fruit trees his father had planted. Sometimes when he awoke in the morning, the house smelled of thin butter cookies and light cakes that they sold in Newbury Park.

The Colony endured the crushing loneliness that each season brought. Pain come in strange bursts, like the first election day when the three widows stood in the yard alongside Ellen, watching while Nils and Ole proudly drove off in their wagon to cast their ballots in Moorpark.

"I would not merely vote my husband's will, were I to vote," Ellen confided.

"Perhaps this is why we are not given the privilege. Only the obligation to pay taxes and toil in place of our men," Karn muttered before turning back to her work.

Christmas was a sad day, especially when one of the hired men brought out Lar's fiddle. Every song held memories of a happier time. The man tried quick tunes, but the women's faces seemed shadowed with memories of the past. Finally Ellen made a quiet suggestion that he give up his attempt. Clearly nothing could keep up the spirits of the children while memories of their missing fathers stole the joy from the holiday. The children played in Lars's barn, where the hay had been pushed aside to make room for the celebration. Ellen noticed her Emma sitting by herself, playing with the kittens while the small children teased one of the mother cats with a tidbit on a string. Her Oscar carved on a piece of wood, making a spoon cradle. When he finished, she took it and pressed her hand to his head with a smile. She had few gifts to give her children this year—the drought had seen to that. Newly knitted socks and carved toys would have to serve. There was no point in including an orange in the Christmas stockings when the trees outside were laden with them. Even the holiday punch made of orange and lemons was not the treat it might be to other children.

In mid-May, Ellen watched from her window as Lina walked through her field to see what her brother's efforts had yielded. The men had held their tongues over the poorness of George's efforts. According to Nils, the planting was sketchy, with missed rows and places where the earth had not been plowed deep enough to trap the moisture. George made a valiant effort to mask his condition, but the sallow skin and the dark circles around his eyes showed that he was not well.

On Sunday, when Nils was reading the Bible and anticipating the first cucumber from Ellen's garden for dinner, he heard the mooing of cattle near his window. Outside, Lina Hansen was running about in her good dress, shouting that his cattle were loose in her cornfield.

"George!" she screamed. But she got no reply. "George, the cows are out! Get help!"

Nils and his son hurried to the field. Ole heard the commotion and came running. They made a quick plan and started in a circle, driving cattle back to the corral where the gate had been pushed open.

When the cattle were penned again, Lina turned to thank her neighbors and heard a loud bang from the direction of her house. "What now?" she asked.

Nils frowned. "It sounded like a rifle." He looked around, a dark suspicion forming. "Where's George?"

"George!" Lina started running toward the yard, her legs flying like drumsticks pumping up and down. She didn't stop to catch her breath until she reached the door.

Nils brushed past, blocking her entry. He crept to the bedroom door and slowly opened it. Using his body to block the view, he growled, "Don't come in. It's bad. You don't need to see this."

He sent a man to Moorpark to place a phone call to the sheriff. It would be hours before the sheriff's buggy arrived to make his report. He kept his eyes peeled and managed to meet the lawman when he arrived. On the way to Lina's shack, Nils explained about the Chilkoot Trail, the headaches, the frostbitten toes and the melancholy that had taken hold in the year since George Ness had arrived. He pointed out the sparse field, the weedy patches and the cow in need of milking. Fortunately, Lina and her daughter had gone to a neighbor's and the house was empty.

The sheriff leaped to the ground and started toward the shack to inspect the bullet that had penetrated the dead man's temple and lodged in the ceiling. He paced the room, checked the view outside where the corn stood trampled by cattle. He closed the door and opened it again. Finally, he quit the room when he heard Lina arrive.

"Anyone who says 'deliberate' is a fool. My brother does not do this to himself," Lina protested. "George was a good man who suffers horribly. He was ill, but he was recovering. I am sure of it. He just needed rest. That was the worst of it. Tired and ill. He cleans his rifle as always after using it. See, he shoots us a rabbit for our supper just this week."

The sheriff studied the dead man's pretty little niece Ella with her long curls and her sad eyes, so concerned over her mother's tears. He looked again at the blood that would need to be scrubbed from the floor by the woman who had loved her brother best. He glanced up and met Nils's eyes, and those of Ole, watching wordlessly. He shrugged. "I'm sure you're right, Ma'am. There's no reason to think otherwise. This was an accident, pure and simple. He was cleaning his gun and it discharged as you have said." He moved to the door and set his hat before adding, "I'm sure the inquest jury will agree. I must convene one. It's the law. But I'm sure they'll say the same, an accidental death."

Lina lifted her chin, her voice strong. "If anyone from Moorpark wishes to attend, we hold the service as soon as you permit it. Some of the hired men serve as pallbearers. Nils will make the coffin. I am sorry for the trouble we cause."

The sheriff moved to where his buggy waited in the darkness, his horse munching the contents of a feed bag. After a hurried meal prepared by Ellen, he tipped his hat and climbed up to light the lanterns on his buggy. The hour was late. He would be lucky to get back to Ventura by midnight.

The next morning the hired men brought buckets and rags to clean the room. They hauled throw-rugs to soak and scrubbed dark stains from the redwood floor. When they finished, they left the door open to air the room of its bleakness while Lina and her daughter walked into the hillside for wildflowers. When she returned, Nils and Ole had already placed the body in its coffin. *George Ness 1871-1902.*

Lina thanked them and returned inside to write her relatives back home. *George will rest beside his friends. I will miss him. I pray he finds peace at last. Should one of my brothers like to come, I would look forward to having his help. There is much work here.*

On the morning of the funeral, Lina led the mourners in a song—even though Ellen joined her husband in thinking the dirge should be eliminated. "Sing," Lina insisted. "We do not mourn in silence. That is a shame reserved for cowardice or suicide. Who here thinks my brother is a coward? Sing loud!" Ellen joined her voice to those of her friends, offering a song to the heavens, just in case.

A few weeks later Lina shared with Ellen a letter confirming that her brother Alfred was sailing to America.

"The house feels cold and dead with only my Ella to cook and care for—and the memories of my two men who sit at the table only months ago," she explained to Ellen one afternoon. "The summer heat burns my corn. And yours as well. What is to be done?"

"Sometimes it is not enough to pray," Ellen agreed.

"The money we save together has gone to settle the death taxes the government requires of us." She thrust her fist in the air. "How unfair that they consider him the owner of our farm when we work long hours together—but in America, that is the way of it!"

"Not like in *Norveg*," Ellen agreed. "What will you do?"

Lina shook her head. "Already I empty my savings. I am not sure how I have money for next year's expenses."

Ellen invited her to stay for supper, but when Lina pleaded a headache, she watched her friend leave with a heavy feeling. Lina felt set apart from them, marked by her troubles. Most days she preferred to be alone. It seemed as though the Colony was breaking into pieces.

Later in the week Ellen realized her fears when Karn stopped by to share disturbing news. "You know, it has been many days—even weeks since my sister-in-law Elizabeth calls on me. But she knocks on my door yesterday with a cake still warm from her Dutch oven."

"You met her warmly? As always?"

"Of course. She is family. Lars was her favorite brother, her support in the early years. Her guardian on the long-ago voyage to America. Even though she is older, she always looks up to him as her hero. But since his passing, her feelings for me have changed. Her heart is broken, just as mine." Karn continued. "We share coffee and chat about the children. Finally, Elizabeth comes to the reason for her visit. 'Karn,' she says, 'Ole and I have been talking. We have relatives living near San Francisco. A small town called Suisun. It is close enough to the city that there makes a steady market for crops. We would be near the ocean again—among relatives.' What about the Colony? I demand. What about the land? Lars would not see you leave this place. We all work so hard for it."

Ellen leaned closer to better understand.

"Elizabeth tells me that this is why she visits me. She tells me the drought has beaten them. They have little hope for a good crop. Ole is discouraged. Lars always claims the land is family. And we agree. Elizabeth tells me she wants me to buy it for my boys. In memory of their father. We are to buy the land. Pay what we can. She tells me that they sell on terms and my hired men will farm it on shares until the boys become men. On that day the land will be ours, free and clear." Karn lifted her chin to look directly at Ellen. "Our boys will farm here together."

Ellen expressed her pent-up breath.

Karn bobbed her small head. "Exactly. I tell her, if this is your wish, then we put it in writing."

"And so you buy the Nelson place," Ellen said. "The idea makes much sense."

Karn hesitated as though she doubted Ellen's words. "Not for now. But the boys do not be children forever. If I must lose these good neighbors and friends—Lar's sister—then at least something good comes of it."

Ellen waited to tell him the news until Nils came in from the fields. He scowled, but she knew the cause. They would have purchased the land for their own boys.

"The Nelsons have made their choice," he stated flatly. "The Olsens will be happy for them."

The neighbors met for Sunday potluck so that everyone could celebrate the news. Elizabeth raised her small glass of wine in a toast. "I want us to still be friends and neighbors, always. Wherever we are."

"When do you make the move?" Ellen asked. "We must have a send-off with all the relatives from Santa Barbara."

Ole laughed. "Not until next spring. We will be awhile harvesting this crop. I travel to Suisun to see the farm that is offered to me, one hundred-and thirty-five acres. I build a proper house this time, with two stories and rooms for the children. Something Elizabeth will be proud to write her relatives back home."

Elizabeth smiled. "If they knew, in *Norveg*, the house we live in, they wouldn't think much of it."

Ole nodded, but his face flooded with color. "We got so busy. There was never time to build a real house for ourselves. This is an opportunity for a fresh start." He looked over at his wife and saw Elizabeth's smile, so beautiful after months of sadness. Their son Harry looked proud and important to have his family be the center of attention. Even little Alma seemed to grasp the importance of the event.

"We will be selling the chickens and cows, seeing to the odd things. My younger brother will come from *Norveg* to help us move and to drive one of the wagons. I cannot handle eight horses by myself." Ole rubbed his son's head and gave him a playful push. "Until this one grows a bit, that is."

His brother arrived to help with the packing of two wagons and the family's belongings. They sold their chickens to one neighbor and their cows to another. The wives cooked a feast for the Santa Barbara folks and friends from Moorpark. For two days the Colony was again filled with children's laughter and the ring of the fiddle and the mouth harps. Some of the others chose to dance, even though Lina refused to join them.

"If you must leave, then let it be on a happy note," Ellen called out in the noisy round of toasts made before a roaring bonfire. "*Best glede varer lengst!* The best joy lasts the longest." She paused to flick away a tear. "You will remain the best of friends."

The Pederson House on Norwegian Colony. From left: Rich, Pete, Karn, Lawrence.

Chapter Seventeen

Make a New Beginning

February 8, 1903. Perhaps a fresh beginning will offer Ellen hope in her grief. A husband might build a new home for a wife.

THE NELSONS PULLED out in two packed wagons before the sun was scarcely over the bluff. Ellen tried to put up a happy face for the sake of the others, but one look at Elizabeth's fixed smile and her neighborly intentions evaporated in a veil of tears. The droughts and the hard years had taken their toll. The Nelsons were filled with hope for the new chapter in their lives, not the sorrows of the past. Ellen watched the wagons start down the road and she wondered if she would be losing Lina Hansen next.

When Lina's brother Albert arrived, Ellen called on her neighbors with a handful of precious iris blooms for their table. She found her friend trying to bottle feed a calf in the yard. Lina straightened and smoothed her shirts. "Never an idle moment, it seems." She swiped at a stray lock of hair and tried to set herself to rights as her cheeks flooded with embarrassment.

Ellen's heart plummeted. "You still think to return to *Norveg?*" Lina set the calf back in its pen. "I have begun a memoir of my life, capturing the Conejo in its fall colors. I write of the friendships and trials God has given me. It might seem otherwise, but I am well-satisfied with all I have been given." She placed the irises in a pottery vase and turned to the photograph of herself, Jorgen, and Ella. "In the past, I imagine my other children in the photograph as well. In my heart all of them are still with me." A shadow crossed her face. "This is what I write about."

"Wherever you live, these memories will go with you. I know this." Ellen said.

"Karn drives her buggy to Moorpark each Sunday so her boys can attend Sunday School," Lina said. "I would do my duty by Ella."

Outside, Karn's boys had hitched their donkey to its cart and were giving the smaller children rides. Later they convinced Nils to lend them a partial roll of hog wire. They took turns rolling across the stunted grass hill with themselves tucked inside.

"Let all the children take a turn, Oscar. See that the girls don't get hurt," Ellen called on her way home to her chores.

When it was time to harvest the scant barley crop, Nils fastened a cowhide under the mower to catch the grain before it was lost in the dirt. The boys followed along, jostling with each other for the privilege of signaling him to halt when the hide filled.

Nils subscribed to the *Moorpark Enterprise*. The newspaper reported that some of the other farmers were shipping their cattle to the Owens Valley until the grass returned. He and his hired man joined the cattle drive to the depot in Simi and loaded their stock into cattle cars bound for southeastern California. It seemed as though God laughed at their lack of faith because the rains returned a few days later. But it was another month before the grass would support livestock again.

When autumn arrived, Ellen joined Lina to wave their children off to Moorpark on the first day of school. Ella rode alongside Oscar on an old, blind horse.

"The walk across the hills will be long, even for a sturdy boy," Lina mused. "My Ella will try it. I worry for her. She is small yet. But she will need book learning if she is to be happy."

When winter arrived, Oscar set off a half hour earlier to check his trap lines. The peddler had convinced them there was a ready market for varmint hides. Oscar learned to skin the pelts and peg them to dry. When he had a stack, he sold them to the peddler for delivery to the fur factories in Chicago.

※

Lina chose a Sunday to visit. Ellen saw her from her window, sitting beside Jorgen's grave, speaking to her husband with her head cocked as though she were waiting for him to agree with something she'd said. She laid a bouquet of chrysanthemums at the foot of the headstone, reminding Ellen of the day the four of them had stopped to explore the Chinese Alley in Ventura. *Much happiness for you two,* the little Chinese man had said when he saw them admiring the flowers blooming outside his shop. *Plant many chrysanthemums in your yard and happiness will surround you.* Lina had done as the man suggested.

In the cemetery, Lina stood and shook her skirt free of dried grass. She summoned her daughter and together they crossed the dirt track holding a fresh spice cake she had baked in her iron skillet. She wore her gloves to show that this was a social call, and drew her tatted lace collar around her dark blue serge dress. She had braided Ella's long blonde hair into pigtails and tied the ends with blue ribbons before pressing a white pinafore for the girl's good blue dress. Ellen had a heavy feeling as she watched them approach.

Lina's knock sounded oddly formal. The children exclaimed over the smells of the still-warm cake while Lina set it on the table and took a seat. She admired Emma's drawing, made from her sickbed, before she greeted the other little girls. Laura and Nora played on the floor with their soft cloth dolls. "Go, Ella. Join them," she urged.

Nils rose to pour three small glasses of his prized elderberry wine. "Medicinal purposes," he murmured, "this being the Lord's Day." He returned to his chair and picked up his Bible once more.

"Oscar and Lud are outside, probably building something," Ellen said.

"They better not be." Nils looked up from his reading. "Sunday is not the day for work."

Ellen and Lina exchanged smiles. "What are we to do? They are boys. They come inside soon and you can quiz them on their verses, Husband."

"How does Oscar get on with his new school?" Lina asked. "Does he get tired walking?"

"The teacher lets him out early in the winter so he can get home before dark. On days when he straggles, I sometimes walk to meet him." Ellen pinched her lips in frustration. "It is a worry, I do not lie. Some days the teacher gives him a ride to the crossroad, but always he has the choice whether to walk on the side of the fence where small black bears live in a cave, or on the side where longhorn cattle graze." She stole a glance outside, but the boys were not in sight. "He is a brave boy. Not many boys his age would be so quick and determined to learn."

Lina nodded. "He is like his father, stubborn." She gave Nils a fond look. "Ellen, you look well, considering. When are you due?"

Ellen patted her growing belly. "A Christmas baby this time."

"You are carrying it like you did the sons. Maybe another farmer?"

"Maybe." Ellen glanced out the window to where the boys were standing and tried to mask the catch in her voice. "Or a healthy little girl. Either would be welcome." Across the room, Nora played with her soft doll in the corner. Perhaps a mother imagined things, until her visitor turned to watch as well. Silence grew between the two and a mother's fear found a name. *Pity*.

Nils set his reading aside and made a vain attempt at clearing his throat. "A cake you have brought us? This is a nice change. Can we expect the lamb roast to be ready soon?"

"Soon enough. And boiled potatoes with pumpkin from the late garden. This was a good year for gourds." Ellen glanced over, waiting for her guest to state the purpose of her visit.

Lina shifted and removed her gloves, blushing at her formality. She cleared her throat and began. "The meal will be wonderful. Everyone knows your lamb is delicious, neighbor. But first I have a matter to discuss with you." She gestured toward the cemetery. "I talk it over with my husband, and he agrees." She fidgeted with her shawl and looked up at Ellen. "I have given much thought to what I might do, and it seems I must return to *Norveg*. My mother is ill and needs me. My daughter needs a good school. She tried it here, but the bullies make her afraid. They knock her from her horse, and she is too small to climb back on. Now she is nervous to go and I see no purpose to it." She glanced down at her hands. When she looked up again tension pulled at the corners of her eyes. "This is a shock, I know. But painful truth is better taken with a quick spoon, my mother always said."

"Certainty is better than false hope. This is for sure," Ellen said. "But how can you know for certain this is God's will?"

Lina shrugged. "Settling the estate has taken all we had saved. I do not see my way out of this."

Nils leaned forward. "We help. The hired men will work the land for shares. The rains return and next year will be better—you will see!"

Lina shook her head. "We take a risk buying Ole Anderson's land. Now there is nothing in reserve—and no hope of saving more. The farm requires a man. I cannot pay labor and come out with anything for ourselves. I must sell. If you are interested, we come to an arrangement.

You could send payments to me when I return home. Something for us to live on."

Nils's face flushed with surprise. He stood and paced, thinking of the problem that had been troubling him. He needed land if his sons were to join him in farming. This would be the solution, but not at the expense of his friends. "Both properties? Ole Anderson's and Jorgen's . . . yours . . . both?"

Lina nodded. "Karn has the Nelson land. She does not need mine. But you will soon have another mouth to feed."

Nils glanced at his wife. "How much are you thinking?"

"My brother has consulted with the banker. He thinks fifteen hundred dollars for Ole's. Twice that for ours." She would not say *mine*. The farm belonged to Jorgen, too.

Nils nodded thoughtfully. "That sounds fair enough." He glanced over at his wife and gave a rueful laugh. "But no more discussing business on the Sabbath. We will break bread together and be family." He reached for her hand. "I miss you already, Lina. But your people will be happy to have you home again." He turned as though he remembered something. "The land will always be 'the Hansen place' when we speak of it. That way you never leave us."

Lina fought back her tears. "The hard part is done. There is no going back after this. Only to go home. But you are right, neighbor. Part of me will always be here on the Conejo with Jorgen and the children we buried."

Dinner was a celebration of happy stories, especially Oscar's tales about school and the friends he was making there. Lina quizzed him on his English and clapped when he recited the Pledge of Allegiance. For a while it seemed that nothing had changed.

Ellen sat unmoving in her rocker after her guests left. She turned to study the plain, drab walls of her home. A faint stream of sunlight highlighted dust motes the children were trying to catch in their hands. "Nils, I want you to build me a new house. Too many memories in this place at the edge of our broken little colony. I want to live closer to the neighbors who remain. Away from here."

Lina Hansen was gone and her house vacant by the time Ellen delivered her baby boy, in a driving rainstorm the first week of January. She gave thanks to God for the healthy child, but her mind was distracted. Her oldest girl was so weak she could scarcely take nourishment, and writhing in constant pain. The younger girl showed signs of the same troubling disease that had taken her two sisters. Ellen sat by the sickbed, stroking her older daughter's hair. The child moaned and twisted, trying to find a comfortable position with little respite provided by the morphine the doctor had left for her.

"You are the oldest of all my girls, Emma. Seven years old. I can scarcely remember my life before you." Ellen massaged the cramps from her daughter's thin legs. Her daughter's pain seemed to ease for a moment before it was back. "Remember how we find the baby owl out of its nest? The butterflies that land on your dress when you sit so very still?" When the girl nodded, she continued softly. "That is what Heaven will be like. Beautiful and filled with wonder. No pain for anyone. Jesus walking with you." Her voice trembled as she continued, quietly so as not to wake the other children.

Emma lay on a cot in the kitchen, staying warm while she watched the comings and goings to keep her mind from the pain in her spine. "I hope my sister doesn't know the pain in the legs. I hope she just goes quietly," the little girl whispered. "That will be better."

Ellen blinked back her tears. "I would have taken my children's pain, but it was not God's will."

She thought of the signs she was seeing each day with her second Nora. Maybe using the same name was an invitation to trouble. She knew her neighbors whispered about this. But she remembered the emptiness of the house without a child's laughter in the months before her second Nora was born. And afterward she didn't have to catch herself when she called out the name and remembered her precious Nora was gone.

From the crib her baby son Ned stirred, wanting changing and feeding.

"Mama?" Emma held out her mended nightgown. "Remember when this wore thin from lying in bed? And the next flour sack was for Lud and Oscar's shirts? You sewed this patch for me. Do you remember?"

Ellen smiled and stroked her daughter's cheek. "Yes, *jentebaby*. And I told you what your grandmother used to tell me, 'a patchwork is better than bare buttocks.'"

Emma's lips tightened as a wave of pain carried her. When her eyes cleared, she lay holding her mother's hand until she dozed.

The weeks of summer and fall passed without improvement. Christmas came and went with little heart for celebrating, only a lamb roast and some carved horses from their father's workshop. Ellen wanted a tree with lit candles like the one she had as a girl, but the mountains were a hard day's drive to the north. Instead, she shared stories about her childhood celebrations.

Winter was in full force, with good rains feeding the thirsty fields, when they buried Emma. A small relief the small coffin did not need to be stored in the shop waiting the land to thaw as in the old country. A tender mercy for a mother. Already grass shoots grew along the road and wildflowers kept a ragged presence in the seepage of the rocks.

Nils carried the marker. He had carved the letters onto the wood days before it was needed, but he had kept it hidden so no one would know. When the last "Amen" passed to awkward silence, he waited for the men to fill in the hole before he set the marker into the earth. *Emma Olsen 1896-1903*.

Oscar stood with his hands in his pockets while the coffin was lowered into the grave. His mother reached for his hand, but he shook it off and stood defiantly, his short legs planted as though he were expecting a strong east wind. Emma was his playmate, a match for his quick mind and his creative hands. His mother watched with a knot in her heart. *So many memories in a small boy's head.*

Later that afternoon, she found him working quietly in the dry, dark room he shared with his brothers and sisters. He had cut a picture of a little girl with long golden curls and a pink frock from the pages of the Sears Roebuck Catalog. He found a picture of a small donkey, like the one that pulled the Pederson boys' cart when Emma could no longer walk by herself. Ellen recalled her daughter, bundled in a quilt with the children running and laughing alongside. She watched from the door as Oscar picked up a small piece of stiff paper and glued the images on it with wheat paste. When he finished, he took his card to the barn. Soon a slow, sad wail filled the barnyard.

She heard Nils hesitate on the porch, making familiar scraping sounds as he removed his shoes. He murmured to the family dog, tied to the clothes pole. When the dog quieted its low whine, begging to be released to chase rabbits and coyotes, Nils shut the door behind him with his heel. He shuffled across her fresh-scrubbed floor in his socks and offered his wife a clumsy pat on her shoulder as though that would make everything right.

She poured him a mug of coffee and placed it next to him. The room radiated smells of fried meat, pickled cabbage and cooking smoke, along with coffee grounds, and with his arrival the musky odor of man's labor. A sweet new scent emanated from the packet he pulled from his frayed grey wool coat.

He bent forward, holding a handkerchief in his toil-stained fingers, a thumbnail torn half across after snagging it on a jagged piece of metal. He slumped into the curved rocking chair and slowly unrolled the newly carved briarwood pipe he had been working on for many days. He had spent long evenings hollowing out the wood, repeatedly checking that the hole was round and centered before bringing it to his mouth to assess the flow of air through the stem.

Tonight he touched the new bowl with his tongue to be sure it was dry of the honey and water he had seasoned it with. He made a ceremony of taking the small red bag of Half and Half tobacco from the mantle. His thumbnail slowly unrolled the first fold and then the second. A faint hint of cardamom, coriander and mace wafted in the air. Satisfied, he took a pinch of burley and Virginia tobacco between his thumb and index finger, enough to partially fill the bowl for its first use. In the half-gloom of the firelight, he gave the pipe a moment's consideration, studying the way the loose tobacco piled against the smooth dark wood. Finally, he leaned into the fire, caught a burning twig and brought it to the bowl. A slow, curling column of smoke rose when the faint red glow bit and caught.

His first puff was unhurried. He sat back, eyes closed in satisfaction that erased a decade from his features, as smoke drew through the stem to fill his mouth and nose. The room filled with the scent of spices and contentment. Ellen darned a sock and then its mate while he cautiously rotated the bowl to distribute the cake of new ash. *So much work for the simple pleasure he permits himself,* she thought. By necessity his can of tobacco would last through the winter months. He kept a seat near the hearth in order to relight the tobacco bowl with a faggot from the fire. *A necessity. So often it goes out for lack of puffing while his mind is deep in thought.*

She looked away to hide the pinch of tears threatening. He had come home with the knot of hardwood, his eyes lit with excitement, she had teased, like a man with a new girlfriend. They had laughed about it.

"What is next for us, husband?" Her question was one she asked too often.

Tonight he surprised her with lines he had drawn on a sheet of paper he pulled from his pocket. "What would you think of moving to the Hansen property? Building a new house to hold us all? I spoke with Martin Overaa, in Moorpark, and he agrees to build it." He searched her face as he did after she visited her daughters' graves, leaving a bit of herself on each visit.

"We have the money?" She felt a faint stirring of hope. Perhaps a new house with better light would help their Nora to recover. "Where would we build?"

"Wherever you want. The Hansen property is between our farms. We would travel less distance for water and wood. The blue gum grove is ours now."

Farther from my girls' graves? "With double walls and no dust between the cracks?" She was gratified to see crinkles in the corners of his eyes like in the old days. "When would Mr. Overaa start?"

Nils indicated the lines, drawn with a lump of charcoal he'd used as a pencil. "I send away for plans for a three-bedroom house with a good porch and a separate parlor. We build a new barn, but we take the chicken pens from here. It will take time. We will need a bunkhouse for a hired man. Oscar will soon be old enough to sleep there. And one day you will have your sewing room."

When my girls are gone? Who would I sew for? "We shall see about that." She turned back to the dress she was stitching for baby Ned from the best parts of a discarded pinafore. He was beginning to walk, and he had outgrown his threadbare, stained baby dress. The child was restless and active, a hard one to keep track of. Maybe he would be her wanderer, eager to find new paths.

Nils took two quick puffs on his pipe, savoring the tobacco. "What would you say to making an investment in Moorpark? I have the offer to buy a good-sized lot for ten dollars. Near the center of town. It's a steep price, but maybe with the rails complete and the train coming through, the town will grow."

A chance to live in town again? She felt a strange quickening in her chest. It was nothing, she decided, just a reaction to his surprising announcement. "I would like that. Maybe you trade hay for more land? Is that possible?"

He smiled. "Once we have a way to get the wagon over the mountain, anything is possible. Oscar is old enough now to help."

"He does well in school. But I hear something disturbing today. Karn tells me she does not send her boys to Moorpark next term. The school board votes to move the school across the new railroad tracks to Charles Street, another mile further. She fears the train whistle will startle the little horse and it will bolt."

"What does she intend to do?"

Ellen hesitated. "There is more. Today, on our walk home, Oscar tells me something. He asks that I don't tell you. But I think I must. After school, he walks near the rail tracks like he always does, even if he knows it is forbidden. A man crouches in the bushes . . . holding a big gun."

"A pistol? One of those long-barreled revolvers? Was he a stranger?"

"Settle down, Nils, and listen. The man tells him to go away, quickly, and Oscar does. But he sees a sheriff and posse riding from the east, from Simi. They find the man and put him in chains. Fortunately there is no shooting. But, Nils, the town is not safe anymore with strangers riding the train and maybe hiding in the boxcars. The town is growing. It is not the place it used to be."

Rage tore through Nils at the image of his eight-year-old son in harm's way, maybe in the line of a shootout or a hostage—a shield from the sheriff. He threw his pipe down on the table hard enough that it caused his wife to start. "Enough talk of Moorpark. If the Pederson boys go to Timber School, then Oscar will also go."

Ellen finished her hemming and snipped the thread with her teeth.

In the early months of the new year, Ellen took walks with her younger children down the dusty road to see how the new house progressed. Martin Overaa was a good carpenter, efficient and skilled, a master builder who made the house rise out of the flat field that Jorgen had used for planting beans. She feared the Hansen shack might be torn down, the wood used for the new house, but it seemed that Nils could not bring himself to erase his friends' existence, either. Better that it remain in use as a bunk house.

In May, Karn and Susie drove their wagon to help Ellen pack up the household. At the new house, Karn arranged furniture and stacked canned goods and dishes in new cabinets while she admired the size of the rooms.

Ellen laughed. "Yours is nearly as large, now that you have added on. We are like rabbits, always building to fit our growing families."

"But what a joy!" Karn said. "We are close neighbors now, only a shout away if one of us needs help." She watched without speaking as

Nils carried Nora past and laid her in a daybed placed near the new woodstove in the kitchen.

Karn glanced at her own daughter, grown hearty playing outside with her older brothers. She broke the silence with an announcement. "My sister has been spending time with a gentleman from Santa Barbara who comes calling. Mr. Dyrkorn. She tells me she gives the right answer to his question. In only a month she and her children will move to his home."

Ellen turned to see Susie's glowing, hopeful face. "Good news!"

Karn picked up a wooden box and carried it down the hall. "I have other news, but I wait a while. Give us all a few weeks to settle into these new changes. One thing at a time, I think."

At suppertime, Ellen poured buttermilk batter into the *vafler* griddle and set it over the fire to cook. After the batter ran out the sides and the steam ceased, she opened the handles and forked the waffle onto a plate before spooning *gjetost* over it. The room filled with the toasty scent of soft cheese melting over the hot waffles. Nora looked up, encouraged by the smell and took a tentative nibble. When her husband and the boys finished eating, Ellen sat at the bedside and tried to tease a few more bites into the child. "Tomorrow we make rosette cookies," she promised. "I don't care that it is not yet Christmas. We don't wait."

A month passed while Ellen adjusted to the activity outside her new windows. Horses pulled the big water barrel on the way to the beanfield. Corn stalks grew in the fields. The winter barley grew to ankle height and beans spread into small bushes. Oscar came home each day with stories of the boys at his new school and their cute little sister, Theresa.

"We play *Annie Over* with a ball, and sometimes when we're running to catch it, the brothers knock their little sister down and I have to pick her up. It happens twice today, but she doesn't cry even once."

Ellen had a plate ready when he returned, tired and hungry from the long walk to Newbury Park. She kept him sitting inside while his younger brothers peppered him with questions. For a few minutes the house was filled with energy. As he talked, she worked cutting down an old dress for Nora, telling herself that it was for when the girl felt better, but really to keep her mind calm in the late hours while she sat by the little girl's side singing the old Norwegian hymns and telling her stories from her childhood. She cradled the girl in her arms and rocked her for hours until the morphine took effect and the child could sleep.

On Oscar's last day of third grade, his sister passed away as he sat by her bedside telling her about the Indian relic he'd found. She smiled and accepted the arrowhead from his hand, and then she was gone.

"Oscar, take the children out and find your father in the field." Ellen felt hollowness seeping into her soul. Her two-year-old was down with a case of poison oak, itchy and fretful in the heat. She attended to him with a strange buzzing in her ears. Her heart fluttered, but she ignored the sensation that confronted her at moments like this.

Oscar ran beside the plow, trying to keep up with his father's long steps as he shouted over the sounds of turning earth. He waited out of reach of the draft horses' heavy feet and swinging heads. The brown mare, Deb, stood patiently, stomping the small biting flies pestering its eyes and nose. His father's face registered little emotion as he unhooked the plow and left it setting in the field.

"Unharness the horses and rub them down," Nils told his son when they reached the house. "Give them a ration of oats. Then milk the cow and carry the bucket to the hogs. No need to bother your mother with the cream tonight."

In the silent house, Ellen smoothed the child's worn dress and arranged her braids. She polished the worn shoes with a can of new brown shoe polish purchased from the peddler. The shoes would be better saved for toddler Laura, but she was determined to have Nora look perfect. When she finished she allowed Nils to place the child inside the plain wooden box. Afterward she watched Oscar kiss his sister on the cheek and tuck the arrowhead in her small hand.

When her son straightened, fighting back his tears, she pressed a small tract into his hand. "For you, Oscar. A prayerbook that comes in the mail. I have saved it for you. *Solglimten*. See, *textblad för de minstra*." She watched as he stared at the picture of a little blonde girl on the cover. He hesitated and opened the book to the inside page with a pen and ink drawing of the Blessed Mother holding her son before the Chief Rabbi in the Temple. She smoothed Oscar's hair with a gentle hand. "When you are lonely or sad, I will read the stories to you. They are written in Norwegian. There is no need for you to remember the words. I will always be here for you." She wrapped him in her arms and felt his body ease against her. "And you will read to me from your English book. We will help each other, *ja?*"

She rose early the next morning in search of summer wildflowers with their buds just opening. She wrapped them in a scrap of dusty pink ribbon, left from the trim on her Nora's flour sack dress, and placed them on top the small, still body.

Lud helped his sister Laura place flowers on each of their sisters' graves while Oscar pulled something from his pocket, the memory card he had made to help him remember his sisters. *Nora Olsen 1900-1905.*

Ellen turned away and felt the baby stirring inside her. Another month and she would have one more to care for. *Please God, this one would be healthy like my boys.* Before they left, Nils and the hired man attended to the marker at George Ness's grave. They righted it and tamped it into the clay like they had the last time.

Later, the ashes in Ellen's cooking fireplace remained cold while she stood at the window, oblivious to the sounds around her. Karn arrived with a creaking of the door almost too quiet to notice. "Ellen, I do not wish to disturb you. I just leave this pot of chicken and dumplings on the table for when you are ready. I feed some to your children and they are satisfied. I leave you now to rest."

Ellen acknowledged her with a nod, but her throat was closed to conversation. She waited to slump into her rocking chair until her neighbor left and Oscar had taken the smaller children outside to play in their toy wagon. The summer heat held steady in the closed room. A board creaked in the hallway. From outside, one of the children laughed. She sat rocking back and forth while she stared at the dirt fields visible through her kitchen window. She was surprised. This death brought no grief, only weariness.

Oscar's grief card, made at age 10.

Chapter Eighteen

Bitter to Test the Marrow

June 3, 1905. Bitter to test the marrow. Karn makes care that we do not despair. We are agreed that we should stay busy and strong amid this new challenge.

"How can this be, neighbor? Not you, too!"

Karn sat at their table, explaining in a soft, certain tone that she had waited a few days after the child's death, but she could wait no longer. Her children needed to be settled in their new home before the new term began. There was much to do. "I have made plans to purchase a small farm in Santa Barbara with the sale of Lars's horses and the money we save. I enroll the children in school there. My relatives, the Langlos, will advise me until the boys are old enough to help. We be closer to our church and the fellowship of other Lutherans. It makes better for the children." She finished her carefully rehearsed statement and waited for the shock to settle.

Nils's face flushed, but Ellen felt nothing.

"When will you leave?" Nils asked.

"In a month, I think. After your baby comes. Susie will be married soon and we will finish packing. The hired men take our things in the wagons and return to farm the lands. We have good men staying. You will have neighbors still." Karn hardened her voice and continued. "When the children have finished their schooling, we return."

"Anna will be happier in town," Ellen said after a moment. "A town is a wonderful place for a girl to grow up."

Nils scowled at the floor of his new house. A house he had built for his wife to be nearer to her neighbors. Karn fidgeted with her coffee cup and waited for someone to speak.

Nils pushed his chair back and stood. "Best I get back to work," he mumbled. "Horses are getting restless."

When he was gone, Karn took Ellen's hand in her own. "I am sorry, Ellen. I know how hard this will be. I wish there was another way. But I must do the right thing by my boys—by Lars."

Ellen nodded. "You have a strong, healthy family. You must protect them. You will be back. And in the meantime, we will be here."

She watched through the window as Karn's shadow moved with her across the yard. In the distance her roosters crowed at some mysterious disturbance that set the chicken house in an uproar. The blue gums shrieked their dismay. Oscar and the Pederson boys were crouched in the dust, playing a game of marbles that never seemed to end. From the window the Pederson girl's praise hymn lilted into the heat, adding a sweet hopefulness to the moment.

Ellen moved from the window thinking to collect the laundry drying on the clothesline. Once outside, she stood inside a row of sheets and heard her friend vent her feelings to her own children.

"Use your English," Karn snapped as she stepped around a ball left in the hollyhocks next to the stoop. "When you talk among yourselves, use English." She mounted the steps and added, "insist I speak to you in English, as well. We are Americans now. We will act like it." The Peterson door slammed with such finality that the boys ceased playing and looked up.

Ellen stood with her head bowed and her arms filled with fresh laundry as the silence of mid-day filled the Colony.

Ellen was proud that her baby was born on Independence Day. She recorded the spelling as *Thora* in the Olsen Bible, before she led her almost-three-year-old Ned over to meet his little sister.

"I love Tora. She my sistah."

Oscar grinned and ruffled his little brother's hair. When he protested, Oscar swung him up on his shoulders and carried him outside to allow their mother to rest. "You can help me hang up the flags."

"Does Tora get flags because she's new?"

"Tora, huh? Is that what we should call her? I guess she does. Let's get Lud to help us hang them from the porch."

One of the hired men fired off his shotgun to commemorate the day. Karn directed her men to lay tables in the yard for the thick loaves of bread, fried chicken and cucumbers she prepared. Susie and her new husband arrived with a watermelon and two cakes decorated with small flags stuck into the whipped cream icing.

Karn gathered her children and saw to the scrubbing of hands and faces. "Boys, you come in and have a bite to eat before the guests arrive. No need to be piggish when it is time for the celebration."

Oscar reluctantly joined the Pederson boys, each with a hand over their heart as they recited the Pledge of Allegiance. Afterward they sang patriotic songs they had learned in school, some of the boys singing louder than others while Oscar mumbled his words. Later the children played tag and ran sack races in the yard. One of the hired men played his Jew's harp. The older boys played with the clay marbles they had formed from adobe earth. Their fathers tossed pen knives into the ground in a game of mumble-peg, outdoing each other in feats of agility as they twisted and strained to reach the last peg.

Ellen made a late appearance, worn out from the delivery of her child. She was glad enough for the meal and the laughter, but she longed for her bed after a long night's labor. As the sun bathed the west in vibrant reds and oranges, the older children slipped away to begin the milking. She stood to join them. Later, night birds and bats flew about the fields searching for mosquitoes.

"This will be a good year," Nils predicted. "We've had a wet spring."

Always like the men to talk about rain and the possibility of drought, she thought. Plenty of food for conversation because their land was always one dry year away from failure.

"When I return, I see to drilling a deep well on our farm," Karn said. "That is what Lars wanted. We will plant trees, hundreds of trees, and water them from a new deep well."

The hired men shared among themselves how a good well would make things easier.

Nils nodded. "We have relied too many years on the shallow well we dug when we arrived. Maybe we will see about a better one for us, too. And a windmill to raise the water."

Ellen tried to speak through the clot in her throat. The wagons stood in the shadows, packed and ready for travel in two days' time. This was the last real gathering they would have, all together like this. "The wells will be something to look forward to when we are together again," she said, glad she was not given to easy tears. She drew her shawl closer.

⁂

Ellen joined her children in waving as the Pederson family rode past, boxes and suitcases packed tightly in three wagons pulled by every horse they owned. Karn insisted on taking her cow. The hired men would be gone a week. Oscar had agreed to feed the chickens and the horses until their return. He was proud of the small payment Karn insisted on paying him.

When they disappeared from view, Nils turned to his workshop. His wife had been asking for a new dresser—something to hold the children's things, and this seemed a good day to begin. He would break the silence with the sounds of hammering and sawing. When his oldest son returned from the Peterson henhouse, the two worked together in silence. From inside the house, sounds of the younger children's laughter rolled across the yard. Nils kept his head down and continued without pausing to scan the empty fields.

For the next three months, each of them tried to ignore the silence hanging over the Colony. The sharecroppers moved into the Pederson shack. Sometimes in the evenings Ellen heard their laughter in the yard. A comforting sound. On their way past her house, the sharecroppers often stopped to chat and to take a cup of coffee. She found her laughter returning in response to the jokes and jests of men who felt as bereft as she. They taught her oldest boys to pitch the cut hay into piles for threshing and held contests to see who could pitch the hay the farthest. Sometimes the hired men let the boys win, even if only by a wisp of straw caught in their pitchforks. The men teased the smaller children, and sometimes brought a toy they had carved from softwood.

Ellen celebrated small triumphs. Oscar moved from fourth grade into fifth. He began playing the flute. She convinced her husband to purchase a violin from a shop in Ventura, but the sound of Lars's Hardanger fiddle was absent from the lackluster efforts of Oscar's playing. With the Peterson boys gone, the parents decided their boys should return to Moorpark School. The two oldest would walk together.

Ellen watched each afternoon for a glimpse of their small heads bobbing over the hill, each carrying a book bag and lard pail—and sometimes a new pelt from one of their traps. She took joy in the small things. The flapping of sheets on her clothesline. The first words of her younger children, their toddling steps and the clever things they brought in from their walks with their father on days when he could be bothered. She and Nils attended school events and met their sons' teachers.

"Oscar excels in arithmetic and science. He has an inventive mind and is quick to find a solution when one is called for," his teacher, Miss Willard, told them. "Are you speaking English with him at home? It would be a fine idea."

Nils nodded. English came easier for him than for his wife, but he had no need to tell the teacher as much. He would pay attention that they spoke English in the house from now on. His wife might feel more comfortable meeting other women if she spoke their language with more confidence.

"Ludvic is a handful. He is inquisitive and quicker than his brother, both in action and in thinking of mischief." The teacher laughed. "But of course you know this. Lud is often in the corner, rethinking his conduct. But he is a sweet boy, and smart. He likes mechanical things—the way the clock works, the pulleys and weights that open the windows. I expect he will be a fine farmer one day."

Lud spun around to stick his tongue out behind the teacher's back, earning a scowl from his father.

"And who is this boy?" The teacher turned to Ned. "I imagine I'll be seeing him in a few years!"

Ellen gripped baby Tora in her arms and nodded. They would wait an extra year on Ned, to be sure he was up to the long walk to the school—barefoot to save the leather. Oscar would take good care of the younger boys. She had no worry on that score.

One thing marred her happiness, an accident that she refused to accept until she could no longer deny it. At first she had attributed it to the change of life, something all the women claimed to look forward to—the cessation of their pregnancies. But one day when Tora was only three months old, she realized with certainty that she was pregnant again.

"How does this happen, wife?" Nils's reaction was predictable.
"As if you had no hand in the matter!" she replied, turning away so that he wouldn't see her tears.

Exhaustion rode her days. The interrupted hours of sleep didn't provide an opportunity to recover before the next day began again. She heard herself snapping at the children, breaking into tears as each chore piled onto the next. With no women to talk to, she felt alone and isolated. There was no time to visit with other women in Moorpark—no neighbor to trade off watching the children, and no man who could spare the time to drive her in the horse and buggy. One day dragged after the other. August would be a hot month for delivering a baby with no neighbor to help out. She dreaded the months of sadness that came after each birthing. She was forty-two on her next birthday, too old for such nonsense, but what choice did she have?

Nils watched and worried. He tried to convince her to take the train to Oxnard to see a doctor. Finally, she agreed. "But only if we take our Laura as well."

The doctor listened to the family's medical history and his eyes grew concerned. He listened to Laura's heart and lungs. Frowning, he tapped on her spine and moved her arms and legs. He consulted with another doctor, but they had no answers. "One day, medical science will provide a diagnosis, but right now it is a puzzle. We have not seen anything like what your daughter suffers from," he told the parents. "I can do nothing for her except to alleviate her pain. Take her home. Give her good broths and plenty of fresh cream and greens. Keep her warm and comfortable. Allow her all the exercise she can tolerate."

Ellen looked at Nils and said nothing. They had wasted the journey.

The doctor turned to her. "You're pale. Would you mind if I examine you while you're here? Laura can keep the baby outside. We won't be long."

When they were alone, he listened to her heart and lungs, and confirmed the pregnancy. "You're exhausted. I'm going to recommend you have this baby in the new hospital in Oxnard. For your own safety and that of your child."

Ellen glanced fearfully at her husband and shook her head. "*Nei*. It is not possible."

The doctor's stern rebuke was directed at Nils. "It's not an idle option. I'm afraid it may be a matter of life and death. I have found something with her heart that concerns me. I will give her some pills. But I recommend—I insist—she return when it's time for her delivery. In the meantime she needs help with her duties. Do you understand? She's not to worry."

Ellen heard herself speaking in halting English. "Doctor, there is a saying in the old country. 'You can give a piece of advice, but not good luck along with it.'" She struggled for words. "A farmer's life is one of worry. The drought is a constant visitor. I fear the rattlesnakes that come in the yard, or once, even to the front stoop."

The doctor nodded, listening intently. "Some women are more suited to country living." He glanced over at Nils. "Is there something more?" he persisted.

Ellen lifted her gaze from the floor. "I am losing my Laura. You tell me to take her home to die. I just last year bury my second Nora. And before that, Emma and the first Nora, and the baby girl. And now you give me no hope for this little girl . . . so precious to me. What do I care about my own health? No wonder my heart breaks. If you want to help me, find a cure for my Laura. It is all I ask."

The doctor turned away, his eyes grave. When he ushered her out of the room, he stood watching at the door as Ellen gathered her baby and took Laura's hand.

On the first day of August, Nils took her by train to the hospital before the baby was due. He engaged a woman from the Methodist Church to cook their meals. After a week of hospital stay, he traveled to Oxnard to bring her home. He was pleased to see her looking rested and happier than she had looked in many months.

"We will call him Nicolay. Nick for short," Ellen said. "The doctor says I've entered the change. This one will be my last. I cannot say I am sorry for that." She looked up from feeding her new son. "How are the children? I have missed them."

Nils smiled. "The boys are too busy to care about a new baby, but the girls are anxious to see their new brother. Laura plays mother with her doll." He saw his wife's hopeful look and added, "When she's up to it, she helps the woman with the baking. Even at six, she thinks to learn. I joke and call her "little mother." I made her a small rolling pin so she can roll out the *flatbrød* with you when you return home. She is waiting to use it."

"Her joints don't ache so much with the new medicine?"

Nils shrugged.

The train ride home seemed shorter than the journey ten days earlier. Steam roiled past the window, a whistle piercing the air along with sounds of clanking wrenches and overhead water tanks filling the hopper. Depots buzzed with people shouting and warning each other to hurry. In Somis, a couple got on carrying their valises for a trip to Los Angeles. Ellen tried to imagine how it might be to travel with nothing in mind but a pleasurable trip. The woman stopped to admire the baby and asked, haltingly, "You are a lucky grandmother."

She nodded, aware of how weary and old she looked. Beside her, Nils's face flared. She patted his arm, letting him know that she didn't mind.

Home again after a taxing journey home, she managed to hug each of her children before collapsing into the fresh sheets of her bed. The room seemed stuffy, the August heat irritable compared to the soft ocean climate of the hospital. Nils scarcely paused to change his clothes before rushing out to see how his oldest son was handling the horses with the late corn harvest.

The woman from Moorpark was persuaded to stay for three more days. Ellen lay in bed with a damp cloth over her eyes while the woman reminded the younger ones to wash their hands before going in to visit.

Oscar surprised her with a package he had purchased with his own money. She opened it and stared at the lens, the levers and black case. "It's a camera."

"We take the film to Moorpark and they will see it is developed," her son assured her. "You can use it any time you want."

She understood what he was saying. She would have a photograph of her children.

Chapter Nineteen

Sons of my Heart

September 19, 1908. Ellen calls them the "sons of my heart." She is the wife of mine. We endure our trials together.

THE NEXT MONTHS were busy, with double diapers to change and scrub, two babies to nurse and meals to cook. Ellen took a photograph of the youngest children in their highchairs, looking almost like twins in their infant dresses and fine blonde hair, but a year apart in age. Ned began school. Laura napped on the daybed in the kitchen.

Oscar dug holes along the driveway to plant a row of trees as a surprise for his mother. He was a serious boy, short for his age but already shouldering the burden of a man. When he reached his twelfth birthday, he moved out to sleep in the bunk house with the hired man. He spent his weekends and after-school hours with his father in the blacksmith shop, the barn or in the fields.

The girls spent time indoors. The oldest helped her mother on days when her stiff joints permitted. Tora was a tiny bird, prodding her younger brother into walking at ten months. She talked for both of them and thought of ways to keep their mother anxious and watchful.

Each night at dinner Ellen looked around at her family. Four boys and two girls sitting on the benches, eating stewed chicken from their henhouse, potatoes and corn from their fields and bread from their grain. She thought of her own childhood in *Norveg*, the songs and cousins, the camaraderie on winter days when fathers drove their horse-drawn sleds to the church for Sunday service, wrapped in quilts with warmers in their pockets, and horses with sleigh bells jingling their quick steps. She recalled the silence of the hills in the snow season, the roar of a distance avalanche, the thin peal of the church bell. The bleating of goats in the summer when the girls joined to play while their herds grazed. The months when the sun didn't set and they took picnics in the hours when everyone should be asleep. Months when darkness outshone the sun.

She recalled singing and laughing with the bitter bite of frost on her lips, neat farms and stout houses as familiar as her own. She longed for the church suppers with kettles kept warm with wool scrap until the time for tasting, food made better by the laughter of good friends and relatives. So much she wanted to give her children, especially the girls. Her oldest was a good cook. The little one would be as well, when she grew a bit older. Barely two, she liked to stand beside her mother and help to stir the soups and whip the cream for pouring over the berries they picked on their walks.

Her last two children seemed determined to grow up. Her duties seemed lighter when they were weaned, out of diapers and ground baby food, free of obstinate colds and sudden fevers. Soon she would have no small children in the house—but she would never be free of the fears that children brought.

One day she heard her older boys teasing the little ones about Nick's fascination with the night sky.

"You can ride on the moon, you know," Lud told him.

"How?" Nick's voice was shrill with excitement.

Oscar laughed and said something about the hill to the east where the moon rose each night.

"You boys stop telling your brother fibs. You'll have him believing them," she chastised as she washed her daughters' hands and carried food to the table. "We have *rømmegrøt* tonight."

"Cream pudding! Use your English, Mother, or the younger ones will never learn," Lud teased. "Look how hard we had to work. Miles we walk to school—and all because we said *rømmegrøt* instead of pudding!"

His mother made a face at the son who was always joking. "The little ones have plenty of time. Nick is only four. But you make him into a foolish boy with your stories, Ludvic." She plunked the platter of meat onto the table and reached to pour the pitcher of milk. "Ned is no better than his brothers for finding mischief. Now eat."

The older boys finished and returned to their bunk house to play cards with the hired man. At half-past nine, on her way to bed, Ellen opened the bedroom door to check on her younger children. She counted heads then counted again.

"Where does Nicolay go?" She turned to see if he was outside before returning to the parlor to demand that her husband help search. He carried his lantern into the room and saw the spot where a small boy's head had lain not long before. "Quick, go see if he's with the older boys," she demanded. "His sweater is missing. And his shoes." She checked the yard, the outhouse, the chicken pens, even the clothesline before she ran into the field calling her son's name. When Nils returned without the boy, she felt her heart racing. "Get the boys to light a lantern and go look. Maybe he tries walking to school like Oscar."

She waited inside the house with the sleeping girls while the men searched. When his father found him an hour later, crying and with a belly no longer full of cream pudding, Nick's tears prevented him from telling his tale. By the time they arrived back at the house, his wail was reduced to sniffles and an occasional hiccup. Inside the warm kitchen, Ellen listened with a hand clapped over her mouth to keep from laughing.

"My brothers say I can catch a ride on the moon if I go to the top of the hill and wait. So I hide my sweater outside and when it is time, I sneak out. Ludvic says to go to the hill where the moon comes up each night, so I go fast as I can. But when I get to the barbwire, my sweater catches. I try to pull it loose, but the moon comes. I try to make it wait. I call, 'Wait, wait—I want a ride.' But the moon doesn't wait. It climbs higher and higher into the sky. I cry because it doesn't listen to me."

The older boys tried to keep their faces straight, but their snickers and jabs only made it worse. Their father gave them a sharp command to stop, but one of them let out a guffaw and they both collapsed in hysterics.

Nick's face got red and he started crying again. "Brother says I can, but the moon doesn't wait. I think it doesn't speak Norwegian. And now my sweater is spoiled."

"Well, we will have a talk with that moon," his father said. "And with your brothers as well. But first, we give your fine sweater to your mother to mend. She will make it good as new."

Oscar finished grammar school at Moorpark when he turned sixteen. The family climbed into the double-seated wagon, lanterns hanging on either side, for the trip to the graduation celebration. Nils made time away from farming to don his best suit and drive the horses. He beamed as he watched his oldest son accept his diploma with a handshake from the superintendent of schools. *A proud moment in a man's life.*

The cake and coffee afterward offered a chance to greet the other farmers. Nils spoke English well enough, but his oldest son stood nearby, listening to the farm talk and occasionally offering an opinion. He could not help but notice the soft looks that some of the girls gave his sons as they stood with their family.

On the way home, Nils gave the horses free rein to pick their way in the dusk. "In Norway, the sun does what it will," he explained to his children. "Sometimes we don't see the sun for weeks. No long winter days like we have here."

Ellen waited until the horses settled to their harness before she spoke. "Nice people hereabouts. Hardworking neighbors who share our same concerns. Maybe Oscar finds work with one of them. It does him good to learn new ways. And then there is high school . . . when the term begins in the fall."

"Our boy has enough to keep him busy here at home. Now he is out of school, he will earn his keep."

Ellen remained silent, but the subject was not settled, only postponed. When they arrived home she placed Oscar's diploma in a frame beside Nils's citizenship paper.

A few weeks later her husband returned home with news. "You will be glad to know I hire a new man so your sons can go to school in the fall. His name is Martin Peterson. He will be here tomorrow, so set an extra plate from now on."

Ellen flashed a quick smile at her son and saw his shoulders slump in relief. The boy had set his heart on secondary school. Now it seemed his way was clear.

Martin Peterson was a good worker and a friend to Oscar. At night in the bunkhouse they talked about many things, including their love of trains. Martin was twenty-six and wiser. He talked about the old country and the places he had traveled. Nils gave his two older sons permission to help out a neighbor, Mr. Waddley, who had purchased a thresher and horses to harvest the grain. For weeks they came home covered in chaff from forking loose hay into the hopper, their faces gray with dust and dehydration, but filled with pride for having done a man's job.

When their own crop of barley was threshed and sacked, Nils gave Oscar the task of hauling it to the grain broker in Hueneme.

"Are you sure he is strong enough to control the team?" Ellen asked as she sat knitting in the yard, after the mosquitoes had settled for the night. "He is so young."

"Old enough to think about more schooling. Old enough to argue when he thinks he's right. I'd say he's old enough to take his share of the work. The farm will be his one day. Time he learns what responsibility feels like."

"Why not let Martin handle the horses this first time? Let Oscar watch and learn?"

"The boy has ridden the route dozens of times. Time he earns his keep."

He assigned the next day's work while the family sat at the table finishing their coffees. "Oscar, you take the horses down the Potrero, tomorrow morning. Mind the ridge at the bottom. It's been trouble for more than one of us. Take it slow." Judging from his son's scowl, the warning didn't need repeating, but it was the father's job to pound the lessons home. "Peterson, you handle the brake. Chain those two wagons together well. We don't have manpower to waste on two trips to Hueneme. We get it done in one if you're careful. Hold tight."

At dawn, Oscar took the reins of the eight-horse team and waited as Martin Peterson climbed on back of the second wagon. He made the right-hand turn at the cemetery before the sun finished climbing the ridge. He drove past the Borchard farm with its vast grain fields already harvested and sheep grazing the stubble, before passing acres of newly planted walnut trees. The route was easy. The team had made the same trip many times and the horses knew what was expected.

At the Potrero, he gripped the reins and hunched forward, tense and alert while Martin leaped out to check the chains and secure the drag. On the downward slope, Oscar turned to be sure his friend was sitting on the sideboard with his hand on the brake. "Keep a good grip, Martin. Once down, we'll stop for water along the road."

"It's not water I need to take in, but water I need to empty."

Oscar chuckled at his friend's crass joke. They would probably both need to relieve themselves, but first they would take the horses down the hill.

He felt the wheels being held back by the force Martin was putting on the brake and the brake-tree thrust through the spokes. At the bottom of the hill he waited to slow, but the wagons rolled faster than he anticipated. He pulled back, but the wagons bumped against the back horses, frightening them. The front wagon hit the bank hard. "Hold the brake, Martin, slow it down!" His shout seemed to do no good. He made a quick half-turn, shouting to his friend, but his friend was no longer sitting on the sideboard.

A low, gut-wrenching sound came from behind the rear wagon. His heart dipped into the pit of his stomach while he brought the horses to a halt, tied them off and climbed down. From the ground he could see Martin, his feet curled in a fetal position as he moaned in anguish. Closer still, he saw that the wheels of the second wagon had rolled across his friend's belly.

"Hold still. I've got you. Can you talk?"

Oscar leaped back onto the wagon and began rearranging sacks to make a bed. He picked up his friend, staggering under the weight. With a mighty thrust, he laid Martin in the wagon before running around to unwind the reins. The horses snorted and danced in terror at the smell of blood, but they managed to pull the load up the other side.

Oscar kept up a steady stream of prattle to distract his friend lying with half-closed eyes, his body dazed in shock and pain.

"I'm sorry, Martin. I didn't know. I would have stopped. You should have yelled. I would have heard you. What happened? Why did you fall off? You've ridden wagons before. I'm sorry."

A ranch house appeared in the distance. Oscar pulled up and left the team at the watering tank while he ran for the door and returned with two men. They carried the wounded man inside and laid him on a bed. One of the women took off the bloody shoes and another lifted the shirt. They looked up at Oscar. "We'll do what we can."

"Send for the doctor. After I unload the grain, I'll be back. Is there anything you need?" The answer was lost in the clatter of boots. He was already on his way out the door to collect his horses.

On the way into Oxnard, a fast-riding vaquero passed him at a run. Farther down the road he saw the man returning with the doctor following in his buggy. At the wharf in Hueneme, he explained the situation and was grateful when others allowed him to break in front of their wagons. Strangers helped him unload while he worked in silence.

Back at the ranch, the same vaquero led his team to water while he hurried to the house. He waited at the door until one of the women saw him and led him silently inside the room to where Martin lay sheathed in a white sheet. "He died soon after you left. I'm sorry. There was nothing anyone could do. Even the doctor. A fortunate thing, truly, for the pain was bad. Very bad," she murmured.

Oscar nodded. He bent to pick up his friend's empty boots, glad for a task to occupy his shaking hands. He remembered thanking the people for their kindness, but beyond that everything was a blur. *I will take him home. We will see to his burial and write to his people. I will take him home,* were the words he remembered saying, but he was never quite sure. He placed the body in the wagon wrapped in the sheet that one of the women insisted he take.

The drive back across the Conejo seemed a dream where the wheels of the wagons scarcely touched the road. He felt none of the ruts and washouts that had plagued the journey earlier. He remembered looking up when the horses came to a stop, surprised to find himself outside his father's house. He hesitated on the seat, trying to summon the courage to step down, already hearing his father's words: *You're sixteen. You should have known better.*

His father was inside the barn when he opened the door to set the harnesses on their hooks. For a moment neither spoke. Oscar stared at his father and saw the look of understanding when he realized the truth of the disaster on his son's face. Oscar felt his lip trembling, but he was grateful. No lectures, only a clumsy arm draped around his neck and a hard shoulder to sob on. Later they worked together to build a coffin.

The next morning the other men joined them at the cemetery. He built a marker and burned his friend's name into the wood. *Martin Peterson, 28 years old.*

He and Lud slept that first night in the bunkhouse hearing Martin's laugh in everything they said until finally they remained silent. They agreed without saying so that his things would remain exactly where he had placed them, even a fine steel pocketknife Martin had carried with him from Norway. Oscar forced himself to write a letter explaining his role in the accident. He had no hope of forgiveness, but his mother had promised he would feel better afterward.

For the rest of the summer he worked his guilt out in a rush of activity. No talk of secondary school was spoken by either father or son. He helped build a windmill and dug a trench from the creek to the house for his father. He cut firewood and picked blackberries along the creek for his mother. He made a little chair for his sister and shod the horses in preparation for the late fall planting. In the evenings, while the rest of the family warmed in front of the woodstove, he sat in the barn, oiling the handles of the hoes and rakes, and rubbing down the harnesses with neat's-foot oil.

His was not the only wagon accident on the Conejo. The Maulhardt wagons went over the side of the Long Grade, damaging the grain, the wagons, and the team. A week later Caspar Borchard lost eight horses and two wagons when the team went over in the same spot—the horses spooked by the sight of the wreckage and the smell of blood. When he heard the news, he understood that Martin's death had been an accident. The grades leading out of the Conejo were dangerous.

Chapter Twenty

Grade-Road Tragedy

Feb 14, 1911. The grade-road tragedy has claimed one of ours.

SUMMER TOOK ITS toll on the entire family, but hardest on Laura, who no longer tiptoed on her little stool to grind the coffee beans before each meal. She found it painful to pull on her socks and often asked her brother Nick to hook her shoe buttons for her. Soon Laura wanted only to climb into the daybed, listless and hollow-eyed, swathed in a blanket in spite of the heat. Her appetite grew peckish and her voice weaker, until she lay for hours without speaking. A different doctor arrived, but this one had no suggestions either. He left a bottle of morphine and suggested hot baths when the pain was most severe.

Two months passed in a blur for Ellen. She administered doses of painkiller to her six-year-old with a growing knot in her stomach. She felt herself rejecting Nils's kindnesses. The youngest children began acting out in a bid for her attention, but she had nothing to give them. She absorbed her daughter's pain until her heart ached with despair. Sometimes she climbed into the daybed beside her little girl and felt her own heart racing as though she, too, were dying.

They buried Laura two weeks after her seventh birthday. Ellen read the dates on the marker Oscar made: *Laura Olsen 1901-1908*. She noticed the same date across the row on another marker. Her Laura had been born the same day Lars Pederson died.

She stood mutely, her mind as blank and vacuous as a planted field waiting for rain. The children ran between worn markers bleached to the color of sand by the sun, some with names scarcely visible. But she needed no reminder of which child lie in each spot. Her memory captured each with the freshness of their passing. It was the details of their living that eluded her, the small features and the quirks. Each girl different from another but melded together in her mind through the confusion of memory and loss.

A cluster of mourners shuffled their feet, in a hurry to return to the business of their lives. They kept a discreet distance and she was grateful. She felt nothing, not pain or loss, only numbness. A sudden gust drove a fly away strand into her eyes, causing them to water, the only tears she shed. She turned to face the bluffs at the edge of the Colony where thatches of stunted foxtail danced like silken threads in the breeze. Her mind recited the litany of names for her daughters now lying side-by-side: *Paula, Nora, Emma, Nora, Laura*—she stopped quickly, horrified that she had almost added *Thora*.

On the walk back to their house, Nils shook his fist at the grassy track where the ragged hill road would one day lead to Moorpark. "That damn grade needs to be finished," he growled. While the church ladies from Moorpark stacked the remains of the meal they had brought, Nils thanked the two Pederson hired men for their respect in taking the morning away from their fields.

"It's time we finish that road. We've had too many deaths on the damned steep grades around here," he raged. His wife blamed this latest girl's death on not having a proper doctor when they needed one, although, in his mind, there was no truth to the matter. Oscar still grieved his part in Martin's death. His wife needed the comfort of being closer to town. "The dynamite work is pretty much done. All that's needed is finish work. Boys are old enough now. Let's finish the job."

The others agreed. They would plant the winter wheat and allow the remaining land to lay fallow until spring. The work began with sporadic days spent digging and prying rocks. Nils's boys helped on weekends and after school—even Nick, who played among the rocks barefooted until he was needed to fetch the water bucket.

Ellen brought Tora to watch, with a warning to stay out of the men's way. At six, her daughter was a sparkling child with health in every limb. The girl laughed and chased butterflies as she trudged alongside the horses when her father led them in from the field. Ellen felt herself easing from her fear and watchfulness. With each passing year it seemed God had heard a mother's prayers. No longer did she fear any stumble or misstep on the little girl's part. The child spun in circles around the house and did summersaults in the yard with her younger brother. Next year she would begin school.

Ellen carried the camera in its black case, handled as tenderly as a clutch of hen's eggs. She clicked a photograph of her older boys as they stood on the side of the mountain with their shovels and picks, working beside the other men to clear the rubble of the last blast. At noontime she set out a picnic lunch. Tora ran to join her father. Nils gave his daughter a chuck under her chin before turning to the bread and cheese. He paused between mouthfuls to describe the work they had accomplished that morning.

"It's coming along. We've had the first rains. Winter will be good for grading," he said. "The men have their heart in this job. We will soon see its completion."

Ellen nodded. "Karn's men are hard workers. But one day the Pederson boys will come home and the men will be working for them."

"The road will be finished long before those boys come back." Nils pared a slice from the block of Ellen's hard cheese. "How is your heart today? Any more spells?"

Ellen shook her head, annoyed at his ability to irritate her with such simple questions. "You have enough to keep you busy. Don't concern yourself, husband. I am fine."

When the men returned to their work, she glanced up at a sky overcast with the promise of rain. God's promise. Thunder and lightning would accompany the storm. Nils's team of draft horses whinnied fretfully in their traces, hitched to the Fresno grader. Best the men call an early halt, she thought. Nils would not take kindly to the suggestion, but the horses would be hard to manage if they sensed an electric storm. She collected food scraps into her woven basket, a wedding gift from the Pedersons.

"Take the younger ones along," Nils hollered where he stood at the head of his team, trying to calm the horses. "Ned, too. Safer with you."

Ned led the way back along the trail the children had made across the field, teasing his younger brother and sister about who would collect the eggs.

"It's your task, Ned. Don't shirk your duty." Ellen heard herself speaking more sharply than she intended as she hurried them along.

Once home, she emptied her basket and handed it to Ned before pulling her apron from its hook. Her white blouse showed need of the washtub. Never a bright color for a farmer's wife, only fabrics that stood up to harsh lye soap and bleach boiling. *I wonder what Nils would say if I showed up in robin's-egg blue? Or red, like the bunards we wore when I was a girl?* She ran her hand over her work table with its blue-checked oilcloth, a purchase from the Moorpark mercantile for a Norska who missed the colors of her homeland.

She motioned for Tora. "Come, help me make dumplings. You can stir the flour. Afterwards, it is your job to grind the coffee for supper."

She was leaning over the table, helping her daughter, when the room lit up like a summer noon. Seconds later a deafening clap of thunder shook the floor and the walls. In the barnyard the cows mooed and kicked the sides of the barn in panic. The chickens set up a racket and she remembered Ned, alone in the barn. In the silence that followed, she heard the sound of hooves and a man's frantic shout. She ran to the door in time to see the boy crossing the yard from the barn, the woven basket heavy in his thin arms.

"Ned, get out of the way. Quick now!"

He stood frozen, his hands clamped over his ears as the air deafened with a second boom. She stretched her hand out, willing Ned to take it, but he was too far away. The horses rounded the corner toward him. She heard herself screaming over the sound of the thunder as she watched him, one moment alone in the road and the next a crumpled heap behind the wagon wheels.

The hired man pulled the team to a stop and tied off the reins before he jumped from the wagon. He glanced over to where Ellen stood in the doorway, her mouth open in shock. They reached the boy at the same time, but there was nothing either could do. Ned's lifeless body lay where it had fallen. "Get a blanket, Missus," he whispered. "Don't let the little girl see him this way."

She took her daughter's hand as the child peered around her skirts. A moment later she returned from the house with the blanket she had wrapped around her daughters in their final sicknesses. She knelt in the dirt, cradling her son's body while raindrops began. "Nils never trusted those horses. And now this." She turned to see the hired man standing uncertainly. Nils and the older boys were already on their way back to the house. The story was not long in telling; the shame on the hired man's face not easily forgotten. The family so long in tragedy, and this one the fault of a man who loved the children and their laughter. The hired man had often said her little boy was a curious one, happy to ask questions and follow him about.

Nils moved the boy from the dirt while the hired man waited outside the circle. Afterward the man stood with his hat in his hands, his eyes searching the hills for an answer. Nils reached for Ellen and they rocked together with heads lowered. The older boys stood with their chins pressing against their chests, faces blank of expression. No tears left for any of them, it seemed. The hired man turned toward the shop, intending to start on the coffin. He was stopped by an arm on his shoulder.

"I'll do it," Nils said. "You go to the bunkhouse. It's been a hard day. There's nothing to blame yourself for. It was an accident. The boy's mother knows it, too. We're sorry for it, but we don't blame you."

"I'd like to dig the grave, Mr. Olsen. It will give me something to do."

Nils nodded. "But first ride to Moorpark and phone for the sheriff. He'll want to know what happened."

Nils left his wife rocking with their daughter on her lap, singing one of the hymns she brought with her from the old country. He escaped into the shop, glad to be alone with his thoughts. He remembered the day she had agreed to marry him. *I promised her a good life, better than she would have back home.* He took a board and began fitting the edge to its mate. Instead of a good life he had given her heartbreak. *Better if I had died instead of Lars.* He'd never spoken of it, but he wondered if maybe she felt the same—better if he had died and the children lived? And yet Lina Hansen had lost both husband and children—now only the one little girl to remind her of the great adventure in America. But would his Ellen think of this as a great adventure? Now with a son needing to be placed into the ground? Surely she blamed him for this rough, dry country. If he had left her in Santa Barbara to marry a town bachelor, she would be happy tonight, tucking a large family into their comfortable beds while the ocean breezes stirred her curtains.

He paused to swipe the tears blurring his work. Behind him he heard the sound of a door opening. He turned in the half-gloom and saw Ellen walking toward him. Her eyes burned with pain and something else, a strange, intense light that he'd never seen in her before.

"Nils, I understand the guilt you're carrying. If you had taken him in hand, if you had handled the horses . . . but blaming yourself does not bring him back. I am the one sent him for eggs." She pulled his head against her as though he were a child and continued in a soft, crooning voice that eased fears carried inside so as not to worry her. "We don't any of us know God's plan. You must rely on the blessings that are ours. Three sons, good boys. And a daughter who will be a comfort in your old age." She ran her hands through his hair and across his cheeks until they rested against his ears. Cupping his cheek against hers, she laid her chin on his head and her words vibrated against his skull. "We will give thanks for what we have. We do not despair. Ned was a good, sweet boy. He will be with his sisters. And you and I go on, together as man and wife. Do you understand what I say?"

He straightened and pressed his forehead against hers. "You are a good wife, Ellen. As good as a man could ask for. I'm so sorry for the pain I bring you."

She ran her thumbs under his eyes and dried the tears that remained. "Just like you, Nils Olsen, to set yourself as the cause of my pain." She smiled through her own tears. "You are my strength." She remained a moment longer, her arms around him until the lantern on the shelf began to sputter and he remembered that he needed to fill it with kerosene.

He gave her a last caress and brushed her cheek with his lips. "What do I need with a lantern when I have you?" He smiled and squeezed her fingers as she turned to leave. "Save me a bit of coffee, if there be any left. I might be late."

"I'll not be asleep."

Alone in the shop, he picked up his hammer and turned back to finish his son's coffin. He hadn't planned on sanding it, but maybe just a light pass would bring out the sheen of the wood. Ned had showed promise as a woodsmith. He would be proud of his father's extra effort.

Nils was still working when his oldest son walked in and picked up his wood carving tools to make the grave marker. When the silence grew heavy, Oscar said, "Ned was born the year the rains came back. I remember. There was a lightning storm. I was his age that year. Strange it was another storm took him." He began carving his brother's name on the wood. "He was proud to be eight. Remember, he threw his hat in the air and gave a shout when Mother made him a cake?" He kept his gaze on the workbench, his hands curled so tightly around a wood punch that his knuckles drained of color. "He thought it was just for him. He didn't want me and Lud to have any of it."

Nils nodded. "He was in a hurry to grow up. He wanted to sleep in the bunkhouse with you. I told him it would be a few years yet." He set a nail and picked up his hammer. "The boy wanted to be like you two. You were good brothers to him. Nothing to regret in that." He hammered the nail in and started on another while his son worked in silence, carving words into the wood: *Ned Olsen 1903-1911.*

CHAPTER TWENTY-ONE

A White Plague Tears our Hearts

November 8, 1912. The white plague tears at our fears. I blame myself, but Ellen will not have it.

NILS UNFOLDED THE letter he'd picked up earlier at the post office in Moorpark and handed it to his wife. "The County people agree to the forming of a new school district, but we must furnish our own school. It's to be the Santa Rosa School. I'm asked to help build it. And serve on the Board of Trustees when we finish." He hesitated. "They've hired a man from Fresno to teach the seven boys who will make up a high school class at Moorpark. Oscar will have a year of high school."

Ellen picked up the letter, struggling over the words that came so easily to her husband. "Santa Rosa will be close-by for the younger boys," she said, forgetting that Ned wouldn't be going. "We start the younger ones in good time. Lud can help Nick with his lessons in another year." She watched Tora playing outside with her brother. It would be good, having all her children in school. She could lie down on the days when her heart took a spell.

Nils set out over the hill each morning to the Santa Rosa Valley with his carpenter's tools. Some days she felt envy at the purpose that consumed her husband's waking hours—him so busy, even in the off-season, working on both the grade road and now the school—his hands so full he didn't have time to dwell on their latest tragedy. People were calling it the Olsen Cemetery now, as though it were an honor.

She was glad when he drove her down the grade for the first time, the day they finished the hill road. People had begun calling it the

Norwegian Grade. She gripped the wagon seat and tried not to worry about the narrow, winding turns where a horse could carry them to their death.

On a Sunday after church, Nils took her to see how the school was taking shape. Ned would have attended, she thought. His death was still so fresh. She didn't speak to her husband about her thoughts. Better they remain unsaid like so much of their sadness. Instead, she drew her son's camera from its box and took a photograph of the building where her children would attend once the school year began.

"Will you be able to spare Oscar for high school once the crops are in?" She'd waited for the right moment to bring up a sensitive subject. Tonight her husband seemed rested.

He frowned. "We make it work."

"His teachers say he is a hard worker and smart." She didn't allow room for his objection. Her family was too precious to leave in the hands of a man now.

"From a mother's mouth." He nodded and glanced away, as if he understood her need to have a say in her children's futures.

She smiled and thought how her relatives in *Norveg* would discuss the matter over their coffees. A boy in secondary school—and such a bright boy! "When you men finish the Santa Rosa School, one day you will build a real high school in Moorpark."

"It's possible. The area is growing. Ten years ago we have only two hundred people. That number is twice that now. I see five or more cars driving to Moorpark every week. In time we may need to worry about meeting another car on the grade!"

The summer months passed with little rest for the family. Father and sons bucked their hay onto the wagon for sale to Germans farming land on the Oxnard Plain too valuable for raising feed. Oscar drove the eight-horse teams down the new grade with no mishaps. All three shuffled in each night, sweaty and filled with chaff from the harvesters. By summer's end they managed to bring in the crops in time to free the older ones for school.

The boys were so different in nature, Ellen thought. Lud, quicksilver and secretive since he was a small boy, always set to do what he wanted despite his father's displeasure; Oscar, serious and brooding, as stubborn as his father and not afraid to butt heads with him on the use of the land. He was studying about the new Sampson tractors that were coming onto the market. In his opinion, the doctoring, feed oats and hay forage were costs of keeping a horse that would be saved by using a tractor. To his mind the savings justified the extra cost of the machine. Her men argued the point each night after dinner.

When the stress of raised voices caused her heart to palpitate, she sent the men out to the barn to finish their discussion. It would end with neither side changing the other's mind. One of these days their father would have to separate the parcels and let each boy do as he pleased on his own farm. But that could wait for a few years.

In September, she stood at the door waving as Lud started out on foot for his new school. Tora wanted to go, but she was too small to keep up with Lud's long steps. She would begin next term when her younger brother was old enough. The younger ones walked with their brother to the bluff, carrying Lud's lard bucket with his lunch inside. At the top of the hill he waved and disappeared. Nick returned to help his oldest brother mend a broken plow. Tora disappeared into the field to tag along behind the new hired man, Olaf, a good worker and happy to have her along.

"Don't get burrs in your stockings, Tora," Ellen warned. "I'll be picking them out all night if you aren't careful." Alone in the house, she finished the dishes and set her milk to simmering for cottage cheese. Her husband was in the fields and would not be back for hours. The Pederson farm with its bachelor shack reminded her of happier days. She turned to the gum tree grove and heard the trees grinding against each other. When she could stand it no longer, she started off to the cemetery with a handful of the garden's first mums.

Ned's fresh grave lay beside his sisters'. Ellen walked among them, pulling a stray weed here and moving a rock there. She bent at George Ness's gravesite to straighten the marker. *The man does not rest easy in his grave.*

On her walk home she saw her husband with the younger children, preparing to haul a load of late corn from the field. It would hold the pigs over for the winter, supplemented with the excess skim milk and the parings of potatoes and squash from the kitchen. With God's grace they would have pork to sell to the butcher, and eggs and butter to trade at the mercantile in Moorpark. The Norwegian whey cheese they would keep for themselves. Americans weren't used to the taste, more the pity for them. The prune-plum trees the Hansens had planted produced a fine crop this summer, sold to a local buyer for drying. Maybe next year they would look into drying the fruit themselves. She had spoken to Nils about it, but he wasn't interested in prunes. It was too bad. Another cash crop with less physical effort would be a happy thing.

Nils came in for lunch with a weary Tora. "The new hired man took sick. I was over talking to him and he looked poorly. He was pale and tired and took a coughing fit. I will see his horses are put away. Must be serious. He does not seem a man to shirk his duties."

Ellen's heart fluttered. "I hope it is not contagious. We have enough troubles."

Nils shook his head and reached for a slab of bread. "Oscar and I aren't likely to catch anything. We're strong stock."

Ellen turned to the window that overlooked the Pederson farm. It wasn't the older two that she worried about—they had reached the age of twelve. It was the younger ones.

When Nick and Tora sat down to supper that night, she studied them for signs of pale skin, clamminess or exhaustion. Lud was filled with disdain for his new teacher and the slate she had issued him for marking his answers. He recited the Preamble to the Constitution at his sister's insistence while Ellen washed the evening dishes. Later she read to them from the Lutheran prayer book. It was in Norwegian, the language they spoke at home. But the boys were helping the younger ones. Even the girl was picking up some English.

Ellen caught one of Tora's curls and kissed it. "You are a sweet girl, my little *lefse*. One day I will give you the *bunard* I wore before I came to America."

Tora smiled. "The dress you let Laura wear when she was alive?"

She nodded. "All my girls have tried it on. Soon it will be your turn."

"Then will I die, too?"

She clutched her daughter close while her heart pounded in unnatural rhythm. "No! You do not have the sickness. The doctor has seen you and he agrees. Even Mrs. Pederson who delivered the others, agrees. You are my healthy girl."

Tora watched her mother with soft eyes. "I will be your helper and learn to cook just like you. Then I will marry a boy in my school and we will live here, too."

"A good plan. You will cook my gruel and help me to remember the names of your babies. And we will sew together and grow hollyhocks and roses."

"I will help Father when you go to Heaven to see my sisters. You promised them you would."

"Yes. In good time, that's where I will go." She kissed her daughter and tucked her blanket tighter. "Now you must go to sleep before the *Hvitebjørn Kong Valemon* carries you off to be his princess."

Ellen turned from the door and considered the big house Nils had built for them, now with only a small girl and a small boy in the room where there should be six girls fighting over who sleeps next to the wall and who has to share the blanket with the kicking toddler. Instead there were only the two. But she was grateful for the time spent with each of her girls. Some more, some less, but good times and lots of fairy tales and songs. And always the plain flour sack dresses with their ugly writing across the front. *I yearned to sew them each a lovely print dress with matching ribbons. But it was not to be.*

Nils was waiting in his chair. She brought him a fresh cup of coffee and watched him stoke the fire. He had taken time off to attend his meeting of the school board. The Board had made a rule that each pupil's family supply a share of firewood, take a turn mowing the grass around the building, sweep, and clean the windows when their turn came. They would try this for a year. If it didn't work out they would hire a janitor. They had already engaged a teacher and provided her with supplies. Her husband seemed at peace with his new responsibilities. All this was enough for him. She wondered if he ached with the loss of their children as she did, but she didn't have the heart to ask him.

Tora was asked to play an angel in the Christmas play, since the teacher lacked enough students for every role. The teacher assured Ellen that her daughter needed only to stand near the manger and not squirm. Nick was a Wise Man. Lud had been asked to play Joseph, but he refused, choosing to sit in the back and scoff at the younger children. He was in his last year, ready to earn his certificate at the end of the year. Because he was a "challenging scholar," as his teacher termed it, he was allowed to spend his time working with the engine that powered the water, as long as he finished his other work.

Christmas Day was quiet, with only the family and two guests to dinner. Pedersons' hired men came to share their dinner, but Nils's new man, Olaf, remained in his bunk house. He was still feeling poorly and didn't want his coughing to disturb the children. She was glad. She had tried to convince Nils that something was wrong, but Nils only saw what he wanted to see.

The older boys had made the younger children toys—Oscar's out of wood and Lud's a toy wagon with a gear he filed with his father's tools. She knitted new socks for each of her boys, and each had a new book to read and a bar of Ghirardelli's chocolate. Pederson's men brought gifts for the children as well.

That night she reminded Nils of his promise. "You say if Olaf does not improve soon you take him to the doctor. It is time."

Nils scowled and nodded. "For a man to miss his Christmas meal over a coughing fit is a serious matter. We go on Monday."

Ellen kissed the top of his head. "It may be nothing. But we must not take risk with the little ones." She blushed at the look he gave her. That he might need to be reminded to keep his children safe! They had both done their share of worrying.

On Monday, Nils returned chilled and weary from a long day's travel to Oxnard and back. She waited until the children were tucked into bed before she asked, "How did it go?"

Nils scowled. "It's bad. The doctor says tuberculous meningitis. It's in his lungs." He shifted and gave up any pretense of reading the book he was holding. "I've told Oscar to leave Olaf stay in the bunkhouse alone. Our boys will be sleeping in the house until the doctor comes to fetch him to the sanitarium this week."

Ellen gave a gasp and stood with her hand over her breast, feeling her heart palpitating. "The white plague!"

Nils glanced around to be sure the little ones were out of hearing. "We need to keep the little ones away. Doctor says children take it harder."

"I should have gone with you! There are things I need to ask the doctor."

"It's a common malady. The doctor has a lot of patients suffering these days. Who knows where it's picked up? That's why it's called a plague." He paused when he saw his wife's face, white with fear. He set his book aside and took her hand. "Come, let's go to bed. Tomorrow comes soon enough for worry."

The doctor arrived on Wednesday to take the hired man to the tuberculosis sanitarium in Santa Monica. Ellen fretted until the doctor's buggy rolled out. She would spend the winter watching for symptoms.

June arrived, and with school's end, Lud's graduation from grammar school. Ellen waited until he came into the house dressed in his new suit so she could take his photograph. He was tall and handsome, with a boyish grin that caused the girls in the class, and even some of the younger women, to stare at him and blush. She felt her husband's pride when as a member of the Santa Rosa School Board, he stood and shook his son's hand. He had helped to hire the teacher, and now his son was in the first class of graduates. Another certificate to hang on the wall.

In August, Ellen was busy stitching a new school dress for her daughter when Tora came down with a slight summer cold. She still had a slight cough when the new term began. The School Board had heard of the hired man's illness and determined that the child not begin school until she received a clean bill of health. Nick was old enough to start school, but Ellen didn't have the heart to ask him to walk alone. She sent Lud to walk part way with him each morning.

Tora's cough worsened. Ellen had Nick sleep in the daybed, and the girl sleep alone in the bedroom where her coughing would not affect the others. She bought a bottle of cough medicine with cocaine in it from the peddler. She woke throughout the night, coaxing the girl to take food and water when the child's small body wanted neither.

Ellen was frightened, but she saw that she wasn't the only one. The older boys stopped teasing their sister after the doctor visited with his diagnosis. The thought stirred her to anger. *Too many sisters buried for them to carry affection for one who will be too shortly with them?* She blamed the hired man for bringing this on them. Tora was her hope. Even though the doctor claimed only half his patients died, he admitted his number didn't include children. *Children younger than twelve die.* She tried to pretend she wasn't doing the same thing as her sons, but she felt herself shrinking. Each night she felt her heart beating its fierce, angry pattern that sometimes woke her husband. She spent her hours in prayer, but her words had a hollow ring to them. She no longer believed that her prayers were heard.

A week into November, Tora passed, weakened and wan beyond recognition. Ellen rushed to line the coffin with flannel before Nils nailed the top down. No time to pick a posy for this one, he insisted; the risk of spreading the disease made a quick burial necessary. In defiance, she plucked a handful of mums from the neighbor's shack and tied them with a blue ribbon the color of Tora's eyes. When she finished she picked up her camera, but her hands shook too badly to continue.

She trudged to the cemetery behind the farm wagon carrying the coffin. A blustery wind caught her skirts, a reminder that she had buried a daughter in all four seasons. November was pleasant, she thought. The heat not so vexing for the gravediggers as in mid-summer. And no rain to speak of. She would remember to thank the two hired men who had done this so many times. Today the men stared with hollow eyes and faint embarrassment for the parents. *It would be nice to have another woman here.* She tried to cry, but her tears were like the adobe—hard chunks of mud that only rain would move. *Thora Olsen 1905-1912.*

When the funeral was over, she returned home, set out a plate of bread and cheese for her men and climbed into her bed. When Nils came in, she heard him hesitate at the door before he softly closed it and left. He understood. There was nothing left to say. *When did silence become the language of my home?* Her boys had never been talkers, nor had Nils. They came and went, taking their meals without speaking. She found it easier to set the food on the table in silence. Her story continued in her head without anyone to share it with.

The doctor came three days later when Ellen had still not risen from her bed. There was no reason to, she explained. Her sons were old enough, they didn't need her. The older boys saw to it that Nick was dressed and off to school in time. The doctor examined her. When she complained about a headache, he mixed an analgesic powder in water and had her drink it.

"It's her heart," he explained to Nils. "This farm life, the memories, everything is too much. She doesn't complain, but her body knows her sadness and it's killing her."

Nils listened, caught between the need to protect the land and his love for her. "You must rest for now," he told her. "One of these days we retire to Moorpark." She heard his words, but they fell short of a promise, and she was glad. Her girls were only a short walk away. She would remain here to tend their graves.

Chapter Twenty-Two

We Bend but Fear to Break

March 1, 1913. I bend but fear to break. My boys can be depended on to do what must be done.

Oscar stopped to catch his breath before the final bend in the grade road. A horse whinnied close-by and he stepped to the side, expecting a wagon to come around the bend. Instead, he heard a man shouting, and afterward the sound of a hard fall. He ran in time to see a man bending over another man with blood seeping from his red hair and beard, who appeared to be dead in the roadway until he gave a low groan.

The upright man turned toward the bank, picked up a rock and started back with it clutched in his raised hands. Without thinking, Oscar charged. He knocked the man to the ground and held him there while the redheaded man struggled to his feet. Between them, they managed to bind the attacker's wrists.

With the prisoner chained to the wagon seat, the red-haired man wiped the blood from a cut on his scalp, stuck out his hand and grinned. "I'm Red Clark, Sheriff of Ventura County. I was taking this man to jail. I make it a policy to never shackle a man when I transport him, and usually they act decently when they see they're treated the same. But this one's a killer. He almost got me." He shook Oscar's hand and admitted, "I have no doubt you saved my life, young man."

Oscar shared the story with his family over dinner that night. When he finished, his brothers broke in with questions.

"Did he offer you a reward?" Lud asked.

Oscar shook his head and smiled. "The sheriff didn't ask my name, so I don't suppose there'll be a notice in the newspaper, either."

"Well, I expect you're a hero, anyhow." Nick's eyes blazed with respect for his older brother.

Oscar thought about the narrow escape on the grade. A hero. The word consumed his thoughts through a week of schooling and chores. One evening he took his time at the barn, pulling the harness off the team while he waited for his father. When the two of them were alone, he got the nerve to state the thought that had captured his thoughts. "I'm taking the train to Los Angeles. I want to see about becoming an engineer."

Nils started as though his hearing had gone bad. "An engineer? A train engineer?"

Oscar nodded. "I've been talking with my teacher and he thinks I ought to give it a try."

Nils remembered the train engineer who was giving Ellen a good time. Or might have if he hadn't proposed. He grimaced in disgust. "You have a farm to run. Who's going to do that if you're an engineer?"

"We can hire it out, like the Pedersons. I'll make more money with the railroad." Oscar stood defiantly, his hands in his pockets. "My teacher says I'd make a good engineer. That I could pass the tests."

"Your teacher knows more than your father?" Nils waited to hear his stubborn Oscar explain himself, but the boy stood scowling. "If that's the case, what do you need the father for? Go. Take your test." He stalked off into the dark before his boy could trouble him further. It would do the boy good to reflect on his rashness. This wasn't the first time the boy and he had argued. Surely this foolish idea would pass as well.

Oscar set off on foot the next morning in his freshly-brushed suit, carrying an overnight bag. His mother packed a sandwich and good, fresh cookies for his journey. From a seat on the train he watched the hills of Simi pass into the San Fernando Valley until he arrived at the depot where he had been instructed to disembark. He had left the name of the company with his mother, after she worried he might not return. But this was only an inquiry. The hiring would come later.

Nils climbed the ladder of his windmill, mulling his oldest son's decision. A train engineer? A man who worked for wages? *A farmer's life is secure. Ask any Nordsmann. Ask those who were thrown off their land what they think of working for wages!* At the top, he pulled his oiling can from the pocket of his old coat. From the narrow platform he saw the place where Jorgen and he had plowed over the tracks of the Butterfield stage after the stage company abandoned the route across his land. He looked west, where the gum trees he and Lars had planted were halfway to the sky. He saw the place where Lars had waved on the day he left to work the Jacobson farm. He saw the cemetery where his children were buried—and his friends. *The land is everything. My son doesn't listen to me. Everything!*

Tears blurred his vision as he reached to oil the open gearbox. At his shoulder the fins screeched and began moving, slowly at first, then speeding up as a gust of wind broke the calm. He looked down and saw the brake rope dangling loose. He had forgotten to tie down the brake. The blades began whipping in the wind, faster and faster until he felt himself knocked off-balance. He reached out blindly to catch himself on the narrow platform and heard the oil can clatter to the ground.

His fingers jammed into the open gearbox. He yelped at his stupidity when a fierce pain ripped across his hand and up into his shoulder. Blood spurted across his face, blinding him. The pain was unbearable, but he clung to consciousness as he clung to the wooden upright—knowing that death watched to see if he failed. His right hand throbbed uselessly, but he fought to keep it raised as he shifted onto the ladder. Lightheaded and bleeding, he hollered into the silent, empty fields that had claimed so many of his friends. Now it was his turn to face this hard land.

Below, Lud raced to the base, took the rope and tied off the brake. Slowly the blades coasted to a stop until the only sound came from the blood pumping in his ears. He wrapped his bleeding hand with his handkerchief and used the elbow of his injured arm to ease his way down. By his second step the throbbing in his fingers matched the beat of his heart beneath his coat.

Ellen was waiting at the bottom. He let her help him to the house. Together they looked at the mangled mass that had been three of his fingers while Lud hitched up the wagon. Afterward his son drove the team to Oxnard with him sitting alongside, his hand wrapped in a rolled towel to stem the bleeding. In the doctor's examining room, Nils heard his wife ask if the fingers could be saved.

The doctor did what he could, cutting the mangled flesh and stitching up the shortened ends before swabbing the wound with antiseptic. When he finished bandaging the wound, the doctor made Ellen lie down so he could examine her heart. He waited until they were both sitting in his office. "Mr. Olsen," he said gently, "I advise you to find an occupation that will be easier on your constitution. Your wife's not well. It's time you moved her into town." His grave tone held a warning.

Nils looked at Ellen, surprised at the relief in her face. He was no longer young, but his sons were. She had not complained, but she would like to live in Moorpark. He owned land now, room for a house and barn, for fruit trees. He could keep cows for her cheese. Even goats if she wanted. What good was a one-handed farmer?

He turned to his wife and slowly nodded. "I send a telegram to the boy before he agrees to something he can't fulfill." He rose and took her arm with his left hand. "Come, we find the Western Union office."

Oscar finished his exam in the late afternoon and rose to thank the woman who waited to receive his test sheets. The mathematics and calculus problems had not been difficult. His teacher would be proud of him.

At the office, a man waited. "Oscar Olsen? You have a telegram."

Oscar opened the envelope with shaking hands. His eyes read the words, but they didn't make sense. *Three fingers? How can this be? Return at once?* He picked up his valise and turned toward the rail station. He would sleep there tonight and take the first train back. *Three fingers?*

Oscar Olsen with Indian Motorcycle

Chapter Twenty-Three

Moorpark Promise

May 1, 1914. Finally I make good on the Moorpark promise. Ellen is a good woman and deserving. Content in her new home.

NILS STOOD INSPECTING his newly-finished house, built on a cluster of lots between Charles and Everett Streets in the early months of the year. He was having the barn built directly behind the house. The chicken pens and his shop would stand a distance from the well. Milk cows would graze on a nearby hill. The house had a nice front porch for sitting, and space for two orange trees with a stone fruit orchard in the rear. He planted a row of cactus between his barn and the house. He could feed the young spines to the cows to save on the cost of hay.

Ellen joined him in the yard. "Who would have thought we would see this day?"

"You will be happy here?"

She didn't bother to nod. Even her words were unnecessary in the fullness of the moment. "I am happy that the older boys will live here. Oscar, on weekends when he isn't boarding in Ventura with his teacher's family. Lud agrees to take a term at the secondary school. That is a good plan."

"We try it for one term, Ellen. I make no promises. When spring arrives, the boy might have to farm fulltime."

She studied him to see if his mind was set. "Those bridges will be crossed when we reach them." Her concern was for her youngest child. "Nick will soon turn eight. Maybe he gets a bicycle for his birthday?"

Nils scowled. "What's wrong with his legs? His brother walked seven miles. Toughened him up."

"Times have changed, Nils. Nick is not his older brother. The older boys suffered and I won't have my last one do the same." She considered. "I will make him a vest to hold bottles. He can deliver his milk route before school."

Nils scanned the hills in the distance. "You won't raise him soft. I won't allow it. He'll learn to farm like his brothers. Take his place on the land when he's ready."

Ellen followed his gaze. "Fremontville. That's what they called the old school. Now our son will start and finish his education just a block from our home. Who would have thought this of an Olsen boy?" She hesitated. "Maybe this boy doesn't be a farmer. Maybe he's for town. Time will tell."

No more was said on the subject. The bicycle would be ordered from the catalog. She smiled as she turned to finish dinner preparations in her new kitchen. *Such things are better left to the woman.*

She walked to the market each morning in her black shirt and white blouse with a simple pin for decoration. No fancy muttonchop sleeves with their high collars or tight cuffs for her. A classic style, sent away for in the Montgomery Ward catalog, was practical and nice enough. The doctor's warning had put fear into Nils. No more canning. No more heavy lifting. A modern cookstove with an oven for baking. On meeting days she donned her new velvet coat with a black fur collar and her favorite black hat, to walk next door to the Fortnightly Club. She carried a plate of *fattigmenje* and a recipe for the puff pastries tucked into her handbag for the cookbook they were compiling. She rolled surgical dressings with her new friends on Wednesdays and collected skeins of yarn from the library to knit socks for the soldiers. On Sundays she attended the Methodist Church, just down the street, and afterward served dinner to her family.

One afternoon a hobo appeared at the door with his hat in his hand, looking for a meal. She sliced a piece of cold pork onto a slice of fresh bread and topped it with another.

"Thank ye kindly, ma'am. Been some time since I seen meat."

She watched as the man tucked the bundle in his pocket and ambled down the road after thanking her again. The following day another man appeared for the last slice of roast and the end pieces of her bread loaf. In the weeks that followed she learned to set aside a meal for the ragged, hungry men who knocked on her door.

One night she rapped Lud's hand as he reached for the last slice of meat. "Leave it for the hobos."

"Seems like we're getting more than our share. Wonder how they know to come here?" Lud complained as he settled for a last scoop of mashed potatoes. "Not like we put up a sign." The next evening he came home with a rabbit he'd shot in the river. He finished skinning it and handed it to his mother. "I think I figured out our problem. Turns out it's not your good cooking the hobos are talking up. Somebody scratched a sign on the bridge with chalk rock." He grinned and waited until his father lifted his head from the newspaper he was reading. "*For a good meal go to Everett Street.* I think they mean us."

Ellen glanced over at Nils. "What does it hurt? Those men are fine people, just like the hired men who work the fields."

Nils glanced back at his paper. "Lud, tomorrow you see to scratching that off. We can't be feeding the whole country."

One Sunday Ellen served a meal of fried pork, boiled potatoes and squash to her husband and three sons waiting at the table. Nils said blessing over the food and passed the meat platter to his oldest. "Time to call an end to your schooling, son. Two years of high school is plenty. The spring crops will need seeding. Money is too scarce to meet your rooming costs."

Oscar ducked his head with his hand still on the meat fork. When he nodded, his gaze remained on the pork chop, not his father's face. "In that case I'll be moving back to the home place. No point in staying here. Just farther to travel."

Lud looked up from spearing his own chop. "I've had enough school. I'll go with him. We can split the work. Partners, like the Pedersons. Share the cooking if it comes to that." He aimed his fork at his brother and grinned. "But we'll come down on Sundays to fatten up on Mother's good cooking."

Nils nodded. "Best let your teachers know. You'll need to return the books and say your thanks. No need for me to see them. Tell them your family comes first."

※

The first Sunday that her grown sons came for supper, Ellen greeted them at the door in her church dress covered by a white apron, with her hair freshly coiled. She wore her cut-glass broach pin because she had no daughter to leave it to. She watched from the window as they dallied in their buggy and team, unsure whether they should knock or simply enter. It was Nick who slipped past to meet them at the gate. She followed, pausing to tuck a stray strand back into place. Thank goodness her hair was still brown and thick with only a trace of gray. In the old days the wives had teased each other over which would lose the color. Not her, for sure.

Lud gave her a lopsided grin and grabbed his younger brother in a headlock on his way inside. Oscar followed with more reserve. He paused at the hat hook to hang his hat next to Nick's woolen cap.

"You may discuss your planting, but you will carry disagreements to the barn," she warned. "I have neighbors now. You will keep a civil tongue with one another."

Lud grinned and pecked her cheek. "We don't argue with Father. We've learned better. After all, we have a guest living in the homeplace, now."

"A guest?"

Lud nodded. "Apparently your old friend, George Ness. Oscar will tell you. Fellow knocks around sometimes at night."

She glanced from one son to the other. "Poor, unhappy Mr. Ness, Just a harmless fellow who lost his way. I hope you be kind to him."

Lud ran his fingers across the new bicycle leaning against the porch. "Father's softening in his old age. Not as hard on Nick, that's for sure."

"Lud, don't. Let it go. It was another time, back then. No going back, even if we could." She gave him a quick squeeze and glanced to see if Nils had returned from his walk.

"How's he doing?" Oscar asked.

"His fingers trouble him, but they don't keep him from milking or tending his chickens and ducks."

"And you?"

"Town living is noisier than on the farm. The little Mexican boys playing in the street remind me of when my children were small." She paused as her thoughts returned to a happier time. "Let us wait for your father and then we eat. And Oscar, you be respectful."

Nils returned with a letter he'd carried from the post office and set it on the mantle before hanging his hat next to his sons'. One of his suspenders had twisted in the back, and his hair was flattened by his hat. She reached to smarten him before she turned to the letter.

Ellen opened it slowly, feeling eyes watching as she slipped the thin sheets from a homemade envelope. "It's from Santa Barbara. From Karn

Pederson. She writes she is busy with the sewing she takes in and the cookies she bakes for sale. Always the industrious one. The boys are coming back to the Conejo. Peder and Richard. They have finished their schooling. She will sell her little farm to drill the deep well for their citrus as planned. She waits until the younger two are confirmed. And Anna is to be married." A fleeting memory caused her voice to break before she returned to the letter. "Anna is seeing a young doctor she met at a dance, a chiropractor who attends school there. And Lawrence is doing well."

She turned the page and laughed. "Karn had an offer of marriage from a gold miner who strikes it rich in the Klondike. He buys her a nice ring with a gold nugget, but she thinks she doesn't love him enough for marriage." She turned to her husband. "The same as Lina Hansen, still carrying Jorgen in her heart."

"When do the boys return?" Nils was more interested in the farming than the romance.

"They're here now. I talked to Pete yesterday. They're working with the hired men to learn to farm the Conejo," Oscar said.

Nils scowled. "Learning how to grow crops with little rain and much aggravation."

Ellen finished the letter and folded it back into the envelope. "Her Anna will not be returning. She will marry in Santa Barbara and remain there until her husband finishes his schooling. Karn and her youngest boy will return after the wedding." She hesitated as a plan took form. "Nils, we will take the train to Santa Barbara and attend the wedding." She gave a sharp look at her oldest son. "But first, my oldest son will drive me to Ventura and I will buy a new dress."

Oscar nodded. "What's for supper? Smells better than Lud's cooking."

"Your mother's a fine cook." Nils smiled and patted her waist. "I've never had a complaint. But she serves it in her own time."

Ellen warmed with her husband's praise. "Lamb roast and butter beans. The way you boys like them."

She had scarcely slid the meat onto the planter before Oscar began. "We bought a tractor. It's a good one. A Sampson. Built in Fresno. It runs on gasoline."

"We plan to hire out after our fields are in. We'll use the money to buy a motorcycle," Lud added.

"A motorcycle? What the fool thing is a motorcycle?" The boys exchanged glances. Their father knew what a motorcycle was. They'd talked about one for a year. But he'd said nothing bad about the tractor

—yet. "You don't be buying this on credit. If you cannot pay cash, then you wait another year."

"We have the money."

Nils scowled and slammed his hand down on the table. "You think you are men now, nineteen and fifteen. I will tell you this! The hard years will come again. Save your money for when the crops don't make. No sense in wasting on things you don't need. Your mother and I sacrificed for that land. You don't be throwing away your opportunity."

Ellen watched her men, always fretting. Nils had trouble letting go of the land. He needed to concern himself with his dairy and his own back yard—not his grown sons.

Nils spoke again. "My name is still on the deeds. The land belongs to me. I have the say in what happens. And I say you should save your money and not take risks with the land."

"We don't take risks," Oscar muttered. "You see to that. But how we do the work is our decision."

Ellen set the lamb roast on the table and handed the carving knife to Nils before he could continue an argument that had no end.

※

The following Thursday, Oscar and Lud rode the train to the sales office in Los Angeles. They remained to take a maintenance class and visited an Indian motorcycle sales office. Lud brought a brochure home.

When the tractor arrived in Moorpark, their parents walked to the depot to see it driven off the train car. At his mother's suggestion, Nils flipped a coin to see who would drive it home and who would follow with the team of snorting, agitated horses. Oscar won the toss. He poured gasoline in the tank and followed the instructions for starting it.

Passersby stood with their hands shading their eyes as he ground the gears and pulled slowly out onto the dirt road, smoke belching over the angry clank of steel and raw power such as the town had never seen. He stood gripping the steering wheel with both hands, surprised at the strength it took to make even the slightest turn. The steel wheels gripped the dirt, chewing a track down the middle of the road while small boys and their fathers watched. And frightened horses fought their traces.

At the bottom of the Norwegian Grade, he slipped it into low range for the long climb. The tractor had only the hand brake which wasn't that good. He stood before the steering wheel, gripping the metal so tightly that his fingers felt numb inside his gloves. Smoke belched out of the stack. Lud waited at the bottom for the tractor to clear the hill before he started up with the draft horses and wagon. If the tractor stalled there would be no way except to back down, inch by inch.

The Sampson climbed steadily, its huge tracks gripping the road while Oscar struggled with the stiff steering at each bend in the road. His hands were sweating and his shirt wet by the time the tractor reached the top. When he saw men farming in the distance, he hit the whistle and heard the air pierce with a shrill sound. Lud started up, his wagon carrying supplies and accessories including instructions for converting their old horse-drawn plow and springtooth to tractor-driven. At home the brothers studied the manuals and figured how they could modify their equipment.

The first week on the tractor was no easier for the operator than for the brother handling the horse team—days that began with the sun and ended when darkness claimed the fields. They worked in dust and heat, trading off with tractor and team.

Across the field, the Pederson boys were digging holes for the orange trees they planned to plant. When they had a line of holes started, one of them stuffed dynamite inside each, set the charges and ran like a jack rabbit. They spent the rest of the spring filling the craters with fertilizer and topsoil before planting trees. The blasts set the horses on edge, until finally Lud unharnessed his team and left his brother to work the field on the tractor.

At the end of the summer, Lud traveled to Los Angeles to buy his Indian motorcycle.

He arrived home at dark, sweaty but exhilarated, wearing a new leather helmet. "Wowee, brother! I don't know if I can see myself on that tractor anymore. How's about I drive around and let the farmers know the Olsen brothers have the only Sampson tractor on the Conejo for hire?"

Oscar motioned for his brother to hand over the helmet. "I have first dibs tomorrow. Your day for the field."

⁂

On the weekend of Anna Pederson's wedding, Ellen walked to the depot with Nils—she in a new dress and he in his best suit, dry-processed and brushed to a nap. Nick spent the weekend with his brothers.

In Santa Barbara, Nils greeted his friends and shared stories old and new. He joined Ellen in walks on the beach, searching for a four-mast sailing ship. Instead, smokestacks and steamships dotted the horizon. After only two days he hinted that it was time to return home.

Ellen smiled. "Remember the serious young man who used to hurry back to his farm? He couldn't decide what was more important, his land or the girl he came so many miles to court!" She took his arm and steered him along the boardwalk. "It seems he has forgotten how to enjoy himself in his habit of worrying."

She felt the passage of time as well. The wedding music was performed by men she didn't know, old tunes for folk dancing and new dances that the younger people enjoyed. She thought of Lars's fiddle, all those years ago. She had suggested Nils take up the instrument. He blamed his fingers, but she knew it was more than that. A fiddle reminded him of happier days.

On her last morning in Santa Barbara, Ellen walked along Stearns Wharf with Mary Ansok, her lungs straining with the effort of talking and walking at the same time. She peered beneath the brim of her hat at the still waters of the harbor. From nearby, a dozen Victorian mansions glittered in the sunlight, a sleepy village grown into a town. "You had an easier life than we did, that's for certain," she said.

"It's ironic. In the end our husbands followed their whims. But everyone says the cost of the children was a great price for the Olsens to pay."

Ellen closed her eyes to shut out the pain of memory. She thought again of what her life would have been if she had stayed here—she, a farm girl with no desire to return to the land except to permit her husband to live his dream. She shook the thought from her head and pointed out a bright sailing ship. "You have the world outside your kitchen window."

"We do that!" Her friend agreed without understanding how wonderful her view of the ocean was to a farmer on the Conejo.

"To a Norska, the ocean is everything." Nils would have said the *land* was everything. She hadn't used the word "Norska" in years. She considered herself an American, but here in Santa Barbara, where the sea brought back thoughts of *Norveg*, she was a Norska again.

She rode the train home in silence. The vacation had been welcome, but the Ansoks and the other Norwegians were from an older time. She recalled nights when her little shack rang with the sounds of girls laughing and playing. She had taught Emma and Laura to sew doll clothes out of flour sack scraps. To bake the good butter cakes, and make cottage cheese. In time they would have been good wives and mothers. And Nora! She sighed. Her sweet Noras. A mother wasn't supposed to have favorites, but sometimes a child fit a mother's heart in just such a way. Her Noras were like that.

And Tora, her healthy girl, the hope that she would have a daughter for company when she grew old. Her feelings for Tora involved none of the guilt she carried for her other girls—a secret fear that she harbored some weakness inside her, passed on to her daughters. She heard this suspicion behind women's murmurs of consolation when she visited the market—and even when she attended church. She had seen doubt in her neighbors' faces each time they walked to the cemetery to bury another of her girls. She had looked for it in her husband's face, but she had never seen it there, the accusation that she was responsible. But his sons were strong and healthy, and her girls were gone. She felt her heart failing a little each day. Soon she would be like her girls, lying in bed, waiting for the end. But it didn't matter. The boys would have their father and the farms.

The miles passed outside the train, giving her time to think while Nils studied the farms from the seat across from her. She reached to adjust a strand of white hair on his temple and he smiled his thanks without speaking. She saw the loose button that would need reinforcing before he wore the suit next. A sharp pain in her chest reminded her that time was precious. By the time the Moorpark Depot appeared, she felt as though she had traveled more than just the sixty miles from Santa Barbara.

Nils stirred in his seat and turned. "Heard you with the other women, discussing the election. Who are you for, Senator Harding or Cox?"

She considered his question for a moment. "Nils, it's not your concern who I vote for. Nor will I take your counsel in the matter."

Anna Pederson and Benjam Albertson, 1914

Chapter Twenty-Four

The Sons Make Courtship

November 4, 1920. It is a wonder the boys got the grain in this season. Neither one is worth much for working. They are both bound for courting.

"Let's take the day off. The county fair won't wait for a spare minute. Let's go see what fun two farm boys can have!" Lud stood at the sink, fresh-washed and dressed in his best clothes. He went into the yard to untarp the Overland and crank it to life while Oscar cleaned the grit from his own skin. By the time he emerged, Pete and Lawrence Pederson were in the backseat.

"I hear there'll be displays for the new Sunkist packing sheds coming to Oxnard. Soon we'll have a ready market for citrus," Pete said.

Lud lifted his hands from the steering wheel and held them in the air while the car maintained a straight line down the center of the road. When the car veered to the right, he gave it a hard turn. "I have no interest in bulls and orange trees. I'm heading for the midway. I aim to win me a stuffed bear and give it to a pretty girl tonight. And find me a beer or two to slake my thirst."

"I want to see the new tractors they're using to farm the Oxnard plains. That's where the money is—Oxnard," Pete commented.

Oscar turned to him. "I wrote about the farmland in my last letter to Rich. Give him reason to get through this war and come home."

Pete scowled. "He should never have gone into that foul war! A lot of local boys went with him, but I don't see what good will come of it. He's fed up with the food. Calls it axle grease. Says the Huns are as sick of things as the Tommies. His letters say things are hard over there, with influenza taking more lives than the bullets. Says it comes in waves. They're expecting another round of the Spanish Flu when winter comes on." He shook his head to clear the wind from his flyaway hair. "Course, he can't write any of that. His letters would be cut into Swiss cheese by the censors. Mother takes the newspaper, and the things she reads don't ease her mind. She'll rest easier when Rich is home again." He turned to Oscar. "Rich writes that you're a faithful correspondent. Your letters are a great help."

"He would do more for the war effort back here, feeding the troops like a good farmer," Oscar said.

"Mother received a letter from Santa Barbara. They're stacking up influenza victims in rows for burying." Pete frowned. "I heard they're taking them out at night, but I don't tell that to Mother."

Lud floored the gas pedal and laughed when the car shot forward. "No talk of influenza or war tonight. This is a night off from worry!"

An hour later Oscar was walking with his brother when they stopped beside a midway barker trying to entice a group of girls into spending their nickel on a game of chance. One of the girls squealed and put her money on the counter before picking up the first of three softballs. Lud stepped up beside her and helped her keep her aim straight. When she lost, she turned and giggled. "Thank you anyway, sir. I guess I'm just a dumb Dora with a baseball. I need lessons before I do that again."

Lud grinned and set his own nickel down. "I'll show you how a guy does it." A few minutes later he handed the cute brunette a little kewpie doll that the barker gave him for throwing fifteen cents worth of rings into the cone. "What's your name?"

"Hazel. I'm here with my friends. We're from the Conejo."

"So are we!" Lud's eyes went wide with surprise.

"You're those Norsky boys! We know about you." Hazel glanced from him to Oscar. "Come meet my friends. This is Theresa and her brother, John Kelley."

Oscar stared at Theresa and saw the color rise in her cheeks. "I see you survived your brothers. I thought you'd be a goner by now," he blurted before he could think better of it. Goner. He blushed at the use of the word to describe so many who had died in the last two months. He didn't want her to think he was making light of the epidemic.

Theresa laughed. "That awful game of tag they used to play at Timber School. I wondered if you still remembered me. I was in first grade. I think you were in third. You were a nice boy to pick me up every time they ran around the corner and knocked me down."

Oscar saw the pigtails and freckles of a little girl transformed into a thick mane of chestnut hair on a young woman so pretty she made his hands shake. He tried to speak and found his tongue tied in a knot of shyness. Before he knew how it happened, she was walking beside him, laughing at Lud's antics as he spent his money showing off for Hazel. When it seemed like everyone was waiting, he picked up a novelty gun at the shooting range and aimed it an inch higher than the paper target. He'd heard about how the gypsy carnies bent the gun barrels to get a farmboy's money. He managed to hit a bull's-eye on his second try. His embarrassment eased when he saw the admiration in her eyes. She wasn't like Hazel; she didn't care if she had a stuffed bear, but she admired a man of ability.

Theresa introduced him to a laughing man who was trying his luck at one of the shooting galleries. "Oscar, this is my father, Silas Kelley."

Oscar stuck out his hand. The father removed his cigar with his other hand as he took a long appraising look. A moment later his face broke into a huge smile and he offered his handshake. "My daughter likes ice cream. Maybe you could find a dish around here."

He noticed a vendor under a poster of a dripping two-scooper. He pulled a nickel from the small stash of coins in his pocket. It turned out that they liked the same flavor, strawberry.

"The first time I ever tasted ice cream was at this fair," Theresa said, smiling over the top of her cone. "I was eight." By the end of the cone she agreed to his suggestion that he drive her home—but not before glancing over at her father and getting his nod.

He wandered around for the remainder of the evening, wrapped in a cloud of happiness. When it was time to leave, Lud offered to catch a ride with friends of the Pederson brothers who were standing at the tractor display discussing the newest farm equipment.

Oscar escorted Theresa to the corner of the field where he remembered parking. To his surprise, her brother John tossed his hat into the back seat and leaped over the side of the car without waiting to be invited. Hazel and another friend joined them while he cranked the starter. "Nice car. Roomy back here." John grinned, enjoying the joke.

Oscar drove with both hands on the wheel while Theresa told him about her strict father and her brothers' tendency for practical jokes. "Dad chased off a fellow one night because he thought the man was too old for me. What do you think of that?"

"Don't go telling Oscar that. He'll think you're too fine for ordinary farmers. Heck, you can ride a horse like a man. And you can shoot, too," her brother said. Giggles from the backseat punctuated his booming laugh. Later, Oscar wasn't sure what they had talked about, but the wisecracks from the backseat made the trip home seem shorter than it had been on the way over. After dropping Theresa and her friends off, he drove home in a haze of happiness. He would be as hung-over as his brother tomorrow, but he hadn't touched a single drop.

He waited through an endless week of farming for Saturday night to arrive again. At the end of the evening, Theresa explained that she would be visiting cousins in Los Angeles for a week or two. He spent endless days harvesting his fields—and when he finished, the fields of his customers.

On the day she had promised to return, Lud halted him as he finished cleaning up. "Brother, it's been two weeks to the day. You don't want to look like an overeager idiot. Give it another week"

The next Saturday, he passed his brother in the hall on his way to the automobile. Time enough for working up his nerve. If he didn't call on her again soon, she would think he was just another windbag.

<hr />

He spent the rest of the summer thinking about possibilities while his nose filled with dust from the tractor's wake. Smoke spewed tiny particles into the air that clogged his ears, his eyes, and even his lungs. One particularly hot afternoon he paused to wipe the sweat from his brow as the sun descended behind the bluffs. He climbed from the tractor with resolute steps.

He bathed quickly and dressed in a fresh pair of trousers and a shirt that his mother had washed and starched for him. Each time they took supper with their parents, he spent the drive fending off his brother's jibes and joking threats to tell their mother about Theresa Kelley. He knew better. Lud might tease, but neither of them wanted to sit through an inquisition about when they were going to meet a girl and get married. Tonight he ate his own cooking, in a hurry to be on his way. It was his turn to drive the Overland, but Lud had been monopolizing it with his new girlfriend and his job at the Potrero Ranch in Lake Sherwood. Tonight he planned to put his foot down. His brother would have to take the motorcycle if he wanted to take Hazel to a dance.

Oscar's weariness evaporated on the drive to the Kelley Ranch. At the turnoff to the farm he squared his shoulders and readied himself for the two little girls who would burst through the screen door and race toward him, plucking at the candy he'd brought. The first time it happened he had been taken unaware, but he'd solved the problem by bringing two bags, one for the little girls and one for Theresa.

Silas Kelley was a laughing father who enjoyed the company of his large family—especially the boys, all of them quick with their practical jokes. A Norwegian boy like himself wasn't used to being the brunt of their Irish foolery. He blushed anew at the memory of the time they pulled his buggy to the top of the barn. He'd had to spend precious hours getting it down again and finding his horses. The lack of sleep and the strain of shame had made for a long day's farming the next day.

He parked his car along the house and knocked. On the other side of the door, the room exploded with sounds of boys jostling for chairs. If there was no dance at Timber School tonight the brothers would sit with their father, talking about farming while he stole glances at Theresa in the kitchen. She would work with a faint blush of irritation, rushing through her chores so she would be free to take a walk with him. Sometimes, just as she finished, the father took out his pocket watch and announced that it was time for bed. Tonight Oscar vowed he would roll up his sleeves and help out. At least he would have time to talk. And maybe the brothers would find something else to occupy themselves.

"Why does your brother call you 'Tracy' when your name is Theresa?" he asked as he dried a dish, aware that the parents could hear and the brothers were snickering.

"Well, we have a lot of *Theresas* in the family. My grandmother, my aunt, me." Her laughter bubbled in a sweet, husky peal. "I expect you don't have that trouble. I've never known another Oscar."

"I guess I know one or two." He felt his face heating. "Probably sounds like a foreigner—or worse."

She looked up quickly and shook her head. "No, it's just different. I'm used to people with plain names."

He knew the German names in her family she spoke of—Caspar, Walter, Antone—not so plain in his opinion. "My father says that in Norway, people use the same names over and over."

"I guess I'll choose different names for my children. No need to stay with tradition. I like to think for myself." She glanced at him with defiance in her expression. "I'm Irish-German and sort of stubborn, if you ask my brothers."

He smiled at this.

He left at nine o'clock, after Theresa's father pulled out his pocket watch and announced, "Time for bed." The evening had gone well. He could see the family assessing him as a sober, determined worker with his own land and a tractor. He knew that his reputation as an industrious man was one of the things she liked about him. He wanted to tell her that he loved the way her eyes lifted in the corners when she smiled. She had a happy nature in spite of the work that was put upon her. Unlike her friend, Hazel, she was serious-minded and responsible. After they were married, he would admit that he wanted to rescue her from the cooking and cleaning, washing and scrubbing required by a father, four brothers and three younger sisters while their mother was hard-pressed and worn-out. She was too fine a girl for the life of a servant, but her sisters, ten and twelve years younger, were of little help.

On his way to the yard he glanced around, surprised that his automobile was no longer where he had left it. He heard the sound of snickering from the bushes and he knew the brothers had found another way to irritate him. The tire tracks led over to the ditch. With a sinking feeling he saw the rear end of the Overland sticking up out of the bushes.

He took a deep breath and turned to face the darkness. "Okay, boys! You've had your fun. Now get the horses and help me get this out of here before the oil all leaks out and your father has to pay the damages."

The sound of his anger brought the father out of the house, followed by his daughter. She stood in awkward silence while the father shouted for the boys to hitch the mules and bring them from the barn. Left alone, he moved to stand beside Theresa, pressing her hand in the darkness to show her that he didn't blame her. He felt the pressure of her hand squeezing his back. It made the whole night worth it.

By the time the car was free and he was on his way again, his heart sang with hope. Soon he would take her away from the crazy family. They would live in his house on the Colony, the house he and his brother were sharing. He had thought about nothing else during the hours he spent on the tractor each day. They could be married when the summer was over.

Nils Olsen Family
Back row: Nick, Oscar, Lud. Nils (note fingers) and Ellen.

Chapter Twenty-Five

Vexed

March 3, 1921. My sons are vexed with each other. Ellen tells me I must be like Solomon to set an example for the new bridegrooms.

LUD WHISTLED ON his way to the table with a pot of scorched coffee in one hand and a plate of lumpy pancakes in the other. "Brother Oscar, you're looking at a happy man. I'm getting hitched!" He set the pot on the table and gave the nearest chair a quick whirl around the kitchen.

Oscar felt his breath catch in his lungs. "To that girl, Hazel?" He hesitated. "Theresa thinks she's not the girl for you. She spends summers at the ranch. Theresa says she doesn't lift a finger to help. She doesn't like living in the country—is that what you need in a wife?"

Lud scowled and helped himself to half the pancakes. "Need? Maybe not, but it's what I want. Hazel's fun to be with. I hate this farming, but I've gotten used to it. She will, too."

"When do you plan on getting married?" Oscar asked.

"Next week."

"How can you support a wife on hired wages? That ranch you're working for doesn't pay enough for two of you."

"I'll quit that job. Start back farming here with you again. As soon as we go to the courthouse and get married."

"At planting time?" His brother would be worthless for the season. Another worry crossed Oscar's thoughts. "Where you plan on living?"

"Here!"

Lud's look of defiance stoked a flare of injustice. Oscar stood up and started for the door. "We'll see what Father says about that. I'm the oldest. You know I'm seeing Theresa. I'm planning to ask her after harvest."

For the rest of the week he stuck to his anger, working the fields and keeping his silence whenever he was around his brother. One day, his rage simmered over. After supper, Lud took off in the car before Oscar had a chance to remind him that it was his turn for it. He turned and started down the hall to the bedroom they used as an office. As he approached the open door, the books and papers he had stacked on his desk flew to the floor with a racket that sounded overly loud in the silence of the room. He felt a brush of air against his shoulder and heard footsteps walking down the hall away from him. For a moment he questioned his hearing, but the proof was there in the scattered books and the fading image of a man in the dark hallway. "George Ness—you back again? Get the heck out! I'm not sharing this house with you, either."

The footsteps faded into silence again. *Anger to raise the dead?* He shut the door and made his way out to the blacksmith shop to pound his confusion into the new set of discs he was welding.

On Saturday, Lud was hung-over with the liquor he and Hazel had drunk the night before. Oscar kicked a rock out of his path on the way to the tractor. It was his brother's turn to do the plowing, but he'd be no good until after lunch and that was a half-day wasted.

That evening his brother was gone before he finished washing the grit off. After making his dinner and cleaning up, he was tired and discouraged, but he managed to ride over to see Theresa. He parked the motorcycle under a walnut tree and warned the brothers that they had better not touch it. The frustration in his voice did the trick. He took the towel out of Theresa's hand and led her to the door. "Let's take a walk." He glared at the father and muttered. "I'm done doing the dishes."

On Sunday, he drove to supper at his father's without waiting for Lud. His brother was already waiting on the porch, grinning. Their mother warned them with a look, that they should temper their disagreement in her house.

"I'm the oldest. I should get the house and the good land," Oscar argued over coffee and his mother's jam cake. He watched his father and mother exchange glances and Lud smile confidently.

"Let Lud live there with his new wife for the time being," his father said.

"Maybe she will settle him down. He's got to quit the alcohol and the late nights if he's to make a farmer of himself. Maybe a family will be the making of him." He turned to Oscar. "You can live here with us in the meantime."

The rest of the week he traveled from his parent's house, up the Norwegian Grade to spend his hours in the fields. At the end of the day he had no energy to go back to Moorpark, clean up and drive the miles back to the Kelley Ranch. Instead he ate his mother's meals in silence and opened a book to avoid his father.

The week turned into two, and then a month. He had nothing to offer Theresa, even if she said yes. Not a house, not even land of his own. Harvest was in its peak and nothing had been decided.

He was making a turn on his tractor at the end of a row when he saw Theresa's father approaching in the little flatbed pickup he always drove. He cut the tractor's engine and jumped to the ground while the truck came to a stop.

Silas stepped out, shading his eyes with his felt hat, its brim turned down in front in the jaunty manner the man favored. He looked over the fields and whistled. "Hello, Oscar. You're one busy man. Your farm looks as good as the Borchards'. Mighty hard workers, you two boys. Everyone says so." When Oscar stood without moving, Silas grinned and reached for his wallet. "I came to see if you have any hens for sale. Coons broke through and got most of ours last night. Thought a fair price might be two bits each. We could use twelve."

Oscar released his pent-up breath. He could spare a dozen hens, even though the man could as easily hatch out his own chicks and spare himself the expense. But he wasn't about to turn down the sale. In the henhouse, they grabbed one and then another hen and stuffed them into a gunny sack. When they had all twelve bagged, Silas stood and cleared his throat as he got to the purpose of his visit. "We haven't seen much of you lately." In the awkward silence, he hesitated and shrugged sheepishly. "My wife thinks maybe we've chased you away with the jokes and the tricks the boys played. Theresa's mad as a hen. Wife made me come by to see if you've had a change of heart."

Oscar felt his face heating. He lifted his hat to wipe his brow before he shook his head. "I've been too busy. When I get this crop in, I'll be back to see her. Tell your wife not to worry." He helped load the chickens and accepted money the man pulled from his coin purse.

Silas was a great talker and today he had news about the armistice. "Bet you're glad the war's over. Course it means the end of wartime prices for the farmer."

He nodded. The price of barley would fall, but Rich Pederson had been fighting in France for two years and now he was home. Everyone had attended the Welcome Home party the community held in Moorpark for the forty-two soldiers who had served. Some of them didn't make it back, but their names were read so that everyone knew who the heroes were. He'd stood with the other young farmers, red-faced and humbled, while Rich and the others who had served glowed with pride.

He waited for Silas's dust to clear before he started his tractor again. He had no quarrel with the man. It hadn't been an easy trip for the father to make. *Theresa missed me!* His heart felt lighter than it had in a long time.

That night he studied a brochure from Pacific Ready-Cut Homes, a company in Los Angeles that offered kit houses. He circled a Craftsman-style house that could be shipped by train from Los Angeles in bundles of strapped lumber and put together by a good carpenter using the blueprints the company supplied. He'd talked to a man in Moorpark, Mr. Florey, who had experience with the company.

In September, with cash from the sale of his grain, he returned to the Kelley Ranch and was gratified to see Theresa's brothers lounging on the porch, grinning as he parked and got out. "Keep your mitts off the car," he warned as he walked up to knock.

"Yes sir," one of them answered. The others nodded seriously.

Theresa's face lit up when she saw him. She took off her apron in the middle of the dishes and left the rest for her mother to finish. Without looking to see if her father objected, she led Oscar out the kitchen door toward the tall oak tree where they could sit and talk. But he had a different plan. "I want you to take a drive with me. Over to see my land."

She walked past her brothers with her head held high and slid into the seat of the Overland, checking that her hat was pinned securely.

He drove cautiously. Time spent with her seemed like a test. Failure would mean a lifetime as a solitary bachelor farmer because he didn't know any other girl he could talk to as easily as her. His responses to her questions came out clunky and dull compared to the quick-witted brothers she was used to. He searched for something clever to say and remembered the story of his little brother trying to ride the moon. She laughed and asked him to point out the spot, but afterward he could think of nothing else to add. The rest of the drive was made mostly in silence. The hum of wind brushing over the open seats made it hard to hear, but it felt good, just sitting next to her. Later they stood on the bluffs and he pointed out the three parcels that belonged to the family.

"I'm the oldest. I get first pick. Which place would you want if you were to marry me?"

"*If* I were to marry you? Are you asking?" Her eyes crinkled and her face brightened.

He thought she was as pretty as the day he first saw her in her little braids, lying in the dirt at Timber School. "I guess I am. If you'll have me."

She fidgeted with her hat before she summoned the nerve to address the concern her mother had insisted she make clear to the Protestant boy. "We have to get married in the Catholic Church in Camarillo. I can't be married in yours."

"I don't have a church. Only the minister from Moorpark. He does some baptisms in the creek at the Finch place, but I don't much hold with that. I guess your church is okay."

She played with the ribbon on her hat as they both contemplated the thought that his parents might not see things as simply. The next words were harder, but they were the condition her parents had imposed in the event the boy proposed, and she had given her word. "You'll have to speak to the priest. And the children will have to be raised Catholic."

"I guess that's okay." For a moment he wondered what his parents would say. But what harm would come of having babies who believed in the same God? The Bible?

She nodded and seemed to relax. Clearly her mother would be relieved. She turned from the creek with its bower of blackberries and pointed to a low rise with a view of the bluffs behind her. "That's a good place for a house." She pointed to the gum trees. "I like this spot. It reminds me of the hills behind my house. I say yes to this place."

"And me?"

"Yes. If you're sure about the children and everything."

He nodded hesitantly, his mind on things that were more within his control. "I'll have to build us a house. Got some ideas you need to look at. There's a carpenter in Moorpark. He can have it up before we get married."

He spread the blueprints on the hood of his car, tracing the lines with his finger while Theresa made suggestions. She wasn't shy, and she had some good ideas.

On the way back, he parked at the cemetery and waited while she adjusted her sweater and fastened her hat against the breeze. She started walking, her shoes leaving small prints in the loose dirt that his tractor had thrown up against the fence. At the first marker, she leaned over to read the letters sanded down by years of grit and blowing dust.

"These were your sisters?" He nodded, unsure what to say. Her curiosity, voiced in reverence and pity, challenged the pain he'd carried in silence from the time of his first sister. "Who carved these markers?" When he remained silent, she studied his eyes, her own darkening in concern. "It was you."

Oscar glanced away. After a moment she moved to take his hand in hers. He waited, fearful to make a move lest she think he was too forward. She lifted her chin until her nose was nearly touching his. When her eyes invited, he took a deep breath and got up the nerve to kiss her.

When the kiss ended, she turned back to the car while he paused to push a marker back into the ground. "George Ness," she read. "Who was he?"

"Just a man who lost his life."

He picked her up on a workday for the drive to Los Angeles. In Calabasas he looked unsuccessfully for a filling station that sold root beer. Fortunately Theresa had thought to bring along a jug of tea. In Los Angeles, she pointed out a café on Figueroa. They agreed on ham sandwiches and lemon meringue pie with coffee.

"When you asked where I wanted to eat, I would have said that Mexican place that smelled so good," she teased. "But a look at your pickle face and I knew you weren't going for that!"

Oscar blushed. "I like food the way my mother cooks it."

She smiled. "Well, we'll have to see about that."

The kit arrived on the northbound freight train. Oscar drove to Moorpark with Lud. In Moorpark, they met up with their father with his wagon and team. After loading the shipment at the depot, they hauled the wagons of wood over the Norwegian Grade in a caravan that included some of the Pedersons. With Rich's help the bundles were laid out in rows according to the carpenter's instructions.

For the next few weeks, Oscar picked up Theresa on Sundays and drove her over to check out the progress of their house. They took picnics on the bluff. Afterward he showed her the shop he was building, and the spot where the chicken coop would stand.

"I'd like peacocks," Theresa said. She walked around, planning her garden. "A circular driveway would leave room for orange trees in the middle."

He smiled, proud that he could give her such a simple thing. "There's room for an orchard in back of the house. What trees will you want me to plant?"

"We should have fig trees. Apricot. Peach. Apple. And a kumquat. And bees?"

"Mother always claimed apples wouldn't grow here. Probably not enough frost."

"Then we'll do without."

They paced off a place for a barn. Oscar hung a clothesline from salvaged twine. He planned the tank house with an Economy hit-and-miss engine to provide power so she could have running water in her kitchen. The carpenter built a bathroom with a clawfoot bathtub and porcelain sink that drained into the orchard. The toilet drained into a septic hole away from the house.

When the wedding date approached and the house wasn't finished, they agreed to help with the finish work. It would give them a chance to work together. Oscar stood in the unfinished shell, describing the built-in china cabinets he would build.

"Do you know carpentry work?"

Oscar nodded. "Norwegian boys know their way around a finish hammer. It's in our blood."

"So you admit it—your father taught you everything you know." Theresa climbed the unfinished porch and turned to face the driveway where the citrus orchard would be planted. "Can we hang a swing on the porch? So we can sit outside and smell our orange trees in the summer?"

Oscar grunted noncommittally, already anticipating the porch swing he had ordered as a surprise. There was no point in spoiling a wife, his father claimed. Another thing they disagreed on.

Oscar and Theresa Olsen wedding day, 1921

CHAPTER TWENTY-SIX

Two Become One

September 21, 1921. Oscar has married. His bride will be a good match for him. Ellen agrees.

IN THE DAYS before her wedding, Theresa went to Los Angeles to stay with her Uncle Frank and Aunt Myrtle while her aunt sewed her wedding dress. They bought a veil, new white pumps and stockings. She had her hair bobbed, after Oscar suggested that short hair might be easier to keep up. She'd considered the idea, but Hazel had warned her that men liked long, luxurious hair on their women. Afterward she admired herself in the mirror, relieved that her new husband would be a reasonable man. She heard her mother telling her aunts that he was a practical man; that much was certain. And a kind man who brought her little sisters candy. Her brothers and her father liked him. And she'd never heard anyone say a bad word about his character.

The wedding reception was held in her father's back yard, with friends and relatives coming from Los Angeles and Oxnard to camp out for the week. The ceremony took place in the new St. Mary Magdalen Church that Juan Camarillo, Jr. and his brother Adolfo had built in thanksgiving for their good fortune. They would be the first or second couple to be married there—an honor, Theresa assured him.

Oscar arrived at the towering Spanish-style church with his parents, his mother looking proud in her velvet coat and his father sweating from nerves. The formal and staid service spoken in Latin, the scent of incense, the gilded statues of saints and the Holy Madonna filled the space until Oscar wasn't sure where to look. Instead he concentrated on the joy on Theresa's face as she turned to him with perfect trust and agreed to be his wife. The rest, he decided, would sort itself out with time.

At the reception he introduced his in-laws to his parents. Theresa had asked her brother, John, to be their best man, after the priest explained that the witnesses needed to be Catholic. "Just as well after seeing that church," Lud whispered to Oscar on his way through the reception line. "I would have just embarrassed myself up there in front of everybody."

Oscar tried a dance with Theresa, but he felt awkward with all eyes watching. Between dances with Hazel, Lud sneaked out to the shed to drink with the Kelley boys and their father. Oscar refrained. He didn't like the taste of beer, he explained to Theresa. She didn't tell him it was one of the reasons she loved him.

"We're going to have a good life," she promised him that night.

Oscar smiled. "I already do." He had driven her to Pismo Beach, to a motor court along the Pacific, but he hadn't counted on the rain that fell in torrents.

After their honeymoon, Theresa moved into Oscar's parents' house in Moorpark, while they worked on the house together. For three weeks they drove back and forth over the Norwegian Grade. Oscar built cabinets while Theresa sanded and painted. They strolled around their new farm, planning where they would plant trees and bushes from the starts that Theresa had collected.

The eucalyptus trees shaded the house in late morning. Oscar saw uncertainty in her eyes when the afternoon wind broke the silence with an unearthly screech. "You'll get used to them," he promised her.

"We'll cut firewood. Start with that big one in the middle that makes most of the noise," she teased.

Each evening, Theresa saw her mother-in-law's slow, careful movements as she tried to help with the supper. "Is there anything the doctors can do?"

"It's nothing," Ellen assured her. "The heart doesn't hurt. It's simply failing." Theresa stirred a pot of rice and waited for her to continue in her halting English. Ellen's dark hair was laced with gray, her face full and unlined except for the lingering heaviness that clung to her like a secret sadness. Her eyes held sorrow as she sighed. "I have nothing left to live for. All my girls are gone now. I'm ready to join them."

Theresa squeezed the handle of her serving spoon and thought of her children who would never know their grandmother. An image of the seven neat Olsen markers in the cemetery brought a question. "Will you be buried with your girls when the time comes?"

Ellen frowned. "The county people say all burials must be done at Ivy Lawn Cemetery now—a requirement for keeping track of people in a growing county, I suppose. But it would be a comfort to be with my girls. And my son." She sighed. "I fear I will be one of the first in the new cemetery. It will be a lonely spot with all that space around me."

"I hope you get to hold a grandchild," Theresa said. "That would be a special thing." Ellen glanced at Theresa's belly for signs of rounding before turning away, disappointed. "You are strong. You will have healthy girls." Her eyes held little hope that she would see a child before she died.

Theresa spooned the rice into a serving bowl and set it on the table. "Oscar's outside with his father. I'll get them. You rest, Mother."

The house was finished and the furnishings placed in the rooms in time for the housewarming Theresa had planned on a Sunday afternoon. Oscar's parents stood beside them at their new front door as the first guests arrived. The housewarming, so soon after the wedding, required no gifts, but she was happy to accept the plant cuttings, vegetable sets and trees that her aunts and sisters carried in.

Theresa followed Oscar as he led her parents through the house, proudly listening as her mother exclaimed over the indoor toilet and the bathtub with its hot and cold water. The wood-fueled cookstove in the kitchen was modern and efficient. The painted wood floors were decorated with throw rugs. The front room featured a border rug under the Queen Anne chairs and a new cherrywood reading table with a crocheted doily. Someone gave them a green kitchen stool as a wedding gift and Theresa had already used it to cut her husband's hair.

Women placed hams and potato salads on her dining room table alongside loaves of her homemade bread. Later Oscar stood beside her with his arm around her waist, watching people fill plates and carry them to wherever they could find a spot. Some stood inside the living room, filling the house with chatter and warmth. Others carried their food outside to the porch. Rich Pederson spent the evening talking farming with some of Theresa's uncles.

When the last person left, Oscar joined Theresa in turning down the oil lamps. From outside, the call of her new peacock broke the silence. "This was a good day," she whispered. Oscar studied the joy in his new bride's eyes. He tried to speak, but a lump in his throat prevented the words.

Within the first month Theresa realized she needed a car. Oscar happily drove her to the market, but it was a burden asking him to drive her to her mother's so they could share a ride to Mass on Sundays. The Pedersons drove to their church in Van Nuys, and Lud and Hazel didn't attend any church, nor did Oscar. He owned a big farm truck and he still had use of the car he shared with his brother, but most Saturday nights Lud and Hazel took the Overland to a dance. When Oscar needed it on Sunday morning, he had to allow time to walk down to Lud's driveway to pick it up. Sometimes the keys were in Lud's pockets, inside his bedroom where he was still asleep. After a few heated discussions the brothers decided to split ownership. Oscar kept the tractor and his brother the car and motorcycle.

Theresa waited until Oscar was sitting in the porch swing with a cool glass of lemonade before she brought up the issue. "My father has a used Buick he'll sell you. If you think we could afford it," she added.

The image of Silas hauling his Overland auto out of the ditch rekindled Oscar's humiliation. "I'll get us a car," he growled.

He brought home a used Model T and called Theresa outside to watch as he cranked it to a start. The car backfired with a blast of dark exhaust that covered the car and their clothing. He waited until it warmed up before he drove it around the house on the circular road where the workshop stood. When he arrived back at the front door, he got out and indicated that she should trade places. "Don't be afraid. It won't bite you," he told her. "Put your foot on the clutch and push down."

She took the wheel and ground the shifter into first gear, slipped the clutch and gave it gas with a confidence that surprised him. A moment later they were chugging smoothly around the corner. "Where did you learn to drive? I thought with all your brothers–"

"My father couldn't spare the boys so he had me drive my mother to Los Angeles when she needed to go. I've been driving since I was fourteen," Theresa said.

Oscar drummed his thumbs on the cloth upholstery without responding. When she finished circling the farm a few more times she headed to the end of the road, dust billowing from the tires, before making a smooth turn at the cemetery to return home. Oscar rode without expression while his brother and sister-in-law gawked through their open front door.

Back at his own house, he waited while she cut the engine. "Don't try cranking it over yourself," he growled. "You'll break a thumb."

Afterward he returned to his blacksmith shop to pound his frustration onto a piece of cold metal. The cost of a used car, the expense of setting up a new house and filling the kitchen shelves with provisions seemed exorbitant. His brother had called him a frugal bachelor. Lud was complaining about his own wife's spending habits, but he had cause. Theresa quietly hemmed new dish towels made from used flour sacks. She made laundry soap from fireplace ash and grease she rendered from butchered hogs. She cooked plain meals and only opened the icebox when it was necessary. Her kitchen garden thrived with plantings and starts brought by her aunts and mother who visited on Wednesdays. She trimmed new cardboard to line his worn shoes and found ways to stretch their income that his mother hadn't thought of. In his workshop he mulled over areas where they could conserve, but with each idea it seemed that Theresa had already applied it.

He returned to the house to enjoy a slice of apple pie Theresa had baked from bartered apples.

With her help he fenced and cross-fenced his land, using eucalyptus posts and hand-split oak. They planted blackberries along the creek for future jams and pies. Theresa sewed their underwear from flour sacks and darned their stockings until some were more darning yarn than original.

⁓⁓

Eight months after they moved into their own house, Theresa woke moody and despondent. "Your tossing kept me awake most of the night, Oscar. And now my feet have to touch the cold floor because you have the rug on your side. Breakfast will be late today. I need to take something for this headache."

She served his breakfast and finished wiping the dishes before she walked outside to feed the chickens, feeling out-of-sorts and dispirited by the quietness. She walked to the edge of the gum trees and stared down the empty road. Even Mrs. Pederson was in her egg house, sanding her son's eggs for sale. She started walking, thinking to stop at Hazel's, but the house was silent. At the end of the road she climbed the cemetery fence and read the names on the markers aloud, squinting at the ones that had faded in the sun and rain. "You poor little things. Think how much Oscar has missed. All the sisters we'll never know."

He rarely spoke of his childhood. She loved him for the raw pain that flickered in his eyes at moments of unexpected beauty or happiness. She saw the way he avoided looking over at this quiet cemetery on their drives past. He held his grief so privately that she was afraid to intrude for fear of what she might hear. She saw the reaction in the faces of people when she told them her new married name. Clearly they wondered if she would carry Olsen babies to term. Apprehension soured her stomach until she feared she would retch again, as she had earlier. She turned toward home with tears blurring each dusty footfall.

Hazel was outside on the front step, flipping through the pages of the Sears & Roebuck catalog without a paper or pencil. Clearly Lud had lowered the boom. She looked up, saw Theresa and gave an exaggerated stretch. "I'm sooo bored out here! Nobody comes by except the Jew peddler in his fancy rig, and Lud says we don't have money for extras. I hear the guy gives haircuts, too. Nick gets his from the man. Isn't that a hoot!" She pulled a cigarette paper out of her pocket, folded it lengthwise and tapped the last of a package of Mail Pouch tobacco into the paper trough. With a sideways glance at Theresa, she licked the edge and twisted it closed. "Lud doesn't care. He smokes too." She sighed dramatically. "I'm so tired of him telling me how poor we are. I keep dog-earing the pages in the catalog, hoping he'll get the hint."

"Oscar says we have to sell the hay crop and pay Nils his share before we buy anything." Theresa felt her stomach roiling at the smell of smoke. "You should unpack your wedding presents. My aunt says your vases and table scarves came from Pasadena."

Hazel shrugged. "Dust catchers out here. Who sees them, anyway? I'm nineteen, not ninety. I'd rather have a wind-up phonograph so I can practice my dance steps. Now that we're married, all Lud wants to do is work on that motorcycle. He comes in at night dirty and tired and expects me to wash his clothes."

"He told Oscar he took you to the movie show last week."

"Yeah, that was swell! But first we had to go to his parents' for dinner, 'cause it was our week and you were at your parents." Hazel stubbed her cigarette out and stood up, making a quick turn to admire the flare of her dress. It was a city style that had no purpose on a farm, but Theresa didn't mention the fact. She turned toward her house.

"I have have bread rising. I better get back."

Hazel looked down the road in the direction Theresa had just come. "What do you do at that cemetery? Talk to the graves?" She laughed at

Theresa's flustered look and her eyes flashed with a sudden thought. "Hey. . . Trace! You know how to drive. Let's take your car into Moorpark and see a picture show!" She brightened and added, "Or even better . . . let's take ours and run to Los Angeles. We can at least window shop. That would be the bee's knees!" She dug in her pocket for more tobacco and scowled when she didn't find any. "I get so nervous out here." She noticed Theresa admiring the hollyhocks that Lud's mother had kept tied to the fence. "Lud's all wet if he thinks I'm going to keep those things up!" She turned and snapped her fingers. "Crackerjack! I'll tell him I need some gardening gloves so I can prune his mother's roses. That'll do the trick."

Theresa glanced toward her house as a wave of nausea rolled over her. "I need to go home. I don't feel well."

"Oh phonus-balonus. You need to stay here until that green glow leaves your skin." Hazel ran in the house and returned with a glass of tea. She peered closer while Theresa drained the glass. "Horsefeathers, Trace, you're pregnant. My sister's going through the same thing." Theresa started. For once her sister-in-law was right; the moodiness, even the sudden fear that she was going to leave another baby in the cemetery—it all made sense. "What's Oscar going to say? Lud would be over the moon if I turned up like that. But I have no intentions of ruining my shape." Hazel laughed. "This tomato intends to keep what she has."

Theresa thanked her for the drink and started home. The tea helped —at least until she made it to the door. When Oscar came in that night, she waited for him to finish his supper before she told him the news. He looked up, surprised and happier than her father had been when he heard about another one on the way.

"We'll have to add another bedroom to the house," he joked. "But this one can hold three kids before we need to worry."

"Do you think your mother's trouble will affect our girls?" Theresa asked the question that had taken root that morning. "Do you think the cause is inherited?" She promised herself she'd never ask again.

Oscar studied her gravely. "Let's not fret about that." He stood and pulled her into his arms. "Doctors are smarter now. And maybe it'll be a boy."

The next morning, Oscar insisted on cranking the car before she drove over to tell her mother the news. At the last minute she stopped at Hazel's and asked if she wanted to ride along.

Hazel squealed and jumped into the car without even checking her hair. "I'm practically one of the family," she said. "Your mother will be so glad to see me."

"Just don't smoke."

On the way over, Theresa felt the car vibrating. She shifted down and coasted to a halt. Hazel remained inside while she climbed out and inspected the tires. "You have to get out, Hazel. Otherwise you'll shake it off the jack."

The right front tire had taken a sharp rock and air slowly hissed from a hole in the tube. She pulled the jack from the trunk, raised the car and wrenched the hubcaps loose. Once she had the tire off, she applied a patch before inserting the tube and pumping the tire full again.

"Tracy, you're just the berries! I could never do that. What a hoot! I thought we were goners, for sure!" Hazel climbed back into the passenger seat and raised her hands high above her head. "Whooeee, we're a pair of bearcats! Wait 'till Lud hears what we did!"

Theresa saw the happiness in her mother's eyes when she shared her news—and the unspoken warning not to space her babies too closely. "Oscar will build you a crib and a rocker. He's good with wood," her mother said. Theresa recalled the drawers and make-shift furniture she'd grown up with. She already had more than her mother.

On the way to the car, Theresa glanced around at the huge oak tree that shaded her mother's yard. She turned to study the oak-studded hills and heard the sound of cattle in the distance. A tinge of nostalgia assailed her. Her farm was so quiet compared to her father's. Her brother John drove up and she forgot her moodiness. "Hello, brother. Have you set a date yet?"

John gave her a slow, lop-sided grin and roped her into a loose bear hug. "I should be as happy as you, sister—is that what you're thinking?" He sobered and added, "Tracy, you look just beautiful!"

She felt herself beaming. They were so different, fraternal twins, but he saw her for what she wished she could be and she loved him for that. "When are you and Olive getting married?"

"She wants you to call her 'Babe'."

"She's not a babe. She's almost out of high school by now." Theresa watched her brother's face redden under the felt hat he wore tilted at a rakish angle. Hazel was watching as well, hypnotized by his charm and dark good looks. Theresa felt an urgency to get her sister-in-law back home again. "I'm glad Babe asked me to be her bridesmaid, but you need to tell her I'll be pretty pregnant by then." She watched as John threw his hat in the air and gave a whoop of surprise. Like her father he found joy in so many things. Beside her, Hazel's mouth was making a perfect 'o' in admiration. It was time to go.

"Babe'll want to see you and Oscar when she comes this weekend. We'll barbecue on Saturday night." John winked at his sister and turned away before Hazel had time to favor him with a dazzling smile.

Hazel was all questions on the drive home. "That brother of yours is a corker. Where does he get his good looks?" She hesitated. "In fact, all your brothers are."

Meaning I'm plain? Theresa half-hoped for another flat tire, something to stop the chatter, and this time she'd take her time changing it. Instead she drove in silence until she dropped Hazel off. As she pulled away, she saw Lud watching them with his eyes shaded against the afternoon sun.

"We'll need to tell your mother and father about the baby before Hazel does," Theresa told Oscar that night. "And my family wants us there this weekend."

Oscar nodded over his plate of pork and fried potatoes. "I have to take a load of grain to the depot tomorrow. You want to ride along?"

Theresa felt her eyes tearing up in gratitude. A day spent with him, telling his parents the good news, maybe even spending precious money on a physic for her stomach—and a chance to wear her nice dress before she outgrew it. A ride to town would eliminate the possibility of Hazel dropping by, asking questions about her brother.

Her joy was short-lived. A few days later a Moorpark neighbor drove over the grade to give Oscar the news that his mother had collapsed. By evening Theresa sat in the small hospital room holding Ellen's hand while outside the door, the corridor whispered with the quiet steps of nuns carrying pills and bedpans. Oscar sat beside them, his expression grim in the semi-darkness as dusk settled outside. Nick and Lud had arrived earlier, but they had taken their father out to get supper. Two visitors at a time. The nuns were strict about visiting hours, even for a dying woman.

She squeezed Ellen's hand and felt her mother-in-law's thin veins weakly pulsing beneath her pale wrist. Her face seemed lined and weary, but peace-filled. When her eyes fluttered open for a brief second, her expression was serene. "I pray it is my time," she whispered. At first Theresa thought she imagined it, but Ellen's eyes glazed with ecstasy. "I want to see my girls waiting for me with their brother."

Beside her, Oscar's lips thinned. Theresa reached for his hand and placed it on top of his mother's, something he could not do so for himself. With the feel of his mother's skin, his face softened. Theresa sat motionless, hoping he could bridge the gulf of silence that captured him each time she asked about his childhood.

His eyes shifted to Theresa. "You know, I was eight years old before I saw my mother's ankles? At the beach when she was wading in the water. She was so private. But such a good mother. She was more forward thinking than Father, and sometimes his ways rankled her. Even if she didn't tell him so." He sat with his thumb caressing his mother's wrist. Before Theresa could respond, he bent to study his mother's shallow breathing. When he turned, his eyes were the shade of a foggy sea in summer. He reached for his wife with such a fierce embrace that she feared for the child inside her. When he lifted his head, his eyes were green again.

Theresa patted the baby and whispered, "Your mother will be here when this baby comes. She's going to meet her first granddaughter. Wait and see." At his hesitant nod she added, "We'll give her a healthy girl. That's all she needs now."

Norwegian Colony looking east. Olsen Farm in front. Eucalyptus grove, Pedersons' citrus trees and grainfield in background.

Chapter Twenty-Seven

A Father's Place

February 28, 1923. Oscar struggles to find a father's place. His children are strong and he will learn. It is Ellen's loss that grieves me.

"It's time. The doctor said we should start in plenty of time," Theresa said. They had borrowed Lud's Overland for the comfort of the back seat and because Oscar trusted it. He had gathered pillows and blankets to make her ride easier. She eased into the seat and breathed with relief.

The baby arrived in the early hours of morning, a fine, healthy girl. Theresa studied the little face, still puffy, the eyes not yet open enough to tell, but Oscar would agree, his mother's round face and nose. For a moment she considered the names she'd read on the markers, to see if the baby generated a connection. Laura? Nora? Emma? Thora was too foreign sounding for her taste. Paula?

A nurse opened the door for Oscar. He lifted his baby daughter with a joke about the strength in her tiny, pummeling fists. The baby kicked off her swaddling blanket and he handed her back, red-faced and embarrassed at his lack of skill.

The nurse laughed. "You'll get the knack."

"And Theresa?" He glanced at the nurse, embarrassed to look at his wife with a stranger in the room. At the nurse's nod he moved to the bed.

"I think we should name her Arthelia," Theresa murmured, fanning the baby's downy hair with her breath. "My dad had a cousin with that name."

"Are you sure it wasn't Othelia? I've heard of that."

"No, he thinks it's spelled with an A. Like Arthel. Anyway, that's how people pronounce it where he was from."

"Nebraska?" He hesitated, but he lacked the will to deny her anything.

A nun slipped into the room with a vial of holy water and checked to see if the baby was in need of immediate baptism. She smiled when the baby squirmed inside her flannel blanket, rooting for dinner. "Visiting hour is over," she said, pulling the drape around Theresa before ushering Oscar out. "Our doctors are firm about the mother's rest. You should return to bring mother and child home when they are stronger. St. John's recommends a week's stay for all new mothers."

At the nurse's station, the nun pointed him toward the door and turned to glide into another patient's room.

Oscar stopped by his father's house in Moorpark to share the good news. When he finished sharing the vital facts, Nils nodded and puffed on his cigar, his expression devoid of emotion. "A child is a delicate thing. You'll want a big family. That way some will survive. It's nature's way."

Oscar felt his nerves bristling. Each time he thought he had something that would satisfy his father, he left disappointed. This time surely he would find the smile, the glad look in the eye, but instead a quiet puff and a warning. He slipped into his mother's room and took the seat beside her bed.

"Hello, son. Happy news?"

Oscar smiled at the joy in her eyes. "It's a girl like you wanted. We'll bring her home when the doctors say it's safe. It shouldn't be but a few days."

"Strong and healthy?" Ellen whispered. "*Ja*. New medicine. New hope." She smiled. "Take your camera and get a photograph of the baby. I will pin it to my pillow." She reached to grip her son's hand until her eyes fluttered closed in weariness.

He returned to sit beside his father while a pot of bean soup simmered on the woodstove. The store-bought bread and butter were already on the cluttered table. A jar of his mother's canned peaches served as a reminder of how hard she had worked before her heart grew too weak for such labor. They ate in silence, heads down, while Nils maneuvered his spoon with his shortened fingers and Oscar considered. Theresa thought he was a lot like his father, but he didn't see the resemblance. Instead it seemed he carried more heaviness than other young men. The Pedersons didn't seem as afflicted by the past. They laughed and shared their burdens with each other and their mother.

One memory especially intruded into his thoughts. A time when he was just out of school, sixteen, and balking at the work his father put on his shoulders. He had quit in anger, stalked off to seek work with a farmer at the foot of the Norwegian Grade. The farmer hired him to wash down the cows, milk, feed, and plow the fields until quitting time—the same work his father required of him. But the farmer claimed his wife was sick and sent his three young children to dog the new hired man's steps so the mother could rest. After a week he took his pay and returned home, afraid to approach his father, but unwilling to spend another week as a babysitter. He stood outside his mother's kitchen, smelling the good odors of pork roast and stewed prunes, not sure what he should do. His father approached from the fields and saw him standing there. "Supper's waiting," he said. That was all. They never spoke of it, but he always suspected his father had set it up with the neighbor to discourage him.

When he finished his meal, Oscar made an excuse to leave. His animals needed feeding. But he looked forward to stopping by the Pederson farm with news of the baby. Mrs. Pederson would be glad for him.

As he drove past their fields, Oscar saw the Pederson brothers beginning to harvest the oranges and lemons they grew on land bought with bank money. They now had a Holt tracklayer to farm the addition to their original holdings. Before she and her youngest son returned from Santa Barbara, Mrs. Pederson had ordered a Craftsman house and paid Martin Overaa to put it up on the road they called "Pederson's Corner." Lawrence's graduation from Moorpark High School was a proud accomplishment for the family. Now Peder was getting married. Even his own brother, Nick, was heading to high school.

Oscar shook off his resentment. Some of the past was no one's fault, but the Pedersons' latest bank loan galled him. He and Lud discussed it when he stopped by to return the Overland and share news of the new arrival.

Lud shook his brother's hand. "What did Mother say? I'll bet she could ride the moon."

Oscar smiled at the wistfulness in his brother's face that made him seem younger today. "Yeah. Pretty happy. Dad, too."

Lud's familiar smirk returned with the mention of his father. "He'll be happier when you have a boy. Continue the name. I don't suppose I'll be doing that." He stood and made his way across the cluttered kitchen to the stove. "Do you see what the neighbors are doing with their land? Soon they'll be gentlemen farmers with hired men to shine their boots." He poured a cup of scorched coffee left over from breakfast and handed it to his brother. "Coffee's old, but it's all we have. I know better than to offer you a beer." Oscar managed a smile. He carried the mug to the table and waited while his brother brushed away a pile of papers to make room. "We scratch out a living on this dry land and wonder what's next!"

Oscar cupped his mug with thick, work-torn fingers and nodded. "They go thirds on all their expenses. Spreads out the risk." He set the cup down on the dirty oilcloth table still piled with the morning dishes. "You and I've been partners for a few years now. It's a good way."

Lud stood and began pacing. "Without money to plow back into the land, there's no chance of coming out ahead. We barely get enough return to carry us through the lean months."

Oscar glanced over to where Hazel sat with a nearly empty bottle of beer, flipping a magazine on her lap with her red enameled fingernails. He lowered his voice and said, "You spend like a town boy who knows where his next paycheck comes from. That doesn't go with our way of life."

Lud's fist exploded on the table, sloshing his beer. "I'm tired of 'our way of life'! I'm ready to try something else. A paycheck sounds fine to me!"

A look at Lud's ruddy face convinced Oscar his brother was serious. He felt his belly knot. "One day you'll own your land and you can do what you please with it. But until then, you're a farmer. The same as me."

"Our father was a farmer," Lud argued. "You're a farmer. I'm not. I never was. The only thing that keeps me here is the machinery. We've made up our minds. Me and Hazel are moving to town." Oscar took a sip, dreading what was coming next. He didn't have long to wait. "Oscar, now that you have a family, you'll be here for Father. He doesn't need me. I doubt Hazel and I are going to have a baby. She doesn't care much for children." Lud glanced over at Hazel. "We're moving to Santa Barbara. I hear they're hiring for road construction. That's what I wanna do."

"What about your land?" Oscar asked. *What about me? What about the Conejo?*

"Farm it, leave it fallow. I don't care. You have the tractor. You can plant my land. Or I'll rent it out to that fellow Erbes. He wants to put his family in the house." He looked up to see his brother's reaction.

"Thought Nick might want to live here when he finishes high school, but he has plans for college in Santa Barbara."

"Where will *that* money come from?"

"I imagine from the rents we pay him for his land. He saves his money." Lud poured another glass of beer and took a long drink. "You'll work your whole life and maybe one day Father will let you make your own choices."

Oscar left a few minutes later, feeling like a stranger in his childhood home. He lay awake far into the night, despite the exhaustion claiming his body. He missed the way Theresa helped him make sense of his troubled thoughts.

The week dragged until he drove to Oxnard again. In Somis, he stopped at a filling station to buy a cold root beer out of an iced tub. Something to mark the occasion. Theresa was waiting for him when he arrived at the hospital to help her into the car. On the way home he made the left turn at the crossroads to introduce his daughter to his parents.

Nils held the baby, searching for something familiar in the little girl's face before he handed her back with a satisfied nod. The words of a few days ago sounded in Oscar's ears: *Wait a bit before you get attached. Have lots of children, that way some of them will survive.*

Ellen was waiting when Theresa carried the baby in and laid it alongside her. The baby's chubby hands batted at her grandmother's frail fingers, bringing a teary smile. "Look, so plump. Like a perfect little dove. So beautiful. With my round face and eyes. It is like I see my Nora again."

Oscar stood beside his mother, watching peace replace the worn look of a failing heart. He spread his fingers across Theresa's, squeezing her as she sat gazing at her baby. He had forgotten the camera, but his mother was satisfied. She had already closed her eyes.

Later, he declined his father's offer of dinner. "Mrs. Pederson will be bringing over a casserole when she sees the car drive past, so we'll have dinner and probably some left for tomorrow," he explained. "We need to go before the February chill makes it hard on the baby."

At winter's end, he started up the big Sampson and began cultivating the soil without hearing the sound of his brother's tractor in the field nearby. Even though he knew better, he couldn't break the habit of looking out to see where Lud's tractor was each time he made a turn in his own field. They had shared the work on Nick's portion, but now the field waited for him to till and plant, and later, to harvest it alone. The tractor broke down and he spent a long night getting it running again without another head to analyze the problem and hand him the heavy tools. He went in to dinner worn out and discouraged. Theresa was a help, but she was occupied with the baby and not getting enough sleep herself. He thought of his father, farming alongside his best friends. He was grateful when Rich Pederson dropped by to visit.

On the last day of May, Ellen passed away.

Oscar stood beside his father and brother at the new Ivy Lawn Cemetery. They were joined by neighbors, friends from Moorpark and relatives from Santa Barbara with their hats in their hands as her coffin was lowered. Later he spent time with Lud, hearing about the new job, the ready paycheck and the cozy house he'd rented.

Theresa reflected on her mother-in-law's life during the drive home. "She dreaded being there alone in that new cemetery. Said she'd be lonesome for her girls." Oscar nodded, but he kept his thoughts to himself.

At the end of harvest, Oscar drove his grain to the warehouse in Moorpark, for shipping out on the train. Afterward he returned home with only Theresa to share the satisfaction. When the rains didn't come and the yield was scant, he listened to his father's criticism without his brother to defend his actions.

Theresa listened as she fussed with the baby. "Oscar, your father frets, that's all. He remembers the hard times. He's afraid you'll suffer, too. But times are easier now. We have a car. Try to understand—he's not trying to criticize, he's trying to help."

He thought about her words while he worked in his shop. The words softened, but they didn't erase the resentment. He watched Theresa's father with his easy laughter and his joking ways, and he wished his father was more like him.

◈

Two and a half years later, Oscar drove Theresa to Oxnard in time to deliver another baby. A week later they returned home with their daughter Eugenia.

Theresa explained, "My mother has a cousin by marriage. A silent screen star, Eleanor Burke. I want to use her name, too. Eugenia Eleanor."

Two weeks later he stood in the church and watched the priest sprinkle holy water over the baby's head, and afterward, accepted the congratulations of the Kelley aunts and uncles who attended the party along with his father and brother, Nick.

On Sunday visits, Nick drove their father over the grade for supper. At dinner his father talked about his life in Moorpark. He was happy with the two orange trees he'd planted in the front yard. He had turned his cows out to graze on the steep hill on Everett Street, and they were producing a satisfactory milk yield, some with new calves. His chickens had kept producing through a mild winter.

Nick was filled with plans to attend Santa Barbara College. Oscar watched his younger brother, tall and good looking like their father in his youth, filled with confidence and a flare for football and music. Lud's wife Hazel had landed him a job at the candy shop in Santa Barbara where she worked. He would roll chocolates each night after class for Hazel to dip later. His girlfriend Sarah was headed to nursing college in Santa Barbara. Their lives seemed set.

Oscar tried to be happy for his brother, but his intentions were undermined by his father's interference over his decision to run sheep on the bluffs. "Think you can keep the coyotes away? And the snakes? Ole Anderson decided against running stock up on those hills. He said the flats were the only way to get ahead."

"He didn't have the money for fencing, back then. And no way to get a herd to market." Oscar shifted. "I'm building a barn. The Janss men found a rattlesnake den over on their place when they were grading. Dynamited fifty rattlers and their young. I think the problem is under control."

Nils acted as though his son hadn't spoken. "About the only use for those acres—sheep or goats. I never liked the taste of goat meat."

On his visits Nils brought a penny for his little granddaughters. He listened to their childish babble with soft eyes, clearly seeing his own daughters. He helped Jean make her first steps, holding out his hands as she toddled across the floor. As the girls grew, he seemed to forget the fears that had occupied him when they were infants.

After Nick left for college, Theresa made a point of stopping by her father-in-law's after church each week so Nils could give the girls a piece of licorice or horehound candy and hear what they had learned that week. She would find him sitting on his porch with his Bible, rereading the bundle of letters from his brothers in Norway while she prepared a pot of beans or stew on his woodstove for the coming week. She brought canned fruit and produce from her garden. When the navel oranges ripened each December, she squeezed juice from his oranges. Sometimes when he needed medical help, she tended his needs.

Nick was a poor correspondent during the school year, but he returned home on summer breaks to take his turn at the tractor. His crops paid for his tuition. Their holiday meals were a combination of Theresa's German traditions and a few Norwegian foods and stories. Nils and his sons sometimes spoke to each other in Norwegian, to the amusement of the granddaughters, but the songs and festive folk tunes of Nils's youth were replaced by new American customs that the granddaughters learned in school.

"It is as it should be," Nils murmured as he watched his youngest granddaughter sing *Silent Night*. "The girls are American now." On one occasion he had news. "Lina Hansen comes back from Norway to visit Santa Barbara. She will drive up with the Ansoks to the Conejo."

Theresa cut his hair and waited while he trimmed his fingernails. She brushed his good suit and saw that his shirt was clean and starched. On the important day she made Oscar shut down his tractor and take a bath.

Lina Hansen arrived on a false spring day. Before the expected hour, Oscar drove down to pick up his father. They were waiting at the Pederson house when she climbed from the automobile, exclaiming over the green hills and the soft breeze feathering the new grass on the bluff. She saw the house and barns that Nils had built on Jorgen's farmland, now leased to a stranger. She toured the new house Oscar and Theresa had built on the land Jorgen purchased from Ole Anderson. She walked down to the prune orchard she and Jorgen had planted. When she saw the trees, dead and abandoned, tears formed in her eyes and she turned away. The Pedersons invited everyone to a fine meal at their house. As they ate on tables set up in the yard, her eyes returned to the changed land and the new methods of farming.

"A new generation takes over," she said. "I feel as though nothing here is the same anymore, not even the memories." Her words were spoken in English for the benefit of the younger people, but she frequently lapsed into Norwegian with her friends.

Karn nodded and passed a plate of chicken. "The gum trees are the same. They never change." Her smile spoke of shared memories of long ago. "I remember helping Lars and Oscar plant that grove."

While Theresa washed dishes in the kitchen, the women talked of other times, of friends who were still living, and those who had passed.

"It seems sad to see Nils without Ellen. She went so young," Lina murmured, out of Nils's hearing.

"She was glad to go," Karn said. "She suffered so."

"Nils looks good. Happy. Living in town agrees with him. He has a light in his eyes for the little granddaughters." Lina lowered her voice. "Are they healthy?"

Karn nodded. "The trouble seems to have ended, praise God. Oscar has a happy little family, and now another child on the way."

"A son this time, I pray. He will need sons for farming." Lina smiled and returned to her coffee. "My Ella is married now and expecting her own child. But as for me, I feel as though no place is my home. Norway once, but no more. And now the Conejo changed beyond recognition. And our prune trees, dead and abandoned. I feel somehow my heart dies with them."

From the kitchen, Theresa blushed for the loss of the trees. Mrs. Hansen didn't understand that the market for prunes had fallen. Oscar's interest was in apricots. Times had changed.

Lina left a few days later. At the end of the month, Theresa stopped by to get Mrs. Pederson's recipe for bread and butter pickles and remained long enough to read the letter Lina had sent. She told Oscar about it that night. "Mrs. Hansen met a man in Santa Barbara who is traveling to China to set up a mission. She has decided to travel with his group and lend her efforts to the cause." Theresa smiled. "That's the way she put it. She says she's happy to have a purpose. *I came here looking for God's plan for me. Apparently, I have found it*,' she wrote."

Meeting the women who had suffered for the Norwegian Colony brought Theresa gratitude that her own life was easier. Still, she suffered in silence as she washed Oscar's dirty trousers in her wash basin, trying mightily not to ruin her hands in the rough lye soap that was the only thing she'd found to take the oil stains out. One day Oscar watched her struggling to twist the water from his stiff denim.

"I saw an old Maytag tub in Lud's barn. And your brother John has a motor in need of the tub and wringer. We talked about it at your mother's supper yesterday. I can build you a washing machine, if that would help." He waited for her quick nod before adding, "But you and Babe will need to share it."

On the next Monday, her sister-in-law hitched a mule to her old car and had the mule tow her from her little shack on the Janss Ranch, through the deep ruts of the dirt road with a trunk load of dirty clothes. She left the mule tied in the gum trees while she drove up to the house.

The two washed their loads together and hung them on the clothesline. What didn't fit, they slung over the bushes. Afterward they retreated to the kitchen to make lunch and share gossip.

"We'll do this every week, Tracy." Babe promised. "John will think I'm turning into a real housekeeper."

Theresa cut a slice of cake for her sister-in-law. Babe was younger than Hazel, but she was bright and witty and told great stories about her life in town. While the clothes dried they took a pail into the orchard and filled it with oranges.

Babe spun in a slow circle that took in the eucalyptus grove, the orchard and the heifers grazing in a nearby pasture. "You and Oscar are making a real farm here. You're hard workers. John says harder than anyone in the family." Theresa kept her head down, but her face blazed with pride for her husband.

Grandpa Nils Olsen with son Oscar's family and Nelda, a young boarder.

Chapter Twenty-Eight

Between Rock and Hard Place

July 28, 1927. My sons find themselves between a rock and hard place. Such are life's lessons.

THERESA DELIVERED HER third baby at the new hospital in Oxnard. The nuns handed her a healthy little boy with blue eyes and a crown of dark hair. Oscar took a chair next to her bed until the nurses carried the baby back into the nursery after only a few minutes with its mother.

"They're monitoring the breathing," Theresa said.

"I want him to have my name. Ivan Oscar Olsen. Junior." Oscar kept his tone low, but he needed her to understand that this was his decision. "And I want him baptized Lutheran, like my father." He looked up and returned his glance to his hands. "You have the girls. This one is mine." He heard his wife's sharp intake and his anger flared. "I'm not changing my mind. This one will be Lutheran."

The nurse entered, sounding winded. "Your baby's wheezing a bit. Doctor doesn't think it's serious, but he wants to be cautious." A moment later she turned and disappeared.

Theresa faced the wall, refusing to look at her husband as the silence between them grew. He stood and walked down the hall. In the nursery, the doctor and two nurses were standing over a crib. One of them looked up and pulled the curtain. A nun rushed past and entered the room. Someone brought a cup of coffee. Oscar accepted it in numb fingers, his thoughts filled with his last argument with his father. *Olsen men are not papists. You need to put your foot down, Oscar. Your wife is a good mother, a good Christian, but you need to stand up to her family. If this child is a boy, he needs to become a Lutheran like his people. Your mother would want this. And I do too.* A chance to satisfy his father, even at such a cost, was not an easy decision. He had given the matter much thought and he realized he felt the same. Coffee soured in his gut, but he drained the cup for something to occupy him. When he finished, he returned to his wife's room.

She glanced up without acknowledging him. He took a seat with anger curdling his belly. He was a good man. She was free to do what she felt was right, but sometimes her whims went contrary to his own, and this was one of those times. Like Rich Pederson was always telling him, he didn't have the reputation for being a stubborn blockhead Norwegian for nothing. He sat with his hat in his hands, waiting for his wife to ask his forgiveness while the tension in the room thickened. It was the doctor who caused her to turn and sit up in the bed when he came in unexpectedly. "Mr. and Mrs. Olsen, I'm afraid I have some bad news . . ." He heard the doctor say something about the blood of the father and the mother, but the rest was lost in a fog of medical terms. He heard enough to understand that the baby had died after only a few hours.

Theresa burst into tears. He stood and leaned over her, but her grief was too powerful to include a husband she had been angry with only minutes earlier. He patted her shoulder, needing her to include him in her heartache, for his own was too intense for tears. But she did not turn to him. He waited mutely while someone brought the baby in for them to have a few minutes alone before the nurse carried it away.

The internment was held at Santa Clara Cemetery, the Catholic cemetery, in a remote area off to the side where babies were buried. Oscar stood beside his wife, watching the tiny box being lowered into the earth while Theresa wept inconsolably. When he could bear no more, he turned and walked back to their car. The ride home was made in silence on his part while she wept her anguish and the little girls slept in the back seat. When they arrived home, he helped Theresa into bed and sent the girls out to gather eggs for supper. Beyond that he could think of nothing else to do.

Weeks passed and the tears continued. He was embarrassed to speak of it to Mrs. Pederson, but Theresa's sister-in-law Babe came to help with the children. Others brought food and helped clean the house and cook meals. Oscar read to his daughters and helped them get ready for school. On days when he worked as a janitor at their school, he gave them rides home and heard their noisy chatter in the silence of the house. His grief returned at odd moments, like when the two of them were in bed at night, a husband and wife who no longer spoke. He ran his tractor in the fields feeling more alone than when Lud had left.

One night, after a silent supper, he sought solace in his workshop. He picked up a hammer and began building a mold. When it was finished he poured cement inside and smoothed the rounded corners. When the concrete was almost dry, he scratched the name of his son into the marker: *Ivan Oscar Olsen, Jr.*

They made a silent trip to the cemetery to place the marker over their son's grave. The girls ran ahead with their mother to where they remembered standing a few weeks earlier. Oscar followed more slowly, carrying the marker. He caught up with his daughters as they made their way slowly across a newly disked field, searching for the metal markers that had been there on the day of the burial. But the markers were churned into the dirt, mangled and ripped.

"Oscar! What have they done? Where's my baby?" Theresa's voice was tinged with anger, demanding that he find out what had happened.

The caretaker hurried over, his worn boots kicking up dust. "I'm so sorry. We had the weeds cleared out by a local man, but he didn't understand to look for the markers in the grass. We didn't think to explain. It was a mix-up. By the time we realized what had happened, the tags were worked under with the weeds."

"Surely you kept records. Our baby is buried here. Where are the records?"

The caretaker's face deepened and he looked down at the hat he held. "The old Monsignor kept the records in his head. And he just passed to his eternal reward."

Oscar turned to Theresa with an empty heart. He shrugged. "There's your answer."

"That's not possible!" Theresa's eyes brimmed with tears. Her brown hat tilted as she searched the ground for a familiar marker in the tilled soil. "I want to talk to someone. It's just not possible."

They returned to the office and a different man repeated what the caretaker had just told Oscar. "Normally, no one asks. People don't return to visit these graves—babies' graves. You're welcome to place the stone in the approximate vicinity, but there's no way to know for certain. I'm sorry."

Theresa shook her head, too angry to speak. Oscar carried the marker back to the car and laid it in the trunk. On the way home the little girls began arguing over a childish matter and he yelled at them to stop. Their shocked silence was worse than the sound of their laughter. At home again he took the marker and set it on his workbench without asking his wife. She might have gladly put it under a rosebush, had he offered, but his anger kept it on his workbench.

A year passed and then another. Sadness broke through at odd times: in the middle of dinner or on a Sunday drive when something set off Theresa's despair. He assured his daughters that their mother was tired, but he missed the old Theresa. Even Lud seemed a stranger. Rich Pederson brought by a stack of newspapers that their friends in Santa Barbara had sent. He had one page folded to a legal notice. Lud and Hazel had separated.

Oscar scanned the page. "Hazel's complaint makes Lud out to be a board-wielding wife beater in need of a bath!"

"It's a shame. We know him for better than that. She was the problem, if I had to guess." Rich shook his head and left before saying more.

Oscar read the report with a feeling of compassion for his brother. "Theresa!" he roared. "We're going to Santa Barbara. Pack a lunch. We leave tomorrow morning."

The visit brought back memories of happier days. The girls played in the surf while he and Lud visited with their cousin, Tom Lee. Theresa had put together a picnic from things she brought from home.

"So what does life bring you, Brother?" Oscar asked.

"Much as can be expected. I'm working as a heavy equipment operator on the San Marcos Pass."

"Still riding that Harley Davidson?"

Lud chuckled ruefully. "Keeping the motorbike. Losing the wife. Suits me just fine. Wife cost me a damned sight more than the motorcycle ever did." He hesitated. "I guess you read the posting in the newspaper. Hazel got her pound of flesh, after all." They gathered driftwood for a campfire on the beach. "How's the old man," Lud finally asked. "I figure he's still okay or someone would have sent word."

Oscar heard the wistfulness in his brother's voice. "You should go see him. At Christmas. He'd like that. We could put you up for a few days."

Lud hesitated before he nodded. "Maybe. I'll see. Does he still think drink is the devil's tool?" He grinned, picked up a pebble in the sand and gave it a toss.

"He'd welcome the visit."

Theresa seemed buoyed by her walk along the beach. She came back and put the children to bed in the tent while the brothers talked. After

Lud left for the night, she turned to Oscar. "I have something I need to tell you." She waited for him to acknowledge her. "When the baby died . . . the nun came in later and told me she had baptized it. I didn't think it mattered to you." She turned to watch the dark waves. "But I want you to know."

He felt air escaping and realized he'd been holding his breath. So the baby had been baptized. The Catholics set great store by that, and so did his father. He took her hand and squeezed it. "If we have another boy, you raise him Catholic."

He felt her pressure in the slight squeeze. Not hard, but enough.

Lawrence and Vida Landru Pederson

Chapter Twenty-Nine

Depression Years

November 10, 1929. Hard times are upon us but the farmer will survive. My brothers in Norway face worse than we.

RICH PEDERSON TOOK his usual seat on the back stoop to talk until dark about farming, the price of crops and the political scope of the world. "My brother's getting married. To a girl he met at church. She's from Saskatchewan. She's had a hard start. Lost her parents after high school. Took her inheritance and got an education. Now she works at a bank."

"They planning to come back here?" Theresa asked from the other side of the screen door.

Rich smiled. "You anxious for another neighbor? I'm sorry to disappoint. Brother has a job in Ventura he likes real well, delivering gas for Standard Oil. I guess he'll do that until he gets the farming bug again."

"The way the economy is going, it may not be long."

"True enough. Has Mr. Olsen changed his mind about the bank? Seems like now Lud's gone and it's up to you, he might see reason." Rich gave him an inquisitive look that said he and his brothers had discussed the matter.

Oscar shrugged. "Bank won't talk to me without Father agreeing. And he's dead-set against it. He won't change his mind. He thinks working harder is the only way."

Rich nodded. "I feel for you, Oscar. It's a tough spot to be in." He stood and shook his trousers before picking up his quart of milk. "I best be getting home. Mother will think I've lost my way."

"How's your mother's health?" Theresa asked from inside the kitchen. "I haven't seen her out lately."

"You know Mother. She's good. Vida took her shopping to Ventura last week." Rich laughed. "Or thought she was. Mother met her at the car with her fishing rod and a thermos of coffee. Had Vida drop her off at the pier like always. Mother spent her day doing what she loves best. And she caught four good sized fish for supper."

After his neighbor left, Oscar remained, thinking of their conversation. With the falling price of dryland grain and beans, soon the return would be hardly worth planting.

Theresa joined him on the stoop. "Grandpa Borchard's failing. The family is getting prepared. There isn't much he needs to do since he already divided his land. His children are taken care of."

Oscar smiled. "Two thousand acres and ten thousand dollars each. Newspaper called him a land baron."

She nodded. "Mom and Aunt Mary have theirs in the Savings and Loan in Thousand Oaks. My brothers recommend it. They say it pays good interest."

"Safe enough, I guess. Your mother's money has been there for eight years. But there's talk of a downturn. What happens then?"

"My brothers say it should be fine. My uncles are for it. They wouldn't give Mother and Mary bad advice." Theresa's tone rose as it usually did when she felt compelled to defend her family.

Oscar decided to keep his opinions to himself. "What's for dinner?"

⁂

Theresa arrived at her mother's a month later to find the house in chaos. Her mother and her sisters-in-laws were in tears. Her brothers were shouting, pounding the walls and the tabletops. She ushered her daughters outside to play with their cousins and waited to hear who had died.

"It's the Savings and Loan," her brother, Charlie, explained. "It's gone under. Bankrupt."

"How can that be? It's a bank," Theresa argued. "Banks are safe or people wouldn't use them."

Charlie scowled. "Walter and I were just there. There's a sign saying they're closed. No one answered the door—it's locked tight. They say the banks are having a run. The stock market failed today."

"What does the stock market have to do with us? We don't own stock."

Her brother tilted back in his chair with his hands cupping the top of his head like he was holding it on his neck. "I don't understand it yet, but we're going to find out. We'll write letters. Go to the County and demand they do something. We know the County people. We'll get to the bottom of this. Mother's money can't be just gone." He rose and paced the room, his voice barely audible over the sound of his sisters' crying.

Theresa went into the kitchen and started putting together a meal while fear spread through her. *What about Oscar's savings?* Maybe she was worrying over nothing. They didn't have much. Bank of A. Levy was supposed to be an honest place. Nils had known him from the time the man was a grain broker in Hueneme.

She took her children home and put them to bed before she explained the events of the day to Oscar. He had already heard the news from Rich Pederson, who had loans outstanding with the bank. "Mr. Levy said the loans wouldn't be affected, but the savings might be."

"How can that be?" Theresa asked.

Oscar shook his head. "I don't know how it works. I'm just glad we don't have much tied up in the bank. Maybe my father was right."

Theresa learned that her brothers' letters had no effect. Her mother's and Mary's money had simply disappeared. She watched them fret over their decision until shame grew into silence. The sisters became quiet and reserved, saying little as they worked in their gardens, growing flowers and produce for their families. Their father sat in his red velvet chair and stared out at the lands he had farmed without voicing his disappointment in them. One thought sustained him, because she'd heard him say it over and over: "My sons managed to hang on to their inheritance. They invested in land, not in a bank."

When Theresa's mother and her sister, Mary, came for lunch, Theresa tried to distract them with stories of the children. She was gratified when her aunt told a story that made them all smile.

"Father had some good news. Last week he answered a knock to the door. A man and his wife looking sore-starved and gaunt. While I saw to plates of ham and eggs, he sat with the folks on the porch listening to how the Depression has taken hold across the country—the man's desperation loud enough to bring shame to the listener. And the wife not saying a word.

"When I walked out with their plates, the man looked past me to that big upholstered chair Father favors, with its red velvet and plain wood frame. The man nodded at his wife, cooling coffee in her saucer and paying no mind. 'Would you like I should carve yon chair? I do you a fine job. Folks have taken to calling it hobo carving. Me and the wife could camp out by the creek and take meals for pay. I figure three days and we'd be on our way.' Father looked at the worried-looking woman, her eyes closed like she'd been without coffee for a spell. He told them, 'I think we could manage that.'

"I set out a plate three times a day, and coffee as well. When they finished, Father thanked the man kindly for his chair and sent them north with a meal in their bellies. I managed a small ham, a packet of coffee and a dozen hard-cooked eggs that the woman tucked in their rucksack." Mary hesitated. "Hard thing, this Depression. Hope they make it through."

Theresa turned to her mother. "See, people have it a lot worse. Now stop fretting about the money. It's gone. No sense in getting sick over it."

She sympathized with her mother, but there was nothing that could be done. The Depression was affecting all of them. She kept the farm books for Oscar, enough to know the price of his barley scarcely covered the cost of gasoline and seed. Her father sent a carload of distant cousins over to their farm to get food to last them until they could afford to return in a few weeks. They told of hard times in Los Angeles; men out of work and relying on food lines. Sometimes even charity food didn't carry them through the month and they arrived nearly starving for meat and potatoes. She was proud when Oscar sent her father's friends off with sacks of dry beans and summer vegetables, whatever oranges and lemons he could spare, apricots in season and always a butchered chicken or chunk of meat.

She drove her children to her brothers' farms to glean walnuts after harvest. When Arthelia and Jean outgrew their shoes, they took the worn leather down the hill to neighbors. "Stop complaining," she told her oldest daughter as she readied the girl's wardrobe for fourth grade. "You girls should be grateful we can afford to buy dress goods from J.C. Penney. Your cousins and lots of others have to wear flour-sack dresses, but don't you ever let on." She held a basted bodice up to Arthelia and marked the seam. "The flour people finally caught on and started using pretty designs on their sacks. In my day we had those ugly brand labels across the front."

One day Theresa waited for Oscar with an open letter in her hand. "It's from Mother's cousin. They have two little girls they'd like to send out to our farm, come June." She gave him a sharp look before continuing. "The parents are hard off making a living."

Oscar considered for a moment. "We got room. Jean and Arthelia could use the company."

Nelda and Betty arrived with their suitcases and stayed until school started again. In September, Oscar returned to his job as the janitor for the Santa Rosa School. He sold honey under his own label and raised hogs that he butchered for customers. "The land will feed you," Nils insisted. Oscar understood his father's logic. But lamb prices had toppled and the price of feed increased. He planted apricot trees and installed a watering system with an irrigation well, paid for with faltering beef sales. Even his daughters helped out by plucking rubbed wool off the barbwire fences and collecting it in a gunny sack for sale to the Jew peddler when he came around—after Theresa used what she needed to stuff her scrap quilts.

He saw an advertisement for a door-to-door sales job for a paint company. The job required him to drive around the countryside offering color chips and delivering cans of paint to farmers who still had money. At the end of the summer he hauled his grain to Hueneme at a price that left little profit. The Pedersons and other neighbors were scarcely better off, their poverty so common as to be unremarkable even in the Sunday collection at church where Theresa allowed her girls each a few pennies for the basket.

The newspaper ran a notice that the new Green Tree Inn and Motor Court was hiring a janitor. Oscar drove over to Thousand Oaks to apply. In the lobby a tall Negro man looked up from his work. Oscar cleared his throat and looked around for someone who might be in charge. He heard a woman laughing from another room as the tall man studied him.

"Yes?" not a question as much as a polite invitation to state his business.

Oscar indicated the newspaper he was holding. "I'm here about the notice. I'm looking for something to fit around my farming. I'm handy with wood. I can handle horses and repairs."

The man observed him with a stiff, dignified air. "Can you wait tables?"

Oscar hesitated. "I could learn."

The man nodded. "Do you have an objection to working for a man of color?" Oscar hesitated, confused by a term he had never heard. *A man of color?* The man took his hesitation as an affirmative and slapped his book shut. "I thought as much. Apparently others in this area share your opinion."

"My opinion of what? I guess you'll have to explain about the color. I prefer blue, but I can go with a dark green."

The man smiled and offered his hand. "My name's Mr. Henderson. I'm the proprietor here. Let's go into the dining room and I'll show you what would be involved." He led the way past the lobby and into a small, elegant dining room with candles on the white tablecloths. Oscar stared from window, to table, to lighting fixtures. He heard a question and realized Mr. Henderson was speaking.

"Mr. Olsen, you have a pair of woolen trousers and a white shirt? I can supply an apron. You would be tending the repairs at first. Washing dishes as the need arises. You might serve tables if you showed an aptitude. You would need to be available evenings and weekends. Are you a family man? How does your wife feel about your being away on occasional Sundays, should we have a banquet scheduled?"

He was given a tour of Mr. Henderson's kitchen where another man of color was preparing vegetables for the evening meal. By the time he left Oscar had learned how to wash the dishes and to bus the tables without clinking the plates or dropping a fork.

In the following days he carried trays of dirty dishes into the kitchen. He watched the way the young waiters uncorked a bottle of wine and answered questions about the thickness and rareness of steaks. He studied the way they took orders and carried their trays over their heads. By the end of his first shift he received a compliment from Miss Pealer, the pretty young woman who showed diners to their tables and rented out the bungalows in the auto court behind the dining room. She explained, when he asked, that she had selected the beautiful furnishings and paintings on trips to Europe with her late father.

For the next few months Oscar maintained the premises after his fields were plowed and seeded, the cattle fed and the fruit picked. Occasionally on Sundays he took extra shifts, working parties and weddings.

One day, as he made his way to his truck at the end of a long shift, a pair of burly men approached. "Don't you have any pride, son? Working for a colored fellow?"

Oscar slipped into his car and rolled down the window. "No shame in earning an honest dollar."

One of them sneered. "You may wish you had another job when we get done here. Y'all go on home now and think about what we said."

The short, paunchy one tipped his hat. "Get along home now, son."

Oscar was angry by the time he arrived home. He woke Theresa when his work clothes hit the floor with a clunk. "What's the matter?" she asked groggily.

"Blame fools stirring up trouble for Mr. Henderson."

By the time he finished telling her, she was frightened. "They're part of a group thinks white people are superior. My brother claims one of them moved in down the street from him and is carrying tales, trying to rile up the town. Call themselves Klu Klux Klan." She reached to light a lamp. "What're you going to do?"

"I'm going to work. This is America. No one tells us what we can or can't do. Mr. Henderson is a good man. He's not doing anything wrong."

Theresa hesitated. "Some people say he's not just working for Miss Pealer."

Oscar threw his shoes down and reached for his nightshirt. "None of our business. Mr. Henderson wants me to start waiting tables. For extra money and tips. We can use the money. Put in the pitting sheds we've been talking about. It's a good opportunity for us."

Theresa cut the lamp, but it was some time before either of them fell asleep again.

A week later, two of the regular waiters failed to show up for their shifts. Mr. Henderson advertised for help, but few people answered the ads. When one did, he didn't last. Oscar was careful to park in the open, away from dark corners when he arrived for his own shifts. On his drive home he watched for lights that might be following him. One day he returned to the house and Theresa met him at the door.

"They were here. Two men. They told me to get you to quit. Said you could get hurt." She hesitated. "Someone made a comment at the market that you should stick to farming and leave the Negroes to their own business." Her face flushed as she rushed to finish. "They're spreading a rumor that the two are living in sin. That it's unnatural, mixing the races."

"They'd rather we stand in a food line?" Oscar looked around at his cattle, the hay in the field, the orchards and the gum trees blowing in the stiff afternoon wind. Stubbornness for everything he'd worked for battled with his fear. With quick, angry motions he found his shotgun and racked in a round. He set it on top of the china cabinet with a warning to keep the girls away. "Anyone comes up, you use this. You know how. From now on we'll do our shopping in Moorpark. I'll only go to Thousand Oaks for work. Maybe the fools'll get tired and move on."

One night a small group of hecklers surrounded his car—strangers he didn't recognize. They catcalled and threatened, but they stayed a safe distance away. When he and Theresa went to dinner at her mother's, her brother mentioned that the town was growing in sympathizers every day. "You need to quit there, Oscar. For your family's sake."

"Would you if you were in my place?" Oscar asked.

John grinned. "I see your point." He aimed a finger at his brother-in-law, fake-fired and blew off the imaginary smoke. "You need help, you let us know. Us brothers will look in on Tracy while you're at work."

His mother interrupted. "You boys aren't shooting anyone. Finish your pie."

The long summer drew to a close. Oscar finished his harvesting and prepared for shearing. Each day that passed without incident made him feel more secure, especially with the Pedersons keeping track of cars on the road.

At the beginning of the fall season he realized he'd engaged in wishful thinking. On his next shift he arrived to find a "Closed" sign on the door. Mr. Henderson and Miss Pealer sat at a table, their faces drawn in worry. "Mr. Olsen, I'm sorry you made the trip for nothing. We're finished here. Ruined." Henderson indicated a letter on the table between them. "It's from my landlord. I'm paid ahead, but that doesn't matter. He's bowed to pressure. Cancelled my lease."

Miss Pealer sat stiffly, her face flush with unshed tears. "What's to be done? Everything is here. Our home. My paintings and artwork. We must form a plan to safeguard our valuables!"

Oscar hesitated. "You can stay at my farm. We'll move a couple bungalows to the back of my property. Make a nice house out of them. You bring your things. Stay there as long as you need. You'll be safe."

The two exchanged looks. "The bungalows belong to us. It's not like we're stealing them. And Mr. Olsen says we'll be safe." Miss Pealer's hands shook, but her face held a spark of hope.

Henderson nodded, but his eyes held reservation. "Only if your wife agrees to the plan."

On a night with ample moonlight, the two men moved the bungalows onto skids and dragged them along Moorpark road with their automobiles. By morning they had two bungalows hidden in the apricot orchard. Henderson helped him convert the buildings into a single house. Miss Pealer's friend, Miss Nielson, moved in with them and the two women draped the walls with Navajo blankets for insulation and covered the floors with Persian rugs.

"Don't bother the folks with your chatter," Oscar warned his daughters.

His younger daughter Jean returned home that evening with a tale of having been invited to tea with the women. She described her adventure over supper. "You should see it, Dad. She paints and sculpts! She's studied in Europe and everywhere. Her house is even better than the pictures in the National Geographic." Jean hesitated. "Why do they have to be our secret?"

Theresa frowned. "Your father's too stubborn to allow injustice against a good man." She was far along with her pregnancy and worn from sleepless nights. Her reply came out crankier than she intended.

"It'll work out. Wait and see. People are stirred up, but they're not all bad." Oscar smiled at his daughter and patted her on the head. "Just don't get in the ladies' way," he warned. "And don't let on to anyone at your school. We don't want Miss Pealer to suffer, do we?" He waited for both daughters to nod before he returned to his meal.

That night he began carrying his shotgun when he checked the sheep.

"Nobody knows if those haters are bluffing, or how far they'll go," Theresa fussed as she readied for bed. "But I suppose, in the meantime our visitors will need to wash their clothes. I'll show them how to use my washing machine in the morning."

"Most of those causing trouble are newcomers. Loud-spoken businessmen bent on making the town into their own ideas. They have few ties to the farmers and townspeople who built this area," he reminded her.

"The girls and I haven't had any more trouble. Maybe the troublemakers will be satisfied with having the Green Tree Inn gone."

"Let's hope so."

Six months passed without further threat. Each morning Oscar saw Henderson walking along the creek on his customary strolls. A few days later he saw Miss Pealer's big touring car drive out early and return in the afternoon. Mr. Henderson came by the house later that evening. He stood with stiff dignity in the living room and accepted an offer of tea before he announced what he had come to say. "Mr. Olsen, as often happens with petty men, the bullies have apparently moved on to other concerns. But Miss Pealer and I will not attempt to revive the Inn." He glanced down with a satisfied nod. "I have been offered a position with a family in Lake Sherwood."

He didn't need to mention that the family he would serve as a butler was wealthy. Oscar understood the value Mr. Henderson would bring to any family he served.

"Miss Pealer has engaged an architect to draw up plans for an estate on the west side of Thousand Oaks, in the hills overlooking the valley. She has taken a temporary residence until it is completed." He held up a hand to quiet Oscar's protest. "I am happy to say we will no longer burden your fine family."

He glanced at Jean. "Miss Pealer has especially enjoyed the company of your younger daughter, a curious and open child. She will miss her, I am sure."

Jean fidgeted with her shirttail, embarrassed by his elegant tone. "Are you leaving today?"

"Shortly. We will leave the bungalow for your father to use as he sees fit." Mr. Henderson smiled at the girl. "Perhaps your father will find a family with children your age. Someone to share your interest in art."

Chapter Thirty

The Final Years

1933-1941. I don't find much to write about. These days my granddaughters and grandsons bring my smiles. Family is the thing. Faith, family and the land. And at the end of it all, Ellen again.

OSCAR TOOK HIS three-year-old daughter Mary along when he went to collect his mail. He set her over the broken cemetery fence to explore while he spent an hour talking with Rich Pederson at their mailboxes. The sun stalled overhead while he shared with Rich the contents of a letter that had just arrived. By the time he finished reading, he'd found reason for optimism.

Back home in his kitchen, he shared the letter with Theresa. "Nick's moving back. They thought it would be better living with Sarah's folks, but he's had enough of working for his wife's people at that furniture store. These days there's no cash for luxuries like furniture." Oscar looked up from the sheet of stationary he was holding. "He applied, but nobody's hiring new shop teachers. Schools can't afford to keep the ones they have." He shuffled the sheets. "He says only three out of the two hundred graduates from his last term at Santa Barbara College got jobs in this blasted Depression. Felt he was wasting money on school."

He continued from the table as he waited for Theresa to prepare his lunch. "Sarah's not set on returning, but now that they have the little boy, Gerald, he thinks to move back. Nick's a stubborn Norwegian and he says they're coming. He talked to Lud about it. They'll set up housekeeping in the old homeplace."

"Your father finally got a grandson. Nils will be happy to have them closer." Theresa looked up from the sink and chided her daughter. "Mary, go see what your sisters are doing while I fix lunch. And no cookies until later."

"He plans on farming his land. Maybe going shares with Lud if that's agreeable with me."

"Is it?" She pulled a bowl from the cupboard and set it on the linoleum countertop. "You've taken on a lot, trying to farm your land and your brother's, too. Maybe it's time to build up your sheep flock like you talked about. People say another war in Europe is coming. The price of wool might be good for a change."

"Makes sense. I talked to a man in Chatsworth with grazing rights for lease. It would save my pastures for winter." He spooned cottage cheese onto his plate. "Father's against it."

"Leave it be, Oscar. Don't bring up the improvement loan again. His mind is set."

"He'll probably sign one for Nick. He's gone easy on him since he was a boy."

Theresa washed her daughter's hands and set her at the table. "Older children all feel that way. Times change. It's just the way of it." She set a plate of steamed zucchini in front of him and reached for the buttermilk. "It'll be good to have your brother and Sarah on the land again." She rubbed her hand across her midsection and smiled. "I could use a good nurse like Sarah. Seems I'm expecting again."

The Norwegian Colony hummed with the sounds of diesel tractors. The Pedersons were expanding their chicken flocks and using the manure on their orchards. Their citrus groves had a ready market with the new packing sheds in Oxnard. Labor contractors bussed in teams of Mexican pickers from Oxnard. Men in frayed clothing climbed tall ladders to pick oranges while their wives picked the lower branches. For a few weeks each year the orchards rang with the sounds of Spanish bantering, Mexican love songs and shrieks of children running around under the trees. At noon their picking halted. Women built small fires in the rows between the trees to cook their tortillas and beans. In the afternoons, babies napped while their parents returned to work.

Rich stopped by one evening to get a quart of fresh milk and talk about the changes the brothers were making. "The times have hit everyone pretty hard, but we farmers are better off than most. My brothers and I haul produce and eggs to our church in Van Nuys for children who haven't seen an orange in months." He locked fingers around his knee and rocked back while the sunset exploded in vivid streaks of orange and splashes of red in the west. "We have much to be thankful for." He glanced beyond the gum trees to his land. "My brother and his wife send news. They're moving back as well. Bringing their little girl Janet to spend time with her grandmother." He shifted and returned his gaze to the sunset.

"I guess we have the Depression to thank for that! Both the prodigals back on the Colony in the same year. Father will like that. So will your mother. With your sister's three—that makes four grandkids. You and your brother aren't keeping up."

Rich grinned. "I don't imagine she'll get any satisfaction from Pete or me." He inhaled a deep breath and straightened his leg. "But it makes her happy to have her youngest back on the home place."

Oscar chuckled. "A wife would take your mother's care off your back."

Rich laughed. "Better not let her hear that! Mother would say she takes care of me. And I'd have to agree." He hesitated. "Too much work to be done around here. A wife would most likely complain about me having no time for her with everything else going on. Best to stay single."

Oscar hesitated. Behind him, his daughters were making a racket in the kitchen. Nothing served in letting Rich know how good it felt to have a growing family. "What are you using on the squirrels now? Having trouble with them in the orchards?" They returned to their farm talk until Rich rose to leave.

During the next weeks the Conejo teemed with changes. Nick and his family arrived with new furniture given to them by his wife's uncle as a housewarming gift. Sarah spent days ridding the house of Hazel's indifferent housekeeping. With Theresa's pregnancy too far advanced for her to drive down the grade, it was decided that Nils should come to stay with them. Oscar drove to pick him up. When they returned from Moorpark, a lantern shone in the windows of the home place. Nils craned his neck to stare at his old home until the light disappeared.

Oscar stood alongside his father the next morning as Nick made his first pass with the plow. Down the road Lawrence stood in the field with his two brothers. Nils pulled off his hat and swabbed his face with his handkerchief. "Lars should be here to see this," he said softly.

Two weeks later he held Oscar's newborn son in his shaking hands for the first time. He took in the plump, round face and downy hair. "A little farmer. He has the look of the Norske. He will be a strong man. And Neil is a fine Norske name. He'll be a playmate for his cousin."

Oscar noticed the relief that having a second grandson brought. He said as much to Theresa as she prepared to nurse the baby. "My father seems to find peace as he gets older. He hopes to see all three of his sons farming together one day."

"He better enjoy what he has," Theresa warned.

The grandfather's joy was multiplied a few months later when Nick announced they were expecting a second baby.

"Soon we fill up our Norwegian Colony again," Nils told them when they gathered at Oscar's for Christmas dinner. "We don't have riches, but we have everything else. Ellen would say the same if she were with us tonight."

"It wouldn't hurt to ask the Lord for a few riches," Nick joked. "My old tractor is held together with wire and prayer."

Shortly after, it seemed that his prayers were answered. Nick was in the field talking with his brother when a black sedan roiled dust down the road.

The man climbed from the driver's seat and introduced himself. "I'm scouting a location for a major film. We'd like to consider your property if you're interested." He scanned the bluffs with a hand shading his eyes, taking in the fields where sheep grazed. "We'd rent your sheep and pay someone to herd them." He waited for their tentative nods before adding, "We'll be back in a few days with a contract and a crew."

Oscar shared the news with Theresa when he came in for lunch.

"How much do you expect?"

"He didn't say. I hear they pay well. Especially for these times."

Theresa nodded. "Anything would be welcome."

A team of men returned to walk the cliffs, measure the distance from the Indian Cave and the creek bed while they took photographs of the fields. The agent returned a week later with a contract.

Theresa listened as Oscar read the figures typed on the form. Eighty-five sheep at two dollars fifty cents a day each. "And five dollars a day to herd them!" Theresa couldn't contain her excitement." They're paying two hundred dollars for the use of your pastures and the bluffs.

Two hundred dollars!" She stared at the paper. "What's the name of the movie?"

Oscar searched the form. "*Wuthering Heights*. The man mentioned big movie stars, but I don't recall their names."

"Will they build a real house?"

He studied the print. "A movie set. On Nick's land. The fellow says after they finish filming, it's his to keep."

In the next few weeks, crews came from Burbank to set nursery pots filled with blooming heather into holes dug into the bluffs that turned the summer-dry grass into springtime, seemingly overnight. The production supervisor warned Oscar that he would have to cut steps up the back of the hill. Oscar watched as the crew laid railroad track for a cart to haul supplies and actors up the hill. The cart was pulled by men and pulleys at the top. After they finished filming the spring scenes, the crew would need to sprinkle the heather with asbestos "snow" that looked like the real thing—they would sweep up as best they could afterward. Crews replaced Oscar's barb wire fences with wooden fences in the pastures.

The mansion set was constructed on Nick's land, with new lumber and quality windows. From Moorpark Road it looked like a wealthy new homeowner occupied the bluff.

Movie stars arrived in a line of cars driven by muscular men in baggy slacks and casual shirts. They disembarked and stretched their limbs. One of them exclaimed over the heather-strewn "Scottish Moors." A make-up tent was set up to transform the actors, with a water truck parked nearby to supply potable water for the caterer and the make-up tent.

Oscar and Nick spent their days watching the filming, ready to bring the sheep when the director needed them. Afterward, the Olsens joined the caterer's lunch line behind Merle Oberon and Laurence Olivier.

Oscar's twelve-year-old daughter, Jean, was hired to dress as a scruffy little boy and herd the sheep. One day the script called for a prairie fire across the grass. The natural grass had been grazed to powder by the sheep, so the crew threw down chopped straw for fuel. They lit the fire and watched it spread in a thin line like the script called for, but Jean couldn't get the sheep to run like they were supposed to. The crew spread new straw on the stubble, relit the fire and tried again.

The sheep milled uncertainly until the director called, "Cut!" Finally, he had Oscar stand off-camera and flap his coat until the sheep ran along the edge of the fire.

Merle Oberon was afraid to ride in the cart to the top of the hillside set so two men were assigned the job of carrying her up and down the hill.

On a day that seemed warmer than usual, the director called for an evening scene to take advantage of the sunset and the full moon. Nick was ready to take his son Gerald home for his nap when he heard a female voice coming from the makeup tent. "It's frightfully hot in here. I'm dusty and tired. Is there nowhere for me to freshen up?" The lead actress, Merle Oberon, who had played her role all morning without complaining stood in the sun, fanning herself while her maid held an umbrella over her. Nick stared at the tents and the water truck parked nearby. "I need a bath!" the actress demanded, her tone fretful and annoyed.

The director rushed forward and waved his hands. "Miss Oberon, we have potable water in your tent."

The actress laughed. "A basin? Ridiculous! I'm hot and cross. My next scene requires that I be dewy and fresh. Absolutely impossible! Not even Claudette Colbert could manage *that!*"

The make-up artist appeared with a basin of water and a folded Turkish towel, but the director waved him away and turned to Nick. "Miss Oberon requires something clean and private."

Nick hesitated. "We have a clawfoot tub just down the road. She's welcome to use it."

Filming halted while Miss Oberon's driver drove her the short distance. Nick and his son rode with the maid and the assistant director in another car. The actress inspected the tub and instructed her maid to run the water while the assistant director followed them into the house, carrying two sets of Turkish towels.

Nick returned to the porch, unsure what his role as host required. His question was answered, in a sharp, angry shriek. "Out! Everyone get out!"

The assistant director came running out the door, red-faced and sweating. "Everyone is to go to the barn and remain until Miss Oberon indicates otherwise." He swept his arm toward the hay barn and yelled, "To the barn, now!"

Nick led the way. The assistant director followed with an expression of humiliation. The driver pulled a dime novel from his pocket and sat down on a stack of hay as though he was used to waiting. He fumbled in his pocket for a rolled cigarette and started to light it.

Nick jumped in front of him and batted at the lighter. "Please, no smoking on the hay." The man shrugged and put it away before he opened his book again. The assistant director paced back and forth without speaking until the actress emerged an hour later. She wore her hair wrapped in an enormous Turkish towel while the breeze fanned the edge of her robe on the veranda. When she turned toward the waiting vehicles, the driver emerged from the barn. He heaved a sigh of relief, lit a quick cigarette and stood in the dirt alongside his car waiting to drive the actress back to the set.

Within weeks the filming ended. The crew left behind the fences and the elaborate set they had built for the outside scenes. Nick had wood and glass to begin building a small house.

CHAPTER THIRTY-ONE

Quitclaim Transfer

March 13, 1940. Cloudy, no rain. Grass is poor. Lud arrived today for the quitclaim transfer. Dad took the signing hard, but it is done. The land transferred to the sons and his name off. Maybe now we will make changes, but Theresa is for caution. Oscar Olsen.

NILS TOOK A dizzy spell. He fell and managed to get to his feet without injury, but the episode reminded him that his years were finite. He saved his news until the next time Oscar visited. Theresa fumed over her husband's casual disregard of the incident when he reported his father's accident to her. "You're as bad as he is. If you don't take him to Oxnard, I will."

When the doctor finished examining Nils, he requested that Oscar and his father join him in his office. He sat at his desk with a file before him and directed his comments to the son. "I find traces of irregularity in your father's heart. Technically, myocardial. And nephritis in his kidneys. He's had a good long life. This is to be expected. But I suggest you take him into your home on a permanent basis and care for him for the time he has left."

Oscar felt his stomach plummet with fear. He glanced at his father and frowned at the stubbornness he saw. "My brother's wife is a nurse. We'll manage well enough."

Nils glowered from his son to the doctor. "I will remain in my own home. Theresa can cook for me there and Sarah can do the nursing. Bring me a pan of soup every few days. I don't require coddling."

The doctor gave Oscar a sympathetic look and helped his patient to his feet. "Eighty years and still feisty, Mr. Olsen. You should be proud to have good sons to care for you."

"Hurrumph!"

The ride home was made in silence until the turnoff to Moorpark, when Nils realized his son didn't intend to make the left turn back to his house. "Never mind the doctor. I don't be a burden on my sons."

"Father . . . we'll talk about it later."

Nils stared out the window while the car climbed to the top of the Norwegian Grade. At the turn onto the Colony road, the cab filled with the familiar tang of orange trees. Nils turned to study the Pedersons' orchards as though he were seeing them for the first time. "Too much too fast, and none of it theirs. Watch and see!"

Oscar kept his tone level. "Let's get you to bed before you take an apoplexy attack like Mother."

That evening Oscar related the doctor's advice to his brother. Nick listened with a growing frown as he anticipated his wife's shock at the task that had been laid on her. "Sarah was never that close to Father. We lived with him for the first three years of our marriage and it was hard on her."

Theresa nodded. "Your dad can be a trial. Your mother was the mediator." She glanced at her brother-in-law, taking his frown as reluctance to get involved. "You and Oscar are the same. Both of you will take yourselves out to your workshops. You won't be much help."

"What choice do we have?" Oscar fidgeted from his seat between his wife and his brother. "He's healthy enough to work in the garden. He can recall the good times he's had up here. The kids will enjoy having him around."

"He's got his good days. He'll want to go home again once he's better."

"He's not giving up, that's for sure." Wants to be around to meet you and Sarah's next one. He dotes on the grandkids. Makes up for the ones they lost, I suppose. You were too young to remember, but I do."

Theresa interrupted. "He's welcome here." She glanced over at her brother-in-law and made the decision for both of them. "We'll share the care. A month at our house and a month at yours." Oscar nodded.

Worry etched Nick's eyes. "The doctor says his heart will fail him in time. What happens next?"

"One day at a time." Theresa turned to her teacup, the conversation ended for her.

"His mind's sharp." Oscar hesitated. "But he wants to see a lawyer before he has a stroke like Mother."

"He's ready to take his name off the deeds. Make it legal so the taxes don't force us off." Nick's relief was palpable.

The county forms arrived in the mail before Lud arrived with his new wife Irene and her son Robert. Theresa sent her girls outside to show the boy their playhouse while she escorted Irene around her home. Lud walked outside to greet his father. Snippets of their conversation floated through the open windows as she showed Irene into the back bedrooms. By the time they returned to the living room the conversation sounded warm and jovial.

"Lud had a couple of beers on his drive here," Irene confided with a wry smile. "To settle his nerves."

Nils sat at the table with a packet spread in front of him. He glanced up and prepared to speak, but his voice shook with emotion. His eyes clouded over. He tried a second time before giving up and shaking his head in frustration. None of the boys could find the words to make the moment easier. They simply waited while he fumbled for the pen, found the proper line and wrote his name in a shaky version of his signature. When he finished signing the last document, Nick helped him to his easy chair and watched as he slumped into it. A moment later he was asleep.

The brothers moved outside to a table on the lawn. Lud glanced toward the car and took a glass of lemonade from a tray. "Hard to believe this ground is ours now, as soon as we file the papers." His voice shook as he stared across the field where Oscar's walnut trees shaded the path to the creek. "A lot of memories here, for sure." He glanced over at his older brother and grimaced. "Some I'd just as soon forget."

Oscar studied his glass as though the lemonade held answers. Some things were just meant to be—like Rich living with his mother. *Someone has to stay on the land!* His father had made his opinion into fact. But his brother made the choice to leave. It was the oldest son's obligation to stay and he hadn't doubted his father's word. In the end, it was a good life.

He thought back to the day Lud had told him he was leaving. He had blamed his brother for their breakup—a partnership made together as young men with boundless energy and strength in their thick wrists and iron biceps. In the end Lud had done what he needed to do. And he, Oscar, had stayed. He glanced over to see if Lud was thinking the same, but his brother's expression was a familiar half-smirk that had masked his feelings from the time he was a boy. Lud looked around for a cigarette, his laughter building as tobacco wore away the resentment. Maybe now that he had a stepson his brother would discover how it felt to have a family.

Lud lit his cigarette and slapped his lighter on the table. "I guess I didn't hate it here as much as I thought. We had some good times, hey, Oscar?" He laughed and took a drag. "But I needed to cut up a little." His chuckle seemed subdued, more rueful. "You know something funny? I always wanted to be one of the Pederson boys." He glanced over at Oscar. "You remember when we were kids, how we could hear them laughing? Running around in the yard while we were shoveling out the barn, or hoeing weeds, or breaking up the clods behind the plow?"

Oscar nodded. "Those boys worked hard. Don't forget that. You did the work well enough, but your heart was never in it. I guess I tried to make it easier on Mother."

"I wanted Father to say something when I finished." Lud held his head low, muttering to the table. "But his answer was just . . . another job. And all the time, those Pederson kids laughing and running around in the dark." He sat without moving. "When I left I thought I was gonna find a better way." He laughed. "I did, too. Nobody works harder. But I love to have a good time. You know?"

Nick shifted from where he sat listening to his brothers. "Dad and I do okay."

"Father went easier on you," Lud said.

Oscar nodded. "Mother said it was because you came along last. Grew up after . . . the girls. I remember once she called you her heartbreak baby."

Nick took a sip of lemonade and turned to look down the road where his planted fields lay. "Dad's never said so, but I expect I'm a disappointment to him in some ways. He wanted me to finish college, but this Depression set me back. Most of those graduated the year before me wasted their time. I figured, why put myself through the expense? So I quit."

"Roosevelt says we'll be out of this Depression soon. I hope he's right." Lud turned to look past the front door into the house where his father was sleeping. "I could have used the money from selling this place, but I had no choice. Now it's mine, I guess there's no hurry to sell." He took another drag and tapped the edge of the pack with a nervous finger. "I may need the land in a couple of years. They say the kidneys are the first to give out on us guys who drive heavy equipment. From bouncing around on those hard springs. I've beaten my body up pretty good. Part of the reason I smoke."

"You've had steady work. Got yourself a house at the beach. I guess you're not doing so bad," Oscar joked.

Lud smiled, but his gaze remained on his own plowed acres where Nick had planted the flats to pinto beans. The field would yield a bumper crop. "The land is everything. You know how many times I heard him say that?" He picked up a stone and chucked it back to the dirt. "'Ludvic, you vork for wages, you vil never be comfortable. I know dis from back home. You vil starve like da others.'"

"Mother was more forward-thinking. She supported a bank loan and drilling deeper wells. Dad was the stubborn one. Set us back a generation."

Lud glanced toward the cemetery at the end of the road. "Hazel and I had a stillborn when we were living here. I might have had a baby buried in that cemetery, too, but she didn't want him left out here on this land. She said she couldn't bear it. So many things here made her sad. We tried, but we were young and both out for a good time. Just different people, I guess."

"She was a pretty girl."

"She sure hated this place." He picked up the pack and took another without seeming to notice.

Oscar watched his brother trying to hide his pain in his brave talk. In his mind he was back in the days when it was just the two of them, working the fields and planning how they would spend their profits when harvest came.

"So now Father's sick." Lud muttered. "I surely don't envy your wives, putting up with him for the next few years."

Nick's eyes lifted in surprise. "You think he'll last that long? The doctor says his kidneys are bad. And the heart muscles are weak." He turned his hands over as though his fingers held a clue. "Sarah knows the technical terms, but that's the gist of it."

Lud laughed. "I'm moving down to Needles for a road job in the desert. I won't be around, but I'd appreciate a letter."

"You really intend on coming back here?" Oscar asked.

Lud stood up and wandered toward the bushes. "You never know. Maybe I'll raise chickens and keep your tractors running!"

When the deeds were filed with the County and the fees paid, Oscar bought a couple of cigars for his father. "I doubt the doctor would approve. Picked them up on my way home."

Nils accepted the gift and lit the tip with his mangled right hand. "I miss my pipe. Cigars are one of the few pleasures left to an old man," he said. "That and watching my granddaughters grow into young women. Ellen would be proud. Arthelia reminds me of her. Sometimes I see the girl and my mind wanders back to the times when Ellen and me were just starting out." He took a puff and stared into the distance with rheumy eyes. "We had such hopes in those days. Lars, Jorgen, Ole, me—even the other Ole," he laughed. "We were land barons."

Oscar heard his father's voice, reflective. As it had been in past nights when they worked side-by-side in the shop. Stories that connected past with present.

Nils sighed and glanced over at his son. "You think the land taught you hard lessons. But you don't know what it was like back in the old country, the men in Norway scratching to make a living for their big families. Sometimes it was a blessing when a child died." His voice grew hoarse, his breathing labored. "But here on the Conejo there was room for everyone. The weather so mild, even in winter. Mild enough that your mother kept a kitchen garden. We watched the children growing . . . and your mother, she taught the girls the sewing, the embroidering, the cooking. They ran around the hillsides. Here, they could be free." He stared at nothing while memories drove the tears glistening in his eyes.

Oscar stared at his hands, mesmerized by the memories he saw in his father's face. His father continued as if he wasn't there. "Ellen lost her girls when they were old enough to be companions. Daughters to share her work with. I stayed in the fields because it was easier, especially in the last days of each illness. I kept you and Lud out there with me so you wouldn't see them so sick and in pain." He gave a frustrated sweep of his hand and Oscar saw the missing fingers. "I left her alone with those dying girls."

Oscar sat by his father's side, both of them rocking in the old chairs they had built together in the woodshop when the long-ago day's work was done. His father took another puff and seemed to lose interest. The red tip dimmed and the cigar went out. Oscar inhaled the scent that would be forever imbued in the memory of his father. He'd never developed a habit of tobacco, but he would miss the smell of it.

He helped his father into bed and returned to the rocker to listen to the sounds of his own children getting ready for bed. The older ones were teens now, but the younger two still liked a tuck-in. It was a shame that Theresa couldn't sing the old Norwegian bedtime songs. He had tried, but the words caught in his throat after so many years. Not a father's job anyway, the singing. In another month it would be time to send his father up to Nick's again. Theresa was getting anxious. It was hard for her to get away to see her own family during the months she cared for Nils, him always needing something—a drink of water or to be taken to the lavatory.

Oscar finished his coffee. He rested his head on the back of the chair, listening to the sounds of the night. In the distance, coyotes howled their hunting calls and peacocks answered with rude squawks from the pepper tree. His hound dog rustled through ivy that grew thick along the side of the house. His first mutt had tried burrowing under the raised foundation to keep warm in the winter against the bathtub pipes that drained into the garden, but he'd fixed that.

Theresa returned from putting Neil down. She sat down in the chair next to him with a weary smile. "I'm too old to keep up with that child. How about you? Are you sore tonight?"

He shook his head, too tired to complain. Nothing a farmer couldn't expect. He glanced around, seeing the room through his wife's eyes. She seemed satisfied with the dim glow of the new electric lamps they had traveled to Ventura to buy, after the power company brought electric lines to the house. "Father always said he had a good life here," he said.

She smiled and reached for his hand without speaking.

Chapter Thirty-Two

Shoes and Sheepfolds

September 1940. Chatsworth. 80 degrees. Sunny and dry. Grass is holding. Nothing to write about but shoes and sheepfolds. Theresa came today with news of the Conejo. Oscar Olsen.

"The county fair's coming up in June. We'll have to go see the animals and maybe get an ice cream," Oscar reminded his wife.

"Mary and Neil will like that."

"I'll need to shear the sheep before the weather gets too hot. Then I'll move them to the Chatsworth lease. I'll put together a sleeping cabin out there while I keep an eye on the herd."

"You need to hold off until Sarah takes her turn with your father. I can't cope with him while you're off. I have enough with the orchards and the vegetables. And now Mary down with another asthma attack. I'm afraid to move her for fear she'll choke."

"Don't know I have a choice. My pastures need time to recover." He lowered his gaze to avoid the flare of frustration in his wife's eyes. The issue not settled, but near enough. He nodded and stood to make his way to bed.

"Take Neil with you. He'll like the adventure and you'll have someone to talk to," Theresa told him the next morning as she hung a basket of clean sheets on the line. "It'll ease my load."

Oscar regarded his four-year-old son, remembering the day his own brother tried to ride the moon. He nodded and turned back to the barn. There was no point arguing. Her mind was made up.

Theresa arrived at the sheep camp at the end of the first week with water and clean clothes, lamb stew, fresh bread, liverwurst, apples and ice for the icebox. Oscar had finished the crude shack he'd built in the middle of the lease. She unwrapped jelly sandwiches and hard-boiled eggs while she shared news of the hard times and hungry families in the Conejo. "Belle Holloway's delivering milk from her dairy. Buys day-old bread and oatmeal out of her own pocket when she finds families with small children."

On her next trip she had more news. "The power company means to shut off Belle's power—despite her need of it for the milking machines. It's all over town she ran off a bill collector climbing her pole to cut off the power. She had her shotgun and was fixed to shoot, she told my brother. But the man left quick enough that no harm was done. Now she's waiting for the other shoe to drop. I hope the power people show some sympathy. She's doing a lot of good for people in need."

Oscar grunted and looked to see if she'd remembered to bring the black tar medicine he'd asked for. He swabbed his brow with a fresh kerchief and gulped down most of a quart mason jar of tepid lemonade, wrapped in a damp dishrag and carried in the trunk of her old sedan. She handed him the mail and the *Moorpark Enterprise* as well as a stack of the *Ventura Star Free Press*.

She opened her purse and extracted a white envelope. "I had a letter. Seems there's a scientist works at Griffith Park Observatory looking for someone to foster his boys. Says he'll pay in advance. I said I'd ask you. I wouldn't mind taking in a couple of boys. They'd be good company for our Neil. And we could use the money."

Oscar scanned the letter and nodded. "Write him to come out. We got the room. And you're right about the boy needing playmates." He hooked a thumb at the shack. "Gnats are pestering him when he naps. Scraped his knee yesterday and fussed for you. I'd say he's ready to go home." He wiped his mouth with his kerchief and slumped in weariness. "Coyotes are almost as thick as the gnats. I'll be glad to see the farm again, myself."

She folded the empty waxed sandwich paper that had held his sandwich and set it aside for another use. "Times are hard, Oscar. But it's going to be over one of these days. I heard my brothers talking."

"More likely it'll be a war pulls us out of this slump. A war in Europe, I'd say—and soon." He lifted his hat to mop his brow again and found a seat.

His son Neil finished off the lemonade and smeared a muddy streak across the dust he'd collected on his cheek since morning. Theresa used the dampened rag to wipe his face. "Clearly someone's ready for a bath and a good night's sleep."

"Best take him home. He's had enough for one summer. I need to hire a man to help with the sheep."

Theresa paused between packing the dirty dishes and loading her son's clothing into her trunk. "That'll mean more cooking for me. But you'll be safer. A lot can happen out here. Myrtle has a relative out from Kentucky, looking for work. I saw him waiting at the hiring office when I drove by." She glanced at her watch. "Be sure you get an experienced herder, not one of those rail bums who hang around the hiring office."

Oscar didn't even have a chance to park his farm truck before a slight man carrying a miner's hat and lamp rushed up pleading for a job. He spoke hesitantly, but the man's bare feet and look of desperation spoke more eloquently than any recommendation.

"Not much call for mining around here. You ever work sheep?"

The man stopped short of nodding. He was honest, at least. "Ah've herded turkeys. One stupid critter the same as another, I reckon." His eyes were bright with hunger and hope. "Name's Tom," he offered, apparently assuming Oscar wasn't the sort who could turn down a man once he knew his name. "Ken feed my wife and kid, I get a job."

Oscar considered his options. He'd stipulated a married man; jobs were scarce and children were starving. Besides, the man's burning eyes would haunt his sleep. "Where's she?"

The man looked over his shoulder. "Over yon a spell. Been on the road and we're some hungry. I'll work you square."

"You handle a rifle okay?" When the man nodded, he pointed to the passenger side of the truck. "Your ribs are showing. Guess we better get you fed."

A barefooted woman and a half-grown kid ran from the shade of an immense oak tree, hoping for permission to hop in the back of the truck. With a shrug, he put the truck in gear and started back. At the camp he pulled a fresh package of liverwurst and a loaf of day-old bread out of the icebox and set it on the table he'd placed in the shade of shack. The family tore into the meal like they had holes in their belly.

"Don't eat all that of a sitting," Oscar warned. "You'll be bilious before night and you'll scare my dog!"

Filled and watered, the three did a credible job of keeping the three hundred sheep bunched. The man had a good eye for coyotes and wasn't squeamish about skinning them after he shot. The wife was a bonus, quick on her feet and not afraid to kill a coyote with her bare hands, she claimed.

By the second day, Oscar was confident enough that he left them alone with the flock when he returned to the camp for a nap. Late in the afternoon he heard a shout. In the distance he could see his new man crouched low, yelling to his wife who was holding a foot as she yelped in agony. She was stranded in a large patch of creeping vine that had managed to sink taproots into an alkaline spring and now sported thorn pods known in the Conejo as goatshead—or some preferred to call it, puncture vine. The sheep had scattered in four directions.

Oscar shook his head in disgust. "Everyone knows the only thing those thorns are good for is puncturing tire tubes and causing colic in horses. Where's her sense?"

The man started in, but his own feet were as bare as hers. She moaned as she looked around for an escape, but the thorn patch stretched the length of Oscar's living room. Forward or backward, she was bound for more of the same torture that had brought her to this pitiful state.

"Stop squirming. Hold up!" Oscar growled. He heaved her over his shoulder in a fireman's carry, her body as light as a walking stick, all arms and legs. They started off with her head bobbing against his back. Halfway out, the woman gave a howl that nearly pierced his hearing on the right side. "Just hang on!" he growled.

On bare dirt again, the hired man carried his wife to the shade where their ragged blankets lay. Oscar pulled thorns from one foot while the man did the same with the other. By the time they finished, they each had a fistful of thorns for the fire pit. Oscar poured sun-heated water into his washtub and thrust an angry, puffed foot in it. "Soap up. Then put some tar salve on. Green goatshead are filled with poison. Take you down with fever." He softened his tone when her beaten-down face told him the woman had suffered enough. "Get in your bedroll and stay put for the rest of the day. See how you feel in the morning."

Sheep were strung out across the fields halfway to Hollywood by the time he returned to the field. He used his dog to get the herd into a circle.

The following morning the man stuck his head around the corner of the shack. "Reckon she'll live."

Oscar nodded and continued toward his old farm truck. Once inside, he cranked down the window and started the motor. "Get some food in her before I get back."

He found a junk store in Thousand Oaks that had a pair of worn women's shoes hanging by their strings from a nail on the porch. He paid for them with the change in his pocket and started back. At camp the woman smoothed the laces over her long fingers and looked up to be sure before she accepted the gift. After breakfast she slipped on her shoes and limped off to finish the day.

When it was time to trail the sheep back to the Norwegian Colony, Oscar let the man and his son ride his horse while he led the herd back with loose hay piled in the bed of his truck. The couple made themselves handy fixing fence and doing odd jobs for the rest of the summer while the boy played with Neil. When walnut picking season started, Oscar dropped the couple off at one of Theresa's relative's farms to help with the harvest. The woman carried her shoes tied by the laces over her shoulders like a live turkey.

The boy hung back, quiet and nervous, but his face was rid of its hollow-eyed desperation. When it was time to leave, he bravely stuck his hand out to Oscar. "I ever get me a son, I aim to name him Neil, sir."

Oscar nodded and solemnly accepted the handshake. He slipped the boy a sandwich Theresa had insisted on sending. "Well, that's just fine. I'll tell my wife. She'll want a photograph if you can spare one."

Rich Pederson, 1953

CHAPTER THIRTY-THREE

Promise Years

December 2, 1941. Cloudy day, light sprinkles. Grass is good. Dad is resting well at the lying-in hospital. Lud will meet us there to say our good-byes. Nothing else to be done. He will not live to see the war with Europe.

NILS LAY QUIETLY between starched white sheets while his family crowded around his bed. He had expressed his wish to die on the Colony, after the doctor who attended him at the Lying-In Hospital concluded that there was nothing more he could do. The end came sooner than expected. His teenaged granddaughters pressed kisses on his grizzled cheek and the younger children patted his hand before stepping behind their mothers' skirts. Oscar leaned against the doorframe to make room for Lud and Nick. They took turns leaning close to comfort their father with stories of another time. When it was Oscar's turn, his father's last words were slurred and low-pitched, but he heard the word *Ellen* among them before his father closed his eyes for the last time.

A caravan of cars followed the hearse to the cemetery, filled with sons and their wives and children. They buried their father next to their mother.

A few friends from Moorpark attended, along with the Pedersons and their families. The celebration afterward was muted, as everyone discussed the bombing of Pearl Harbor the previous Sunday.

"So the end of an era," Nick said. "I'm glad he doesn't have to live through another one."

"On my way over here I had to pull aside for a military convoy." Lud fished in his pocket for a cigarette. "Looks like my job's ended. Won't have to wait long to see what's in store for the country."

Theresa and Sarah eyed each other with barely-hidden relief that their burden was lifted, their sacrifices sufficient to assure that their husbands did right by their father.

Later, Lud summed up their feelings with a speech that brought tears to Theresa and Oscar. "Dad came here with nothing but his strength and his stubbornness. The land tried its best to beat him, but he stayed because it was his dream. And when he grew old, he found peace and it rubbed the hard edges off. He was a good man. A staunch husband. A loving father who gave us a better life than he or Mother ever knew."

War prices raised the value of Oscar's crops, even as hired help disappeared to enlistments. Overnight, black-outs and restrictions became the new reality. He dug out his father's old flag and hung it in a corner of the dining room. When a call went out for volunteers, he and his daughter Jean joined Nick as volunteers for air defense. After memorizing manuals outlining the shapes and markings of their own and enemy planes, they heard a government man explain the secret code required when they called in their watch reports. Because the Conejo lacked phone lines the lookout was stationed over the hill in the Santa Rosa Valley.

Rich Pederson stopped by to warn Oscar to keep his daughters from riding their bikes or horses along the road for a few weeks. "We've had to replace the Mexican pickers. Can't get them across the border anymore. We got a new bunch doing the picking until this war's over. German prisoners. They bring them in a convoy from Filmore. Don't want to alarm you or your girls, but just to be safe."

"Labor shortage is going to take its toll on all us farmers."

Rich smiled. "You're lucky you have the older girls. Put them to work. Our dads had us milking at the age your boy is now. Didn't do us any harm." He grimaced at the cup of weakened coffee he was offered. "I sure miss real coffee and chocolate. That's not the half of it. I miss not having sugar for Mother's sweet desserts. Coffee and her blackberry pancakes sure make a day better." He took another sip. "I'll be glad when this is over. Right now, we're buying war bonds while we keep our trucks running on busted wire and a prayer."

"Be grateful for your beehives. Lots of people would give an eye tooth for honey to supplement their sugar rations. Our hogs and mutton keep meat on the table. Still, it seems like our lives are plagued with shortages." Oscar glanced down at his worn work boots.

The next day he waited for Rich to get his mail before he reached into his own box. An application from the state Motor Vehicle department lay on top. He read the name the letter was addressed to and frowned. "Have to tell my daughter to put off getting her driver's license. Only enough gasoline for work and shopping. She'll take it hard."

"Wartime sacrifice hit us all, one way or the other. What do you hear from Lud?"

Oscar rummaged through a pile of letters and tore one open. "Lud writes that his construction job ended when their heavy equipment was needed for the war effort. He's working in an aircraft factory now. Using a new material called *plastic*. Company's hoping it will have other applications after the war. He and Irene brought some pieces of jewelry made of scrap. Gave the little one a necklace in the shape of a red heart." He laughed. "Light as a marshmallow. Probably be the end of pot metal if it catches on."

"Maybe they can figure out a way to make bombs out of the stuff."

Oscar picked up another piece of mail from the pile, a booklet for farmers printed at the government's expense. "You read this warning about not holding back our citrus for private sales?" He thumbed through to a page and read: *Farmers are allowed a specific amount for personal use, after they meet their quota. Remember, you are working to feed the troops."* He scowled. "We may be too old to serve, but we farmers are as patriotic as the next man."

Overnight, ordinary household staples disappeared from market shelves. Sanitary napkins went for war-effort bandages, and stockings became a pencil mark up the back of the leg. Oscar ignored most of the complaints his daughters made, but one thing bothered him more than anything else. One morning he walked into the kitchen anticipating coffee with his bacon and eggs.

"We used the last yesterday," Theresa told him with a look that discouraged further complaint.

He slammed his mug down in disgust. "What's the point if we run out early every month?"

"I run water through the grounds twice, but even without the girls drinking it—"

"Ration Board suggests folks switch to tea."

Theresa looked skeptical. "My family always drank coffee—"

He held up his hand. "Well I'm fed up! For the rest of this war we'll do with tea. After that, we'll decide."

Theresa served her first pot of bitter black tea sweetened with honey and diluted with milk until it was the color of caramel candy and lukewarm.

By the end of the summer the girls were out of the house.

One day Oscar discussed a problem with Theresa while his daughters were away. "My hired man's been drafted. I'm going to need one of the girls to come home and help out."

"Arthelia's never been the outdoor sort. And we promised Jean she could finish her business course in Los Angeles. We were lucky my brother-in-law had room to board her. Got a letter today. My sister says their little house is packed—with her girls and ours sharing a room. Some sleeping on the floor, crowded together like sardines. They eat beans five days a week and jelly sandwiches the other two, but the girls don't seem to mind."

"The hired man's leaving next week. I'm going to need help. Can't do it on my own."

"Jean's like you—always the one for reading. Let her finish her course. She's so close."

Oscar hesitated. "Write and tell her she can finish out the term. When she gets her certificate she returns home." He glanced toward the door where his idling tractor was wasting diesel. "She always liked working outside. She won't mind."

"With her sister working in town!"

"It's the times. The best we can do." He didn't need a reminder. He could already see the disappointment in his daughter's face. "When Neil turns eight, he can take over!" He stomped out, slamming the door behind him.

Oscar watched from the blacksmith shop the day his daughter returned home in a clattering Ford driven by her aunt. After tea and ham sandwiches, Theresa produced precious gasoline stamps and two lamb roasts to pay her sister for their trouble. With a quick look in his direction she stepped into the orchard to fill a gunnysack with oranges and lemons.

His daughter disappeared into the house and returned moody and quiet, dressed in her work jeans. He waited until she made her way to the sheepfold before he explained their dilemma. They started shearing the next morning, with his son helping to tamp the bundles into the long burlap sacks. The girl's resentment eased when the buyer stopped by to make his inspection and offered the comment: "You handle those shears as well as any man." He explained that they would need to finish in time to add their pelts to the bulk shipment. Box cars were waiting on the siding in Moorpark and most of the Chatsworth sheepmen had already begun bringing in their shipments.

The three of them worked from dawn to dusk, shearing, stomping, catching ewes and flopping them on their backs, pausing only to guzzle tepid lemonade or to brush off a tick when it made its way across a bare arm or neck. Few words were spoken beyond. "Sew er up," "catch the gate," "another over here." With the boy handling the gate, one sheep faded into another and one day into the next.

When the last ewe was shorn, the final bag loaded in the flatbed and the sideboards fastened, they drove to Moorpark with dread ears listening for the warning train whistle. Jean helped load the wool into the boxcars. When the last bag was stowed and the door rolled shut, she joined her little brother already slumped against their father's old truck.

Oscar led his two helpers across the street to Castro's Market to choose a soda from the icy slurry in the icebox. "The shipment is bound for the woolen mills in Utah," he told them as he downed his root beer. "Soldiers will have new uniforms from that wool." His daughter's fingers were shiny with lanolin from the pelts, her fingers filthy and bruised from clippers and flying hooves. Her cheeks were sunburned, but her eyes shone with satisfaction. He remembered Theresa at nineteen, already weary and hollow-eyed with responsibilities. He looked over and was gratified when she returned his smile. "We get the apricot trees pruned, you can take that job with Allis Chalmers, Jean. They'll be lucky to get you. Neil turns eight, he can learn to milk."

Oscar sat on his porch studying a set of blueprints the day Jean brought a young man to hunt doves in the pasture. Her eyes held a look of pride as she introduced her young sailor still in his duty blues. The young man was soon to ship out for the Pacific, and Jean was changing jobs to work at the Rationing Board. *Changes happening every day.* His father had left undeveloped lots in Moorpark to his granddaughters. To his sons and grandsons he left small rental houses. Nick got the barns and outbuildings. With post-war shortages, houses were in short supply, and his father's house and barn held good redwood waiting to be repurposed. By the looks of things, his older daughters would be needing their own houses before long.

"County will only allow one driveway shared between the two lots. Doesn't care which side it's on as long as there's a legal easement," he told the girls. "Arthelia's the oldest, so she gets the larger house with the dining room. I'll have to fit the driveway on Jean's side and eliminate her lawn. It'll be tight, but there's room for two garages. Best I can do." When his younger daughter objected that she would be married before her sister, Oscar heard his father's voice quelling the argument. "My decision stands."

Lud arrived from Santa Barbara for Jean's wedding the following year looking haggard and ill. Oscar took him aside. "You don't look so good, brother. What's ailing you?"

Lud ducked his head and laughed. "It's because I stopped drinking. Not even a beer."

Oscar saw his brother's sallow skin and the unhealthy look of his eyes. "You need to see a doctor. Not something to delay. Mother was only a few years older when she took sick. We have too little family left. We can't afford to lose another stubborn blockhead."

"Everybody goes sometime, I suppose." Lud's lopsided grin lacked his usual cockiness.

Lud's call, a month later, was one of the first Oscar received on his newly-installed telephone. He took the receiver from his wife with a quick moment of panic before the static cleared and he remembered to hold the earpiece tight against his ear. He heard his sister-in-law asking them to come to Santa Barbara. Not an invitation, but a summons. He drove to the hospital with Nick and the wives in time for visiting hours. Once in the sterile hospital room he tried to make light of his brother's condition, but Lud was in poor spirits.

"What is it?" Oscar turned to Lud's wife, Irene, who sat at the bedside looking dazed.

"It happened so quickly. Only a belly ache. And then much more. Cancer of the stomach." She wiped her eyes on a crumpled linen hanky and whispered, "There's nothing to be done."

Lud opened his eyes and smiled wanly at his two brothers. "So, the Olsen brothers are together again."

"Are you in pain?" Nick wanted to say more, but these words were easier.

Lud shook his head, frowning with the effort. "Morphine. I should have discovered it years ago."

Unable to find words, Oscar gave his brother an awkward pat on his shoulder and stood back so Theresa could step forward to squeeze her brother-in-law's hand. Oscar couldn't recall later what she said, but she put his brother at ease while Sarah conferred with the ward nurse.

They rode the first miles home in silence until Oscar said, "Only forty-seven."

Nick nodded from the passenger seat. "Yes, but he lived a lot in those forty-seven years. More than we did. With that Harley Davidson he had a good time, that's for sure. In his own way he's satisfied."

Lud passed a few days later. His wife agreed that he be buried in the same cemetery as his parents—their plots as separated as their lives had been. After the funeral Oscar spent a few minutes with the widow. "Theresa and I are in agreement. We can spare money for family."

Irene shook her head. "I'll be all right. We had some assets. Don't worry about us." She hesitated, and added, "I know your family had concerns about him, but he was a good man. He stopped drinking and he was good to my son."

Oscar stood for a few minutes at his mother's grave, where her headstone was already taking on a faint patina of age. When he heard Theresa talking to the Pedersons, he started toward them.

⸙

Oscar was in the field when Nick flagged him down with a letter in his hand. He suggested they walk back to his house for a cup of coffee. "Shame neither of us drinks anything stronger," he joked. They crossed the road and Oscar saw his mother's old hollyhocks, newly pegged to the fence again. His brother and the family had made a lot of improvements to the old home place. Inside, he hung his sweaty hat on a hook before taking a seat at the table.

Nick scanned the letter with growing agitation. Finally he forced out an explanation. "Lud's widow has married a man named Hank Haynes, a farmer. The fellow plans to raise chickens on the land she inherited from Lud." He looked up and waited for the words to settle. "What are we going to do? This is Mother's home. My family lives here!"

Oscar looked around at the room where he had done his homework almost from the time he could remember. Irene hadn't waited even a year and now she wanted Lud's house, even if he'd left it behind. "The banks might loan you money to buy it from her."

Nick shook his head, too distressed to notice that he was still wearing his hat in his wife's kitchen. "She says she won't consider selling. Her husband wants to farm."

"When are they coming?"

Nick handed the letter over, but he'd already committed the words to memory. "She's grieved to have to write, but times are hard and her new husband is determined. She's agreed to give me time to build a house on my own land. She hopes it will be sooner rather than later."

Sarah stood twisting the towel she was using to dry the dishes before she moved to the stove to prepare coffee. "It's the only way we'll ever get a new house, Nick. This house was wretched when we moved in."

Nick swept a hand toward the eastern end of the road. "We've walked the property, planning the day we could afford our own. We know where the new house would stand, in the saddle where we can see the entire Conejo—and if you climb higher, even the ocean and the Channel Islands on a clear day." He glanced at his wife and saw her nod. "We have the lumber from the *Wuthering Heights* set. The school in Camarillo plans to tear down its gymnasium. We can get the flooring for a savings if we tear it out."

"We would have to do the work ourselves," Sarah added. "The children are old enough to help."

"How long will Lud's widow give you?"

Nick indicated the letter. "She didn't say, but I'm thinking a year." He turned to inspect the fields. "I could start clearing ground as soon as the rains come. She'll just have to wait."

When the rains arrived to soften the adobe, Nick spent his time preparing the ground and laying a foundation for the house he intended to build while the county looked over his plans and issued its approval. The work was hard, and slow-going. "New wood would be a heck of a lot quicker," he complained to Oscar one afternoon while they were tearing apart an old shack with usable redwood. "This project is turning out to be harder than I thought. Going to end up taking two years instead of one."

"Maybe it's time you took out a construction loan. Buy new wood before Lud's widow decides to kick you out!"

"Working on it. Banker says it has to be a personal loan. Land isn't enough collateral—nobody would want it. They'll loan enough to get started. He thinks we're crazy with just the wife and kids helping. But we'll show him."

Oscar helped out when he could. Both of them worked around their farming and other chores, but the project was Nick's from start to finish, crafted with modern touches that belied the cost. His pride and joy was the foyer that he created from the movie set, with its wide windows and fine craftsmanship. As a finishing touch, Nick hooked one of the chicken coops to his Caterpillar and dragged it on eucalyptus poles up the hill to the rear of the garden. In the same manner he cut the workshop in half and rolled it to a spot he had leveled part way up the hill.

The morning they finished the house the family woke to snow—the first anyone could recall. The Norwegian Grade was too slippery for the bus to come up, so his children spent the day sliding down the slope and trying to make a snowman out of a quarter inch of snow.

When they finished moving in, Nick invited Oscar's family to an open-house party along with their neighbors and friends.

"The best thing that could have happened, brother," Oscar said, taking in the view from the veranda. "It takes necessity to get a stubborn Norwegian off his duff."

"We have a mortgage hanging over us now. Sarah and I have talked it over. She's making her top salary at St. John's Hospital, and with the travel it isn't enough. She's had an offer as a psychiatric nurse at Camarillo State Hospital. I'm applying for a job there, too. Head of the furniture workshop. We'll get that loan paid off in a year or two."

Oscar joined friends and neighbors admiring the setting sun from the veranda. He was happy for his brother. Jealousy wasn't the issue—nothing as simple as that. But Nick was still a young man. He had already been asked to run for school trustee—and now both husband and wife with good jobs to supplement the farming. Nick was a talented woodworker. He could see an ornate grandfather clock in a cherrywood case and reproduce it in his workshop without blueprints. Now he could teach others.

Oscar was the one who should have finished school. Instead, at sixty-two, he was working for Ventura County as an agricultural inspector, responsible for the plants and bees on his end of the county. He was proud of his job, but Nick had the benefit of education. Nick would have his loan paid off in two years if he set his mind to it, and keep his land in production on weekends and vacations. Rich Pederson had just shared news that his brothers had been offered a contract with the State Hospital for eight thousand eggs a day. The three of them would take turns delivering the shipments from their new production facilities.

Oscar watched his neighbors and friends congratulate his brother. When the laughter and conversation tapered off, he drove home with the proof of other men's success in his rear-view mirror.

Theresa read his thoughts. "Two brothers still on the land," she said. "You should be grateful for that."

Oscar glanced over at Lud's empty house and decided to concentrate on things within his control. His name was coming up on the post-war list for a new pickup. His oldest daughters were married with babies on the way. He would measure success with a different stick.

Olsen Cemetery after the fence was removed for reinterment in 1957.

CHAPTER THIRTY-FOUR

A Hard Farewell

September 25, 1957. 76 degrees. Clear and sunny. Grass poor. Neil thinks to begin college. Theresa agrees that selling is inevitable with the changes to the Colony. It will be a hard farewell for us all.

"GOOD NEWS, OSCAR. I'm getting married."

"You—Rich? After all these years?"

"It's all in God's plan, I suppose. Strange for a man to wait until he's sixty-three, but with clean living I figure to have a good twenty years with her. Marrying my army buddy Pearson's widow, Ruth."

Oscar heard his neighbor's news before Rich shared it with the others, a compliment to their friendship. They sat at his kitchen table with iced teas while Rich clenched and unclenched his fingers around the frosty glass. Theresa refilled their glasses, her gaze lingering on Rich's face. He'd done his best with his mother. But after she lit a fire in the new gas oven, he and his brothers moved her to a Lutheran care facility in Van Nuys. They visited her each Sunday after church.

"Of course you'll come to the wedding."

Oscar nodded, but he saw his friend's hesitation. This wasn't strictly a social visit, not on a Tuesday, with Rich's eggs just finished shipping and the record keeping yet to be done. He waited while his friend came to the real point of his visit.

"There's something else. I'm retiring. Moving to Santa Barbara. I'm donating a hundred and forty acres of my land to be used for the benefit of young people. I never had children of my own and I want to do this. Four Lutheran organizations are going in on the deal. My wife and I will have an annuity to live on, but the balance will go to establishing a college here on the home place."

Oscar cleared his throat and croaked, "When?" Rich shrugged. "It won't happen immediately. Probably take a couple of years before everything is finalized. We won't get married for at least a year." He lifted his gaze to include both of the Olsens. "Once word gets out, you'll probably be getting calls. You can retire a rich man if you decide to sell." His gaze shifted to the open door where the sun was setting beyond the bluff. "They'll want to develop the area where your father built his first shack."

Oscar tried to grasp what Rich was telling him. "That's the cemetery."

Rich nodded. "Bodies will need to be moved."

Oscar reached for his glass and took another swallow, but the liquid caught in his throat. After seeing Rich off, he walked out to his barn to absorb the news of the last hour. Too much to consider at one sitting—like the Santa Ana winds that drove through the eucalyptus grove each fall. He heard the trees groaning against each other and he wondered how he could live without the sound.

Theresa joined him as the last straggling bees flew home to their hives from the orange grove, their hum replaced by the click of crickets. Silence filled the night so profoundly that the rush of a night bird sounded loud. An owl hooted in the nest he had built in the barn. When he turned back to the house, his heart remained conflicted; to remain on the farm and watch the valley fill with heavy equipment, dust and noise would be like suffering a lingering death. Watching Rich's orange trees being uprooted for college classrooms would feel as though his own limbs were being severed. Rich wasn't staying to watch. Probably his brothers wouldn't either. Pete and Lawrence would sell to developers—an opportunity to retire, like Rich said, rich.

The following afternoon Nick knocked on his door, his face white with shock. He took a seat and toyed with the sugar spoon while he took a quick glance out Oscar's kitchen window. "Rich came by this morning."

Oscar nodded. "He said he would. Talked with him yesterday."

"He was shook up in the telling." Nick gave a strained chuckle. "But the news was no easier for his delivering it in person."

"He suggested a meeting between the five of us, Sunday afternoon. Give us time to let everything soak in."

"Sarah and I are thinking to sell off the land across the road. We'll stay, no matter what. It'll be hard, though." Nick set the spoon down and picked up his cup.

A few weeks later a typed letter from the County arrived in their mailboxes, informing them that the family cemetery would need to be abandoned in order for the sale to close. The exhumation and reburial at Ivy Lawn Memorial Park would be done at their expense. The County would provide a tractor and driver. The Pederson and Olsen brothers would serve as witnesses.

"We'll need new caskets," Nick said.

Oscar nodded. His cracked thumbnail worried the corner of the envelope holding the County letter while he considered. "We can put the little girls together. They'll be—"

"One will work," Nick agreed. "What about the two hired men?"

"Martin Peterson." Oscar could still recall his friend's cocky grin the morning they set off to Hueneme. But the details had faded and that was a blessing.

"Will you mind putting him in the same casket with George Hess?" Nick waited for his brother's answer.

Oscar gave a thoughtful nod. "It's been so long. They've made their peace by now."

"The Pedersons will make arrangements for their father and uncle. Mother always said the little Jacobson girl was buried with her father," Nick wasn't sure why he mentioned it, but the fact seemed important to recall. He took a deep breath, suddenly weary, as though the significant events of his life were behind him. If he asked, Oscar would say he was a young man still, only fifty, but he felt old today. "We'll buy a single lot at Ivy Lawn and bury them together."

⁓⚬⁓

Nick was waiting with his brother and the Pedersons when the coroner's vehicle pulled up, followed by a truck carrying a backhoe. In the morning sunshine, quail called from the sagebrush across the road, in the wild area of his land too steep for farming. He liked seeing the rabbits and the birds with their nests in the bushes, the small tracks that led into the cacti. It was as though nothing had changed since the day his father found him trying to ride the moon on this hill. He glanced around at "the flats," fields the six sons had farmed all these years—and before them, those resting in the graveyard. The land belonged to the fathers as much as to their sons; maybe more because some had died working it.

Nick watched Oscar making small-talk with Rich Pederson. The men looked like brothers in their identical chino trousers and tan shirts, felt hats, ruddy cheeks and faded eyes. They were friends from birth, set here on this Norwegian Colony by fate and by the determination of their fathers. He felt his eyes filling when a soft breeze fanned the air, rippling the summer barley crop. He turned his attention to the clatter of chains coming from the tractor being unloaded. A line of metal caskets lay with military precision on the ground.

Soon the tractor began taking bites from the earth. The first coffin uncovered was that of George Ness. Lina was gone now, her daughter Ella married to a Dutchman and never returned to this place where her father was buried. Jorgen Hansen's body would be reinterred with the others. Already the coroner stood with a clipboard ready to record the names and dates into his records.

Another coffin was unearthed, decomposed by dry-rot and termites. The men gathered the remains and laid them inside a common casket. Nick watched as the third plot was unearthed. This time Oscar shouted to the tractor operator to halt, drew on gloves and carried his shovel to help the county employees. The tractor arrived at Lars Pederson's grave. The Pederson brothers turned away from the exposed bones, but Oscar shoveled, his head down, the blade pressed into the hard soil.

When the shovels exposed a set of tiny bones, Oscar straightened and stared across the fields. For a moment Nick envied the memories of an older brother for whom the bones held form and substance rather than just a name and a story. But as he looked again, he saw the naked heartache. On reflection, he was fortunate to have been spared such sorrows. Time and birthplace had cushioned him from the emotions he saw in his brother's face.

Suddenly the shovels struck another coffin, but this time the sound was solid. The driver waited while the men used their shovels to free the coffin. It was intact, the only one so far. The diggers lifted it to solid ground and began to pry the lid open.

"No! Keep it closed!" Oscar's voice, loud in the silence, startled the workers. They set their tools aside with looks of embarrassment and waited to be told what to do. The tractor engine cut to silence as the men gathered closer to see for themselves. When they realized they were blocking the view, they backed away to make room for Nick. He studied the coffin. A miracle—or merely the result of a chunk of hardpan clay that hadn't allowed moisture to pass through? Truth to the adage his mother was fond of saying: Faith always leaves a window open for doubt.

"Emma." Oscar's whisper was meant for himself alone.

The sorrow in his brother's welling eyes seemed to capture the essence of this day. Nick remembered his camera. Without thinking, he snapped his brother, maybe not to share, but as a reminder of the bond between them and this place.

Oscar stood next to the box, its wood discolored but the redwood boards still sound. It was as though his memory recalled the image of a small girl, her dress fresh and unfaded, her hands folded as though in prayer; in the corner a nosegay of flowers, picked by a mother's hands so many years ago, still bright with their spring colors and tied with a faded ribbon that matched those in the little girl's blonde curls. He lifted his head to address the workers who were staring mutely, waiting for his instructions. "Lift the coffin gently. We'll bury it with her sisters, just as it is."

The sun was setting behind the bluffs by the time the last truck was loaded. Tomorrow they would travel to Ivy Lawn Memorial Park in Ventura, to Section F, Block 25, Lot 6, where the caskets would be reinterred.

Nick joined his brother standing beside the three Pedersons, each of them trying to find a reason to remain. The day's events had taken a toll. Each man's face was grave with weariness by the things he had seen. He said something that brought a low round of laughter to break the tension. He was the only man who had not known these children as playmates. Only Tora. In his mind it was Tora whose coffin remained unbroken, but he would never be sure. Oscar had another opinion. Maybe they would speak of it on another day, but this one was too full.

He watched his brother and the others leave, some in cars, some on foot. After they departed and he was left alone in the barren place of broken earth and rotting markers, he bent to straighten a sliver of wood with the faded letters: "Geo Ness." He tucked it in his pocket before he started up the hill to his own supper. He would have a light meal—maybe just soup tonight. Sarah was working a long shift and he didn't have much of an appetite for his own cooking. He was just tired. From the western edge of the Norwegian Colony, the sun descended behind the gum tree grove highlighting the neat sections of farmland with no fences separating the fields, just as they had always been. He turned to where a crescent moon would rise in a few hours, at the spot where he had once chased a rising moon, begging for it to wait for him and his snagged sweater. He still owned that sweater, created by his mother's hands.

In a few months Oscar would be gone from the land. He had announced this morning that he and Tracy were taking a trip north to see about a farm. He intended to leave before the college started developing Rich's land. Nick understood his brother's thinking. If Oscar left beforehand then it would be his decision, not one he was forced to make. But he, Nick, would remain. He would sell off a portion of his land and travel to Norway to meet the cousins. Maybe meet Ella Hansen and show her the photos of her father's grave. She would appreciate having a link to the place of her childhood memories. He would watch from his patio as the orange trees were ripped up, but he was still of an age to appreciate change. A college would offer opportunity—even as it broke with the past. Both are good, he thought. *Both are good.*

He paused to watch the lights of Oscar's house flicker on at the end of the road. With a final glance at the gathering dusk and the Norwegian Colony, he turned to go inside.

Author's Note

The mysterious disease that took five of my grandfather's sisters was not understood by doctors of the time. Descriptions of the malingering illness have not been sufficient for modern physicians to suggest a cause. Some of the girls were born stiff and never developed normally. Others had difficulty walking and were eventually confined to their beds in extreme pain.

Thank you to Candace Simar, award winning author of Norwegian-American historical fiction including *Shelterbelt*, Jeanette Morris, Robert Natiuk, and Martha Burns for substantive suggestions. Mary Olsen Rydberg provided historical records and research. Eva Fjorstad, Gerry Olsen, Janet Pederson Reeling, Helen Honerkamp Androsfay, Eugenia (Jean) Olsen Thompson (dec.,) and Neil Olsen (dec.,) shared their family photographs and stories of the Norwegian Colony.

About the Author

Anne is a descendent of one of the Norwegian Colony families. A fifth generation Californian, her love of the West was fueled by stories of bandits and hangings, of the stories recreated in this book, of Indian caves and of women who made their own way.

She earned a B.S. in Social Science from Cal Poly State University, SLO. Her first job was waitressing at a truck-stop cafe in Cholame, near the spot where James Dean died.

Anne is past-President of Women Writing the West. She lives in Southern Oregon with her husband, two Labs and several free-range chickens. She is a proud grandmother of two. Her interests include: reading, discovering new historical sites, hiking the Pacific Northwest trails and hearing from readers.

Blog: **http://anneschroederauthor.blogspot.com/**
Facebook: **www.facebook.com/anneschroederauthor**
Website: **www.anneschroederauthor.com**
Email: info@anneschroederauthor.com

If you enjoyed this book, consider leaving a review on Amazon, Goodreads, Bookbub or your own social media.

The Caballero's Son
Book Three, Central Coast Series
(Five Star Publishing, October 2021)

Chapter One
Mission San Miguel, California
October, 1850

"Mamacita!"

Miguelito's fierce whimper was swallowed by a gust of sand on the wagon track of El Camino Real, carrying the sound across empty fields strewn with the dung of mission cattle that had grazed the field to dust. Leaving not even a mustard stalk for a small boy to chew on. He glanced hopefully to the track behind him, but his plea had not softened his mother's unblinking stare, nor was it bringing her running to his side. Wind whipped the ends of his coarse black hair. Grit blew into his lashes and made his eyes water. He ground his grubby fists into his sockets to hide his tears and glanced quickly to see if anyone noticed, but Jose Toma was scanning the road ahead, too concerned with safety to care about a small boy's battle to be brave.

His mother watched from the shadow of the abandoned mission church. For a moment he thought to turn and run back to her, but she would be shamed if he did—he, a boy of almost four summers. He did not want to act like a baby, but he could not make his legs move forward either.

"*Apùrate*. Hurry. We must go." Jose Toma's whispered words brought a quiver to Miguelito's small lips as he stood frozen, afraid to move.

"I can . . . not."

"Miguelito, come." A grown-up who must be obeyed, Jose's quiet voice brought the awareness of danger. Miguelito mutely stared at a dust-devil spinning across the field.

"Miguelito." Esperanza's soft pleading reached his ears, but he remained with his feet planted in the middle of the road while he waited to see if his mother would change her mind. Surely she would arrive to take his hand, and they would return to their little room in the mission ruins of San Miguel de Arcángel where they would be safe. But his mother did not run toward him. Instead she stood stiffly, a small figure in the distance, her face smooth and unmarked. Her eyes dead.

He silently willed her to lift her arms and call him back to her, but she remained like the stones in the courtyard, not even blinking. Anger fed the flame of his thoughts and he turned away, swiping his thick black bangs from his eyes; straight, course strands singed by his mother with a burning stick in the old neophyte tradition to show that baptized Indians mourned their loss of freedom. But he did not lack freedom; he was free to starve and to hide from enemies, just like the others. His mother mourned the old times. Her eyes were sad and she often knelt on her knees and rocked back and forth, crooning a low, sad hymn. Perhaps she was glad to be rid of him in this world of hunger.

He heard sounds of impatience from the others and hurried to catch up.

Jose's grunt sounded like a deer snort. "Walk as I do. Softly. Leave no trace." Miguelito nodded, even though a boy of four summers did not need to be reminded. "If *Yanqui* riders come, we will die. *Comprende?*" Miguelito nodded, eager to show that he could be trusted, but Jose Toma hurried on without looking behind to see if a small child followed.

At the place where the road made a sweeping turn, Miguelito peeked back for a last look, but the shaded oak forest had swallowed the Mission, and his mother as well.

For many hours he trudged without complaining, even when his muscles twisted like knotted ropes and fire burned his calves. He kept his head down and hoped that Jose Toma would kill a rabbit for the evening meal with one of the rocks that lay strewn across the wayside, but Jose showed no sign of stopping. Small pebbles caught between his toes, making him wince. Adobe mud caked his feet, making every step feel as though he were dragging a great weight. But still they walked.

During the long afternoon, a train of six ox-driven *carretas* lumbered past, the first cart loaded with brown-skinned children laughing and eating tortillas smeared with honey, their household goods stacked high behind them. The girls wore long, black braids on each side of their faces and the boys wore woven hats with the feathers of small birds tucked into the bands. Miguelito watched as they rode without a care in the world, it seemed. These were *Sonoreños*, on their journey from the Mexican desert to the newly discovered goldfields in the Sierra Nevada;

families pressed by the Mexican government to populate the land to keep it from falling into the hands of the Yanqui foreigners who were flooding Alta California in search of gold. Each day Sonoreños came in droves past the Mission, some of them to pan for gold like they had learned to do in their native region of Sonora, for which they named their new gold camp. Miguelito watched the fathers walking wearily beside their oxen with dust from El Camino Real covering their feet. The older boys rode spirited horses like he would do when he was a man—his mother had promised—these budding young vaqueros sporting thin mustaches that would one day make them look fierce. Meek peasants who did not possess a horse plodded at the head of their oxen, some looking as frightened as their women.

A passing carreta forced Miguelito into scratchy patches of mustard growing along the roadside to a height that nearly hid him from sight. He felt stems tickling his legs while he waited for the caravan to pass. He caught the aroma of honey on the sticky fingers of Sonoreño children while his belly growled with hunger, but he kept his gaze to the ground so that his hunger would not show.

One of the older boys smirked and tossed a rock that he had been holding for a likely target. When it struck Miguelito in his leg, the boy called, "Hey, digger brat. You eat lizards in your belly?"

Another called out, "My papa says you live like dogs on the road. Arf Arf." The others joined the laughter until a butterfly flew into the cart and they turned their attention to capturing it.

Miguelito edged closer to Esperanza's skirt until the wagon passed. When he finally ventured out of her shadow he was sorry he had shown fear to these foreign boys. For the rest of the day he walked with his head down while the sun crept across the sky, pouring heat onto the earth and burning the soles of his feet. Finally he could stand it no longer.

"Jose Toma, I thirst."

Jose Toma leaned over and picked up two shiny pebbles. He stuck them in his mouth and indicated that Miguelito should do the same, but he didn't offer to pick up more from the sand. Miguelito ran his tongue across his cracked lips. He found two small stones, popped them into his own mouth and felt a bit of moisture on the inside of his lip.

Through the hours of remaining sunlight many rabbits crossed their path, but Jose did not seem to notice. The sun chewed up the hillside and disappeared. The moon replaced the sun and day disappeared, but still they walked. Darkness descended and an owl began its night call before Jose declared it safe to stop.

"There is little chance anyone will find us here," he murmured at last.

Miguelito glanced around at the strange surroundings and longed to hear the barking of a dog or the crow of a rooster, but this dark place carried a strange spirit that stirred his apprehension. He choked back his fear, not wanting to shame his mother even if she were not here to see. He needed to be brave like the stories she told of his father, the bravest caballero in all of Alta California.

Darkness swallowed the sun and a sliver of moon begun its slow journey over the land. An owl hooted from where it kept watch in the high branches of a valley oak, a tree so massive that its branches filled a green glade where they made camp. In his bed on the forest floor Miguelito listened for the night birds' rustling. The forest was dark—darker than the small room at the Mission where his mother slept beside him on a tule mat, covered with a worn woolen blanket that she had woven back in the time when the world was happy—or so she said. He had never known such a time.

"*Mamacita, yo te amor.*" Alone in his bed he whispered his love to his mother. With his eyes clenched to stem his tears, he listened to the owl. *Whooo. Whooo, Miguelito?* His mother said the owl was a good omen, but tonight its call brought him no peace. His body was worn from many leagues they had traveled, and knotted muscles caused him to bite his lip in agony. Nearby, Esperanza packed away their dinner scraps into her burden basket with soft rustling sounds that made him feel safe. He had known Jose Toma and Esperanza for all of his life. They were not his father and mother, but they would not allow harm to come to him.

The second day was easier. He had no energy to think about his mother, only to put one foot in front of the other. Jose Toma had no reason to look back over his shoulder and scowl in his direction, for he had no energy to stray into the fields searching for butterflies. That night Esperanza rubbed salvia on his legs and kneaded his muscles until the pain went away and he could sleep. The small bundle of jerky in her burden basket had lasted only two days. Even though they nibbled slowly and held the dried meat in their mouths to savor the juices as long as possible, his belly ached with hunger. He joined Esperanza in stripping moss from the trees and picking miner's lettuce from underneath the oaks.

The third night they camped beside a tributary of the Long River, the Salinas. Jose Toma crouched in the water, searching for fish under the banks where tangled vines and roots created dark hiding places. Miguelito silently watched from the edge of the sand, his arms motionless. The small crescent moon had risen before he saw a trout hiding in the hollow of knotted tree roots. Jose Toma scooped it out and tossed it to Esperanza, waiting on the shore, before he bent to find another. Afterwards they tore pieces with their teeth while the taste of the cool, sweet flesh exploded on their tongues. Esperanza ate slowly, chewing carefully, but a small boy was too hungry to have shame over his greediness. She smiled at him and did not correct his manners. When she had eaten her share, she spread what remained on a rock to dry for the next day when they would leave the river and have no chance to fish.

"It is better to travel in the sagebrush," Jose Toma told them. "The Yanquis will claim the river for their travel. Always they take the best and leave the useless parts for us. Even kill for their right to cheat us."

Many hours passed the next day while they walked without water. Miguelito's tongue swelled with thirst, but he kept his head down, remembering the feel of cool water running over his body. But the memory did not slack his thirst. He was glad when Jose Toma halted and signaled for them to crouch beside a fallen oak. Instinctively, he froze in case it was a deer that captured Jose's attention. But it was only a log. Jose rolled it aside while Esperanza scooped larvae from the rotting leaves underneath. She collected their dinner in her ragged linen shift and he helped when the maggots squirmed out of her hands. Afterwards the three of them had a good meal.

Miguelito's toes were cracked and bleeding, but he did not open his mouth to complain. Still, Esperanza noticed. She soaked leaves from a plant that grew nearby, and wrapped them around his feet while he laid waiting for sleep. The next morning the pain was better and he no longer limped. She whispered something to her husband and the pace that day was not as fast as it had been the day before, but although Miguelito was glad, he did not say so. Now that they were in the forest they walked cautiously, as silent as the deer watching from the shadows, listening for the blue jays and the forest sounds to tell them it was safe. They kept an ear out for the sound of horse hooves. Yanqui devils rode like giants. They would come crashing through the underbrush, shouting from atop their horses and killing without reason. With their long guns they feared nothing, but three Indians without a horse or a weapon had everything to fear.

They came upon another Indian family, their sounds familiar even to Miguelito. He recognized them by the soft, regular "chud", "chud" of the woman's stick as the family dug roots in the shadows of the oaks. It was Socorra and her children, digging wild onions and camas. Esperanza joined the other woman and Miguelito reluctantly followed. When they had each dug enough, the women prepared their meals together and Esperanza shared their meager supply of fish. Clearly the children had not tasted such a treat in many days. They nibbled quietly while the grown-ups talked in soft voices.

"Where is Enciro, your husband? Is he not with you?" Esperanza asked quietly.

The woman looked up with dead eyes. "Gone. Flown away like a condor in the air."

"How has this happened?" Jose Toma glanced up with a worried look.

The woman's gaze shifted to where her children were eating before she spoke in a low tone. "Some of the others were tricked into thinking that life would be easier if they followed the Yanquis to the Sierra Nevada to pick nuggets of *oro amarillo*. My husband remained behind, but we heard the Yanquis say that these gold nuggets are as plentiful as shells on the sand and that if our people went with them, they too will be paid with much gold. My husband tells the others, 'What would we do with this yellow gold?' His words anger the foreign men. But my husband is lucky that the Yanqui spares him and does not punish him for daring to speak. But others question the men on horses and they grow weary. When one of our friends whispers a warning to the others, the foreigners kill him and beat the other men and bind them like goats. Some of the men are not so easy to capture. They escape into the bush, including my husband. Later, he thinks to follow, hoping to find a way to release them, but when he is discovered, he too is tied and dragged behind one of the horses."

"He is there still?"

The woman looked down at the ground. "I saw him taken with my own eyes. Three moons past. Now my children and I make the journey to find him. He will suffer with no wife to prepare his meals. And even if there is nothing to eat, like here, at least we will be together."

Esperanza nodded. "We must keep the old ways."

Jose Toma considered Sorocco's earlier words. "*Oro amarillo*, this yellow gold lies upon the earth? For anyone to pick up—even us?"

The woman nodded. "My husband says we could trade this yellow gold for food and we would not be hungry. Do you think this might be so?"

Jose Toma's eyes seemed to search for the truth inside himself. For months the roads had been filled with Sonoreños rushing to get to the goldfields. Maybe this Yanqui oro was all gone by now. But maybe some was hidden in pockets of the earth where the gringos wouldn't find it. It would be good to have gold to pay for food. He looked up and saw Esperanza and Miguelito watching. "*Si*. We go to this gold field to pick up oro amarillo."

"And to find my husband?"

His eyes flickered to the children and he lowered his tone. "God willing—if this is possible."

Other Books by Anne Schroeder

Memoir

Branches on the Conejo

Winner, William Sayoran Persie Award for Non-Fiction

"Anne Schroeder draws a detailed picture of the first farming families who settled in the Conejo Valley overlapping the 19th and 20th centuries…She successfully describes the interdependence of the varied heritages that came together to build a strong community."

— Amazon 5-Star Review

Branches on the Conejo Revisited

(October 2020)

Revised and updated with added historic photos and stories of early pioneers of the Norwegian Colony and the Conejo Valley. Introduction written by Wyatt McCrea.

A timely memoir of what life was like in Southern California before the land was paved and the memories lost.

Victor Davis Hanson, author, *Fields Without Dreams* and *The Land was Everything*

Ordinary Aphrodite

https://www.amazon.com/dp/B0051ADYW0

"*Ordinary Aphrodite* literally offered my sense of being a woman in this world a wonderful tune-up! I found myself placing penciled checkmarks beside those passages that rang my chimes, that resonated within me in a kindred-spirit kind of way. Anne's book of essays about her life is now more than a favorite. Her memoir is a keeper."

— Amazon 5-Star Review

Historical Western Fiction

The Central Coast Series

Maria Ines

Finalist, Will Rogers Medallion Award, Western Inspirational Fiction

https://www.amazon.com/dp/1432832778

"This accurate and well-researched historical fiction pulls you in to a past world not frequently explored, delivering an eye-opening account of what women endured during this dark time. It's a tale of one woman's strength and fortitude as she fought to live and love amidst death and desolation. Truly inspirational."

— Amazon 5-Star Review

Cholama Moon (Central Coast Series)

Named "Best Non-Traditional Western Novel,"
Stu Rosebrook, *True West Magazine*

https://www.amazon.com/dp/B07JCLDHSH/

"Anne Schroeder writes a story that is not only great, she write with amazing detail. When you are reading one of her books, you feel as if you are watching a movie. In fact I would love it if this was a movie!"

— Amazon 5-Star Review

The Caballero's Son

(Fall, 2021, Five Star Press)

A love story in the tradition of Helen Hunt Jackson's *Ramona*. This stand-alone novel, the third in the Central Coast Series follows Miguelito's tumultuous life from the time his mother, Maria Ines, sends him away to safety. A mother's love has no bounds, nor a son's sense of betrayal.

— Beta Reader Review

Walk the Promise Road

Winner 2019 Will Rogers Medallion Award for Western Romance

https://www.amazon.com/dp/B07C7H5WP8/

"The history and detail is some of the best I've ever read about the Oregon Trail. Engaging characters make this hard to put down. I've been a fan of Oregon Trail stories my whole life, and this book definitely is at the top of my all time favorites list."

— Amazon 5-Star Review

Boy in the Darkness

Shortlisted, 2020 Will Rogers Award for Western Short Fiction

https://www.amazon.com/dp/B07SV52KPN

"His struggle to survive occupies his mind, body and spirit with surprising results. A hundred and fifty years later the echoes of his struggle remain when a Lakota Indian advisor finds signs of his passage in the limestone cave."

— Amazon 5-Star Review

Short Stories
Gifts of Red Pottery

https://www.amazon.com/dp/1976467977

"A collection of emotion stirring short stories gathered together from her (Schroeder's) many years of writing and given as a gift to her readers. Men and women alike will be touched by her stories—current and past, dark ones and light ones, tough and gentle; each tale a stand-alone gem."

— Amazon 5-Star Review

Made in the USA
Monee, IL
25 April 2023

32408518R00174